"A charming and delightful read. Th[...]
place—so strong one can smell t[...]
—Alexander McCall Smith o[...]

Praise for th[...]
Seaside Knitters Mysteries

Angora Alibi

"Ms. Goldenbaum writes such interesting and likable characters, the reading of one of these [novels] is like a reunion with old friends."
—Fresh Fiction

"The sights and sounds of the latest Seaside Knitters story will enchant readers. The mystery unfolds nicely with some surprising and clever turns."
—RT Book Reviews

A Fatal Fleece

"Goldenbaum offers credible characters, a mystery that's uncomplicated without being too obvious, and the knitting content her fans demand in a very readable package."
—Publishers Weekly

The Wedding Shawl

"Like the best marriages—mystery, romance, and lots of charm."
—New York Times bestselling author Nancy Pickard

"This might be Goldenbaum's best so far."
—Booklist

"A very pleasant read that evokes summers by the sea."
—Kirkus Reviews

A Holiday Yarn

"Goldenbaum's plotting is superb, her characters richly drawn . . . and her prose is seamless."
—Richmond-Times Dispatch

"Goldenbaum's cozy mystery features appealing characters whose relationships will matter to the reader."
—Booklist

continued . . .

"A powerful story." —*Midwest Book Review*

"A good series is like taking a break and going to spend some quality time with friends you've never met. Goldenbaum has constructed a town and its people with care and attention to detail."

—*Gumshoe*

Death by Cashmere

"Murder in a truly close-knit community—a knitting circle in a New England seaside town. Peopled with characters we come to care about. Add a cup of tea, a roaring fire, and you've got the perfect cozy evening."

—Rhys Bowen, author of *Queen of Hearts* and the Agatha and Anthony award–winning Molly Murphy mysteries

"With all the dexterity and warmth the women of Sea Harbor knit into their sweaters and shawls, Sally Goldenbaum weaves us a tale that combines friendship, community—and crime—without dropping a stitch."

—Gillian Roberts, author of the Amanda Pepper series

"Sally Goldenbaum's appealing world will draw readers to return time and again to Sea Harbor. In this wonderful launch of a vibrant new mystery series, the characters ring true and clear."

—Carolyn Hart, author of *Death at the Door*

"[A] vibrant and earnest portrait of friendship. This is a whodunit with a big heart." —*Richmond Times-Dispatch*

"[A] charming debut . . . a cozy many will find an ideal beach read." —*Publishers Weekly*

Angora Alibi

A SEASIDE KNITTERS MYSTERY

Sally Goldenbaum

AN OBSIDIAN MYSTERY

_Sk_

Goldenbaum

OBSIDIAN
Published by the Penguin Group
Penguin Group (USA) LLC, 375 Hudson Street,
New York, New York 10014, USA

USA | Canada | UK | Ireland | Australia | New Zealand | India | South Africa | China
penguin.com
A Penguin Random House Company

Published by Obsidian, an imprint of New American Library, a division of Penguin Group
(USA) LLC. Previously published in an Obsidian hardcover edition.

First Obsidian Trade Paperback Printing, May 2014

New American Library Trade Paperback ISBN: 978-0-451-41535-6

The Library of Congress has cataloged the hardcover edition of this title as follows:

Goldenbaum, Sally.
Angora alibi: a seaside knitters mystery/Sally Goldenbaum.
p. cm
ISBN 978-0-451-41534-9
1. Knitters (Persons)—Fiction. 2. Mystery fiction. I. Title.
PS3557.O35937A83 2013
813'.54—dc23   2013000646

Printed in the United States of America
1   3   5   7   9   10   8   6   4   2

Set in Palatino
Designed by Elke Sigal

$15.00
11/17/15
DC

i14120070

For readers everywhere

Acknowledgments

My special thanks to Dawn Slugg, previous owner of Ruhama's Yarn and Needlepoint Shop in Milwaukee, Wisconsin. Dawn graciously designed the pattern for the baby blanket Nell is knitting in *Angora Alibi*.

Thanks also to Nancy Pickard, who provided me with a shady deck, a duck pond, daily encouragement, and a comfortable brown leather chair, all of which were instrumental in writing *Angora Alibi*.

And thanks to family and friends from Minnesota to Kansas City who imagine my story lines with me, explore the characters' motivations, and help me keep the Seaside Knitters fresh. Their suggestions and ideas send me off in welcome new directions.

Cast of Characters

THE SEASIDE KNITTERS

Nell Endicott: Former Boston nonprofit director, semiretired and living in Sea Harbor with her husband

Izzy (Isabel Chambers Perry): Boston attorney, now owner of the Seaside Knitting Studio; Nell and Ben Endicott's niece; married to Sam Perry

Cass (Catherine Mary Theresa Halloran): A lobster fisherwoman, born and raised in Sea Harbor

Birdie (Bernadette Favazza): Sea Harbor's wealthy, wise, and generous silver-haired grande dame

THE MEN IN THEIR LIVES

Ben Endicott: Nell's husband

Sam Perry: Award-winning photojournalist married to Izzy

Danny Brandley: Mystery novelist and son of bookstore owners

Sonny Favazza and Joseph Marietti: Two of Birdie's deceased husbands

SUPPORTING CAST

Alphonso Santos: Wealthy construction company owner; Gracie Santos' uncle; now married to Liz Palazola

Andy Risso: Drummer in Pete Halloran's band; son of Jake Risso

Annabelle Palazola: Owner of the Sweet Petunia Restaurant; Liz and Stella Palazola's mother

Archie and Harriet Brandley: Owners of the Sea Harbor Bookstore

August (Gus) McClucken: Owner of McClucken's Hardware and Dive Shop

Ella and Harold Sampson: Birdie's longtime housekeeper and groundsman

Esther Gibson: Police dispatcher (and Mrs. Santa Claus in season)

Father Lawrence Northcutt: Pastor of Our Lady of Safe Seas Church

Franklin Danvers: Wealthy investor; Elliott Danvers' uncle

Gabrielle (Gabby) Marietti: Birdie's ten-year-old granddaughter

Harry and Margaret Garozzo: Owners of Garozzo's Deli

Henrietta O'Neal: Wealthy Irish widower

Horace Stevenson: An old man who lives near Paley's Cove

Jane and Ham Brewster: Former Berkeley hippies; artists, and cofounders of the Canary Cove Art Colony

Jake Risso: Owner of the Gull Tavern; father of Andy Risso

Janie Levin: Nurse practitioner in the Virgilio Clinic; Tommy Porter's girlfriend

Jerry Thompson: Police chief

Justin Dorsey: Eighteen-year-old distant cousin of Janie Levin's

Kevin Sullivan: Ocean's Edge cook

Laura Danvers: Young socialite and philanthropist; mother of three; married to banker Elliot Danvers

Lily Virgilio, M.D.: Izzy's obstetrician

Mae Anderson: Izzy's shop manager; twin teenage nieces, Jillian and Rose

Martin Seltzer, M.D.: Works in Virgilio clinic

Mary Pisano: Middle-aged newspaper columnist; owner of the Ravenswood B&B

Mary Halloran: Pete and Cass' mother; secretary of Our Lady of Safe Seas Church

Merry Jackson: Owner of the Artist's Palate Bar & Grill

Pete Halloran: Cass' younger brother and lead guitarist in the Fractured Fish band

Tamara Danvers: Franklin Danvers' wife

Tommy Porter: Policeman

Tyler Gibson: Esther Gibson's grandson

Willow Adams: Fiber artist and owner of the Fishtail Gallery

The web of our life is of a mingled yarn,
good and ill together; our virtues would
be proud, if our faults whipt them not;
and our crimes would despair, if they
were not cherish'd by our virtues.

　　—SHAKESPEARE

Angora Alibi

Chapter 1

"These are the glory days. A unique and special time in your life."

"You're glowing, Izzy."

"Radiant with life."

Izzy pulled the blue fleece tight across her heavy breasts and jogged along the wet sand. She welcomed the salty spray that slapped her cheeks like a reprimand, forcing her into wakefulness.

Special.

Miraculous.

Joyful.

Everyone agreed.

And everyone was right. Of course they were right. That's exactly how she had felt. For months and months.

Ever since the day that innocent-looking little stick had turned pink and she and Sam, dizzy with thoughts of having a baby, walked the beach for hours, hand in hand, wrapped in dreams. When nightfall came, they wrapped themselves in a Hudson's Bay blanket on the deck and watched the stars come out, marking the day that began a new chapter in their lives. The day their world changed and their hearts grew so full they thought they might burst.

A heady, joyous time.

The joy was still there. But dim, restless. Fuzzy.

And Izzy had no concrete idea why.

As her body grew, so, too, did the number of her visits to Dr. Lily Virgilio, until lately she found herself in the clinic once or twice a week, feeling a kinship with the doctor and with the office staff. It was a place filled with people whose only concerns seemed to be for her and for the life growing within her. That was how it had been.

"No worry," Dr. Lily assured her, explaining her scheduling of frequent visits. "The baby is fine. I just want to keep a close watch on your blood pressure. And I want you to relax." Her liquid voice and warm smile comforted Izzy as the baby rolled from side to side inside her.

But Izzy wasn't really worried about the baby. She knew this baby intimately. And she knew that he or she was strong and safe and content in the warm cocoon of her womb.

It wasn't the baby who was playing with her blood pressure.

If not the baby, what? Sam had asked with increasing frequency.

And then he'd answered his own question, knowing none would come from his wife. *Hormones.* He had read up on them. They happened to moms-to-be. Changes in the body's chemistry could cause all sorts of things.

Izzy only half listened to him. Maybe it was hormones. The pile of books stacked beside her bed told her that pregnancy was an emotional ride. Tension and anxiety came and went. Moods came and went.

Running helped some. Working in her yarn shop was therapy, too. And Thursday . . . Thursdays were a cure-all. Knitting night with dear friends whose love alone could surely ease the irrational emotions squeezing her heart.

And they would ease the feeling that something in the universe—something *out there*—wasn't at all right. A feeling. A premonition.

Izzy slowed her jog, then stopped along the edge of the half-moon beach and sucked in huge gulps of air, her fingers splaying around her ponderous belly. It was a natural position these days—cupped hands embracing her unborn baby.

Somersaults beneath a thin layer of polyester responded to her embrace—a rippling wave that rolled from one side of her belly to the other.

Izzy patted what felt like a tiny heel. She lowered her head and whispered intimately, "Soon I'll give you a whole world to move around in, my sweet baby. Be patient."

A peaceful, safe world.

But the world wasn't ready yet. She felt it in her bones. Not ready to welcome this tiny babe with gentleness and peace.

At this far edge of the cove, the beach narrowed to a path, then disappeared around a pile of boulders, where it threaded its way up a hill to a neighborhood of elegant homes hugging the sea cliffs. Most of the houses were old estates, many renovated, with extra rooms and porches, guest cottages, and boathouses making the already enormous spaces even larger.

Izzy looked up at them for a few minutes, then turned away and picked up her pace again, heading back in the direction from which she'd come, her ponytail flying between her shoulder blades, her head held high.

Step after step after step along the seaweed-laced sand.

She waved to another jogger, picked up speed, and didn't slow down again until she reached the steps to the parking strip that ran alongside the road. With one foot on the bottom step, she breathed deeply again, her head low.

It wasn't until her heartbeat slowed that she forced herself to look.

It was still there.

Sitting on the sand next to the low stone wall, as patiently as a well-trained pup.

A baby car seat. With a corner of a yellow knit blanket peeking over the side of the padded seat.

Yellow. Angora, Izzy suspected. A blend—the kind she sold every day to young moms and grandmothers wanting fuzzy hats and mittens for the cold Sea Harbor winters.

A baby car seat.

Without a baby in sight.

Izzy scanned the cove just as she had in the days before. Some people called the cove the mothers' beach, a small protected area that vacationers rarely visited. With low waves and boulders at each end of the carved-out area, it was an easy place to keep track of children as they skipped in the waves and built sand castles during the day. But the June weather had been too cold and the only people frequenting the area were scuba divers in their wet suits, some local fisherman who kept boats nearby, and strollers or joggers such as herself.

No moms strolling the beach.

No party leftovers from college kids who took over the sandy area at night.

No children.

No baby.

Old Horace Stevenson, as predictable as the sunrise, walked near the water's edge with his golden retriever, Red, at his side. Not a day or nighttime passed without the Paley's Cove Sentinel, as the neighbors called the old man, walking the beach, his bare feet and Red's paws making intricate patterns in the sand. Every now and then Horace tossed a piece of driftwood into the sea and Red dutifully waded into the cold water to retrieve it for his master.

Horace's eyesight was failing with the years, but his other senses, his hearing and smell and touch, were keen and sharp, and he always knew when Izzy was jogging along the beach. It was her scent, he told her once—and the particular slap of her tennis shoes on the sand. Today, as always, he tipped the bill of his Sox cap in her direction, then continued his slow walk down the beach. They were friends, she and old Horace, bound together by their love of this sandy cove.

Izzy turned again toward the car seat, staring hard, as if the sheer power of her glare would make it get up and fasten itself into the backseat of a car, where it belonged. Welcome a baby into its safe curve and keep it safe.

But the car seat didn't move.

Chapter 2

Coming upon it from the west, the Anya Angelina Community Center looked as if it grew directly out of the land and thick woods surrounding it. There it stood, a beacon at the edge of the rise above the pounding surf. In daytime, sunlight reflected off its tall windows—glass stripes between stretches of cedar walls. But tonight the center glowed with hundreds of flickering candles that filled the windows and welcomed guests.

"It looks like the whole town's shown up tonight." Sam Perry drove slowly past the center's entrance. Inside they could see crowds of well-dressed guests milling around. He searched the lot for a parking place.

"Over there." Izzy pointed to a narrow space between Cass Halloran's new truck and the edge of the woods.

Sam maneuvered his car into the small space.

"Good causes bring out good people," Nell Endicott said from the backseat, where she was wedged tightly between her husband, Ben, and tiny Birdie Favazza.

"Tonight's event is definitely that," Birdie said. "Bless that Lily Virgilio. Her free health-care program has grown like wildfire. She's a gem and I hope this party raises a truckload of money to help it along."

Ben agreed. "Free screenings, children's vaccinations, prenatal vitamins—it's an innovative way to use a part of this great facility.

And from what I hear, Lily has corralled nearly everyone in town with an M.D., D.O., or R.N. behind their name to help her out."

"Your obstetrician has her hands in everything, Iz." Nell touched the seat in front of her. "Good lady."

Izzy nodded. "Of course. Nothing but the best for this baby."

Sam looked over at his wife, his hand leaving the wheel to lightly graze her belly.

Nell watched the intimate gesture from behind, saw Izzy lift Sam's hand and kiss his fingers lightly before letting go and climbing out of the car.

Izzy's mood seemed to have shifted during the day. Earlier, when Nell dropped by the yarn shop, she had seemed unusually quiet. She'd brushed aside Nell's concern. The shop was filled with customers. Payroll was due. She was busy, that was all.

Tonight, her smile was larger, her laughter less forced. Ben told Nell she was watching Izzy too closely during her pregnancy, imagining emotions that maybe weren't even there. Her niece had always been independent, and Nell needed to respect that.

He was probably right. Of course he was.

"Does the sweater fit, Izzy?" Nell asked, catching up to her niece in the parking lot. She touched the edge of the soft blue gossamer sweater. Nell had started knitting it the day Izzy announced her pregnancy. Something for summer nights, something that wouldn't impose on Izzy's changing figure. The short lacy knit was tied loosely in front, its abbreviated sleeves just long enough to ward off ocean breezes.

Izzy looped one arm through her aunt's and hushed the sentence. "You're as transparent as this lovely sweater, Aunt Nell. Of course it fits. And what you are really asking me is how I am. I'm fine. Honest, I am."

On her other side, Birdie Favazza laughed, a rich, wind-chime laugh that always made those around her smile. "This baby is well loved, Isabel," she said. "And sometimes love brings a bit of unnecessary concern."

Nearly a foot taller than Birdie, Izzy smiled down at one of the wisest women she knew, then looked back to her aunt. "Why don't you come with me this week when I see Dr. Lily? You can hear her report for yourself. You might hear baby Perry, too. This baby is noisy, just like his dad—" She glanced over her shoulder at Sam, then looked down at the baby's form and added, almost as if talking to herself, "When he bounces around so much, I'm sure it's a mini Sam. But when I play Norah Jones and the baby rolls so gracefully to the music, I think it's a little girl in there, maybe a dancer. But we'll all find out soon enough, I guess."

Nell's smile was hidden in the darkness of the night as she listened to Izzy dream aloud about her baby. It was foolish for her to worry about her niece, just as Ben and Izzy and Birdie said—yet they put up with Nell and treated her concern kindly.

"So, Aunt Nell? What do you say?"

"Thanks, Izzy. Of course. I'd love to go with you."

Birdie was the first up the steps, her diminutive figure shimmery in a short silver dress. Her gait was lively, belying her eighty-plus years. She hugged one of the young women handing out programs at the door. "Janie Levin, you are a vision tonight."

Birdie had known the young nurse her entire life and, along with the other knitters, had cheered Janie on when she left an hourly job to go to nursing school, and then they had welcomed her back with open arms when she returned, degree in hand, to pursue her career in Sea Harbor.

Janie blushed at the attention and slid a palm down her watery silk dress. She lowered her head, a thick red curl falling over her forehead. "Do you recognize this dress? I got it at Laura Danvers' garage sale. A designer dress! Who knows the glamorous places it's been?" She laughed and pushed the stray lock back into place.

Without her hair, Janie might have been considered pleasant looking, but one would never describe her that way. *Gorgeous* was used more often. Twenty-five years before, she'd made her way into the world with a headful of valentine-colored curls, surprising the entire medical team, not to mention a black-haired mother and father who wondered briefly if their tenth child had somehow been dropped off in the wrong delivery room. Along with her deep green eyes and tall, lanky body, Janie stood out, no matter how hard she tried not to.

"No one will ever know. It looks like it was made for you, Janie," Izzy said

Janie laughed again. "Laura walked right by me tonight without even noticing I was wearing her dress—of course it's shorter on me, but short is 'in,' so I'm fine. I paid four dollars and fifty cents for it, can you believe it?" She held up four fingers.

"Yes, I can," Izzy said. "That's why you're the garage sale queen. You're the best bargain hunter I know."

"It's easy to be frugal when you grow up with nine siblings. I love garage sales. And now I get to use my hobby to buy things for my boyfriend. I never tell Tommy where things come from—he thinks the shirts and designer ties I give him are new."

They laughed at the thought of the young policeman, whose shoes were always shined, his uniform pristine and pressed perfectly, dressed in garage sale finds. "Tommy Porter's a lucky man," Birdie said.

"And Dr. Lily, too," Izzy said. "As if being head nurse isn't enough, Janie seems to have her hand in everything over there."

"It's my dream job—and I want to be involved in everything. I get to train the new nurses and all sorts of . . ." Janie's words fell off and were replaced by a frown as she looked over Izzy's shoulder and down the steps. Several young men, dressed in khaki pants and light blue shirts, stood at attention at the curb. A VALET sign was posted in front of them.

Izzy followed Janie's look. "You worry too much, Janie," she said. "He'll be fine."

Justin Dorsey, a ponytailed young man with dimples and an infectious smile, had taken a set of car keys from the construction magnate, Alphonso Santos, and was eagerly climbing into his shiny yellow Porsche.

Janie fidgeted with of the evening's program, bending a corner back. Finally, once Justin had eased the car away from the curb, she relaxed. "I know, I know. I shouldn't worry about him. Tommy thinks I'm crazy. He'd be happy if Justin would disappear. But it was so nice of Laura and Willow to hire him to park cars tonight— even though I had to talk him into it. There was a party at the beach—a bunch of college kids—and he really wanted to go. They needed him, he said. He'd make his money down there. 'How?' I asked him. 'Selling hot dogs?' He just doesn't think. I know he doesn't make much at the clinic—and frankly, we needed him to-night, so I forced him to come. He's like a little kid and lives in the moment, doesn't think about the consequences. And I just worry. You know?"

"Well, stop worrying, dear," Birdie said, patting her hand. "It accomplishes nothing but wrinkles. Justin can drive a car as well as anyone. If he's related to you, he has to have a few marbles up there."

Janie's worried look remained. "Well, he's related to a cousin of a cousin out in California. But everyone in the family kind of cast him aside. I felt sorry for him."

A few minutes later the young man walked back across the parking lot, waving to arriving guests and swinging Alphonso's car keys from his one finger.

The worry began to disappear from Janie's face. "He's okay . . . and can be sweet. He just doesn't have much faith in himself. Tommy says I'm not the one to put it there and I should just let him grow up." She shrugged. "Maybe he's right. But Justin doesn't seem to have anyone else."

They knew the story, how Janie had met the several-times-removed cousin at a reunion where no one paid much attention to him. But Janie had, and by reunion's end, Justin had developed a puppy-dog crush on her, like a youngster on a young teacher or a camp counselor. And much to her surprise, a few months after the reunion, he'd hitchhiked his way to Sea Harbor, showing up on her doorstep. Justin would move the sun for Janie Levin if she asked him to—but he sometimes tripped over a few planets in his attempts.

"You've done a lot for him. But maybe Tommy is right—now he needs to stand on his own two feet."

Janie nodded to Birdie. "Sure, you're right, Birdie. And even Justin tells me he is figuring out how to make money on his own. He doesn't need me to find him jobs, he says. The clinic gig is enough. But . . ." A line of people forming behind Birdie and waiting for programs interrupted her thought, and one hand flew to her mouth. "Jeez. Fine volunteer I am. I'm going to be fired!" She gave a small wave and stepped aside to greet the next guest.

The threesome left Janie to her duties and moved into the center hallway.

Birdie looked back to the doorway where Janie was graciously greeting each guest. And where, beyond her, Justin was stomping out a cigarette and taking the keys to another fancy car. Once again, she saw Janie's eyebrows lift, her forehead furrow, and a flicker of anger in her eyes as she spotted the crushed cigarette.

"Sometimes that girl takes on too much," Birdie said.

"Are you saying Justin is too much?" Nell asked.

"Perhaps he is."

"Janie has gotten him odd jobs everywhere," Izzy said.

"But he has a tough time keeping them, from what I've heard," Nell said.

"Well," Birdie philosophized, "he's just a kid, really. He'll grow up. They all do." She waved at neighbors filing by and followed their eyes to the large posters hanging on the walls.

Everywhere in the high-ceiling entryway, people stood in groups, looking up at the large posters hanging on the walls that outlined auction items donated for the event. The entryway flowed into a larger room, its ceiling reaching two stories. The skylights, windows, and doors created an amazing open space filled with elegantly set dining tables and lined with white-clothed bidding tables that groaned beneath the donated items.

Nell looked around at the opulent setting. "I suspect you're right, Birdie. Lily's free clinic will be on its way to being well funded by the end of tonight."

Izzy lifted herself on tiptoe as best she could manage and looked around the crowded space, peering over the tops of heads. "Where do you suppose the men are? We may never see them again in this crowd."

Nell pointed toward the far end of the building, where a long bar had been set up in front of the veranda doors. "I suspect they're back there. And I think I see Cass and Danny, too."

Izzy volunteered to lead the way, her bulk providing an invitation for others to step aside. She greeted friends and customers as she rotated her body through the crowd.

Cass greeted them with a laugh and a hug for Izzy. "Have you noticed how easily crowds part when you walk through? I think I'll take you out on the *Lady Lobster* with me and see if you can part the sea."

The group laughed and moved into easy, familiar conversation, wrapped up in the comfort of longtime friendships. Ben passed glasses of water and wine around. "We thought we'd lost you for a minute there. This place is packed."

"I figured you'd be checking out the silent auction items, looking for treasures." Cass smiled up at the quiet blond-haired man standing next to her. "Like Danny here. I think he's going to surprise me by bidding on something amazing. Right?"

Danny Brandley walked his fingers up her bare back. "Who knows? Word has it that someone donated an expensive necklace, dripping with gems. . . ."

She wrinkled her forehead. "I was thinking more of those new lobster buoys Gus McClucken donated."

They all laughed. Cass tried hard to maintain her tough fisher-woman image, but it didn't fit her tonight, no matter how hard she tried. Tonight she was all Cinderella, her thick black hair loose about her shoulders. Torn jeans and a yellow slicker had given way to a midnight blue, spaghetti-strapped dress that in no way spoke of hog rings and head netting.

And Danny, her mystery writer friend, seemed to be enjoying every bit of his Cinderella.

Behind the bar, a dark-haired man shook a silver carafe, half listening to the group's friendly conversation, a smile on his face.

Nell looked over and her face lit up. "Kevin Sullivan!" She leaned over the bar to hug the bartender. "I didn't realize it was you. I think it's the beard."

"You like? I got tired of being carded when I was in New York."

"Well, we're happy to have you home again. Birdie tells me people are flocking to the Ocean's Edge to taste your specialties."

Kevin's face reddened with his grin. "Aw, shucks."

A year at the Culinary Institute clearly hadn't rubbed away the young chef's gentle veneer. "Head chef. Good for you, Kevin." The others clapped their approval.

"So, master chef, what are you doing tending bar?" Cass asked.

Kevin poured a rose-colored drink mix into a glass. "How do you say no to Laura Danvers and Willow Adams—and both of them at once? They've mastered the fine art of getting free help." He nodded toward a tall man farther down the bar. "They also figured I'd bring one of the Edge's real bartenders along with me."

"Who's that? Just when I think I know the whole town, some great-looking guy appears," Cass said.

Birdie slipped on her glasses and looked down the bar. "Oh, for heaven's sake. You know him, Cass. It's that sweet little Tyler Gibson, all grown up. He's been back home for a couple months now."

Cass took a closer look. The man's wide smile was concentrated on several young women walking by. "Ty? Good grief. I used to babysit the Gibson kids." She stared at the well-built blond bartender until he finally looked their way.

He grinned, then shrugged and walked toward the group, lifting one broad hand in greeting. "Hey, Cass. I thought for a minute you weren't going to acknowledge me."

"The bane of my babysitting career." Cass followed her words with a whooping laugh. "You were a mess."

Tyler matched her laugh. "Hey, give a guy a chance. I've reformed. I haven't snuck a beer past a babysitter in, what, a dozen years? I even mix drinks now—legitimately." He puffed up his broad chest and cocked his thumb at the line of bottles behind him. "Believe it, O ye of little faith."

Cass shook her head and looked around at the others. "This kid was a handful—and sweet-talked his way out of everything."

Birdie waved her words away. "I've known Tyler since he was knee-high to a grasshopper. He's a wonderful boy." She pushed her glasses into her cap of silver hair and smiled at him. "Your grandmother is happy you're back. Esther always stood by you even when your parents were ready to sell you to the highest bidder." Birdie reached across the bar top and patted him on the cheek, a gesture only Birdie Favazza could carry off graciously.

Ty laughed. "Having a grandma who was the town's police dispatcher was a pain when I was in high school, but she's a great old gal. My folks retired to Florida, but Grams talked me into coming back to Sea Harbor. I got laid off a construction job in the city, so she paid for a quickie course in bartending and then sweetly talked Kevin into giving me a gig at the Ocean's Edge."

"Of course she did," Birdie said. "She'd move the earth for you, and we're happy she did."

A group of college-aged women sidled up to the bar, their eyes and seductive smiles focused on Tyler.

"Business." Tyler lifted one shoulder in a playful shrug, then moved back to mixing martinis and smiling his way into the women's hearts.

"Who would have thought?" Cass said. "A nice kid with lots of visible attributes, but as his grandma Esther would say, 'not always with the sense God gave a donkey.'"

Birdie laughed. "She didn't say donkey, if I remember the conversation correctly. But I do remember her worries about him growing up. Everyone loves Ty. And he loves everyone back in equal measure, but not always wisely."

Nell motioned toward a table she'd claimed nearby just as a bell tinkled in the distance and a microphone whistled to life.

Willow Adams, cochair of the event, stood as tall as her five-foot-one frame allowed and welcomed them all to the first annual charity auction. "But before you head off to the amazing food stations or to view tonight's amazing donations, my cohost tonight, Laura Danvers, and I would like to thank a few people."

Elliot, Laura's banker husband, led the applause as his wife hurried over to Willow's side. In her mid-thirties, Laura Danvers was already a well-respected leader in Sea Harbor society. It was a rare charity that didn't have a touch of Laura in it somewhere.

"So many people to thank, so little time." Laura laughed, then gestured to the programs scattered on all the tables and waved for those at the bar to find a place to sit. "The program lists everyone who generously supported us tonight, but there are a couple of people we want to mention because their drive and generosity are what we are all about. Dr. Lily Virgilio, please join us."

The crowd applauded again as the attractive doctor came forward to give a brief explanation of the health program the community center was initiating for the families of Sea Harbor who couldn't afford care.

"I wonder if Lily's associate is as supportive of the program as she is," Izzy whispered to Nell and Birdie. She nodded toward the table where Martin Seltzer sat, his long face solemn and pale, his eyes never leaving Lily's face.

"Not terribly happy, is he now?" Birdie frowned at the man, as if her look could coax him into being a bit more cheery for the festive event. "Poor Martin. I think this is the last place he wants to be. He told me once that he'd rather have a root canal than attend obligatory cocktail parties."

They watched the doctor cradle a glass of water in his long fingers, his eyes never leaving Lily as she handed the microphone back to Laura and stepped off the stage, returning to their table.

Willow picked up the praise. "And next, a huge thank-you to Franklin Danvers." She put her palms out and shook her head. "Okay, okay, we all know he's Laura's uncle and there's no way he could have turned us down when we went to him begging."

She paused for brief laughter, then went on. "But Mr. Danvers didn't just agree to help, he said yes in a most generous way, underwriting all the food and drink you're enjoying tonight. And it's my guess he'll be reaching in his pockets again before the evening is over, once his beautiful wife sees our auction items."

Laura looked over and encouraged her uncle to stand. He and his wife sat at the head table, along with the Drs. Virgilio and Seltzer.

"I think the new wife has definitely softened Franklin," Ben said, laughing at Franklin's courtly bow.

"I think it's a bit more than that," Birdie said. "Not only is Tamara beautiful, but she's giving Franklin the one thing in his life that's been missing. An heir."

A perfectly coiffed Tamara Danvers sat with a look of pride on her face as she lifted her hands in enthusiastic applause. A diamond ring sparkled on her finger. She leaned over and said something low to Martin Seltzer, and to their surprise, the somber doctor managed a smile.

Ben lifted an eyebrow. "She's pregnant?"

"Newly pregnant," Izzy said. "You're just not on the cutting edge like we are, Uncle Ben."

"Maybe that explains Franklin's recent largesse. He was in Europe for a few weeks a short while back looking into new business opportunities for his firm. A successful trip, I gather, but a side product was that he brought back some ideas to increase tourism for Sea Harbor. A group of us got together at the library last week to talk about it. On his way in, Franklin noticed some damage a winter storm had done to the roof and wrote a check right then and there to fix it. And then he suggested that the children's room at the library looked a little ragged and needed some improvements. He offered to cover those costs, too."

"So, Sam, when are you going to pull out your wallet?" Cass asked. "How about a new school for baby Perry?"

Their laughter was drowned out by Willow, once again taking the microphone as she encouraged people to fill their plates at the gourmet food stations, enjoy the music and dancing, and above all, bid on the many treasurers awaiting signatures at the auction tables.

Izzy dropped her purse at the table. "While all of you are enjoying your alcoholic beverages, I'm going to indulge myself in other ways. I'm going shopping."

"I'm right behind you," Cass said, dropping a lacy wrap on a chair back and asking Danny to fill a plate for her.

They walked across the room, passed the veranda where Cass' brother, Pete, and his Fractured Fish band were warming up. Brightly decorated banners—courtesy of Canary Cove artists—hung from fish line above the auction tables, designating the auction categories.

"Jewelry," Izzy read, heading toward a white-clothed table with tiered displays.

Willow was already there. "You have to see this," she said, waving them over. "This came in late today, just as we were finishing the setup."

It was a platinum necklace—two gold hearts the size of pretzels hanging from the chain. Roped around the hearts, binding them together, was a string of sparkling sapphires, diamonds, and rubies.

Izzy gasped. "Good grief."

"It's big," Cass said, touching the hearts with the tip of her finger.

Nell walked up and looked over Cass' shoulder. "My. It's certainly large," she said, moving in for a closer look. She frowned. "It looks familiar."

"It'd be difficult to forget," Izzy said. "But it's not exactly your taste, Aunt Nell."

Nell laughed. No, it wasn't. It looked expensive. In fact, it shouted that fact for all to see. Nell's taste in jewelry ran to far more simple items.

"Are those stones real?" Izzy asked Willow.

"Real as you and me. At least that's what the papers accompanying it read."

"It must weigh a ton," Cass said.

Tamara Danvers walked up behind them. "It's beautiful, isn't it? I could look at it all night."

"Beautiful . . . and big," Cass repeated. "Very big."

But Tamara ignored the teasing. Her eyes grew large as she examined the clear, perfect diamonds, the rubies and sapphires circling the hearts. She leaned closer to the velvet display.

Izzy looked at the card describing the gems. "It was an anonymous donation."

Anonymous. Nell looked more closely at the hearts. "Someone was generous to part with this."

Tamara couldn't take her eyes off the necklace. "I have a bracelet and earrings with jewels slightly bigger, more expensive, but it would go beautifully together. It's very nice."

"And big," Willow whispered to Cass behind Tamara's back.

Tamara touched it gingerly, almost as if a diamond would explode before her eyes. Then she pressed a finger to her throat, as if feeling the necklace hanging there, measuring it, touching her skin. "Franklin will want something to celebrate our news. This might be just the thing." Her smile was coy. She wrote down his name.

They waited for a moment to make sure of the good news being celebrated.

Tamara touched her abdomen lightly. "The heir," she said, then scribbled a bid behind his name. "People say it's too early to be telling people, but I can't seem to keep the news private."

"Good news can be like that," Nell said. She smiled at the numbers Tamara had scribbled on the bid sheet. "Franklin is very generous."

"Yes, he is. He spoils me, especially now that we have a baby coming."

"The necklace will look great on you," Izzy said. "Not too many people could wear a piece of jewelry like that—but you can, with your height and figure."

"And these new breasts that pregnancy has given me," she laughed. "Unexpected but quite nice." She looked down at her body with obvious pleasure.

They all smiled, not sure where to rest their eyes.

But it was true—the business mogul's younger wife's figure was even more voluptuous with the increased blood supply of early pregnancy. She wore her beauty carefully, as Birdie put it, as if it might break. It was well tended, made possible by Franklin's wealth. Tonight her figure was highlighted by a shimmering strapless gown and gold necklace collar. Yes, she could wear the entwined hearts comfortably. They'd settle between her breasts and beg to be admired.

"I love jewelry. And, well, that dear man owes me—he left me home alone for nearly a month while he traveled the world." Her words fell away as she looked at the necklace again.

Willow wedged herself in beside Tamara and picked up the necklace, holding it up to catch the light. "Just so you know, I heard Alphonso Santos say that the sapphires matched his wife Liz's eyes," she said, her dark eyebrows lifting. One finger trailed down the lined sheet. "Hmmm. It looks like he's interested in this necklace, too."

"Oh?" Tamara picked up the sheet and scanned the names, finding the generous Santos' bid immediately. She quickly scribbled Franklin's name on the sheet again and, alongside it, a new, higher bid.

Across the room, Franklin Danvers stood at the bar, watching his wife as one would admire a fine painting. Tamara's husband wasn't a tall man, but his solid stance, strong, handsome features, and intense gaze granted him a power lacking in other, larger men.

Several Cape Ann businessmen approached him and he turned away, moving easily into a weighty discussion of some sort, seemingly impervious to the party atmosphere spinning around them.

Tamara looked at the bid sheet once more, gave the necklace a proprietary pat, and moved on down the jewelry table, dutifully scribbling generous bids on additional item sheets.

Once she was out of earshot, Nell looked at Willow. "You're devious—you know that, young lady? You intentionally got her to add several numbers to that bid."

Willow chuckled as she checked Tamara's latest bid. "I am devious, aren't I? And so good at it." She wrinkled her nose at Nell—her second mother, as she called her—and moved along to another table, checking items and encouraging bidders along the way.

"Tamara deserves that necklace, showy as it may be. Life with Franklin Danvers can't be all fun and games," Cass said. "And he has two ex-wives to prove it."

Izzy agreed. "He seems kind of . . . well, sedate, I guess you'd say. Nothing like his wife."

"Pete says she's a party girl," Cass said.

Izzy frowned. "Party girl?"

"Well, not now that she's pregnant, I suppose. But he used to see her at the Gull Tavern when the band was playing there a couple months ago. Her husband was traveling, Europe or somewhere, and Pete said she was probably bored, being alone in that huge house."

They watched Tamara as she walked over to the bar and stood beside her husband. Her platinum hair was pulled straight back, reflecting the lights from above. Mrs. Franklin Danvers was every inch the glamorous executive wife tonight, not looking much like someone who partied at the Gull. She was put together perfectly, almost too perfectly, as if pulling one thread would cause her to unravel like a poorly knit sweater.

"She probably was lonely with him gone," Nell said. "Even when he's home, he works long hours, though I suspect a baby will keep him home more often."

Izzy nodded. "Tamara comes into the shop often for that very reason. She doesn't like to be alone. There's always a group in the back room and she likes sitting around talking to them. But it's funny, after she leaves, I realize I don't know her, not really."

"You're never sure what's really there, right?" Cass said.

"Something like that. Although sometimes she comes out with really personal things. Like a couple months ago—it was before she was pregnant—she told a whole group that before she got married, she had a checkup to make sure she could have a baby. Franklin suggested it, she said."

Nell lifted her eyebrows in surprise. "That's *very* personal."

"And weird," Cass said.

"Well, maybe not," Nell said. "If it was important to both of them, maybe it was wise."

But it was definitely an odd thing to share with people you didn't know well. Tamara was Franklin's third wife—and the first two marriages had obviously not produced a baby. Perhaps that fact played into the decision. Nell looked back across the room.

Tamara was laughing at something her husband said, one hand resting on the sleeve of his Italian suit.

He's mine, her posture seemed to say.

When Franklin turned his attention to the businessmen and more serious talk, her eyes wandered around the room, to the tables of jewelry, the well-dressed couples, then back to the bar, where Tyler Gibson was disengaging himself from a bevy of beauties. His eyes caught hers, and he paused briefly, his smiling look traveling over Tamara like a beam of light.

His attention seemed to startle Tamara, as if she'd been caught looking when she shouldn't have been, and she quickly turned away.

The bartender looked surprised at the rebuff, then shrugged it off and walked the length of the bar to where Justin Dorsey stood waiting, a bag of ice in his hands.

Justin nodded toward Tamara with a grin, apparently noticing the brush-off. Tyler laughed and took the ice, shrugging off Justin's teasing.

A minute later the mayor approached the Danvers group, and together they moved out to the veranda, where more appetizers and music filled the sea air.

"Have you seen Justin?" Janie asked, coming up to the group. The worry lines across her forehead had returned.

"He's working." Izzy pointed toward the bar. Justin held the ice lid open while Tyler dumped it in.

"It looks to me like he's making himself useful," Cass added.

Janie's smile returned. "Good. Which I guess I should be doing, too. I promised Willow and Laura I'd keep an eye on the auction items." She hurried off, waving to Justin as she disappeared into the crowd.

The evening passed quickly as plates were cleared and more desserts made the rounds. Willow, Janie, and Laura wandered through the crowd, encouraging bidding and making sure food and drink were plentiful. Justin and the other valets set up extra tables in the entry hall for checkout, and boxes and bags were discreetly piled up behind them to carry off winning items.

Finally Laura brought the bidding to a close, and the volunteer staff moved quickly, collecting bid sheets, circling the winners.

Laura motioned for the bevy of volunteers to stand behind the tables where people would bring their receipts and claim the portable items.

"Do you need help?" Nell asked.

"I think we're fine," Willow said. "Laura could organize a roomful of toddlers. She's amazing. And Kevin and Tyler will stick around after the bar closes and help the other guys handle any of the heavy stuff. They've all been taking turns patrolling the tables, too, keeping an eye on things."

Laura laughed. "Our very own muscle men." She turned to Willow. "Time to read off the top item winners. Want to do the honors?"

Squeals and cheers greeted the generous winning bids as people stepped up to claim their winning sailing adventures and vacation homes. When Willow read Franklin Danvers' name as the highest bidder on the last item—the diamond, sapphire, and ruby heart necklace—Tamara leaned over and kissed him fully. The crowd cheered, and the organizers declared the evening a wild success.

As people headed to the entry hall to claim their items, Nell looked around for Birdie and Ben.

Birdie waved from a table where she was claiming a cartload of items. "Ben is loading his art winnings into the car."

Nell laughed. "All we need is a few more walls in our house."

"They're all Canary Cove artists. Ben couldn't resist."

He appeared then, taking Birdie's box and motioning toward the entryway. "If Izzy has to stand for one more minute, I think she'll have that baby in the middle of the community center. She's drained."

He nodded toward the jewelry table where Izzy and Sam stood talking quietly to Laura and Willow. Behind them, Janie Levin, along with several other volunteers, huddled together, listening intently to what Laura was saying.

"Something's wrong," Nell said as they made their way toward the group.

On the table was the black velvet stand that once held the sapphire and ruby diamond necklace.

"It's gone," Laura mouthed, meeting Birdie's eyes.

Nell turned and looked at her.

Birdie's hand went to her throat. "Gone? As in . . . "

Laura nodded.

"Oh, my," she said, and moved to Laura's side.

"Tamara or Franklin didn't claim it?" Nell asked.

Willow shook her head. Her eyes were moist.

Nell watched Birdie's face, composed and in charge, as if it were her job now to calm the event organizers. Suddenly she remembered why the necklace looked familiar. She'd seen it before—in Birdie's den, when they were looking for some papers in the safe behind Sonny Favazza's portrait. "It was your necklace, wasn't it?" she said quietly.

Before Birdie could answer, Laura spoke up, her voice choked. "Birdie, I'm so sorry. I don't know how this could have happened. The volunteers were watching the tables all night." Her face was the color of her snowy white Versace dress.

Birdie waved away the concern. "No worry. It isn't really a problem—except maybe for your uncle Franklin's wife. Tamara was determined to get that necklace." She looked beyond Laura to the bar, where Tamara Danvers stood chatting with Ty Gibson and Kevin Sullivan, oblivious of the drama unfolding behind her.

"I'm calling the police—"

"No, dear, you won't." Birdie placed one blue-veined hand on Laura's arm. Her voice allowed no room for arguing. "Perhaps it was misplaced. But either way, the jewelry is insured. Besides, my mother always said that when one lost something to theft—if that's what this was—the thief most likely needed it more than you do. And in the best of worlds, one would find that person and give her something to go with it."

"So we should find a bracelet to match?" Izzy asked.

Birdie chuckled. "That would definitely be the answer. But I doubt if such a thing exists. So instead, we'll forgive and forget. As I'm sure dear Carl would have done."

"Carl?" Cass asked.

"My second husband. He gave it to me. He was fond of such weighty and expensive embellishments, even though I wouldn't have been able to stand up if I had tried to wear any of them. Somehow he thought bigger and brighter and more expensive was always a good thing." She smiled brightly. "Now, let's not ruin a wonderful party over a necklace that I never liked. There's no need to talk about this with anyone."

She glanced across the room again, and then looked sadly at Laura. "Except perhaps with Tamara and Franklin Danvers. And I suspect you are the best person to handle that, my dear."

Chapter 3

"**F**ranklin Danvers was gracious about the whole messy incident Saturday night," Birdie said. She sat on the patio at Coffee's—Harbor Road's always crowded coffeehouse. Her small hands cradled a steaming cup of dark roast.

A blue sky and Coffee's dark roast. Certainly a good way to begin another week, in Birdie's opinion. All was right with the world.

Across from her, Nell and Ben listened with interest to the happenings since Saturday night when Birdie's necklace went missing. Laura and Elliot Danvers had taken her to Sunday brunch and filled her in on all the details.

"Franklin honored his bid—even though he didn't get the necklace. He assured Tamara he'd find something equally as beautiful for her. On my end, I'll funnel the insurance payment back to the community center fund, so nothing is lost, everyone wins nicely."

"Even the thief," Ben said.

Birdie laughed. "Yes, even the thief. Although whoever that may be is doomed to having a sore neck should he or she ever try to wear it.

"Franklin Danvers was adamant Laura and Willow call the police, but Laura held her ground, as I'd asked. Not an easy task, standing up to that man." Birdie tossed a crumb of croissant to a waiting gull.

"It would have been a shame to end that lovely evening with flashing blue lights," Nell said.

"On the other hand, Franklin's right—someone committed a crime," Ben said.

"I suppose," Birdie said. "And I believe people should accept the consequences of their actions. But last night simply didn't seem the time or place. And perhaps the person truly was needy. How do fines and jail time help such an individual?"

Ben covered Birdie's hand, his large one causing hers to disappear. "Just one reason why we love you, Birdie. But what if the guy is buying drugs with money he makes off the jewels? We don't know that, now, do we?"

Birdie shushed him and suggested he forget he once had gone to law school.

"Does Laura have any idea who might have done it?" Nell asked.

"Not really, and she was reluctant to guess. There were hundreds of guests, lots of college kids helping out, people in the kitchen, catering, bartenders."

Nell thought over the evening. The tables were always crowded—so crowded it wouldn't have been too difficult to sweep the necklace off into a pocket. "It happened late in the evening or someone would have noticed the piece missing earlier."

Ben nodded. "It was a valuable necklace." He looked at Birdie over the rim of his coffee mug.

"That's all relative, now, isn't it? Valuable to whom? It dawned on me recently that things sitting idly in a locked box could be put to much better use—like Lily Virgilio's free health program."

"You're right, as always." Ben pushed out his chair, then leaned over and patted Birdie's hand. "And with your wisdom ringing in my ears, I'm off to a morning meeting with the yacht club directors. I'll leave you and Nell to figure out the world's problems."

"And solve them," Birdie said sweetly.

Ben laughed as he walked off down the street, his long legs taking him quickly out of sight.

"Ben wears retirement well," Birdie mused. "Though that's a bit of a misnomer. He's as busy as anyone I know."

"But he can pick and choose now; that's the secret. He only has to attend a few family business meetings a year. That's the stress that was wearing down that heart of his. He finally could see what his brothers had already agreed to—that the nephews and nieces could handle things just fine. Let new blood take over."

A shadow fell across the table and their words.

Mary Pisano stood at Nell's elbow. The bed-and-breakfast owner wore her customary hospitable smile, one that also served her well in drawing out information for the local newspaper column she delighted in writing. "It was a perfectly lovely party, but it would have been better without someone stealing your jewels, Birdie," she said. "Theft. It's everywhere."

Birdie just shook her head. "Mary, you amaze me. You know the unknown. I imagine you know the Sox score before the game is played. Surely you know who took that necklace."

No, she said. She didn't know that. But she wished she did. And she'd certainly work at finding out. And when she did, her thoughts about it would appear in her "About Town" column immediately.

The sound of shouting from down the street stopped Mary from the questions they knew she had on the tip of her tongue.

"It's Archie Brandley," Birdie said. She stood up and shaded her eyes against the sun. "It's not like him to yell like that unless someone is spilling coffee on one of his books."

Nell had already gathered her sweater and bag. "I'm headed that way. Let's see what's up."

Mary tucked her laptop into a backpack and led the way across Harbor Road and down the block, the diminutive columnist moving as fast as her sneakers could carry her.

A small crowd had gathered at the end of the alleyway that separated Archie's bookstore from Izzy's yarn shop. Standing in the middle of the gravel road was a red-faced Archie Brandley, his hands on his hips and his booming voice shouting at a young man teetering at the top of a wooden ladder. "You're not going to kill yourself in my alley, young man," they heard Archie boom. "I won't allow it."

"Good grief," Nell said, staring up the ladder. "What are you doing up there, Justin?"

Justin Dorsey looked down, a dimpled smile appearing instantly and one hand releasing its hold on the ladder to wave. "Hey, Ms. Endicott."

"Hold on to that ladder. You're going to get yourself killed."

"Nah. I'm good with ladders. I painted a whole house last summer. This is my first time at window washing, though. Can't be that hard, right?"

"He's a fool," Archie muttered. "I don't trust that kid farther than I can throw him. He's already dropped a wet sponge on poor Hemingway's head." He looked down at his aging Lab, lying calmly in the middle of the alley. "Janie needs to get herself another project. This one is trouble, I guarantee it."

"Does Izzy know you're washing her windows?" Nell looked up the old ladder. A bucket of water hung from a rusty hook attached to its side. She wondered briefly about Izzy's insurance policy. Perhaps it was indelicate of her, but she also didn't want Izzy's baby to be subjected to any stress that an accident might incur.

Justin shifted his weight and Nell held her breath as the ladder moved, creaked, then settled back against the two-story building.

The side door slammed and Izzy appeared on the steps. "What's going on out here?" She stared at the crowd, at Nell, Birdie, and Archie, and then at the wooden ladder leaning up against her building. Her eyes moved up until they locked into Justin's.

"What are you doing up there, Justin?" Worry lines creased her forehead.

Justin started to wave again, then thought better of it and held on to the swaying ladder with both hands. "Sorry to cause such a commotion," he shouted down. "I just wanted to help Janie."

"Janie?" Archie demanded.

"Janie?" Nell and Birdie said together.

"Oh, jeez," Izzy said. She looked at Birdie and Nell. "I was going to tell you about it. Janie Levin is moving into the apartment above my shop. That little house out on the highway that she was renting is up for sale." She took a step back and looked again at the young man on the ladder, then over at a beet red Archie.

"I guess he thought the apartment needed cleaner windows. He's probably right. He's not so bad, Archie."

Archie's thick eyebrows pulled together, his frown telling Izzy what he thought of her personality assessment. But before he could articulate it, a metal bucket plummeted to the ground, its contents spraying old Hemingway and Archie Brandley's new khaki slacks.

The ugly gray stain was demonstrable proof that Izzy's windows did, in fact, need cleaning.

A call from Dr. Virgilio's receptionist told Izzy that her morning doctor's appointment had been interrupted by the birth of three babies. Izzy agreed to come by after work the next day instead—a better time, anyway, since her shop closed at six on Tuesdays.

Nell was fine with that, too. Perhaps they'd have more time with the doctor. Although what they would do with it, Nell wasn't sure. Izzy had seemed better the past couple of days. And Sam had told Ben that she was sleeping better. No worries, Sam said. And Ben brought the message home forcefully.

"So, my Nellie, you need to throw that worry right out the window. Right now," Ben had said the night before, wrapping his arms around Nell and trying to understand her concern for such a natural happening.

Maybe it was because her own efforts to have a baby had never been realized. The years of trying, of miscarrying, of having an adoption fall through, had been put to rest over the years, relegated to a quiet corner of Nell's heart. But now, in the time it took for Sam and Izzy to show up on her doorstep with the news that she was to be an aunt again, they reared up—the worries, the fears, the wondering. All overshadowed by enormous joy, but still there, lingering at the edges of her happiness.

Ben suggested it wasn't fair to Izzy for her to hover. He was right. Did all mothers go through this when their daughters announced a pregnancy? But she wasn't Izzy's mother, and even Izzy's own mother didn't seem to share Nell's anxiousness. Nell's sister called her once a week, but mostly Caroline talked about nurseries and showers and baby names for her first grandchild. Not anxieties.

She'd finally decided it was Izzy herself who was making her anxious. She and her niece were so closely connected, and some days she felt Izzy's mood shifts as acutely as if they were her own.

"Aunt Nell?" Izzy's voice intruded, pulling her from her thoughts. They were standing at the door to the Virgilio Clinic.

"Where did you go? You were far, far away. . . ." Izzy smiled, searching Nell's face. She rested one hand on the doorknob, then leaned over and brushed Nell's cheek with a kiss. "I love you," she whispered. "Thank you for being with me."

A push from the other side of the door caused Izzy's hand to fall from the knob and they looked up into the smiling face of Tamara Danvers, her husband, Franklin, right behind her.

"Greetings, ladies," Franklin said. He nodded slightly, then took Tamara's arm and ushered her down the steps as carefully as if he were carrying a basket of eggs.

A long black car pulled up at the curb and a uniformed chauffeur hopped out and opened the door. Tamara looked back at Izzy and Nell and offered a small wave. She lifted one shoulder slightly as if apologizing for her husband's unnecessary gallantry—but the smile was more one of an Olympic swimmer winning a gold medal.

The door closed and the car sped away.

"Laura says her uncle is crazy with joy," Izzy said. "He insisted on extra tests, precautions, recording blood types, all sorts of things, even though Dr. Lily assured him that the drugstore pregnancy test was fine this early in the game."

"Well, I suppose when you've waited this long, you want to be sure everything is covered."

Izzy watched the car disappear around the corner. "I suppose, although I think of having a baby as a more natural happening, something that shouldn't be weighted down with all of that."

Nell listened, her own thoughts about Franklin's odd behavior filtering into the mix. Rumors had surrounded Franklin Danvers over the years, something that often accompanied great wealth. It seemed all that had come from his previous marriages were tales of wives' infidelities—not children. Perhaps history and experience colored a person's approach to events, even to the natural order of things, like childbearing.

It was certainly true in her own life.

She followed Izzy into the waiting room and closed the door behind her.

Once the great home of a sea captain, the Virgilio Clinic still held a grandeur and spoke of the ocean. On every wall were framed paintings of Cape Ann's heritage—majestic storms, stately schooners, and brave, weathered fisherman. In the reception area, soft couches were angled discreetly, offering a sense of warmth and comfort—and privacy. At the far end of the room, Janie Levin stood behind the reception desk, looking down at a computer screen.

She looked up as the door clicked shut, and almost immediately her face flooded with apologies. The news of Justin's recent escapade had clearly made its way to the clinic. "I don't know what he was doing today. I'm so sorry, Iz. Justin doesn't think before he acts."

"He could have fallen," Nell said. "That was the concern, Janie. The ladder was ancient. Justin found it in a shed behind the bookstore."

"And simply helped himself to it," Janie said. She looked around to be sure no one was within earshot, then lowered her voice. "It's a pattern with him. Do you think he'll learn?"

"A pattern?" Nell said.

"He's been in trouble his whole life. But no one ever tried to help him or give him a chance. I thought I could make up for some of that." She leafed through a few papers on the desk. "Sometimes I bite off more than I can chew, but I really thought I could help him. He can be so charming—when he isn't trying to think up ways to get rich. Having money is so important to him, but I guess when you've never had any, maybe you think it's an answer to all your problems, I don't know."

"Well, Justin was right about one thing—those windows were filthy," Izzy said.

"Like he thought I needed clean windows? You're so generous to rent me that beautiful place, Iz—I'd love it if it had no windows."

She bit down on her bottom lip. A slow flush of frustration worked its way to each cheek. "Tommy is upset with me. He'd like to wipe Justin off the face of Sea Harbor, if not the earth."

"Justin's heart is in the right place," Izzy said, trying to coax a smile back to Janie's face.

"But that's the problem. Sure, he means well, and he's really smart—he's a genius with computers and he loves all the lab stuff. He even won some science awards in high school before he dropped out, if you can believe it. But he still acts like a kid—he's nineteen!—but he does really dumb things. He always seems to be a step removed from the real world, like he's living in this dreamworld or something, making up his own rules, coming up with silly schemes to get rich fast." She sighed. "I can't imagine that a pail of dirty water on Archie and his beautiful dog is going to endear him to anyone in town."

"Archie will be fine," Nell said, waving away her worry. "And so will Hemingway."

Janie brushed a handful of hair from her forehead and picked up a folder from the desk. She glanced over her shoulder toward the offices. "I shouldn't be dishing on him. At least he showed up for work on time."

"Justin's here?" Nell asked.

"He works here. Dr. Lily has him doing odd jobs around the clinic. He fixes things—jammed printers, computers. He's great at details, keeping files and reports and papers in the right place. But washing windows? Not so much. Now, on to other things." Janie's voice was dismissive as she turned back into the efficient, in-charge, competent head nurse of the Virgilio Clinic. "This is about you, Iz. It's time to hear baby Perry's amazing heartbeat."

She held open the door to the inner offices, then led them through the maze of hallways that defined the old house. On the other side of the building, Dr. Alan Hamilton and a younger partner ran a family practice, sharing some offices and a dispensary. On this end the hallways wound around examining rooms, offices, and a library that housed Dr. Lily's busy obstetrics and gynecology practice. Unlike some other old structures in Sea Harbor that had suffered through many renovations, the clinic still stood tall and proud; the most recent architect had done a masterful job of keeping the quaint touches, the curving hallways and tall windows that looked out onto the sea, the wide stairways to the upper floor and a winding, narrow one that led to a widow's walk at the very top of the house. But instead of dark corners and the smell of ships and stormy seas, the walls were white and bright and smelled slightly of antiseptic, freshly laundered linens, and soapy creams.

Nell followed her niece around a corner, her eyes lingering on Izzy's rolling walk. The newfound sway on her tall, well-toned niece was still unfamiliar to Nell, making her wonder if she'd recognize Izzy if she were behind her on the street. She'd heard it called a waddle, a result of the ligaments loosening for the baby to be born. But that word didn't resonate with the lovely sway her niece had adopted. To Nell, it was beautiful.

As they turned another corner, Nell glanced through a half-open pocket door into a small office. Martin Seltzer, dressed in a white jacket, stood near a window, murmuring in a low monotone. His hair was bright white, his shoulders narrow and pushed slightly forward. He turned his head, words still falling from his lips, then spotted Nell before she could turn away. White eyebrows lifted, as if in surprise at seeing a woman watching him. Slightly embarrassed, Nell smiled and murmured something about having a good day.

The doctor smiled back—a grave smile—as if clouded by thoughts that he needed to get back to. As Nell began to turn away, she noticed someone else in the room and realized the doctor hadn't been murmuring to himself. It was Heather Gruen, a young woman Nell knew from the hair salon. Heather was pregnant with her first child and openly nervous about every change her body was undergoing. She waved to Nell, then turned her full attention back to Dr. Seltzer and he to her, releasing Nell to hurry down the hall after Izzy.

The man was certainly an enigma, so uncomfortable in social settings, yet obviously patient and understanding with anxious mothers-to-be. She and Ben saw Martin around town often, but he never encouraged long conversations and sometimes bordered on rudeness.

Birdie thought Nell misjudged the man. He was simply a loner, she said. Some people found pleasure in being alone. Or maybe, Birdie said, he simply hadn't met anyone interesting enough to befriend. At that Nell had laughed and given in. Birdie was often right about such things. And he'd certainly seemed comfortable with Heather Gruen.

She followed Izzy into an empty examining room and waited while Janie chatted, carefully recording Izzy's weight on the chart.

When Lily Virgilio walked in, a bundle of professional efficiency, Janie headed off toward a ringing phone.

"The receptionist went home early," Dr. Lily explained. "Janie is wearing several hats today." She gave Nell a hug. "I'm so glad you came with Izzy. It gives me a chance to gush about that wonderful event. I'm still overwhelmed by the amount of money raised for the free health clinic. This town is simply wonderful. My thanks to all of you who made it happen."

"It was a great evening—and a great cause. Besides, we love an excuse for a party."

Lily laughed, then turned toward Izzy and patted the paper-wrapped exam table. "So—let's see what's going on with you, Izzy. Sleeping any better?" She wrapped the cuff around Izzy's upper arm and began pumping air into it. She watched Izzy's face, reading it with practiced eyes.

"Somewhat better. Running helps. Except for . . ." Her words fell off.

"Except for what?"

Images of the empty car seat flashed before Izzy's eyes. She blinked them away. "Except for the fact that I eat everything in sight."

"You can afford it, Izzy. No worries there." Lily released the air and watched the needle flicker as the cuff deflated. "Still a little higher than I'd like it," she said, scribbling a note into the record.

"Dangerously high?" It was Nell asking the question. Izzy's eyes were on the open window, as if the darkening sky was dramatically more important than talking about her vital signs.

"No," Lily answered, her voice reassuring. "Not dangerously high and there's nothing that needs to be done. Blood pressure often rises in doctors' offices and that may well be what's going on here. I am just being overly cautious. Izzy seems a little stressed sometimes so I'm keeping a close eye on her."

"Without reason," Izzy said, rejoining the conversation. "It's all silly. It will pass. It's just a feeling—like a sixth sense that developed along with my pregnancy. Things just don't seem quite right. I don't want my baby coming yet, not until things are peaceful." Her arms instinctively circled her belly.

Lily sighed. "You want a perfect world to bring your baby into. Wouldn't that be nice? I'm afraid you might have to wait a long time."

Izzy just smiled.

Nell watched the look that passed over Izzy's face. She meant it;

she sensed something and it didn't matter if it sounded silly or man-ufactured or crazy. To Izzy it was real.

Until Izzy got pregnant, Nell always thought the similarities between her niece and her sister, Caroline—Izzy's mother—were confined to their tall, slender builds and glorious thick hair. But pregnancy unearthed a few more. She remembered Caroline saying similar things during her three pregnancies. She was vehemently protective of her unborn baby, wanting to keep the baby safe inside until she declared the world ready for him or her. Nell had listened to Caroline with a certain wonder, marveling at the miracle she con-sidered each pregnancy to be and whatever that fierce protective in-stinct was. And now she saw it in Izzy, too, that sureness that she knew what was right for her unborn child.

"So," Lily was saying beside her, "I suspect we have a little bruiser here."

"That's not a surprise." Nell smiled. "His father is one."

"Where's all this 'his' coming from?" Izzy asked.

"I stand corrected. He or she." Lily laughed. The examination complete, she helped Izzy sit up and drop her legs over the side of the table.

A knock on the door was followed by Janie's voice with a re-quest to talk to Dr. Virgilio. The words carried a sense of urgency, and Lily quickly moved outside, leaving the door ajar.

"One of us must have failed to record it, Janie," they heard the doctor whisper. "I'm sure that's what it was. Don't worry. I'll take care of it."

When she returned, a smile was back in place. Again, she reas-sured both Izzy and Nell that the baby was in fine shape. "Probably finer shape than any of us," she added.

"Thanks, Dr. Lily." Izzy picked up the sweater she'd left on the chair and slipped it over her shoulders, tying it above the large mound of baby. "Even though I know my baby is fine, it's always nice to hear it from you. And Sam hangs on every word. He'd be here today if he weren't doing a photo shoot in Boston."

Lily nodded and smiled, but her mind seemed to be elsewhere, beyond the confines of the small examining room. "Next week, then?" she asked absently. "Check with Janie when you leave. She'll set you up."

Lily walked out of the room and disappeared down the hall.

Nell and Izzy walked back toward the waiting area. It was dark outside now, the neon lights in the hallway casting shadows along the painted walls. The office door Nell had looked through earlier was closed, no sounds indicating life on the other side.

But as they turned another corner, Janie's voice stopped them short.

She was standing between two doorways at the end of the hallway. One opened into a large, well-lit room filled with computers, filing cabinets, and bookshelves. The other doorway was partially open, but enough to see a winding staircase leading upward.

Janie's hands were on her hips, and her cheeks were nearly as red as her hair. "You're supposed to be fixing that computer, not roaming around the clinic. What were you doing up there, anyway?" Her hand pointed toward the staircase. "That door shouldn't be open like that. Dr. Seltzer is adamant about it."

Justin dropped his head.

"No, don't tell me. I can smell it—your darn cigarettes. You can't smoke up on the widow's walk. Dr. Lily told you that, Justin. You're going to burn the place down!"

"It was five minutes, Janie," he began, but Janie didn't allow any more words.

"Dr. Seltzer lives on the next floor, and that staircase goes right by the back door to his apartment. He'll kill you if he finds out you were up there. What are you thinking?"

Justin tried once more to talk, but Janie put out both her hands, stopping him. "It's too much, Justin. And look at all these files scattered every which way. Dr. Seltzer says you've lost some of them. I've had it, Justin. Just leave. Forget about everything and just go away."

Justin's reply was a plea, his voice pouring out into the hallway. "Hey, I'm sorry, honest. I'll fix it all, the charts, everything. One more chance, that's all I need."

Janie walked in, scooped up an armful of files, and began backing out of the room.

Justin jumped up from the chair and started to follow her. "I'll make it up to you. Things are going to be better now. Honest, Janie. I'm going to be making some real money. Don't be mad." His voice was a plea, so warm and heartfelt it would have melted chocolate had the air-conditioning not been so high.

"You don't *think*. That's your problem. One of them, anyway," Janie scolded, trying to stay firm. "You've missed a dozen shifts at the Artist's Palate—Merry is ready to kill you—and you messed up a whole order of books at Archie Brandley's bookstore. He was so mad he wouldn't even tell me about it. Not to mention the scene at Izzy's shop today. Justin, sometimes I could . . . I could just strangle you."

But the last choked words held a softness, like those of a caring aunt or mother or teacher trying to hold on to an anger that was slipping away into a warmer feeling.

She turned, moving into the hallway quickly. Too quickly. Her elbow cracked against the door frame, sending the files in her arms flying in all directions.

"Oh, no," she cried. One hand rubbed her bruised elbow.

"Let me help." Izzy hurried forward.

But Justin was there in a split second. "Nope. I got it, ladies." He crouched down and began scooping up the folders.

Janie shook her head and managed a smile for Nell and Izzy. "I can't even blame him this time. It was my clumsiness."

Justin stood up, his arms full of files, his eyes begging for another chance.

"Those need filing," Janie began.

"I know, I know. I'm good at it. I like filing." Before she could change her mind, Justin headed back into the room and toward a row of filing cabinets.

"And don't forget the lab reports that need to go into them. Dr. Seltzer put them on the desk in there."

She shook her head once more and began walking toward the reception area, reclaiming her professional demeanor. "You need an appointment, Izzy. That's much easier to deal with than Justin. Next week, right?" She tapped the computer to life.

As Izzy and Janie looked at the appointment screen on Janie's computer, Nell stood back and looked down the hall, hoping to say good-bye to Lily.

But Lily was nowhere to be seen.

Instead, silhouetted against a window a short distance away from her was a figure. For a minute, Nell thought it was just a shadow, a trick of the light shining in from an office at that end of the hall. But when the figure moved, she recognized Dr. Seltzer. He had taken off his white coat and replaced it with a tweed jacket and English hat. In one hand he held a walking stick, his fingers gripping it tightly.

As her eyes adjusted to the hall light, she could see his face more clearly. Steely gray eyes sat deep in the pale, chiseled face, eyes focused beyond her, not seeing anything but what was at the end of the hall—two open doorways. The kindness Nell had seen in his smile earlier had disappeared completely. She turned and followed his stare.

Justin Dorsey was clearly visible, sitting on a chair near the long row of filing cabinets. His body was swaying to the music pumping through the giant headphones fixed to his head. He was fully immersed in opening one file after another, stopping now and then to glance at lab reports, carefully rearranging papers, then opening and closing the heavy metal file drawers.

He was oblivious of the deadly look fastened on his back, and the headphones prevented him from hearing anything around him, including the words that slipped from Martin Seltzer's thin lips:

"Foolish, foolish child. If I have to take care of it myself, your days here are numbered."

Chapter 4

Thursday morning gave rise to a sun so bright the light bounced off the sidewalks and warmed the ocean air. A warm June day, the weatherman said. Beach weather.

Nell walked the few blocks to Izzy's house, smelling the grass and lilac bushes. The tang of the sea.

When Izzy had suggested she and Nell do a morning run together, it made Nell chuckle. Nell's idea of a run no longer matched Izzy's, even though for years they'd pretended it worked. Pregnancy was definitely slowing down her niece's speed.

"Maybe I can keep up with you at last," she'd said, and happily agreed to join her.

Nell rounded the corner onto Marigold Road and spotted Sam and Izzy out front.

"G'morning, Nell," Sam called out as she approached the small frame house.

The Perry home sat in the middle of the block, surrounded by well-tended lawns, leafy trees, and nicely painted houses. Unpretentious and inviting. Friendly, was how Ben described the street.

Once Sam's bachelor home, it had become a reflection of both Izzy and Sam after she moved in and added her own touches. The clean lines, airy rooms, and white walls highlighted Sam's photography, while the sleek wooden furniture and brightly colored cushions spoke of Izzy's warmth. It was homey and perfect, with a deck off the back and a lightly forested trail that wound down to the sea beyond.

"You're running with us, Sam?"

Sam's laughter closed the space between them. "You know I don't punish my body that way, Nell. Now, give me a boat to sail or game of pickup basketball and you'll see a healthy, happy guy before you." He lifted the camera hanging around his neck. "But today I'm off to take some photos for a magazine article on scuba diving and surfing in these remarkable waters we call home. I'm just keeping my bride company for a few minutes."

Izzy was kneeling down beside the sidewalk, tugging out a few stray weeds. She sat back on her legs, shielding her eyes against the sun. "He's being vigilant, Aunt Nell. He's starting to hover. Sam's as bad as you are. Thinks if I hiccup, labor will begin. And to top it off, he insists on taking snapshots of me every time I turn around. This baby is going to be seeing tiny dots of light its whole life."

Sam's response was a kiss to the top of her head, followed by a gentle pat to the round of her belly—a good-bye touch to his soon-to-be-born child.

"See what I put up with, Nell?" he called back as he climbed into his car. "Sass. Nothing but sass. That's what pregnancy has done to her." He blew Izzy another kiss and drove off, his sandy hair flying in the breeze as he drove down Marigold Drive toward the beach.

"I do love that man," Nell murmured, watching him disappear.

"Yeah. Me, too," Izzy said, still crouched on the ground beside a growing pile of weeds. She finally pulled herself to a standing position and peeled off her gardening gloves.

"So, where to?" Nell asked. "Somewhere easy, I hope."

"Definitely." Izzy pulled on a Sox cap and tugged her hair through the band in back. "I was thinking maybe Paley's Cove? We can go the long, easy way, through Cliffside, then down to the beach. It's warm and sunny—the ocean breeze will feel good." Izzy began walking down the street while she talked.

"That's not too far for you?"

"Nope, it'll be fine."

Nell looked at her sideways, catching an odd tone of voice that didn't fit a carefree run with her slow-moving aunt. It was slightly clipped, a tone Izzy didn't use often. As if she had a mission beyond that of good health.

"You okay, Iz?"

Izzy nodded. "Fine."

They moved on in silence for a while, Nell effortlessly matching Izzy's pace for a change. Soon the road twisted and turned and the smaller homes in Izzy and Sam's neighborhood disappeared, giving rise to the elegant estates that spread out over the rise of land called Cliffside. The roads here were lined with centuries-old granite walls, waist-high and broken only by iron gates that marked entry into well-manicured yards and stately homes. Stands of hemlock and sweet bay magnolias partially hid the homes from view.

Most of the homes were owned by longtime residents. Some were older than the town itself. Every now and then a narrow pathway meandered between two properties to the sea beyond, the serpentine path opening into the vast blue of endless water.

"Franklin's place is the largest of them all," Izzy observed as they passed an elegant estate. The house behind the wall looked as if it had grown directly out of the granite rock upon which it was built. Several smaller houses were positioned about the property, discreet and private.

"It's the original family estate, according to Birdie. Generations of Danverses were born and died in this house. It's magnificent."

"Tamara talks a lot about the house when she's in the shop. She loves living here—the mystery, the glamour, the dark hallways. She says the place is full of secret passages and doorways that open up below the cliff, right onto the beach. It's interesting how a place can change a person. I swear her voice is even changing. Can you imagine bringing up a baby here?"

The shrill of a siren behind them drowned out the end of the sentence. Izzy and Nell spun around just as Tommy Porter rounded the corner in his police car, a light flashing on top.

Instinctively, they stopped and looked around to find something worthy of Tommy's sound effects. Just then, the wide electric gate guarding the Danvers' driveway opened. Franklin and Tamara stood just inside. Between them, his head hanging low, a tangle of wet blond hair falling over his forehead and a surfboard strapped to his back, was Justin Dorsey.

Tommy slid out of the car and walked over to Franklin Danvers, his eyes taking in the silent Justin. "Hey, Mr. Danvers, what can I do for you?"

Franklin shook Tommy's hand and motioned toward Justin. "We've got a little problem, Tom."

For a minute Tommy didn't say anything. Then, "So, what's he done now?"

Justin looked up briefly. Then he spotted Nell and Izzy standing on the side of the street, and a sheepish look of relief washed across his face. *My rescuers,* it said.

"Trespassing," Franklin said. "And upsetting my wife."

Tommy looked over at Tamara. Through a slit in her silky green caftan, a strip of tan skin and bikini straps peeked through.

She looked upset, that was true. Nell felt a strange urge to protect the young man—not for personal reasons, really. But accusing him of trespassing on the Cliffside Beach was silly. At one time or another, nearly every Sea Harbor teenager spent time on the private coastline that wound around behind the properties. Izzy herself had probably spent some time on the rocks, watching surfers master the high waves that often developed where the land jutted out.

"Trespassing?" Nell looked at Justin, then Tommy.

"Well, sure," Tommy said. "Legally speaking, anyway. There are signs all over saying it's a private beach."

But his reluctance to immediately slap a fine on the young man—or arrest him—was as evident as Tamara Danvers' uncomfortable stance.

She stood silent, as if she wished she were anywhere but standing between her husband and a young ponytailed surfer, his hair still wet and sand coating his legs. She took a step closer to Franklin and away from Justin.

Justin looked uncomfortable, standing in a sleeveless wet suit. He shoved one hand in the thigh pocket, his feet shifting back and forth.

"Justin?" Tommy focused all his attention on Janie's cousin now. "Is there anything you want to say?"

Justin shrugged. Then the familiar smile came back, but forced this time. "Hey, Officer Tom, I was, like, trying to catch a couple waves."

"Waves, my foot," Franklin said. "I came home from the office unexpectedly and it's a damn good thing I did. I went up to my bedroom to get something and spotted this kid through the window, down there on the lower terrace, hands outstretched like he was a moocher expecting a handout." He glared at Justin. "You don't belong here."

Justin hung his head again and managed a weak "Hey, sorry. We were just talking, hanging out for a minute. Didn't mean any harm, Mrs. Danvers."

Tamara looked away, her jaw rigid.

"Hanging out? I don't think so." Franklin looked over at Tamara, who was now distancing herself from both Justin and her husband.

"I need to lie down," she said. "Just let this go, Franklin." A flash of anger appeared in her eyes, but it wasn't clear who the object of her anger was.

Franklin frowned. "Tamara needs to rest—and I'm sure we all have more important things to do today than continue this conversation." He looked sternly at Justin. "But I suggest we come to an agreement, young man. This is private property. You are trespassing and harassing my wife. I'll ignore it this time because Tamara needs to get inside. But if you want to surf, try Good Harbor over in Gloucester. Or Long Beach. Not my backyard. I don't want to see you back here again."

With that, he nodded to Tommy, offered a polite smile to Izzy and Nell, and walked back through the iron gate.

While the gate slowly began to close, they caught a fleeting glimpse of the wealthy investment banker wrap his younger wife in a protective embrace and walk her slowly back down the cobbled drive to the house.

Justin heaved a sigh of relief.

Tommy walked over to him. "What is it with you, Dorsey? Mr. Danvers is a decent guy. He wouldn't have called me just because you were surfing back there or walking the beach. You shouldn't be bothering the people who live around here. Don't you ever use that thick skull of yours to think?"

Justin stood in silence, one hand cupping a worn fanny pack on his waist and the other balancing his board.

"I think Franklin is just being overprotective of his wife, Tommy," Izzy said.

"That's his choice, right? Justin upset her apparently."

"She's pregnant," Nell said.

Tommy shrugged. "Sure, makes sense, I guess. My ma always got prickly when she was having another one. You touchy, Iz?"

Izzy laughed. "You'll have to ask Sam, Tommy."

Tommy laughed, too, but when he looked away from the women and back to Justin, the smile fell away and his voice was stern. "As for you, I suggest you listen to what the man said. You're becoming a major nuisance around here, and whether he's overprotective or not, he could have slapped a fine on you for trespassing. You were lucky this time."

Without waiting for an answer, he climbed back into the squad car, made a sharp U-turn, and drove back toward town.

"Close call, huh?" Justin said, catching up with Nell and Izzy as they headed down the hill toward Paley's Cove.

"Tommy's right," Nell said. "You need to do as Mr. Danvers says."

"Yeah, sure." He shrugged, as if he'd already forgotten the suggestion—or the incident. He tucked the board beneath one arm and shifted his fanny pack, checking the clasp. "But Tom was cool, right? Do you think he'll tell Janie?"

Izzy picked up a slow run down the hill, and Nell kept pace, both women ignoring the obvious answer to his question. Of course Tommy would tell Janie. In fact, he had probably already called her on his cell. *Justin Dorsey is trouble,* he'd be telling her.

"Where are you headed, Justin? Do you need help getting that board somewhere?" Nell asked.

"Hey, thanks, but no. I was running some errands for the clinic and used Janie's car. It's down at Paley's Cove." He picked up a little speed to keep abreast of the two women, his flip-flops slapping against the firm dirt path.

They rounded a curve in the road and began the gentle descent down to Paley's Cove, spread out below them like a glistening half-moon.

Nell knew Izzy liked running here along the smooth sand, even though she seemed distracted today as they neared the curve of beach. Perhaps it was a result of the ruckus up at the Danvers place.

Or, as Ben would be quick to say, perhaps it was simply Nell's imagination. Worrying without cause. She'd done too much of it lately.

"Guess I'll leave you ladies here," Justin said as they neared the water's edge.

He looked around the beach for a minute, as if half expecting to see someone—perhaps Franklin Danvers coming after him with a shotgun. Then he forced a smile back to his face. "Gotta get back to the clinic. The printer doesn't work again. I'm becoming indispensable over there, but they're going to have to figure out how to get along without me soon." He waved at old Horace Stevenson, sitting across the road on his porch, and then called out with a jubilant smile, "Have a great day, ladies! I sure am going to."

And he was off, sprinting across the beach to the narrow parking lot.

"Great day?" Nell murmured. Justin seemed to be unaware that he'd almost gotten thrown in jail. She watched him as he strapped his board to the top of Janie's car, wondering if Janie knew her car was running errands that included a trip to the beach—and a visit to Franklin Danvers' wife.

Justin reached into the front seat, then closed the car door and walked a few yards to the steps, bending low over the granite wall, as if in thought. The tip of a cigarette glowed in profile. Nell wondered if something was wrong. But before she could call out, he crushed out the cigarette, climbed into the car, and was headed toward town and the clinic.

What did he mean, he'd be leaving the clinic soon? Nell wondered if Martin Seltzer was finally getting his way. But Justin seemed happy about the possibility, not sad. Was he quitting? She turned toward Izzy, wondering if she had the same thoughts about this unpredictable young man.

But Izzy's thoughts seemed to be elsewhere. She had stopped running and was staring across the beach at the parking lot, one hand cupped over her eyes, squinting.

"Izzy?"

She didn't answer. Instead, Izzy turned and scanned the beach, her gaze on the scattering of people. A young couple, lolling on a blanket. In the distance, some teenagers frolicked in the waves, pushing one another and laughing, the morning sun warming their tan, firm bodies.

"Are you all right?"

Izzy nodded slowly. "You'll think I'm foolish. No, you'll *know* I'm foolish." She pointed back toward the stone wall that separated the parking lot from the sand, to a gray object near the spot where Justin had been smoking.

Nell hadn't noticed it before—she'd been focused on Justin. Or perhaps she wouldn't have given it a second glance even if she had seen it. People brought all kinds of things to the beach. From where she stood, it looked like a small beach chair.

"It's the baby car seat," Izzy said.

Nell looked again, nodded, waited.

"There isn't a baby anywhere on this beach," Izzy said. "And there wasn't a baby here yesterday when I ran, or the day before that, or . . ." She stopped, her words falling to the sand. When she looked up, her face was pinched with worry. "It's the same car seat that's been here every day."

"Maybe the mother is walking with her baby along the shore, beyond the breakers where we can't see her," Nell suggested. "Perhaps over on the Danverses' beach. I'm sure it's fine, Izzy."

Izzy shook her head. No, the mother wasn't walking along the beach. Izzy was sure of that.

And the baby wasn't there, either.

There was only a car seat.

Chapter 5

"Are you sure you want to take on a renter right now?" Birdie asked. She sat in the yarn shop's back room, in Ben's old leather chair. It was Birdie's favorite spot after a long day. On the coffee table in front of her was a chilled bottle of pinot gris and four glasses. In her lap sat the infinitely soft beginnings of baby Perry's first romper— the creamy cotton glacé begging for shape—the arms, the legs, and a figure of a bunny near the row of buttons. She fingered the yarn, imagining a sleeping baby in folds of soft cotton.

Thursday night. The comfort of yarn and friends. At last.

Izzy stood at the old library table, tossing Nell's arugula salad. A sweetened pecan made its way into her mouth. "No worry about a renter, Birdie. It's Janie Levin we're talking about, and I kind of like the idea of someone other than ghosts living above the shop."

Nell glanced over at her. Ghosts in her apartment. Ghosts on the beach . . . Earlier that day, while getting the quesadilla ready to grill, she had told Ben about Izzy's strong reaction to seeing a baby carrier on the beach.

Ben had brushed it off, but then, he hadn't seen the look of distress on Izzy's face, as if she wouldn't rest until she found a baby for that car seat. As if it were a scene that needed fixing.

"Janie's working like a demon to pay off a boatload of nursing school loans," Nell said. She looked at Izzy. "You're probably charging her next to nothing. This will be a huge help to her."

"And here's another plus," Cass said. "Her boyfriend's a cop. Great way to get free extra security."

Izzy laughed. "I'm not sure I need that. Yarn doesn't seem to be high on thieves' 'things to steal' lists."

"Do you suppose cousin Justin will be hanging out here?" Cass asked.

"No," Izzy said. "He stays over at that old boardinghouse that Mrs. Bridge runs. She agreed to a reduced rent if Justin ran errands for her. He doesn't like the arrangement—she's a tough lady—but Janie thinks it's good for him and maybe keeping him out of trouble."

Nell unwrapped a foil cover from the pan of quesadillas. The sweet smell of orange sauce wafted up with the steam.

The growling of Cass' stomach was more effective than a dinner bell, and in minutes they'd heaped their plates high with arugula salad and spicy quesadillas and settled on the slipcovered sofa and old leather chairs near the stone fireplace. The casement windows above the window seat were open wide, bringing in gusts of salty air that ruffled napkins and sent Izzy over to close them partway. "There's a storm coming in," she said, looking up at a parade of clouds racing across the sky.

"Not a serious one. Just some nice rain for the flowers," Birdie said. "Harold's arthritic bones are the best weather predictor in the world. He says this will pass over with little damage, but we might want to bring the trash cans inside."

"A groundskeeper with telepathic bones," Cass said. "Only Birdie could have found such a man."

Before anyone else had a chance to chime in on Birdie's amazing household staff, a booming noise from the alley sent a framed print of Gloucester Harbor falling to the floor.

"My Winslow Homer print," Izzy cried, pushing herself up from the chair.

"Thunder?" Cass wondered.

But it was coming from the alley, not the sky.

Izzy reached the side door first and flung it open. A distraught

Janie Levin stood in the alley, staring at the ground. Behind her, packed full of boxes and chairs and knickknacks, was Tommy's pickup truck.

But it was what was in front of her that caused Izzy to rush over to her side. "Janie! Are you okay? What happened?"

Inches from where she stood, the remains of a large packing box, mangled and open, lay on the ground. And scattered as far as the eye could see were shards of colorful pottery.

In answer to Izzy's question, Janie looked up the steps leading to her new apartment.

Standing at the top of the outdoor staircase, just outside the apartment door, was Justin Dorsey, a torn flap of cardboard dangling from one hand.

"It slipped," he said. "I was trying to open the door."

Janie fought hard for composure. "I'm sorry for the mess, Izzy. Tommy let me use his truck to move some things into the apartment. Justin showed up to help, and then . . ." Her voice broke.

"What lovely pottery," Birdie said, bending over and picking up a hand-painted piece.

Janie bent down beside Birdie and began scooping up the larger pieces, placing them in an empty box. She held one in her hand, looking at it as if imagining it whole. "I'll make a mural with the pieces. A coffee table or mirror, maybe," she murmured, more to herself than those around her. Then she looked up from the mess and pushed a smile in place. "Everything is from garage sales. Nothing matched. It'll be okay."

"The real problem would have been if the box had landed on you," Nell said. Her frown was aimed up at Justin. "That wouldn't have been okay."

Justin looked sheepish and took a few steps down. "I'll buy you more, Janie. Promise. And no more garage sale stuff. You deserve better. Quality stuff . . ." He pointed to a patch of alleyway nearly hidden by the Dumpster. A shiny motorcycle leaned against it. "Like that."

Janie looked over and frowned. "What's that?"

"It's a Honda. A used one, but so, like, cool. Like it? I'm trying it out. Gotta get it back tomorrow."

"Trying it out?" Janie asked, the mountain of broken pottery forgotten. She stared at the bike.

The question was answered with a shrug, and Nell watched Janie's frown deepen as her look passed from the bike to Justin and back again.

Cass walked over and looked at it. "I'm not an expert, but it looks like a nice bike, Justin. Not cheap, but very cool."

Justin reached the bottom of the stairs and stood with his hands shoved into the pockets of his jeans. He beamed at Cass' words. "Yeah, I think I might buy it."

"Hey, folks." Tommy Porter walked down the alley and wrapped an arm around Janie's shoulders, pulling her close and missing the look of consternation on her face. "Got here as soon as I could, babe. Crazy day at the station, and I had to change clothes." Then he spotted the broken dishes littering the alley. "Oh, jeez. Sorry, Janie. I shoulda been here to help you. Did you hurt yourself?"

"Nah, it was me, man," Justin said, taking a step toward Tommy. "I dropped 'em. But no worries. I'll replace 'em." He lifted one palm in the air. "Scout's honor."

"Dorsey." Tommy's whole body tensed as he stared at him. Finally he took a deep breath and unclenched his fist. "Sure. Sure you will, man."

Tommy's voice dripped with disdain, something Nell had never heard there before. She'd known the mild-mannered policeman almost since his birth. As a teenager he'd mowed their yard and run errands for them and their neighbors. And when he graduated from the police academy, she and Ben joined the whole town in celebrating his success. He was well liked, and when he and Janie started dating a couple of years ago, it seemed the stars had lined up perfectly. *The policeman and the nurse*, they'd come to be called, once Tommy convinced Janie to go back to school. It was a match made in Sea Harbor heaven.

Tonight they all saw a new side of Tommy, maybe one reserved for police work—arresting thieves, dealing with hardened criminals. Or maybe one reserved for someone he disliked intensely.

Justin sensed it, too, and without another word, took the broom Izzy handed him and began cleaning up the littered alleyway, his whole being concentrating on the pieces of pottery.

Tommy looked over at the truck. "Weatherman says rain tonight, so how about we move these things inside?"

As if receiving stage directions, everyone moved, the scooter momentarily forgotten. Birdie and Cass began pulling things out of the truck and handing them off to Tommy, Janie, Nell, and Izzy. Slowly the hand-to-hand brigade transported things from the truck, up the stairs, and into the small, airy apartment above Izzy's shop.

"How many people are moving in with you, Janie?" Cass joked, looking at the stacks of books, furniture, towels, and clothes.

"Oh, it's all just garage sale stuff," Janie said. "It's not all for me. You never know who might need something. You'd be surprised."

Tommy stopped short when Birdie handed him a high chair. "Janie?" He looked back at the truck and pointed to a bassinet and two booster seats, crammed in between a car seat and a changing table. "Something I should know?"

Janie laughed away the embarrassed blush that colored her cheeks. "Garage sale finds. How can I turn down barely used things that someone else will need? Most of Dr. Lily's free clinic patients can't begin to afford those kinds of things."

"Yeah," Justin said. "So Janie buys 'em. She's a real pack rat. Like you should see all the stuff she's given me." He turned toward Janie and held up one palm. "But no more. I promise, now I start paying you back. I've finally hit big m . . ."

Tommy stopped Justin's words with a single stare. Clearly he wasn't in the mood for Justin's chatter. It seemed a bit severe, Birdie observed later. Not the usual reaction from sweet Tommy Porter. But then, Janie was his girlfriend, and he was clearly protective of her. And it was also very clear that he didn't like Justin Dorsey.

It was pitch-dark by the time they finished piling things into Janie's new apartment and went back outside. They stood beneath the gaslight in the alley next to Tommy's empty pickup.

"Great job. You're all the absolute best," Janie said, looking at the semicircle of weary faces. "I can't believe I thought I could manage this alone."

"When will you move in?" Izzy asked. "Purl can't wait." She pointed toward the window where the calico cat sat, watching the group with infinite patience.

"There's a secret passageway in the shop," Izzy explained. "An unused return vent—above Mae's checkout counter. It's just big enough for Purl to crawl through and along the two-by-fours into the apartment above. I thought I had lost her once until I heard her sweet meowing coming through a light fixture. Now she comes and goes freely. I hope you don't mind, Janie."

"I've always wanted a cat," she said, her eyes lingering on Purl. "With ten of us kids, the last thing my parents needed was a pet. Purl and I will be wonderful friends. I'll never be lonely."

Tommy looped an arm over her shoulder. "And, hey, if Purl needs any help on the lonely front"—he brushed a thick wave from her eye with the tip of his finger—"I'm a great stand-in."

Janie laughed.

Justin coughed for attention. "Yeah, Janie. Me, too."

Nell shook her head. Poor, naive Justin. Tommy's disdain for him—not to mention his protectiveness of Janie—seemed to escape him. Social nuances were definitely not Justin's strong suit.

Janie filled in the awkward quiet that followed. "If it's okay, Izzy, I'll move in for real on Saturday."

"Sure. And we'll be around to help." Izzy began walking toward the door.

"We're off, then?" Janie looked up at Tommy.

"Yep. Gracie's Lazy Lobster Café." With two hands on her shoulders, he turned her toward the truck. "I'm starving. Bring you anything, ladies?" he called back.

"I'll be sound asleep before you get to Gracie's amazing key lime pie," Birdie said.

The knitters waved them off and walked back inside to reheat their dinners. It wasn't until Nell glanced out the window that she noticed Justin. She had almost forgotten about him. He was sitting in the shadows of Archie's bookstore on the seat of the shiny bike. Although Janie hadn't said anything, it was clear she wondered where it had come from. An expensive toy for someone with little money.

Justin looked up and noticed Nell watching him. Gaslight lit his face, and he waved, a large sweeping movement that ended with a thumbs-up and the familiar dimpled smile.

Justin Dorsey wasn't sad. He looked like a child on Christmas morning with a new toy, content to spend the evening in other ways.

Nell's returning wave was lost in the rumble of the engine starting up, a thundering sound that filled the alley and broadened the smile on the cyclist's face.

In the next instant, he was gone, leaving a cascade of flying gravel in his wake.

ommy was right about the rain. When Izzy finally locked up the shop, waved the others off, and climbed into her car, fat drops were falling onto the windshield. She sat there for a minute, switching on the radio as she watched the taillights of Nell's car disappear down Harbor Road.

After Janie and Tommy left, they'd reheated the quesadillas in the microwave and stayed long enough to fill both their stomachs and the need to make a little progress on the booties and rompers and tiny sweaters that needed to be finished for the baby shower. Willow and Jane Brewster had insisted on planning it—small, they promised Izzy, just good friends. They hadn't decided on the theme yet, but no matter what it was, the tiny outfits needed to be finished soon.

Janie's move, however, had interrupted the usual rhythm of their Thursday-night knitting—the slow, easy hours they looked forward to all week. Their tonic, as Birdie put it. Their pocket of peace.

But they'd make up for it as they always did when unexpected circumstances cut their Thursday evening short. A Sunday morning together when the shop was closed or a knitting rendezvous on Birdie's veranda or Nell's deck. It was a need as deep as their friendship—the joy of casting on and binding off, of slipping strands of silky yarn through their fingers, of creating warmth and softness to cradle a newborn babe or protect an old fisherman from harsh winter winds.

Izzy turned out the lights and followed the others out, locking the shop door behind her.

"Don't worry, it's not a nor'easter this time, folks," the radio weatherman had said. "Just a good old-fashioned summer rain to make the grass and flowers grow. Enough to wash off the sidewalks and docks and freshen up the town. 'A good rain.'"

A good rain.

But not good for everything.

Not good for a yellow angora baby blanket, for starters.

Izzy slipped her keys in the ignition and started up the car, the methodical sound of the wipers filling the small car. She sat still for a minute. And then, as if the car had made up its own mind, she turned sharply at the corner of Harbor Road and headed toward the winding beach road.

She drove carefully, past joggers scurrying for cover, past the turn off to Canary Cove, Sandpiper Beach, the yacht club, and on north toward the cove, where she and Sam spent many hours. Sometimes they'd sit on the rocks that anchored it at both ends and watch the moon turn the water into a changing kaleidoscope of night colors. Or curl up on a blanket, pressing their bodies into the sand as deep night sounds surrounded them. Then they would gather their things and walk slowly back up the hill and through the sleepy neighborhood to Marigold Street, to home.

Filled with children in the daytime, Paley's Cove frequently hosted bonfire parties and packs of college kids at night. But tonight it was quiet, people heeding the weatherman's advice.

Izzy pulled off the road and onto the gravel parking area, just a single car deep and curving along the stretch of beach. Her beach. That's how she thought of it.

Her beach.

She left the headlights on and climbed out of the car, barely noticing the rain, which fell heavier now. Her hair hung in damp multicolored rivulets, her sweater smelling of wet cotton. She tucked her chin to her chest and hurried along the wall until she reached the three small steps to the beach. At first she just stood there, staring out past the deserted beach to the ocean, unable to tell in the heavy night where the water ended and the black sky began. It was a thick sea of darkness. She closed her eyes, wiped the rain from her forehead, then slowly moved her head to the side and opened them again.

Of course it was there, just as she knew it would be. The edge of the yellow blanket sticking out, soggy and limp.

Without a second thought, Izzy tugged the offending car seat from the sand and carried it back to her car. She opened the trunk and in one clumsy movement hefted the wet seat inside and slammed the trunk shut. In seconds, she was back behind the wheel, her wet fingers grasping the leather covering. She pulled slowly out of the parking lot, an irrational relief flooding her body.

Hormones. In full rhapsody.

The rain came down in glassy sheets now, and Izzy stopped along the side of the road, letting the wipers do their work. A light from behind drew her eyes to the rearview mirror, but it wasn't a car. Far down, at the bend in the road, a single steady headlight pierced through the darkness. A bike? she wondered, and almost turned around to see if the rider needed help.

But at that moment an engine gunned into life and the headlight began to move. Relieved, Izzy pulled back onto the road and made her way home.

Chapter 7

S am was still drinking his Saturday-morning coffee when Izzy noticed the problem. But then, as Sam said, it wasn't *really* a problem. A stuck car trunk was all it was. Easily fixed.

Izzy had tried to open the trunk so she could take a lamp into the yarn shop, one she thought would look nice in the apartment above the shop. A housewarming present for Janie. But the trunk didn't open. Not with her key. Not with the spare.

She stood there in the driveway for a minute, thinking back to Thursday night when it had opened just fine. Easy as pie. She'd tossed the abandoned car seat inside, closed it tightly, and relished the peculiar sense of relief that flooded over her, right along with the rain.

Out of sight, out of mind. And it had been. She came home, parked the car in the driveway, and tumbled directly into bed. In minutes, she was sound asleep. And an early-morning run along the cove the next day had been peaceful and serene.

Sam came outside in his bare feet, set his coffee mug on top of the car, and poked at the lock for a minute, putting the key in, twisting it hard. He stood back, his brow furrowed, and ran his fingers around the lock. Then he glanced over at Izzy, an amused smile creasing his face.

"You tried really hard to open it," he said. "What did you use, a sledgehammer?"

She smiled sweetly. "No, darling. I treat my little VW with great respect. I used a key. I save the sledgehammer for your car."

Sam looked at the lock again. It was surrounded by dings and dents. The lock itself looked as if a tool had been forced into it and twisted hard, to no effect, other than messing it up.

"It looks like someone tried to pry the trunk open. What's in there? Anything important?"

Izzy looked at the trunk. Certainly nothing anyone would want. A drenched baby seat that had sat on the beach for days and played havoc with her dreams? No, Sam would definitely think her crazy. She looked up and shrugged. "Nothing important."

He looked at the damaged hood again, then retrieved his coffee cup from the roof.

"It's not a big deal, Iz. I'll call Pickard's Auto Shop on Monday and take it in." He took the lamp and fit it into the backseat of her car, then opened the front door while Izzy tossed in her bag and slid in after it. Sam leaned through the open window and held Izzy's head between his two large hands. He looked into her eyes, then pulled her close and kissed her soundly. Pulling slightly away, he whispered into the sliver of air between them, "But next time, Rosie Riveter, give me a holler before you take the blowtorch to it."

The voice was the same, but the doelike figure that flew down the yarn shop back steps a few hours later was a little taller, the tan legs longer by an inch than the summer before. But there was no mistaking the wild dark hair that flew in all directions and the freckles dancing across her nose.

Gabby Marietti was back.

In one flying leap, Purl was off the window seat, landing squarely in Gabby's outstretched arms.

While Gabby hugged Purl, Nell hugged Birdie's young granddaughter—cat and all. Gabby Marietti belonged to all of them, or at least that's how they looked at it. Since coming unexpectedly into

Birdie's life the summer before, Gabby and her uncle Nick had made the trip to Sea Harbor every chance they got—Thanksgiving, Christmas, spring break. She had to check on her nonna, Gabby would say. But it was also because whenever Gabby left Sea Harbor to return to her father and her Central Park condominium, she left a little bit of herself behind—and the lure to return and fill that hole grew stronger and stronger.

"So, tell me what you've been doing since you got back in town," Nell said.

"She's been one busy girl." Izzy walked down the steps carrying a basket filled with summery cotton yarn. "She's already signed up to teach a class for me and it's nearly full. We're going to pick out a project today. You're just in time to help, Aunt Nell."

Gabby took the basket from Izzy. "Yep, it's true. And I'm helping Willow in her art gallery *and*," she said, her voice lifting nearly to the ceiling, "I've been fishing with the cool Ocean's Edge guys. You know Kevin? And Tyler, he's Esther's grandson. Did you know sometimes Kevin catches his own fish to try out new recipes? And yours truly helped him and Tyler catch a cod. A *cod*! Huge. This big!" Her hands stretched as wide as the doorway.

"Amazing. What can I say?" Nell said.

Gabby laughed. She dropped the basket of yarn on the library table. Her hair flew along with the movement of her body, the halo effect rivaling any of Izzy's angora yarns.

Gabby grew serious, squeezing a skein of the yarn. "But you know what one of the very best parts of this summer is? I'll be here to welcome baby Perry." She turned and wrapped her arms around Izzy. "I'm going to help Willow with the shower—and we need to start right now playing music for the baby. We should talk and laugh a lot so she'll know our voices when she arrives."

"I doubt we'll have any problems on that front," Nell said, laughing.

"She?" Izzy's eyebrows lifted. "Everyone except me seems to have very definite ideas about the sex of this baby. I'll have to have twins, though, to satisfy everyone."

Gabby giggled. "Okay, a baby Sam will be great, too."

"Sam will be happy you think so . . . ," Izzy said, then paused, looking up as footsteps and a jumble of words rumbled across the floor of the upstairs apartment.

"Good grief, not again," Nell said.

Mae Anderson, Izzy's shop manager, appeared in the doorway just as the voices reached a crescendo. She moved her palms up and down as if to quiet the air and calm everyone down. "Don't get excited, Izzy, or that baby will drop out right here. Janie Levin knows how to handle herself. She'll be fine. And no plaster has fallen loose from the ceiling, far's I can tell, anyway."

"I hear a guy's voice. Who's that?" Gabby asked.

The voices continued, rumbling across the floor above.

"It's no one," Izzy said, then stopped herself. Clearly it was *someone*. "I don't think you know him, Gabby. His name is Justin Dorsey. He's a distant relative of Janie's."

"Justin? Oh, sure, I know him. He gave me a ride on the coolest bike yesterday. A Honda—really fast."

Nell dropped a skein of yarn. "You what?"

"He was down on the dock talking to Tyler and Kevin. He's cool. We drove down to Paley's Cove. Then back up here. He was real careful with me on the back, and I had a helmet on."

Nell sighed. Would she be like this with Izzy's child? So cautious, frightened by things that made noise and went too fast?

Izzy rummaged through the balls of yarn, then began sorting the skeins into piles by their lyrical names—tourmaline, goldenrod, plum crazy, driftwood—trying with each luscious color to force her mind off the ruckus above.

"I think something's happened," Gabby said. "Janie sounds upset."

Janie Levin rarely raised her voice. They all looked up again.

Mae crossed her arms across her chest. "Well, you know what they say about too many cooks. I say just leave the girl alone. Janie can certainly care for herself."

But neither Izzy nor Nell subscribed easily to the "leave alone" school of thought, especially when a large thump rattled the window blinds. Finally Izzy stood. "Justin was supposed to be helping Janie move the last of her things. But something is obviously wrong up there."

The words from above were muffled, not easily discernible, but Gabby was right: Janie Levin was terribly upset.

"I'm going to check on them," Izzy said finally, heading for the shop's side door.

"You're not going up there alone," Nell said. "Gabby, maybe you can help Mae in the shop. Back in a minute."

It wasn't until they reached the apartment door that Nell realized Gabby had followed her up the outside stairway.

"In case we need to call someone," Gabby whispered, holding up her cell phone.

A light knock on the door went unanswered. Izzy opened it a crack, just as Janie's voice filtered through the crack.

"Sometimes I could kill you, Justin Dorsey," she said, her voice choked with tears. "There must be something wrong with you. Please, just get out and stay out. I don't care where you go, just away from me. This time I mean it. Out!"

With that, she jerked the door wide-open and found herself face-to-face with Izzy, Nell, and Gabby, pressed together on the small porch landing.

Her hand dropped as if the doorknob had been on fire.

Behind her, Justin stood with his hands shoved in his pockets and a confused expression on his face. A child caught with his hands in the cookie jar, and wondering what all the fuss was about.

But Janie's face reflected something more serious than a cookie jar theft. She was furious. Her forehead was damp and tears rolled down her face.

She wiped the tears away with the back of her hand and looked at Izzy. "I'm so sorry. So sorry."

Before she could say anything further, Justin walked around her and through the door. He half smiled as he brushed past Nell, Izzy, and Gabby.

"It's okay," Janie called after him. "Go ahead, just take it." A set of car keys flew through the heated air. Justin caught them in one hand. "Janie, I'm—"

"Just go," she said.

Justin turned and, taking the steps two at a time, headed for the small car parked in the alley.

Nell, Izzy, and Gabby watched the fleeing figure as he hopped into Janie's small car. The engine roared to life and in the next instant, Justin backed out of the alley and disappeared down Harbor Road.

Izzy turned toward the door. "I'm so sorry we barged in like this, Janie. Clearly we interrupted something—"

"No, no. It's your apartment, Izzy." Janie shook her head back and forth, a tangle of crimson waves falling over her forehead. She stepped back and motioned them into the apartment. "You must have thought I was tearing the place apart. I'm sorry you had to hear all that." She looked at Gabby and managed a small smile. "Honest, Gabby. I don't usually yell like that."

"Well, I do," Gabby said. "Our cook, Sophie, says sometimes you just need to yell. It's the only thing that works."

Janie gave her a quick hug.

"Are you all right? Did Justin break something?" Nell asked, looking around. She half hoped that was the problem, but suspected this was worse than a broken dish.

"No. In fact—" Janie turned around and pointed toward a large box on the floor.

The lid had been removed and inside, on pads of tissue, was a set of pottery, one easily recognized. It came from the Brewster Gallery in Canary Cove—each plate uniquely designed and fired by the artist. Each a collector's item. Each beautiful—and expensive.

Nell leaned over and picked up a piece. "These are so beautiful, Janie. Ham and Jane are amazingly talented."

"Justin gave them to me."

Gabby frowned. "You yelled at him because he gave you a present?"

Jane shook her head and tried to smile. "No, sweetie, it's not that. He did something else that made me angry." She looked again at the dishes. "But if he had any practical sense, he wouldn't have done this, either." She looked up at Izzy and Nell. "How could he afford these?"

"He probably wanted to replace the ones he broke the other day," Izzy said.

Janie's voice turned cold. "One month ago, I had to pay Justin's rent at the boardinghouse because he was broke. I had to give him money for food and begged Dr. Lily to give him more hours."

For an awkward moment they stood side by side, looking down at a gift that should have elicited happiness. Instead, Janie's anger was pressing down on the room like a dark cloud.

"All right, then," Nell said, breaking the silence. "Justin seems to be working all over town. Jane and Ham often need help packing and shipping at the gallery—and more than once, they've paid in art if someone prefers it. Maybe that's how he got this lovely pottery."

"Sure. That's probably what happened. It's a smart way to be paid," Izzy added. "They're so generous and I'm sure they gave him a great deal. You know how they are, Janie."

Nell nodded along with Izzy's affirmation. It *was* true. Nell was fully aware of the Brewsters' generosity, especially if they felt they were helping someone in need. And Justin, clearly, was in need.

"Yeah. That's the truth," Gabby added with great conviction. "I have the coolest mermaid statue Ham gave me last summer and all's I did was sweep out the studio for him—and I'm not a very good sweeper. Really bad, in fact." Her hands flew out in the air.

It was Gabby who finally drew a smile from Janie.

But the dishes couldn't have been the source of the argument. Nell looked around the room, wondering what else Justin had done to upset Janie so badly.

"What else is going on here?" Izzy asked. "Maybe we can help?"

"No," Janie said. "Nothing." But her voice betrayed her denial.

"Why don't we help you unpack some of these things?" Nell

said, sensing Janie's need for distance from whatever her cousin had done. She looked around at Janie's collection of garage sale finds, the boxes stacked along the wall, a pile of towels and sheets.

The apartment seemed smaller with all of Janie's things piled around, but no less wonderful. Nell loved this space and hoped Janie would, too. Shortly after Izzy opened the yarn studio a few years before, Nell and Ben had helped Izzy turn the second floor into a cozy apartment, thinking she might want to live there. It was open and bright, with skylights and a butcher-block island separating the galley kitchen from the living area. Beyond the kitchen and living area, a wide archway led to a bedroom with a high wooden bed, once a guest bed in Nell and Ben's Boston brownstone. But Nell's favorite space, what made it the perfect Harbor Road apartment, was the window seat below the mullioned windows, a perfect match to that in the room below—along with the same perfect view.

But Izzy decided early that she needed a place separate from her work—her short tenure as a defense attorney had shown her that in a hurry. Work and life could merge so easily. So even though she loved her yarn shop and the wonderful apartment above it, she wanted—needed—to nourish the other part of her soul as well.

"We could help hang some pictures, empty some boxes. You'll feel better," Izzy said. She walked over and picked up a small box near the island

Janie frowned at the box, then walked over and took it from Izzy. She opened the flap and pulled out an old T-shirt. "This is Justin's. It's just like him to mix our things up."

"That's not a problem," Nell said. "I'll drop it off at the boardinghouse on my way home."

Janie looked at the box as if she wished it would disappear right in front of her. But when she looked back at Nell, she simply looked sad.

"He'll be back. He borrowed my car for that scuba dive tomorrow—and he's meeting someone after it over in the Ravenswood neighborhood so he needed a ride. But . . ."

They waited.

Janie took a deep breath, then forced a sad smile to her face. "But as of today, it would be useless to drop it off at the boardinghouse, because he no longer lives there." She took another breath, her anger creeping back. "Mrs. Bridge would probably burn it if you dropped it off."

"He moved?"

"Not exactly. Mrs. Bridge locked him out and told him never to come back. He wouldn't tell me why," Janie said quietly. "He just kept saying he was planning to leave anyway. But the truth is, he must have done something awful to make her so mad."

Nell agreed. "Mrs. Bridge is blustery, but she's not unfair."

"She was so nice to give him the room, the reduced rent, and this is what he does. It's the last straw. I truly mean it this time. Tommy was right. Once he returns my car, I don't ever want to see him again."

When they left the apartment a short while later, Janie's resolve was still in place—and the steely determination in her voice said she might truly mean it this time.

Justin Dorsey was out of her life forever.

Chapter 8

Saturday night, at last. Nell felt her body relax beneath the hot shower massage. She looked up through the skylight at dozens of stars filling the sky. A perfect night to relax on the deck. Just Nell and Ben . . . a bottle of wine . . . soft, smooth jazz. And a blanket wrapping them up together against the ocean-chilled air.

She turned off the spray and grabbed a towel, rubbing herself alert, pushing aside the dreamy thoughts of being alone with Ben. Another night. Soon.

She slipped on a silky blouse, a pair of black slacks, and a new pair of strappy sandals Izzy had talked her into buying, and made herself presentable—a sweep of blush and light lipstick. Her summer face, Ben called it. She gave her hair a quick brush, noticing several new streaks of gray nestled into the dark mix. They'd become too plentiful to pluck out months ago, and she'd come to like the contrast, the streaks of silver defining her dark, shoulder-length cut. Some people paid for highlights. Hers just walked in on their own.

Ben was downstairs mixing martinis on the deck, rehashing the week with Ham and Jane Brewster. Their voices floated up through the open bedroom windows, familiar and soothing, punctuated now and then with Jane's throaty laughter.

An evening with friends. Perhaps it was just what the doctor ordered.

. . .

Friends, and then some. Birdie had reserved a table at the Ocean's Edge to welcome Kevin Sullivan back to Sea Harbor—and, not incidentally, of course, to enjoy his culinary specialties. Word had it a food critic for a popular travel magazine was expected. Knowing a crowded restaurant would be a plus, Birdie had spread the word to everyone she knew.

The Ocean's Edge was packed.

"The Favazza party is out back," the bartender called out as they walked through the door. Jeffrey Meara had tended bar at the Edge for as long as anyone could remember, and no one passed by him without a greeting and, if he wasn't busy, a hug to go with it.

The hostess matched his warm greeting and led them through the crowded restaurant to the open back doors. Outside, the wide covered porch was filled with colorful pots of daisies, ageratum, and zinnias. Tiny white lights circled the outdoor bar and the eating area, hanging from pillar to pillar and casting shadows across the flagstone floor.

Nell waved to several neighbors sitting at the bar before spotting the Danverses—both generations—sitting together at a nearby table. Franklin was engaged in a lively conversation, complete with gestures and an occasional hug for his wife. His niece, Laura, her long auburn hair pulled back and tied with a ribbon, was laughing at something that he said. Her dress was simple and elegant, the emerald green matching her eyes, which now were on her husband. Elliot, usually stiff when around his formidable uncle, looked relaxed tonight. Tamara completed the scene, relaxed and happy, and eye-catching as always in a brilliant red dress.

Another couple stopped to greet the Danverses, hiding the diners from view, except for Tamara, who slipped away from the table. Nell watched her head toward the restroom—something Izzy was also doing these months with increased frequency.

Tyler Gibson, tending the outdoor bar, spotted Tamara, too, and greeted her with a huge smile, waving her over.

But Tamara, clutching her purse to her breast as if to protect herself from an intruder, gave him a cold stare and hurried inside.

Tyler stood there for a minute, scratching his head, a confused look on his face—as if a friend had refused to greet him or a beautiful woman failed to acknowledge his charms, something that probably didn't happen to him often.

But as Nell watched, he quickly shrugged off the rejection and, with a grin back in place, moved toward a group of young woman eyeing him from the other end of the bar.

"Here we go, folks, this way," the hostess said, pulling Nell's attention from the odd little scene.

Nell glanced back at Franklin. He was looking at the bar now, but whether to get the cocktail waitress's attention or for some other reason, it wasn't clear.

"Nell and Ben, we're over here." Birdie's blue-veined hand waved in the air. Sam and Izzy were already there, sitting at a table overlooking the water. The sea was quiet tonight, lit by the moon and a canopy of stars.

"Sam wanted to be sure we were seated near a quick getaway point, just in case," Birdie said. "This is perfect, don't you think?" She nodded to a flight of stairs that wound down to a wide green space used for picnics and clambakes. Nearby was the dock for the Ocean's Edge taxi that shuttled people back and forth to Rockport, Gloucester, and the northern edges of Sea Harbor. "We'll just usher Izzy down those steps and off to Sea Harbor Memorial if baby Perry should decide tonight is the night."

"Sam's a crazy man," Izzy said, rolling her eyes. "He needs distractions to stop thinking about childbirth every second. This baby's going to come when the two of us want him to—but it's not going to be tonight." Izzy pushed her chair back from the table and rested her hands on the curve of her belly. A narrow plate of appetizers sat in front of her: Greek cucumber cups, stuffed with spicy lime shrimp, olives, and tiny slices of avocado.

"I have plenty of distractions in my life, Isabel Chambers Perry," Sam said, pulling the appetizers away from her. He bit into one of the cucumber cups. "For example, tomorrow I'll be up at dawn, and not to drive you to the hospital. The baby can't come tomorrow, either, because I'm shooting that early scuba dive over at the cove."

"For that *Travel and Leisure* series, right?" Ben ordered another plate of shrimp cups along with some of Kevin's beer-battered calamari.

Sam nodded. "It'll be a good for tourism. Gus McClucken's dive shop is offering free dive equipment for some of the guys we've recruited in addition to the regulars."

"That'd be me," Danny Bradley said as he and Cass walked up. "Can't believe I let you talk me into it, Perry. But I figure, assuming I don't die, that I'll fit it into a book somehow. I took some lessons once but don't remember much."

Sam laughed. "We needed a token famous author's name for the article."

"I keep telling him he needs to try new things," Cass said. "Something to keep those murderous ideas flowing. Danny's way too mild—"

"Still waters run deep, Catherine," Birdie said, accepting Danny's peck on her cheek.

"You tell her, Birdie. She can be pretty incorrigible."

Cass offered him a poke before sitting down and waving to a well-dressed couple walking by. "Hey, you two," she called out. "Don't you look snazzy? So hip and with it."

"Me, hip?" Tommy Porter's laugh was full. "You used to call me a nerd when I helped scrub your dad's boat, Cass. What's with the compliment? At least I think it's a compliment. . . ."

"Well, you were a nerd, face it," Cass said. "But look how Janie has cleaned you up! Geesh, who would have thought? A *GQ* model in the making."

Tommy blushed, the policeman clearly not completely at ease in his skinny denim jeans. He tugged at the knot of a narrow tie, already loose at the open collar of his plaid shirt. Uniform blue trousers and a jacket with a shiny badge were clearly more at home on Tommy's tall frame.

They laughed as Tommy's blush passed to Janie, knowing what was coming next. *Garage sales.* That's where she had found Tommy's True Religion jeans, and his cool plaid shirt and tie.

"Twenty dollars for the whole outfit," Janie said, warming now to the topic. "And those jeans cost over two hundred dollars new!"

Birdie winced at the awful thought, then smiled up at him. "You look splendid, Tommy dear."

Tommy immediately changed the subject, explaining in great detail how they'd just repainted the jail a pale pink to calm prisoners down.

While the rest of the table engaged in a discussion of "drunk tank pink," Janie stood quietly looking off toward the water, her mind clearly elsewhere.

Nell watched her, searching for remnants of the distress that they'd witnessed earlier that day. Slight worry lines remained on her forehead, but the anger seemed to have faded.

"You look lovely, Janie," Nell said softly.

"Thanks, Nell," Janie said. "I know what you're asking, though, and I'm fine. Really I am. But terribly sorry about my outburst today. I hate it that our sweet little Gabby saw me at my worst."

"Oh, nonsense. Did Justin come back?"

"No. I guess he got the message. Sometimes I think he is truly confused when I get upset with him, like he doesn't get why. And then he assumes everything is fine. That's probably how he is this very minute, happy as a clam, thinking all is forgiven. Do you think it's because he had such a bad upbringing? He never even knew his dad. And his mother was a mess, ending up in jail a couple of times."

"That's a difficult way to grow up."

"It must have been awful. I took a psychology course in nursing school, and he's like one of those people who has had to fend for himself for everything, and he needs instant gratification. It's so strong in him that he does what makes him feel good right then and there because he might not get a second chance. He doesn't ever think about consequences. He just wants to have fun and be rich—fast."

Janie seemed to warm to the subject, clearly articulating thoughts that had been filling her head.

"Like the texts he sent me after he left today. They weren't about how he's going to clean up his act or find a place to stay or hold on to a job and earn his riches. Instead, he texted about how great it is that he's going on the scuba dive tomorrow and might get his picture in a big-time magazine, and isn't that cool? And then he added that maybe he'd take me to Duckworth's in Gloucester to celebrate."

"Celebrate?"

"I know, I know. Celebrate what!"

She shook her head, then looked at Tommy to be sure he wasn't listening. "I don't think I have a single friend left in Sea Harbor who Justin hasn't let down. And now this latest thing at the boarding-house. And the thing is . . . the thing is, he doesn't even care. He says he was going to leave there anyway. He's got his eye on those new *expensive* condos on the north shore—"

Janie stopped, her eyes widening as she looked across the porch to the outdoor lounge area. Nell sat tall and followed her look.

Justin Dorsey stood alone at the very end of the long bar. He was motioning to Tyler Gibson, standing a few feet away, pouring drinks and shaking martinis.

"But he's not even twenty-one . . . ," Janie started.

Tyler handed the drinks off to a waitress and moved toward Justin, a swatch of blond hair falling across his forehead.

Justin high-fived him and pulled up a stool, his manner busi-nesslike, as if delivering some news. Tyler listened carefully, nodded, ignoring the waitress waiting with drink orders. Every now and then he looked up, as if protecting the conversation from bystanders' ears. When Justin tugged something from the fanny belt strapped around his waist and placed it on the bar between them, Tyler stood back, staring, a surprised grin on his face. Then he slapped Justin on the shoulder as if in congratulations.

"Maybe Justin is looking for a place to stay tonight," Janie said, a touch of regret slipping into her voice.

"Maybe," Nell said. She watched Tyler offer another high five and walk down the bar to waiting customers and waitresses.

Justin stood there for a few minutes, watching the activity spinning around him, a solitary figure in the middle of the crowded, happy space. But he seemed puffed up somehow, satisfied with himself. Then his gaze drifted over to the Danverses' table and settled on Franklin's distinctive profile.

He stared intently at the older man, and Nell wondered what he was thinking. There was certainly no love between those two. But Justin's look was one more of curiosity than dislike, as if he was trying to figure the man out. Janie said Justin was obsessed with money—perhaps that was the intrigue Franklin Danvers provided: Justin was trying to figure out his secret to being rich.

Tamara looked up and spotted Justin staring at their table.

She lifted one hand to her mouth, but before she had a chance to react further, Justin turned back toward the bar, grabbed a handful of pistachio nuts from a bowl, and disappeared down the porch steps and into the night.

Beside Nell, Janie shivered, then followed Tommy to their table nearby.

Hours later, after devouring Kevin Sullivan's signature dish of pan-roasted cod, floating on a pool of minted crème fraîche, even Ham Brewster declared himself full.

"Magnificent," Birdie said when Kevin stopped at their table, doffing his white toque and smiling broadly.

"A step up from my scones?" he said.

"No, dear. Nothing will ever top your scones, but this was truly delicious."

The accolades came from all around the table, and Kevin thanked them profusely, before moving on to other tables, other friends, and more compliments.

"Take me home, Bill Bailey," Jane said finally, looping her arm through Ham's.

"Izzy's nearly asleep at the table," Sam said, helping his wife up.

"Sleeping for two," Izzy murmured, as they all made their way through the restaurant and out to the parking lot. Janie and Tommy were leaving at the same time, leaning nicely into each other.

"Young love," Jane Brewster said, looking over at them as Tommy unlocked his car.

"Old isn't so bad, either." Ben wrapped Nell into the curve of his body.

"Who will we see tomorrow at Annabelle's?" he called out as everyone climbed into their cars.

Tommy spoke up from two cars down. "Rumor has it she's making a special Swedish pancake, not to be missed."

Izzy waved out her window. "Count me in for sure."

"Danny and I'll come by after the dive shoot," Sam said.

Sunday breakfasts at Annabelle Palazola's Sweet Petunia Restaurant were sacred.

Ben looked over at Birdie, climbing into Sam's backseat. "Pick you and Gabby up, Birdie?"

"Not tomorrow, Ben."

"No?" Nell said. "Gabby loves pancakes—"

"Gabby is hanging out at Willow's studio tomorrow, helping her get ready for the next Art at Night event—and possible a baby shower. As for me, I have a date."

They all looked her way.

She leaned through the window, her smile wide. "Oh, hush, the bunch of you. It's not that kind of date."

"What kind is it?" Danny asked. "The kind in fruitcake?"

"It's a *conversation*—that kind of date. A handsome young man named Justin Dorsey is coming over to have coffee with me."

Standing beside Tommy's car, Janie Levin tensed at Birdie's words.

Nell tried to read the expression on her face. *Embarrassment? Puzzlement?* She couldn't be sure.

But she was sure of what she didn't see there: *happiness.*

Chapter 9

The pancakes looked to be everything the blackboard at the restaurant's front door described: buttery, sweet, fresh. Sinfully delicious.

"That last description is for Father Northcutt. He likes straying every now and again," Annabelle said, leading them through the restaurant to their usual table out on the deck.

The Brewsters and Cass were already there, enjoying a second cup of coffee.

"She's amazing, no?" Ben asked, pointing to the platters of warm crepes passing them by. He wrapped an arm around the owner and cook.

"Who would have thought that you, Annabelle Palazola, would be perfecting Swedish pancakes?" Ham said.

Annabelle laughed. When her husband had died at sea years before, the fisherman's wife did what she knew how to do best—cook—and opened a restaurant that would provide for herself and her children, sending each to college. And she had succeeded beyond her expectations. The Sweet Petunia was beloved by all of them.

Before they'd finished the freshly squeezed orange juice, Annabelle was back with the special, plates piled high and smelling of fruit, butter, and cream.

Rolled around fresh lingonberries, the crepes were lightly

browned and sprinkled with powdered sugar, then topped with dollops of sour cream and Annabelle's promise that there were more in the kitchen.

"More fruit, too," she said, nodding toward the mint-lined bowl heaped full of melon balls, berries, pineapple, and bananas. Then she was off, back to her more comfortable place behind the cast-iron stove that Birdie had loaned her the money to buy all those years ago.

"This is it for the week," Nell warned Ben. "I swear. No more food."

"That's what I told Sam when we got home last night," Izzy said. She checked her watch and frowned. "Maybe he took me seriously."

"He'll be here. He's such a perfectionist with that camera—and underwater photography can be tricky," Ham said.

His wife agreed. "Sam's a true artist and he treats his photos with great care. But what's up with this dive? I only heard snatches last night."

"The dive club that Andy Risso heads up is organizing it," Izzy said. "Gus McClucken offered to take care of the equipment for folks who didn't have their own. It's a great deal if you like that sort of thing. And then, of course, Sam needed a buddy and someone to write down people's names—so Danny got roped into going along. Sam wasn't sure I'd make it down the rocky slope."

"Sam is wise." Nell added a bit a maple syrup to her pancake.

"He asked me to go along, too," Jane said around a bite of pineapple. "But I told him the truth—if God wanted me to be at the bottom of the sea, he'd have made me a dolphin."

Soon the talk turned away from scuba diving and focused on summer concerts, gardens being planted, the upcoming shower for Izzy and Sam, beach cleanups, and other easy and pleasant Sunday-morning topics.

When the waitress refreshed their coffee cups for the third time, Ham and Jane pushed their chairs back.

"Ham would eat another plate of those," Jane said. "But he'd also fall asleep in the hammock outside the gallery as soon as we hit home."

"Who, me?" Ham joked. He stood and helped Jane tug her enormous cloth tote from beneath the table. "But she's right. Canary Cove is hopping on summer Sundays—and that's just the way we like it."

Nell watched her dear friends make their way down the porch, greeting the Sunday-morning crowd, waving, hugging. Jane's long peasant skirt swished around her legs as she walked. Minutes later they disappeared down the hilly path on their way to the art colony below.

Father Northcutt caught Nell's eye and waved. The priest was sitting with Cass' mother, Mary, just as he did most Sundays. The truth was that it wasn't the pastor but Mary Halloran who really ran Our Lady of Safe Seas Church, and she used their Sunday brunches to outline for Father Larry the events of the week, telling him where to be and when—and to watch his cholesterol. Farther down Nell spotted Lily Virgilio, not looking like a doctor today in a summery blouse and pants, her high cheekbones pinked by the sun, large sunglasses shading her eyes. She was eating alone, with a plate of pancakes in front of her and a book propped up against a vase.

She looked peaceful in her aloneness, Nell thought. Most often Nell would catch sight of Lily in restaurants with Martin Seltzer. But today he was nowhere in sight and for some inexplicable reason, Nell was happy for Lily that she had some time alone. Without wanting to be a matchmaker, she hoped for a more lively companion in Lily Virgilio's life. She couldn't figure Martin out, and for unknown reasons, that fact bothered her. There was a bit of mystery about him.

The day before, she had seen him walking down Harbor Road, his white coat flapping against his long legs, his shoulders slightly stooped. He stopped at the scuba equipment display in McClucken's window, peering through the glass for a long time, as if choosing his gear of choice. He disappeared inside. But when he reappeared a few minutes later, all he carried was a bag of mulch.

A gardener? Where would one garden at a clinic with no yard? she'd wondered at the time.

At the end of the porch, Annabelle's restaurant was shadowed by a thick stand of evergreens climbing up the hillside like sentinels, and that was where Henrietta O'Neal always sat. Henrietta was of some undetermined age—some said eighty, some thought older, and Henrietta thought they were all crazy for caring. Although she lived alone, the wealthy widow rarely ended up alone in public places. She loved to talk, loved to argue, and loved people of all shapes and sizes—even those, she was proud to say, who were dead wrong in their political leanings.

The ringing of Ben's cell pulled Nell away from her people watching, and she looked over at the offending phone as if to remind it that they were eating.

Ben glanced at the caller's name, scratched the side of his head, then stood and stepped away from the table to take the call. He moved out of earshot, over to the service area, but the others at the table watched and saw the concerned look that fell over his face. "That was Sam," he said to the table of expectant faces. He motioned for the waitress and handed her his credit card.

"Sam?" Izzy pushed herself back from the table. A flash of fear lit her brown eyes. "What's wrong? Is Sam all right?"

"He's fine, Izzy. But he and Danny won't make it for breakfast. There's been a delay. They asked us to meet them back at the house." Ben took a deep breath, then cleared his throat, an uncomfortable sound in the expectant silence.

"Our house?" Nell said finally, though her question was rhetorical. She began gathering her things, trying to convince herself it was a normal request. Danny and Sam were too late for breakfast at Annabelle's—they wouldn't want to tie up the table any longer. So they'd have coffee with all of them back at the house. And then they'd all be off and about their Sunday. It made sense.

And yet it didn't.

"Why?" she asked quietly.

"There's been an accident," Ben said, starting toward the door.

Izzy, Cass, and Nell stood at the table, refusing to move.

"Speak to me, Ben Endicott," Nell demanded. "What kind of accident?"

Ben paused and turned back to the table. His voice was low.

"Justin Dorsey is dead," he said.

Chapter 10

S am and Danny were already sitting at the kitchen island when the others arrived at the house. The smell of coffee filled the air. Sam got up and met Izzy in the middle of the family room, wrapping her in his arms as if to protect his unborn baby from tragedies and bad news.

"Justin . . . ?" Cass moved to Danny's side.

"But he can't be . . . ," Nell began, then realized there was no "because"— no reason she could give that it couldn't be true.

Suddenly her thoughts turned to Janie, the harsh scene between her and Justin the night before flashing across her mind.

"Janie," Izzy said softly, as if reading Nell's mind.

"Tommy came to the dive site along with the ambulance. He wasn't on duty. He just heard the sirens. It's like a moth to light, I guess. He headed over to talk with Janie as soon as Chief Thompson got there," Sam said.

"Birdie was supposed to have coffee with Justin later this morning, after the dive," Nell said. "I should call her."

As if responding to her name, Birdie walked into the room from the front hallway, her face already lined with worry. "What's happened? I heard sirens earlier. Harold was out getting the Sunday paper. He has this uncontrollable urge to follow fire trucks. So he did. They went to the cove, he said, but he couldn't get close enough to see, so he came home. Is it old Horace Stevenson? Did something happen to him?"

She frowned, took in the somber faces around the kitchen island, then looked over at the coffeepot. "Ben, I need a strong cup of coffee. No cream. And then I need someone to tell me why Justin never showed up at my house this morning."

Ben piled the coffee mugs on a tray as Nell ushered them out to the deck. Perhaps the warmth of the morning sun would cut through the chill that had filled the kitchen with Sam's news.

"Justin was so excited about this dive," Sam said. "Most of the divers—especially at that early hour when they're still shaking off sleep—are kind of quiet before a dive. But not that kid. He talked a blue streak—about how good a diver he was, about wanting to buy a surf shop, about how people would see him differently now that he could afford things. How he raced over to McClucken's to sign up. Nonstop magpie. He had everyone laughing. I finally had to shut him up to find the equipment Gus was loaning him." He took a drink of coffee and continued.

"Gus and Andy Risso had brought down the extra equipment the night before and locked it up in that boathouse the dive club uses. Everything was marked with the diver's name and ready to go. So Andy gave his little safety spiel, some basic instructions, and then we all went down. I got great photos. Tons of mussels, anemones, lobsters. Sometimes it's hard to tell who's who down there, but I tried to get everyone in a shot. I know Justin was right along with the rest of us, swimming with the fish."

He looked over at Danny, who agreed and added, "Being the wimp I am, I mostly stayed close to Andy—I figured the dive leader oughta know what he was doing. Justin went by us a couple of times. His suit had the McClucken mark on the back, so I knew it was him."

"I guess we were down there—what, Danny?—twenty minutes, tops, when Andy motioned us back up. With relatively inexperienced divers along, he didn't want to stay down longer, he said.

"But Justin didn't surface with the others," Sam said. "Andy always takes a quick roll call, and he just wasn't there. Andy and I went back down right away, couldn't have been more than a matter of minutes. And that's when we found him. Down at the bottom, down between some rocks, his arms wide."

"How awful," Nell said. "This will be hard on Janie, especially after throwing Justin out of her life last night."

Some eyebrows lifted, and Nell and Izzy repeated the episode in the apartment. "I think Janie was at the end of her rope. And when Justin's careless behavior started to affect her friends, she couldn't take any more," Izzy said.

"Tommy thought she should have sent him away weeks ago," Sam said. "He was a nice enough kid, but he didn't have much direction."

Birdie had been unusually quiet, her head back against the chaise and her forehead creased, listening and thinking. Finally she sat forward and asked, "Why did he die, Sam? I used to scuba dive with Sonny a thousand years ago. People don't normally die unless something goes wrong or they have a health problem."

It was the question they'd all been toying with, the one hanging there at the fringes of their conversation.

"Justin was just a kid," Cass said. "He seemed as healthy as the next guy. But I suppose he could have had a heart condition no one knew about."

"We'll know soon enough. They'll autopsy him. Andy had Chief Thompson and the crew out there in minutes. They collected the equipment and took lots of notes," Sam said. "Protocol, Jerry said."

"I've read plenty of stories of malfunctioning equipment," Ben added. "But when Gus McClucken opened that dive shop in the back of his store, he insisted he'd only carry the most trustworthy equipment. Andy Risso and the dive club say his shop is one of the best."

"But it can still happen," Sam said. "Justin himself could have inadvertently misadjusted his regulator."

"Was anyone around? I might have been running in that exact spot this morning if I hadn't been lazy," Izzy said.

"I saw old man Stevenson," Danny said. "He was walking his dog."

Sam nodded. "I talked to the old guy briefly. He'd been up all night, he said. The full moon keeps him awake. But his eyesight is bad. He wouldn't have seen anything.

"Franklin Danvers was a little way down the beach, too. That diving spot straddles the edge of his property, and Andy always lets him know when there's going to be a dive. He lets the club use the storage shed for their equipment. Franklin's a diver himself and appreciates the sport, so he probably came down to watch—or maybe the police lights brought him down to check."

"Franklin says walking that beach is better than sleeping pills," Ben said.

"Speaking of walking," Danny said, pushing himself up from the chair, "we gotta go." He turned and held out a hand for Cass.

"We're fixing some broken traps at the dock with Pete today," Cass explained. "It might be good to be down there anyway, to put some reason to the rumors as they start rumbling around the boats. It doesn't take long for rumors to grow."

"Cass is right," Nell said to their departing backs. "It won't take long for the word to get out. I wonder how Janie's doing."

Izzy and Birdie began gathering up coffee cups and taking them into the kitchen. "Last night would have been her first night in the apartment," Izzy said. "I was going to call her first thing, make sure everything worked. And now this—"

When the doorbell rang a few minutes later, they all stared toward the front of the house. Rarely did anyone ring the Endicotts' doorbell.

Ben headed across the room. In minutes he was back, one arm around Janie Levin's shaking shoulders. Behind her, Tommy looked helpless, as if he wanted to pick Janie up and carry her off to a place where bad things didn't happen. Where divers dived—and didn't die.

Janie's eyes were swollen, her hair flying haphazardly around her tearstained face. "I pushed him away." She looked at Nell and Izzy. "You heard me. I told him I hated him. I wanted to kill him." And then she began to cry, giant sobs that shook her slender body.

Ben and Tommy guided Janie to the couch while Nell brought a glass of water and a box of tissues. Tommy sat beside her, his face sad and his arm wrapped around her shoulders.

"I didn't know where else to go. Tommy said we should come here, maybe you'd know something. He knew you'd be here, Sam—and you were there . . . down there . . . with Justin. . . ."

Sam sat across from Janie. He leaned forward, his warm brown eyes focused on her face. "It was a freak thing, Janie."

"But he used to dive in California. He knew how to do it."

Sam nodded. "Was Justin's health okay? Did he have any heart condition?"

Janie shrugged. "I don't know. I know so little about him. We're related in one of those ways that people can never figure out. The second cousin of a third cousin . . . that kind of thing. Other relatives said he was kind of a castoff. I thought that was so sad. When he showed up for our family reunion, most people didn't know who he was." Janie took a drink of water, then pulled a band from her wrist and tried to capture a fistful of hair. "I'm rambling. I'm sorry. I'm just so sad."

"Of course you are," Nell said, laying one hand on top of hers.

"I don't know what to do." The tears began again. "Tommy had me call my mom to see if she could get some personal information that the police will need. Like where his mother is and where to send the . . . body."

When Janie and Tommy finally got up to leave a while later, Janie's tears had stopped but her step was slow. She walked over and hugged Ben tightly, as if she'd somehow find protection in his strong arms.

Sam looked at Ben, his eyebrows lifting with a silent question. Then he looked at Izzy and she nodded, knowing exactly what her baby's father was thinking—and that today wouldn't be spent putting the new crib together after all.

"Hey, you two," Sam said to Tommy and Janie. "I think the best place to be during troubled times is on untroubled water. With a glass of wine and takeout lobster rolls from Gracie's Lazy Lobster Café. What do you say?"

Izzy pushed herself off the couch and wrapped her arms around Sam's waist, squeezing hard. "And you can't turn this man down because he's desperate to show off the new sail he and Ben just got for the boat."

Tommy looked relieved, as if Sam had just given him a great gift. Something far removed from the direness of the morning's news. An escape.

"Any other takers? All are welcome," Ben said.

Nell watched the scene with a lump in her throat and her body leaning comfortably into Ben. For that one moment, the sadness of the day was pushed into the shadows as she basked in the knowledge that her niece had quite possibly married the one man in all the world who was just about perfect for her.

Nell couldn't have chosen better herself.

Chapter 11

The news of Justin Dorsey's death didn't resound as robustly through the Sea Harbor community as it might have because many of the residents didn't know the young man personally. There were some—like Archie Brandley and Mrs. Bridge—who knew him but didn't like him much, and their reaction to the news of his death was one of slight guilt, as if their dislike had somehow played a role in his death.

Moreover, townsfolk wouldn't even be able to learn more about him at a funeral because he wouldn't be buried in Sea Harbor.

All things being equal, the news might have fallen off people's radar within a day or two or three.

But all things were not equal.

The tide began to change late Tuesday afternoon.

Ben was at the yacht club when he got the call from Chief Thompson.

Nell was standing in front of a room of well-dressed women at a late-afternoon library meeting, having finished a talk on writing grants, when she glanced down at her phone and read Ben's succinct text.

Birdie received Nell's text while at the Ocean's Edge Restaurant with a small group of white-haired women having tea, although the term *tea* was a holdover from the days when the matriarchal group really did have tea, instead of the afternoon sherry they were drinking today.

Janie Levin didn't get a text. She was back at work at the clinic, comforted by Dr. Lily and by the familiarity of the nursing job she loved. But she would receive the news very quickly.

And Tommy Porter got word while on duty at Sea Harbor police headquarters. He was surprised when the chief called a special meeting, but more surprised when he found out why. He immediately called Izzy and Sam.

Could they go over to the clinic—be with Janie until he was able to leave?

Justin Dorsey was murdered.

He hadn't been ill, he hadn't been drunk, he hadn't been any of the things that the rumor mill had bandied about since news of his death traveled through town.

Justin Dorsey, age nineteen, had been killed.

The night passed in a blur. Izzy and Sam stopped by the Endicotts' to report on Janie. They had stayed with her until Tommy showed up. She had eaten a little, Izzy said, but mostly sat in disbelief, her face chalky white and her hands shaking. Tommy told them he would spend the night there. Janie shouldn't be alone. And who knew what kind of crazy person was out there? Who knew if he had further prey?

They were all grateful. Janie had taken the news hard. First not believing it. Then trying to make sense of it. Which, of course, was impossible. One day she was arguing with him, telling him she'd like him to fall off the face of the earth.

And the next day he did.

"I feel like there's an awful cloud over my head," Janie had said. "And it keeps getting darker and heavier. If only the sun would come out, the blackness would all go away and Justin would come back."

Izzy and Sam had few reassuring words for her, and Tommy even fewer.

No matter if the sun came out or a nor'easter reared its head, someone in Sea Harbor had wanted Justin Dorsey dead. And that was the awful truth of it.

The headline in the Wednesday morning *Sea Harbor Gazette* was intended to get readers' attention. And it succeeded, though the facts were few.

SCUBA DIVER MURDERED AT SEA

It hadn't taken the coroner or the diving equipment experts long to determine what hadn't killed Justin—or what had.

On first examination, he didn't appear to have any health problems that would explain a death, according to the coroner.

And it wasn't an equipment defect, according to the mechanical experts who examined the diving cylinders and other equipment, although these would be scrutinized further.

It was, in fact, a human deed—the clear manipulation of a piece of equipment that had caused Justin Dorsey's death, so read the *Sea Harbor Gazette*.

"It makes me wonder about Izzy's premonitions," Nell said as Ben spread Wednesday's paper out on the island so they could see it together. "She's been feeling that something wasn't right. And now this."

The article was short, not more than a couple of inches of newsprint. No one knew much about Justin or his family, just that he was distantly related to Janie Levin, nurse at the Virgilio Family Clinic.

Specifics of the equipment problem hadn't been spelled out, but the thought was that someone had gotten a hold of Justin's regulator and made sure it would get him down to the bottom of the sea—and not up again.

And that was about it, except for a quote from Justin's landlady, Mrs. Bridge, who respectfully declined from saying anything other than that he had lived at her boardinghouse for a time but had ceased his residency there on Saturday. She had added that she never spoke ill of the dead, and the reporter had dutifully recorded it.

"It's sad there isn't more to say about his life," Nell said.

"It's sad that someone disliked a nineteen-year-old boy enough to kill him."

"Dislike? Is that what you think killed him? Someone hated him?"

"Hate is a strong motive," Ben said.

"But do you honestly think anyone in Sea Harbor knew Justin well enough to hate him? Janie knew him best and—"

"And she said she hated him."

There was silence for a few seconds while Nell processed the truth of Ben's statement. And then she punched at it.

"That's silly, Ben. And you know it is. Janie is young and she was very angry with him. But she wasn't expressing the kind of hate that makes someone kill."

Nell could feel her cheeks reddening as the emotion of her words took hold. Of course Janie didn't hate Justin. Not really. She was devastated by his death.

Ben turned from the paper, set both their coffee mugs on the island, and pulled Nell to him, holding her close. His cheek pressed into her hair. "Of course she didn't hate him that way, Nellie. You and I know that. But her words will be dissected now, pulled apart, and examined carefully. And anything anyone else said to Justin. Or about him."

Nell pressed closer to Ben, her heart sinking. He was right. It was the beginning of all that. The questions, the fears, the looking over one's shoulder.

And all this when preparing for the most joyous birth of a baby. She thought of Izzy's comment about her sixth sense. *"All's not quite right in our universe,"* she'd said. *"And I don't want my baby coming until it's better."*

Noises at the door and the slap of flip-flops across the hardwood floor brought Gabby Marietti into the kitchen. Birdie was close behind.

Gabby hugged them both. "Nonna said someone killed Janie's friend," Gabby said. Her dark blue eyes filled her face. "It's awful and so sad. Why would someone do that? He was nice."

Birdie wrapped an arm around her granddaughter's waist. Over the winter Gabby had grown taller, filling in the small difference in their heights, and now they were eye to eye. Granddaughter and Nonna on an equal plane. Both questioning the irrational and tragic happenings in life.

"Yes, indeed, sweetheart," Birdie said. "Why?"

Harold had dropped her and Birdie off, Gabby said. And now they needed a ride to the market. Wouldn't Nell like to come?

"Ella needs a bunch of things and Nonna needs fresh air," Gabby said.

And she did, too, Nell realized. The whole town did. Fresh air.

The day was bright and cool, a contrast to the heated news that was being discussed up and down Harbor Road. The summer farmers' market was set up near the Ocean's Edge, on the great green expanse of grass that ran from the parking lot down to the water's edge. It was already crowded, with people pulling out their cloth bags and filling them with early summer produce—lettuce and spinach and arugula, slender stalks of asparagus, carrots, and baby corn.

But in between the stands of vegetables and fruit, people huddled together as small bits of information of a murder were passed along, inch by inch, like some insidious weed. A mixture of emotions washed across people's faces—disbelief, curiosity, fear—all a sharp contrast to the fresh garden items around them.

Gabby led the way to a stand with an abundance of green and buttery lettuce. "It looks like an oil painting," Birdie said.

Nell looked around as Birdie and Gabby examined the lettuce heads. Not far from the booth, on a slight rise of land, stood a white gazebo. Today it hosted a high school band playing an assortment of old Woodstock songs.

Henrietta O'Neal stood in front of it, tapping her cane and singing along to an old Joan Baez tune.

Farther down the greenway, apart from the market activity and closer to the water, stood a tall, lone figure, looking out to sea. Nell pushed her sunglasses to the top of her head, squinted, and recognized Martin Seltzer. A lumpy market bag hung from one shoulder, and a bony hand grasped the back of a park bench.

Henrietta noticed him, too, and immediately stopped her tapping and headed his way, her head leading her small round body as it bobbed across the grass.

Birdie looked over and laughed. "My tea ladies told me that Henrietta has been trying to socialize Martin Seltzer. He's her new project, they said. Do you think I should warn him?"

"I suspect the man can hold his own," Nell said, remembering the look he had given Justin that day in the clinic. Daggers with very sharp points. "If Martin doesn't want company, I have a feeling Henrietta will know it very soon."

Martin turned as Henrietta approached. But before he could speak, she raised herself up on the toes of her sneakers and, waving one blunt finger in the air, let loose with a string of words that startled a group of gulls into flight. The distance was too great for Birdie and Nell to hear, but Martin clearly did. His head dropped at the torrent of words, but before he could reply, Henrietta spun around and walked back to the gazebo. In minutes she was mouthing along to an encore of "One Day at a Time" in true Baez fashion.

"Hmm," Birdie said. "So much for socializing the good doctor. I'll have to see what my tea ladies think about that."

Nell watched Martin shift his market bag to the other shoulder, then walk slowly back up to Harbor Road. A part of her wanted to catch up to him, to talk to him about Justin. What would his thoughts be, now that the young man he had so clearly wanted out of the clinic was dead?

"Life is interesting," Birdie said, and turned back to see Gabby standing with Kevin Sullivan. The bearded chef was dressed in old jeans and his head was bare, his hair blowing in the breeze. He was holding up a bunch of arugula, explaining its merits to Gabby.

"So this is why the Ocean Edge salads taste market fresh," Nell said, eyeing the arugula. "They *are*."

Kevin grinned and nodded. But the smile gave way to concern as he stepped away from Gabby and lowered his voice. "Hey, I heard the awful news about that kid. He was Janie's cousin, right?"

"Distant. But yes," Nell said.

"That's a tough one. Tyler said he was a good kid. A little goofy sometimes, but not, like some are saying, a bad kid."

Tyler turned at the sound of his name. He stood behind a nearby table heaped high with everything from beets to cabbages to fresh herbs. The smell of basil filled the booth.

He smiled over at the group and gave a wave. "Hey, Birdie, Nell. And if it isn't Gabriella Marietti!" Tyler rolled the *r*s in Gabby's name, drawing giggles and a blush.

"Gabby and I are old buds," he said to Birdie. "She helped me pick my gram's garden nearly clean the other day, didn't you, gorgeous?"

"So that's where all this came from." Nell laughed as she eyed the produce. "Esther Gibson's plot in the community garden puts all the rest of ours to shame."

"Yeah, so you've seen it? Every doggone thing she plants comes up like it's going to take over the earth. She gave a ton of this to Father Larry's soup kitchen, but it just keeps coming."

"It's like the loaves and fishes," Gabby said. "That's what Father

Larry says—it keeps on multiplying." She picked up a bunch of green onions and some arugula and dropped them in her basket while Birdie handed over a bill.

Then Gabby's eyes narrowed, her eyebrows pulling together. "Hey, Tyler, remember that day? Justin Dorsey came by to ask you to stop by the beach or something?" Her frown deepened. "Justin . . . and now he's dead."

Tyler looked at her for a minute, as if doubting her recollection. Finally he nodded. "Yeah, Gabby, I think you're right—he came by and helped us. Jeez, it's awful, what happened. You don't expect this kind of thing here in Sea Harbor."

"You and Justin were friends?" Nell asked.

"Yeah, well, sort of. He was younger, but a friendly guy. He seemed to get around." He shifted from one foot to the other, then looked back at Gabby. "Hey, look at these beets, Miss Italiano. Have you ever seen anything so beautiful in your whole life?" He held up a bunch and raised his eyebrows, drawing a new round of giggles.

Gabby replaced her grin with a firm expression. She held out her hand, palm toward him, pushing away his words. "Italians don't eat beets."

Tyler laughed and ruffled her dark mop of flyaway hair. Then he noticed a woman holding a head of Esther's cabbage, gently testing the end for moisture, then lifting it to her nose and sniffing it.

"Oops, business calls." Tyler gave them a wave, then turned this attention to the woman, expounding on the merits of cabbage. A welcome escape.

"Justin seemed to know everyone," Birdie observed.

"It's like Tyler said, he was friendly. Kind of a wheeler-dealer, you know? Always wanting to make a quick buck, especially if it didn't take much work." Kevin examined some onions, then slipped the vendor a few bills and dropped them in his bag. "He'd come into the Edge now and then when Tyler or some of the college kids were working, just hanging out. Not drinking, though. Tyler's good about carding kids. He knows all the tricks since he tried most of them himself at that age."

"We saw Justin there last Saturday night," Nell said.

"Yeah. I did, too. It was the night before he died, right? Eerie to think about it now. I asked Tyler about him that night because I noticed Justin flashing a roll of bills in the parking lot, like he'd won the lottery or something."

Nell remembered Justin pulling something out of that fanny pack he wore. He'd put it on the bar between him and Ty—a show-and-tell gesture. She supposed it could have been bills.

"Who'd want to hurt a kid like Justin?" Kevin asked.

"That's the question, I suppose," Birdie said.

"The paper said he was from California. Maybe someone from there tracked him down here, someone with an ax to grind."

Nell half listened, knowing the stories were just beginning, all the possible things that could have happened that fateful morning. Strangers, vagabonds. Sinister outsiders. And even as people were clinging to those possibilities—to the assurance that Justin's death was a freakish deed committed by someone no one knew, someone who had immediately left the area and would never come back—more rational minds were dismissing the tales as unreliable and without merit, without rhyme or reason.

The more likely scenario, the one no one wanted to mention out loud, was that Justin Dorsey was killed by a neighbor or an acquaintance or a friend, or someone who at that very minute was wandering around the farmers' market, looking for the perfect cabbage or bunch of beets.

Chapter 12

By Thursday, the news of Justin's murder had created a rock-solid undercurrent of fear and suspicion—one fueled by gossip, innuendo, and the bits of factual information that made it onto the front page of the *Sea Harbor Gazette*.

Or inside the paper, in Mary Pisano's "About Town" column.

"All right, Birdie, what does Mary have to say?" Nell stood at the old library table in the yarn shop back room, tossing a handful of spicy pecans into a salad. They'd all shown up early for Thursday's knitting group, as if the week's events had stretched out the days interminably and they were desperate for the comfort of Izzy's back room. Although they talked and texted daily, nothing was as therapeutic as a lapful of yarn, a calming sea breeze, and being with dear friends. It was a formula that defied failure, and Nell's seafood surprises and salads and pastas were icing on the cake.

Birdie sat in her usual place near the fireplace, her enormous knitting bag beside her and an open bottle of chilled pinot gris on the coffee table in front of her. She smoothed out the newspaper on her knees and read aloud from the column, entitled "A Season of Hope." After scanning the beginning she skipped to the last paragraph:

> *Our beloved town has been rocked mercilessly with this recent tragic happening. Justin Dorsey was not a Sea Harbor native,*

but he was a Sea Harbor tragedy, and it is the responsibility of each and every one of us who loves our town dearly to right this awful wrong and bring the perpetrator to justice. We need to retrace our steps, to plumb the recesses of our minds for any strangers who might have crossed our paths in recent days or for any unusual happenings we may have overlooked, and report them promptly to the authorities. We shall all be citizen deputies until this is put behind us.

It is the worst of times, as the Great Writer wrote, and it is up to each one of us to help our stellar police department bring back the best of times, and to make this summer our season of hope.

Birdie took off her glasses and looked up. "So . . . ," she said.

"Mary's gone literary on us." Cass walked over to the table and tore off a piece of sourdough bread. "Do you think she forgot Dickens' name?"

"I think she just wants people to look it up on their own," Nell laughed. "Mary fits more facts into that almost preadolescent-sized frame of hers than Wikipedia." She walked over to the library table and began pulling food containers out of her oversized bag.

Birdie agreed. "Mary is very perceptive, and her heart is always in the right place. But I'm wondering how Chief Thompson feels about her plea to help the police department do their job."

"That poor guy," Izzy said. She grabbed a handful of silverware and napkins. "Although by now he's probably used to it."

"And who knows? Maybe Mary's piece will actually draw some leads. Maybe someone saw someone down there near the beach, or saw Justin talking to someone, and will think twice about it," Cass said.

Nell put two wide forks into a large pottery bowl and suggested they fill their plates. She motioned for Birdie to take the first one.

Nell never called the Thursday-night libations a meal, although Cass claimed that the leftovers kept her going for at least a few days. "Except those days may be disappearing," she grumped. "Now that

Danny is hanging around so much, it's sometimes gone before it hits the refrigerator."

Tonight's shrimp and fresh pea salad, which Nell spiced up with pepperoncini, capers, cilantro, and a light yogurt dressing, would be no exception.

Izzy heaped salad onto her plate, added a chunk of warm sourdough bread and pat of sweet butter, and followed Birdie across the room. "Mae's nieces were working here today and talking nonstop about Justin's murder. Jillian and Rose said lots of them knew Justin, or at least who he was. Somehow the twins seem younger to me, but actually there's only a couple years between them. And Justin loved the boogie boards and all their beach fun."

"This must be difficult for them. Teenagers think themselves immortal," Birdie said. "And to have it be someone they knew is just all the more difficult."

Izzy nodded and swallowed a bite of salad. "The kids liked Justin. He was a regular guy, they said."

"And just enough older to make him seem cool," Cass said.

"Has anyone talked to Janie today?" Nell asked. "I wonder how she's doing, poor thing."

"She's been working. Lily Virgilio has become her surrogate mom. She loves Janie and feels so bad for her," Izzy said.

"Janie knew Justin better than anyone," Nell said. "The police will be questioning her."

"Tommy is pushing for some breathing room for her," Izzy said. "She's still in shock."

Cass refilled her plate and returned to her chair. "I'm sure the whole awful mess hasn't sunk in for her yet." She looked over at Birdie. "Justin was supposed to meet with you Sunday, right? What was that about?"

"Now, that's a mystery, isn't it?" Birdie said. "I don't have any idea. I didn't know him all that well, except for his connection to Janie, whom I love dearly."

"But people like to talk to you, Birdie. You have that aura," Izzy said. "Maybe he wanted to talk to you about Janie."

"Aura? Oh, sweet Izzy, I don't have an aura. I have *years*. Lots of them. Sometimes that is comforting to people because they know that there's little that can surprise me." Birdie gave a laugh, though it had a sad edge to it. She pushed herself up straighter in the chair and wiped her hands on a napkin. "I've been thinking about it, though. I have. It wasn't a casual 'let's talk sometime' invitation. Justin had something specific he wanted to talk to me about. He called me late Saturday afternoon—probably after he left here—and said it was important he see me. He sounded anxious, so I suggested we meet right then, but he couldn't. He was on his way to 'an important business deal,' he said. So we settled on Sunday morning."

Nell frowned. "Business deal?"

"I think sometimes Justin was full of himself. He probably meant Lily was giving him a paycheck."

And before they saw him at the Ocean's Edge. So a late-Saturday business meeting. Nell stored away the information.

"So, why did he want to talk to Birdie? Any ideas?" Cass carried her empty plate to the small galley kitchen and called back over her shoulder, "Maybe someone didn't want him talking to you?"

"I can't imagine why. I thought he might be looking for another job. I have that big place—maybe he thought Harold could use some help with the yard or driving the car—he seemed to like driving the cars at the Community Center event."

"That doesn't seem to fall into an 'important' category, though," Nell said.

"If you need money badly, maybe it does," Birdie said.

While Izzy cleared the remaining plates and hands were washed, they tried to get their arms around a crime that on the surface made no sense. A young life lost. And many other lives affected.

"I don't think it was for a job," Izzy said. "Not the way he was acting."

They settled back in their chairs and pulled out needles and yarn and half-finished projects. Izzy traced the tiny shape of her latest pair of booties, no bigger than a thumb, knit from a green-and-yellow-striped angora blend.

Between the four of them, baby Perry would have a knitting wardrobe to match any of the Hollywood babies that filled the popular magazines. Nell reached over and touched the tiny stocking.

"Why don't you think he needed another job?" Birdie asked. She tightened the last row of stitches on the tiny romper. With the legs finished, she was beginning the main body—creamy soft and cuddly and ready to hold a tiny baby.

"He was considering buying that motorcycle, for starters. And he invited Janie to Duckworth's for dinner. He told Sam at the dive that things were picking up for him—'big-time,' he said. Maybe he'd saved a little money and was feeling more secure. Janie was in the dark about where this sudden money came from. I think she was concerned about the bike—and certainly that set of pottery."

Nell brought up the roll of money he'd had on Saturday, which they all thought strange.

"Maybe he wanted investment advice," Cass joked. She smoothed out the small sweater she was knitting for the baby, a miniature fisherman's sweater knit in a cotton so soft the baby would feel as if he were on a cloud. "From his fisherman aunt," Cass had said when they questioned her choice of a cable sweater for one so tiny. "It's important he know from the start there will be lobsters in his life."

"Whatever the reason, he knew you, Birdie—or about you, anyway," Izzy said. "And Janie clearly thinks you set the moon. He probably just wanted to talk to you about his life, about Janie, jobs. Mistakes he's made. We've all done that at one time or another."

They pondered that possibility. Even Birdie had to admit it was possible. She was like a confessor without the penance. No matter who it was, she always listened, always cared, and was always fair and wise in her answer. Birdie never sugarcoated life's problems, but life, in her clear gray eyes—and in Mary Pisano's and Dickens' words—was always a season of hope.

"I'm wondering if he was in trouble," Nell said. She fingered the edge of the baby blanket, her fingers rolling over the seed pearl stitches. It was the softest merino blend she could find, a touch of silk on a baby's pink cheeks.

Heavy footsteps pressed their thoughts into silence as someone walked up the outdoor steps to Janie's apartment.

As if choreographed, four pair of hands stopped moving, needles and yarn dropped to laps. All eyes looked up at the ceiling, the room suddenly still.

Izzy leaned forward and started to push herself up from the chair. Then she stopped and shook her head, murmuring more to herself than the others, "What am I doing? How silly. It's Janie's apartment. She's an adult. She can handle visitors." But her voice was tight.

No one spoke.

They waited. Minutes later the footsteps came back down the stairs, more slowly this time, and then there was a knock at the door.

A quick knock, but urgent and insistent.

Cass got to the door first.

Tommy Porter stood on the doorstep, disheveled and alone. He looked as if he hadn't slept for days.

"Do you know where Janie is?" He was out of uniform, his shorts and shirt wrinkled.

"I thought she was working," Izzy said.

He shook his head. "I went there first. Lily said she got a phone call about an hour before closing time and seemed upset. Lily told her to go home. But she doesn't answer the door."

Izzy frowned, looked around. "Purl," she called out.

The cat didn't respond.

"I don't think I've seen Purl all night," Birdie said. "That's unusual. She's always here on Thursday night."

Izzy nodded. "Purl loves Janie. And she seems to have this sense that tells her when she's needed. Since the cat isn't here, she must be up there—with Janie."

She grabbed a ring of keys from the bookshelf. "Come on, Tommy."

They all got up and headed for the door.

No one spoke aloud the fear ringing in their heads. For some reason, harm coming to someone else they knew was unthinkable, and so they pushed the thought as far away as their fears allowed.

Janie should be answering her door. Everyone loved Janie—she'd handled her jobs, her life, her friends with good common sense and great compassion. No one would ever dream of hurting her. . . .

Izzy was the first one up the stairs with Tommy's breath an inch from her neck. She knocked lightly. "Janie, are you all right? I was wondering if Purl was up here with you."

At the sound of her name, the cat jumped to the windowsill and looked out at them, her green eyes glinting in the moonlight.

"Janie," Tommy called out, louder, an urgent cry. "Are you in there?"

"If Purl is there, Janie's home." Izzy tried the doorknob. It opened easily. They walked slowly and carefully, one by one, into the darkened room. In the small kitchen alcove, the stove clock added an eerie light to the area.

Purl was off the sill in an instant and flew toward the bedroom, as if leading them along. *Come, follow me.*

Janie was curled up on the bed, her hair a blaze of color spread out on the downy white comforter.

She didn't move.

Tommy hurried over to the bed. He shook her arm gently. "Janie?"

Janie pulled her eyes open slowly.

An audible wave of relief passed through the room.

She shifted on the bed, and a half-empty box of tissues fell to the floor. As her eyes adjusted, she saw the circle of concerned faces just behind Tommy.

"I . . . I must have fallen asleep," she said.

As soon as the words were out, the tears began again, running down her cheeks in rivers, falling onto the bedclothes. Purl pressed herself against Janie's chest as if to stop the flood.

"But you're okay?" Tommy's words were barely audible.

Janie nodded and reached for another tissue.

Birdie took one of her hands and held it in her own.

"Janie, these are dark days, but they will get better and we'll find out who did this."

Janie's head rolled back and forth on the pillow. "It's a nightmare. I want to wake up and have it all go away." She tried to focus on Birdie's face. "If I hadn't thrown him out like that. If I had helped him more, maybe—"

"Justin's death had nothing to do with you, Janie," Tommy said. His voice was firm.

Janie took a deep breath and pushed herself up in the bed, as if Tommy's words had turned a switch. She swung her feet over the side and forked her fingers through her hair, pushing it back from her face. She wiped the tears from her cheeks with the back of her hand.

"You think your life is almost perfect," Janie said. "I have you, Tommy, and this wonderful apartment." She looked at Izzy. "I love my job so much. And then little things start to happen. Things got a little crazy at work—the clinic is tense, you know?" She looked at Izzy. "Do you feel it, Iz? It didn't used to be that way."

"A little, yes, I do."

"Sometimes Dr. Seltzer doesn't seem to be tracking completely. Then some things go missing and Lily and I can't figure it out. And then Justin . . . Where did that perfect life go? I don't know if I will ever get it back."

"Sure, it's tough now, but we'll make it better. I promise." Tommy sat next to her and rubbed her neck.

She turned her head toward him. "They called me at work, Tommy."

"Who did?"

"The police."

"They'll probably want to talk to all of us, Janie," Nell said. "Right, Tommy?"

Janie shook her head. "No, it's not like that." When she looked at Tommy again, it was with great sadness, as if she had done something terrible to hurt him.

"I said I wanted to kill Justin—I told all of you that. I even told Archie Brandley when I left the house that night." She pulled Purl onto her lap.

"And the police think maybe I did."

Chapter 13

"Tommy was wonderful," Nell told Ben at breakfast the next day. "He hugged her and tried to get her to laugh. She was talking to the wrong person, he told her. After all, *he* was the police. And he knew firsthand she couldn't kill a spider if her life depended on it."

Ben downed the last dregs of his coffee and got up from the island. "Tommy's a good man. I'll see Jerry today at the chamber meeting and see what I can find out. Tommy's absolutely right— Janie couldn't hurt a fly."

But the furrow in his brow told Nell what she already knew. The police were on the fast track to get this murder solved. Not only did the town need the peace of knowing there wasn't a murderer in their midst, but it didn't help tourism any to have stories about the scuba diving murder—as the press called it—on visitors' radar. The yellow tape had finally been taken off the beach, but that wasn't nearly enough. Someone had to be behind bars before the collective sigh of relief would come from the town.

They'd talk to and consider anyone who had had any relationship with Justin Dorsey, the ponytailed kid from California. And they'd certainly not overlook his friend and distant cousin— a well-loved young woman who let it be heard that she wanted to kill him.

"It must have sliced right through her to realize she was a suspect," Ben said. "Janie really cared for the kid."

Nell put the breakfast dishes in the sink and began rinsing them off. "She saw the good in him, just like she does in everyone. And Janie is a natural caretaker. It's in her blood—and Justin needed lots of caring."

"I liked him, actually. We had a great talk one day about his love for the ocean—Atlantic or Pacific, he wasn't fussy. He thought our sailboat was great."

"Which of course would endear him to you."

"Absolutely." Ben walked over and wrapped his arms around her while she held a cup beneath the spray. "And speaking of endearing—" He nuzzled the side of her neck. "You're not so bad yourself."

Nell turned slightly and rubbed a soapy finger across his cheek. She smiled at him. "Then you won't mind picking up some fish for tonight?"

"Hmmm," Ben responded, then pulled away and checked his watch. "Not exactly what I had in mind, but I guess it'll have to do for now. Duty calls." He dropped a kiss on her cheek, picked up his keys, and was out the back door, off to help plan a summer regatta for the Boys' Club kids. Something, it occurred to both him and Nell, that might have made a huge difference in Justin Dorsey's life, had the opportunity been there.

It was noon before Nell finally got away from the house.

She'd sat at the kitchen island finishing a short grant application for the Canary Cove Arts Association, a task that should have taken an hour or two, but thoughts of Justin Dorsey and Janie Levin played havoc with her concentration.

Four hours later she grabbed her errand and grocery lists and drove down toward Harbor Road.

Birdie would meet up with her a little later at Izzy's shop, she'd texted Nell earlier. *No reason*, she said, except that Harold was off getting the car detailed and she needed some things at the store, so they would shop together.

And, Nell thought, Birdie knew she would like the company. They all had a sense about that—Nell, Birdie, Cass, and Izzy. There was a time to be alone, but a time when a close friend filled that space so much better.

Just as Nell turned onto Harbor Road, a car pulled out of a parking space directly in front of Gus McClucken's hardware store. A good omen, she thought. Perhaps the whole day would unfold that way—good, fortuitous things happening.

She pulled in and sat for a minute behind the wheel, her thoughts on the conversation she'd had with Ben. On Janie. On Justin. She looked across the street at Izzy's shop. The windows in the apartment above were open slightly. Izzy had called early to say she'd talked to Janie that morning. She had slept some, felt a little better—although she looked haggard, Izzy thought. But she was on her way to the clinic. Back to living her life, she'd said, though it would be forever changed.

And it would, Nell knew. One didn't experience the death of someone close without it having a lasting affect. Pairing that with murder made it doubly so.

Ben had said he liked Justin. She did, too. There was something about those engaging blue eyes and dimpled smile that was endearing. That was probably what Janie had seen at the family reunion and what drew her to him and him to her. He needed someone to care for him, and Janie was an ideal person to fill that need. Justin had an intriguing innocence, a kind of naiveté that made him seem younger than he actually was. And that, she realized with a start, could certainly exasperate those who cared about him, especially if it led to foolish decisions. Like washing windows on a rickety ladder or skipping job shifts in favor of surfing . . . or buying expensive presents without the money to pay for him.

"Yoo-hoo, in there. Anyone home?"

Nell looked over at a smiling Henrietta O'Neal, tapping on the passenger window with the handle of her cane.

Nell rolled down the window. "You caught me, Henrietta. I was deep into daydreaming."

Henrietta leaned in. "But from the look on your face, I suspect they're not especially nice dreams."

"It hasn't been the best of weeks, has it?" she said.

"Sometimes bad things happen."

"Justin Dorsey's death is certainly that—a bad thing."

"Murder, you mean, Nell. One must call it as it is, as distasteful as that may be. *Murder*, it's such an ugly word, not one we want to linger here long."

Nell slid out of the car and walked toward Henrietta.

It wasn't until she stepped up on the curb that she noticed Horace Stevenson. He was sitting on the bench outside Gus' store, his dog, Red, on the sidewalk beside him. Nell smiled over at them both, and Red thumped his tail in greeting. The only place she ever saw Horace on Harbor Road was in that exact spot. He'd buy his weekly supply of dog food, then wait contentedly for Gus to give him a lift home. His social life, he told her once. A chance to people-watch.

He tipped his ball cap to Nell before turning his attention to a group of skateboarders rolling down the street.

Nell turned to Henrietta. "Did you know Justin?"

Henrietta tsked at the racket the skaters were making, then pulled her white eyebrows together, as if Nell had asked her a difficult question. *Did she know Justin?* Finally she said, "I knew who he was—let's put it that way. He was always friendly when I'd see him around town. But then there was another side to him. . . ."

"Another side?"

"How shall I say it? Something wasn't quite right. His attention span seemed to be minimal. He didn't seem to know his boundaries, like an untrained puppy, but not suitable behavior for someone nearing twenty."

"How so?"

Henrietta waved one chubby finger in the air, as if scolding herself. "I'm being a fuddy-duddy. But that being said, I know he was a problem in the clinic. Doc Hamilton told me Lily hired him to do odd jobs, fix computers, file things. Apparently the young man was smart enough. But when I'd go in for my weekly blood-pressure screening, I'd see him wandering around, checking doors, snooping, you might say. Recently I went over to Martin's office to say hello, and there was Justin, standing outside the office door, as still as a mouse, like he was listening to what was going on behind the door. I suppose what I'm saying is that he was a tad inappropriate— though Martin would say that's an understatement."

She shook her head and laughed. "Goodness gracious, I *am* a fuddy-duddy, aren't I? And who am I to talk? I've been known to 'accidentally' overhear a conversation or two myself."

"That's an understatement, Henrietta dear." Gus McClucken walked out the front door of the hardware store carrying a giant bag of dog food. He set it down next to the bench and scratched the dog behind his ears. "I'll get you home in time for lunch, Red," he said, and then nodded at Horace. "He can come, too."

"All right, Gus," Henrietta said, "tell us what you think about all these goings-on."

Gus' smile disappeared in a flash. "It's pretty damn awful, is what I think. It's been a mess over here, with the police checking records, equipment, and what have you, trying to figure out who had access to it, that kind of thing. I knew Justin—he hung out in here because he loved all the toys, the surfboards and boogie boards and gear. He was dying to do a dive. . . ." He paused at the unfortunate choice of words, then said, "It's a cryin' shame. All of it."

Nell looked over at Horace. His watery eyes were on the street traffic, but she suspected the old man's ears were tuned to the conversation going on beside him.

The bell above the door rang again and Martin Seltzer walked out of the store, carrying a bag of fertilizer.

"Hey, Martin," Gus said, touching the bill of his cap.

Nell smiled a hello, but Henrietta was more effusive, walking up to the doctor and touching his arm. She looked up and smiled warmly—though her words were pure Henrietta. "Martin, you're skinny as a rat's tail. I hope you've come down here to eat."

Martin frowned at her, then lifted up his bag and stared at it. "You think I eat fertilizer?"

They laughed and Nell worked at swallowing her surprise. Martin Seltzer had a sense of humor. Who knew? But it was nice to see. Perhaps Henrietta brought it out of him, in spite of their disagreement at the market.

"My buddy here's a great gardener," Gus said, his thumb pointing back toward Martin. "He's one of the few that knows you get what you pay for. Always buys premium quality. Organic."

Henrietta frowned, as if she couldn't imagine Martin planting anything but his feet.

"You were talking about the kid who died—what Henrietta was saying was right. It's all true."

They waited.

"Lily thought he needed a break, so she paid him to work at the clinic—for doing nothing, in my opinion. I told her to fire him. He was no good, believe me, I know. He was a snoop, a common thief, a kid who didn't know right from wrong. I'd like to have killed him some days. But Janie Levin stood up for him, too. Foolish woman. She's a great nurse but a bad judge of character. That kid was bound to meet a bad end. And then he did. I warned him." Martin's face grew agitated as he talked and the toe of his long brown shoe tapped nervously on the sidewalk. When he spoke again, his voice was angry, his words carried on a wave of emotion.

"Sometimes people ask for it. They're warned, they don't listen. And then they get what they asked for."

Up and down Harbor Road, people laughed and chatted and children walked by eating giant ice-cream cones. Cars honked. The smell of garlic and tomato sauce floated out of Harry's deli down the street.

In front of McClucken's Hardware Store and Dive Shop, all was silent.

A gravelly voice finally broke the silence. "Who asked for what, you crazy fool?" It was Horace Stevenson, leaning toward the group.

They all looked over at the old man, his face carved by the years. His eyes were rheumy but his voice was strong.

"We were talking about the young man who was killed," Nell said. Horace lived a stone's throw from the dive site. He must have heard about the murder.

With a wave of his hand, he dismissed Nell's comment. "I know what goes on," he said. "Sometimes it takes a while for what I see to become clear in my head, to connect to my thoughts, you know?" He thumped his head with his knuckles as if knocking things in place. "But I was there . . . out on the beach. It was dark as doom. Shadowy. But the sounds were there. And the smells. Strong and tingly in my nose.

"And I know this much for sure: no one has the right—no matter who they think they are—to go in that shack and fiddle with the gear. No one deserves that kind of end—to sink down there below that water, your breath cut off. No one, not even that crazy surfer."

His face came alive as he talked, as if saying the words out loud was somehow clarifying some confusion in his own mind. As if murky thoughts were becoming clear, rational, connected. Even his weary eyes, cloudy with cataracts, seemed to be seeing something that was becoming clear in his mind. "Now it fits together." Horace reached down and scratched his dog's head, his words softening to a murmur meant only for Red.

Gus nodded. "The old man's right, Marty. No one deserves that kind of thing. Not even you."

Martin's face faded to the color of the sidewalk. The vehemence of his own words seemed to have taken a toll on him. He coughed into his hand and stared at the ground.

"I knew him," he mumbled.

"Maybe you did, maybe you didn't," Henrietta said, tapping his arm with the handle of her cane. "But the one thing I do know is you better watch your tongue. I think you're half starving and it's affecting your brain. We're going to get something to eat. Maybe it will turn you into a decent human being."

With that she picked up her cane, motioned toward Harry Garozzo's deli, and began to walk in that direction, her cane tapping authoritatively on the cement. *Follow me,* it said.

Martin Seltzer followed.

An hour later, Nell walked into Izzy's yarn shop. She'd been to the post office and the cheese shop, then picked up old-fashioned candy dots from Lulu's Sweets, the new candy store next to the bank. And all along the way she'd wondered about two men—the doctor and the old man who walked the shore—both who seemed to have unusually strong opinions about a young man's death.

Her last purchase was an impulse buy—the long chain of candy disks reminded Nell of Izzy's colorful window display. The twins had created a nursery, complete with bassinet and rocking chair. And overflowing from the bed and chair were giant balls of alpaca, angora, dreamy cottons, and fine merinos in every color of the rainbow. Tiny infant sweaters, plush blankets, and hats—donated by customers for the children's shelter—were a colorful background, hanging gaily from a white clothesline that stretched from one side of the window to the other. The candy disks matched the colors perfectly.

"Great candies," Mae Anderson said as Nell handed her the bag. "We're overrun with mothers these days—I think it's the wonderful display plus folks wanting to check out Izzy's progress. The little ones that tag along will love a special treat."

"Is Birdie around?"

"Yep, and ready for an escape, in my humble opinion. When I stuck my head in a minute ago, the talk was focused on the merits of drug-free childbirth and the wonders of a father cutting the umbilical cord. My Jerry would have been flat on the floor at the very mention of it."

Nell laughed and headed toward the back room, following the iPod sounds of someone singing about love, stars, and long summer nights. She stood in the archway for a minute watching the activity swirling around the knitting room. Heaped on the library table were baskets of needles, measuring tape, scissors, and markers. Pattern books were strewn about, and groups of women sat at the table or on the couches and easy chairs with balls of yarn at their side, knitting and purling tiny sweaters and hats.

Birdie sat near the open casement windows, relishing the brisk afternoon breeze. Purl was curled up on her lap. Nearby, Laura Danvers and several of her friends sat with piles of baby Suri alpaca yarn on the table between them.

Nell walked over and admired the half-finished sweater on Laura's lap. "A baby sweater?"

Laura smiled. "Don't even think it, Nell. Our two girls keep Elliot and me plenty busy." She held up the tiny garment. "This is for Uncle Franklin's baby. It seems early to be knitting something, but Tamara says it makes it more real to her. In nine months we should be able to open a store with everything she's suggesting we make."

"Franklin seems overjoyed with this pregnancy."

"It's this *heir* thing he has. It's so important to him. He really wants a boy."

Franklin Danvers was a private man, but it was an often-repeated rumor that the lack of offspring contributed to the failure of his previous marriages. "But there's no guarantee of that," Birdie says.

"Exactly. So, what if it's a girl?" one of her friends asked.

The question lingered there, then was silenced as Tamara Danvers walked into the room, spotted them, and walked over.

Nell hadn't talked with her since the morning Franklin had called the police on Justin Dorsey. *Years ago*—that's how it felt. But it wasn't years; it was just a few days before he died. Tamara had been agitated that day, or maybe upset by the commotion Justin had caused.

Today her color was better, her face composed, and her blond hair pulled back and fastened with a wide gold clip at her neck. She wore sneakers and stretchy, formfitting black pants with a pink tank top and a vibrant nylon jacket on top.

She held up a skein of angora yarn, bright blue, soft, and luscious, and looked at Izzy. "Do you like it?"

"Another baby sweater, Tamara?"

"No. This is for leggings for when he crawls. Gwen Stefani's boys wore leggings. I read that she knit a pair herself."

"Not angora, I bet. This isn't strong enough. And it'll have a halo effect, not great for a bruising boy." Izzy took the yarn and was back in a minute with a cotton acrylic in the same majestic blue. "This'll work better." She looked at Tamara's figure and sighed. "I never looked like that. Even before I was pregnant."

"I'm keeping up my routines. Exercise. I think it'll keep things tight during the pregnancy. It's early, you know. I want to keep active."

They knew. But no one told Tamara that she was dreaming.

"We may even try some diving this summer, though Franklin is afraid of every little thing, as if I'm a china doll."

"Diving . . . ," Laura said quietly. "That's not a pleasant topic around here right now."

Tamara took a sharp breath and fingered the yarn in her hand. "Of course it's not, that was stupid of me. It was right near our place, you know. Franklin dives a lot. He could have been down there with the club that morning. He could have been the one killed."

Or Sam. Or Danny. Or Andy Risso. All wonderful men. But not men whom anyone would want to kill.

"I don't think the police think it was a random thing," Laura said. "Someone wanted to kill a specific person, not just any diver."

"So who was he?" Tamara asked. "Franklin said the paper didn't say much."

"Justin Dorsey," Izzy said. "You've met him, Tamara. He was the guy who came up on your veranda that day. Franklin was upset about him being there, remember? He called the police."

Tamara paused for a moment, then said, "Of course, I remember now. I hadn't made the connection. Good Lord. Franklin was really mad that day. I thought at first the guy was just friendly, someone with a board, walking the beach. But he walked right on the terrace, as if . . . as if he had a right to be there. It was frightening. But after Franklin called the police, he never came back. At least as far as I know."

"No. He probably didn't," Nell said.

Laura frowned. "Uncle Franklin called the police? That's crazy. Every kid in Sea Harbor has surfed and boogie-boarded down there. It's a great beach, gets good waves. And nothing against you, Tamara, but most of the people who live up there rarely use the beach."

Tamara looked defensive. "Franklin was just trying to protect me from someone who didn't know how to take no for an answer."

Laura was undeterred. "Maybe. But it's still a little crazy."

"Franklin thought he was a troublemaker."

Nell watched the exchange and wondered about the relationship between the two women. Tamara wasn't much older than Laura, although their husbands were a generation apart. Laura was already a prominent figure in Sea Harbor, no matter her age. She was devoted to her family and nearly every charitable cause that reared its head in Sea Harbor. People liked and respected the young community leader. Nell wondered if that was a problem for Tamara.

But Tamara didn't seem affected by Laura's comments as she proudly passed her legging pattern around for everyone to see.

When the conversation moved back to young motherly topics, Birdie rose from the window seat, gave Purl a final pat, and gathered up her shopping bags. With a nod to Nell and a wave to the group, she headed up the stairs.

Nell followed. Birdie's manner of leaving was one of the things they all cherished about her. None of those prolonged and awkward good-byes at a door. Birdie simply got up, waved, and was gone. Sometimes squeezing a quick hug in between the two, depending on whom she was leaving.

"People don't know what to say about it all," Nell said as they walked through the shop.

"But 'say' they will, making up things, if need be. No matter, Jerry Thompson is a smart man. He'll get to the bottom of this soon."

Nell nodded absently, looking into the Magic Room, the name Izzy had given the yarn shop's playroom. It was filled with the shop owner's own childhood toys—dolls and doll beds, puppets, stuffed animals, and Tinker Toys—along with newer ones donated by the mothers who appreciated a place to leave their toddlers and pre-schoolers while they picked out patterns and took classes. Mae's nieces Jillian and Rose loved watching over the kids, wiping noses, playing games, and retrieving mothers when needed. Today they seemed to be cuddling their charges more, watching each child more closely.

It's what happens when a town has been wounded in such a horrific way. Mothers all over town were paying attention to their teenagers' curfews, requesting frequent check-ins, worrying about parties and days at the beach. The wonderful carefree things that made up summer were now potential dangers, something to put under a magnifying glass.

Outside the yarn shop they paused, putting on sunglasses and adjusting to the bright light.

"Humph."

The two women turned toward the sound, and found themselves looking into the small beady eyes of Mrs. Bridge, owner and manager of the Bell Street Boardinghouse, perhaps one of the last remaining boardinghouses in North America. Justin's last-known address.

Mrs. Bridge had a first name, but she never used it and over the years it had fallen from everyone's memory—even the postmistress couldn't remember her mail addressed to anyone but "Mrs. Bridge."

"This is where Janie Levin lives, they tell me," she said to Birdie and Nell. Her chubby index finger pointed to the upper windows.

"That's right, Mrs. Bridge. But she isn't here right now."

"It was her friend who was murdered," Mrs. Bridge said.

"A distant relative," Nell said.

"He lived at my place, you know," she went on, as if Nell hadn't spoken. "The police have been by, of course, and they said there wasn't much there. Old clothes, a surfboard. They took what they wanted. The rest is right there." She pointed to a cardboard box on the sidewalk beside her old Chevy. "I'd like it to be gone."

Her tone of voice indicated that the rest of Justin's belongings would turn her house into a deadly virus if allowed to remain.

"We'll give it to Janie," Birdie said. "Was Justin a problem?"

Nell picked it up and put it inside the yarn shop door to deal with later.

Mrs. Bridge seemed troubled by the question. Then she said, "I shouldn't speak ill of the dead. But that young man wasn't my kind of tenant. I told him he had to leave."

"To leave?"

Mrs. Bridge looked down and rubbed her palms down the sides of her wide-legged polyester pants. Finally she met their eyes again. "Yes." She sighed heavily. "I banished him."

"He wasn't a good tenant?"

Again, Mrs. Bridge was silent. She shifted her considerable weight from one foot to another. Finally she spoke. "There were the late-night rendezvous a while ago. He let a friend 'use' his room, if you know what I mean. I heard about it, of course I did. I looked the other way at first, then finally warned him I wasn't running that kind of place, and it stopped. As for his recent shenanigans? I've no proof, not now, I know that. But I also know this. Justin Dorsey was a charming con man. He told all my tenants he was on his way to being rich. And I don't doubt it. As sure as I'm standing here, he was helped along by the cash that went missing from my apartment last week—two weeks' worth of rent money, waiting for me to take it to the bank."

Chapter 14

" A con man."

Ben considered Mrs. Bridge's words as he rummaged through a kitchen drawer, searching for the grill lighter. "The romantic version of a con man is of a charming, likable guy. Justin seems to fit that. Maybe that's exactly who he was."

"Harriet Brandley came out of the bookstore while we were talking. She didn't say much at first, just listened until Mrs. Bridge left. But then—very reluctantly, I thought—she said that Justin didn't do right by Archie, either, when he helped out there a couple months ago."

Nell set a bowl of basting sauce for the tuna on a tray and continued her story. "It had something to do with the day's cash not matching receipts or something. But it happened weeks ago, Harriet said."

"I wonder if people's reluctance to call Justin out on things was because of Janie. She was trying her damnedest to get him jobs and turn his life around," Ben said.

"Probably." Everyone in town loved Janie. "But all those things—none of them add up to murder. You don't kill someone for being a petty thief. At least Sea Harbor folks don't."

A noise at the front door announced Birdie, Cass, and Danny. Cass' brother, Pete, and Willow Adams were close behind.

Birdie carried a platter of buttermilk brownies and lemon

squares. "Sinful," she said. "And all made by Ella and Gabby—who, I am sorry to say, have become master dessert makers."

Although Nell and Ben never knew how many people would show up on the deck Friday nights, they knew that good news or bad news was a magnet that pulled people together—to hug or laugh or cry or simply to sit around a fire and *be*.

Tonight they'd be surrounded by friends.

"And don't even ask if I made this sourdough bread," Cass said, setting down two round loaves. "No, of course I didn't make it. Not only has Danny become a better knitter than I, but he's learning how to bake bread. Jeez."

"Way to go, Brandley," Pete said, and clapped the writer on the back.

"She's right. I mastered cables this week. There's no stopping me now," Danny said. He gave Nell a hug.

Jane and Ham Brewster followed soon after and Izzy and Sam brought up the rear.

"I tried to get Janie to come," Izzy said. "Tommy was working tonight and I didn't want to leave her alone. She's still not used to the apartment and . . ." Izzy paused.

But Nell knew exactly what she was thinking.

And we still don't know who is out there, and if there's anyone else he wants to kill. Janie was too closely connected to Justin for them not to worry about her.

"Anyway, she said no. She was going to do some knitting, and then spend some time with Dr. Lily."

"What does she do with all of those baby things she knits?" Ham asked, handing Ben a bottle of olives.

"Most of them go to the free health clinic. She loves to knit. She's says it's her therapy," Izzy said. "I get that. It's mine, too."

"The police talked to her again yesterday," Ben said. "I know that's taking a toll on her. And Tommy's miserable but can't do a thing about it."

"The police can't possibly think she has anything to do with Justin's murder," Jane said.

Ben shook a silver martini pitcher and poured the liquid into the glasses he'd lined up. "Pretend you're the chief," he said, adding olives to each. "Janie said she hated Justin. She'd gone out on a limb for him more times than she can count, and he messed up every time. Apparently he even screwed up some things at the clinic, and Janie loves that place. She must have been mortified."

"But kill?" Ham said.

"Okay, sure, we know she wouldn't, couldn't. But the police need to look at it from a distance."

"Ben's right. They called my dad down to the station this afternoon," Danny said.

"Archie?" Jane said. "Good grief. What for?"

Danny repeated the story his mother had told Nell and Birdie earlier. "My dad had misgivings about Justin from the beginning, even though my mom liked his smile. Dad thought he was trouble and only hired him to help out because Janie asked him to."

A familiar scenario. Janie had asked her friends to help him— and Justin had screwed up. For a brief moment, Nell wanted to kill him herself. She took the tray of marinated tuna steaks out of the refrigerator and set it on the counter.

"Justin made bad decisions," Ben said.

"And that's probably what got him killed," Sam said. "But if everything we're hearing is true, there were lots of people who might not want him around. People here are generous—but they don't like being played for fools."

"But here's a funny thing you should know," Ben said. "I had a meeting with Father Larry a few days ago—before we knew the whole story of Justin's death. We were talking about the church's project for underserved youths, some of them orphans. He said he didn't normally reveal people's contributions, but he felt this was appropriate, and he told me that Justin Dorsey had come by Our Lady of Safe Seas last Saturday—the day before he died—and given him a contribution envelope marked for the project. When Father Northcutt opened it later, he found ten one-hundred-dollar bills inside—a thousand dollars."

Nell's eyes widened. She pulled a stack of napkins from beneath the island.

"Where would he have gotten money like that?" Cass said.

"You think Justin had a little bit of Robin Hood in him?" Sam asked.

Robin Hood. It somehow fit this young man who had mastered the art of making bad decisions and yet could win people over with a charming, sweet smile and then give money to kids who, like himself, didn't have a very good start in life.

"It could be a dangerous profession," Ben said.

Nell handed Izzy a platter of shrimp rolls, picked up a cheese and fruit platter, and ushered everyone out to the deck. "Fresh air," she said.

Ham Brewster shuffled through a stack of Ben's old CDs until he found some old seventies tunes and let Simon and Garfunkel sing to them of peace.

Drinks and appetizers were passed around, chairs and chaises pulled together, and the same Friday night magic that had embraced the group through births and deaths, through the best of times and the worst of times, took hold.

"Janie's the one suffering through all this. Not only is she suffering from having to be questioned about his murder—as if she might have had something to do with it—but she is convinced that if she had done more for Justin, he wouldn't have done whatever he did to get himself killed," Izzy said.

"I wonder if Janie knows about the donation he made to the church," Nell said. "I think she'd like hearing that."

"But where did he get that kind of money to give away? Certainly not from the hodgepodge of part-time jobs he had—or even the kind of petty theft he seemed to have enjoyed," Jane said.

"Did you hire him, Jane?" Nell asked, remembering the beautiful set of hand-thrown pottery Justin had given Janie. "Was that how he paid for the dishes he gave Janie?"

"I almost forgot about that. He came in the other day—it was Saturday morning, I think—and was looking at the most expensive collection I had. I tried to steer him away from them, but he refused to budge. He wanted the best, he said. So I suggested maybe he could help out in the gallery—we're always in need of people to mail things for us, take orders off the Internet. He said no, he was busy— he might be getting into business for himself."

"What?" Ben said. "What kind of business?"

"A surf shop, I think he said. Can you believe it? Some crazy thing that would cost a lot of money. Anyway, he said he'd pay for the pottery with cash. And he did. Lots of it. He had a fat wad of bills, all shoved in a fanny pack."

"He didn't even give Jane a chance to give him a discount, which she would have done because he had a nice smile and my Jane can't resist dimples."

Jane wrinkled her nose at her husband.

But it was true. The Brewsters' generosity to friends and family was limitless, and Ben sometimes wondered how they made any money.

"Okay, so somewhere, somehow, from someone, Justin was getting cash," Danny said.

"And from what we're guessing, it wasn't through legitimate means," Pete said.

"But some of it went to good things, like the children's fund," Izzy said.

"And dishes for Janie."

"Birdie, I'm still curious about Justin wanting to see you," Willow said.

"Now that I know he lost his room at Mrs. Bridge's boarding-house, I'm wondering if he was wanting a place to stay."

"I don't think so," Ben said. "Even for a young man who somehow thinks the world will provide for him, that seems a bit presumptuous."

Birdie agreed. But the young man had *something* on his mind, something he thought she could help him with. And that be-fuddled her.

Ben put the bluefin tuna steaks on the grill and brushed each one with the basil, garlic, and lemon butter sauce Nell handed him. The conversation fell silent while the intoxicating aroma of the fish and herbs wafted up from the grill in a white smoky cloud.

"Ben, will you marry me?" Cass asked, her full attention given over to the appetite-enticing aromas around her.

Willow and Nell disappeared inside, returning with Willow's lobster risotto, Danny's sourdough bread, and a leafy avocado and pecan salad.

The dining table, already set for dinner and warmed by the glow of hurricane lamps, was comfortable and worn, and nestled beneath the protective branches of Nell's favorite maple tree. They gathered around while Ben filled wine and water glasses, then held one in the air. "Birdie, my love. Please do the honors."

Birdie's short silvery hair moved as she looked around to each person sitting at the table. Her words were clear, filled with the moment. "We give thanks for friends, for family, and for new life," she said, her eyes lingering on Izzy and Sam. "And to those we shall protect, no matter what. Peace."

In minutes plates were filled with tuna steaks, the herbed aioli sauce was passed around, and conversations picked up.

"So, Izzy dear, how did Jane and Willow ever talk you into this baby shower they're planning?" Birdie asked.

Izzy put down her fork and looked across the table at the two women in question. "Have you ever tried to say no to those two?" she asked. Her dark blond eyebrows lifted into streaked bangs as she glared at them. "I thought not."

They laughed.

"Gabby is helping, too. It will be lovely and intimate and fun and make all of us feel good for having done it, so that's that," Jane said.

"As long as we don't have to play those crazy games, I'll come," Cass said.

"Are guys invited?" Danny asked, and the conversation escalated to a heated discussion of whose baby was it, anyhow?

Nell half listened to the conversation circling around her and leaned back, looking up at the impenetrable black sky, broken only by one or two flickering signs of a solar system. A majestic and infinite sea of darkness.

"Nell?" Ben asked.

Nell focused on Ben's voice, and only then on the sound of the doorbell. It was becoming routine—interruptions to Friday-night dinners. At least when there was turmoil in their lives.

"I'm up. I'll go," Ben said.

For the second time in as many weeks, Janie Levin stood at the Endicotts' front door, shivering, even in the warm June night, and was ushered inside.

She apologized for the intrusion, but she needed to talk to Birdie.

Janie's face was pale as Ben led her to the deck. He pulled out a chair next to Birdie and insisted she sit and have a glass of wine.

Birdie saw the stress in the nurse's face. "We need to coax that lovely pink back into your cheeks, Janie," she said.

Janie sat down. She dropped her bag in her lap and took a sip of wine. "I think I should get this over with or I may just drink the whole bottle of wine."

"Would you like to talk in private?" Birdie asked.

Janie shook her head no. It was clear she'd been crying again, but for the time being, the tears had stopped, and the determination on Janie's face told them she would keep them at bay as best she could. She looked around the table. "You're all my friends. I care about you—"

Birdie placed a blue-veined hand on top of Janie's. "And we love you, Janie. You know that. This is about Justin, I suspect. And we all have a soft spot in our hearts for him, too. No matter what."

"No matter what?" Janie said.

"Of course. He might not have been the most responsible person in the world. He made some mistakes along the way. But the saddest thing about that is that one of those mistakes may have got him killed."

Janie looked down at her lap. Her fingers played with the buckle on her bag. "I don't think this mistake is the one that got him killed,

Birdie. But I don't know, had I known about it . . . I might have been tempted. . . ." She managed a small smile and wiped away a tear that had somehow escaped and threatened to roll down her cheek. "But the thing is, Justin meant a lot to me. He was like a little brother, I guess. And I think underneath it all, he was a good person. I don't want you to hate him. And that's why this is all so hard."

"Janie, that won't happen," Nell assured her. "Absolutely not."

Janie took another deep breath and plunged in. "I was driving over to Dr. Lily's tonight and thinking about everything that's happened, and of course I started to cry again. So I pulled a tissue out of my glove compartment before going into her house. An envelope dropped out with the tissue. I thought maybe it was from a checkup, but then I spotted a scribble on the front that looked like Justin's blocky print—and I remembered that he had borrowed my car last weekend."

"Yes, I remember," Nell said. "We were with you that day."

Janie threw her a silent thank-you. Somehow having all parts of her story believed and verified seemed to be important to Janie.

"Go on," Birdie said.

"It was bulky—the envelope. So I looked inside. I think it's why he wanted to see you on Sunday."

Janie fumbled in her bag and pulled out an envelope. While everyone watched, she opened the end and poured the contents onto a napkin.

A platinum chain fell out first, followed by a handful of diamonds, rubies, and sapphires, sparkling in the candlelight. Finally Janie stuck two fingers back in the envelope and pulled out the remaining piece—two large entwined hearts.

Birdie looked down at it. She fingered the hearts, and the trace of a smile lifted the corners of her mouth.

"Goodness. Even with the jewels pried out, it's still quite an unattractive necklace," she said. She looked around the table. "I don't believe it would even have looked nice on Tamara Danvers." She shook her small white head and smiled in a comforting way, patting Janie's quivering hand. "And most certainly not on Justin."

Chapter 15

I t was late Friday night when they finally went their separate ways.

Ben had called Tommy at the station and invited him to drop by after his shift. He mentioned the double chocolate brownies—but also said Janie was there. She'd had a long night. His company would be welcome.

Tommy showed up soon after and stayed close to Janie's side, mostly listening while she filled him in.

When she finished, Birdie looked at her long face and gave her a hug. "So much sadness isn't productive, dear." And then she told Janie about the donation Justin had made to Father Larry's under-privileged children fund. "He wasn't all bad, you see. You taught him some things, Janie."

"I knew kids like Justin when Ham and I lived in Berkeley in the early seventies," Jane Brewster said. "Those were different times, but stealing didn't seem so bad to runaway kids—and we met plenty of them. They had their own way of thinking: the store would always have more wallets and more knives. Rich people had more jewelry. Who would care? And if some of that money went to help someone who needed it, even better. And often it did. Like Ben said, there was an element of Robin Hood about it all—redistributing the goods to make the world a more equal place."

Birdie smiled at Janie. "We think Justin may have been playing Robin Hood."

For the first time that night, they saw the shadow of a smile on Janie's pale face.

The condition of the necklace was interesting, Tommy said. Justin had probably removed the gems because they'd be easier to sell. Certainly less recognizable than the distinctive necklace from which they came.

"And he didn't know it was Birdie's," Janie reminded them again. "None of us did."

Even Tommy agreed he'd probably not have done it if he knew whose necklace it was. And for Janie's sake he held back the words they all knew were trying to get out: *But it was still wrong.*

"And who knows what he planned to do with the money he'd get for the jewels?" Ben reminded them. "Buy something for Janie? A Boys' Club contribution? Put it in Father Northcutt's collection basket?"

The more they peeled away the layers of Justin Dorsey's personality, the more of an enigma he became.

Janie pointed to the scribble on the envelope. It was Birdie's phone number. "He asked me about the necklace recently," she said. "He wondered if it had been found." She winced when she repeated his words, the lies still a fresh affront. "I told him it was Birdie's jewelry and she had decided to simply let it all be, not report it.

"At the time, I thought his reaction was kind of strange," Janie went on, her eyes on Birdie's face. "He was shocked that it was yours. And seemed very bothered by it. He liked you. He said you were one of the wisest women he'd ever met, and then he asked me to get him your phone number." Tommy brought her a glass of water, and she went on.

"So now I suppose I get it. As wrongheaded as his thinking was, Justin didn't steal from friends or people he liked. Stealing from anonymous sources, like a store or an auction that had anonymous donations, was apparently okay, but not from real people, especially ones he knew I loved. So he was going to meet with you and make amends. He shoved the necklace in my glove compartment so he could take it to you Sunday after his dive. But . . . he never got that chance." Her voice was filled with such sadness that they looked away and began bringing in the dishes, leaving Janie to her moment of grief.

They looked at the necklace again, and thought of his other small thefts—books, a few small items from stores that Janie had found in his belongings, some wallets, fancy knives, scuba gear. But none of them could imagine anyone killing him for those things—and certainly not for an ornate necklace that its owner was happy to be rid of.

After Tommy finished off the pan of brownies, he and Janie left, promising to be in touch. Soon the crowd had dwindled to a few.

Ben scooped up the necklace pieces Janie had left, tossed the envelope on the kitchen island, and found a sturdier container for it. "There's always next year's auction," he teased Birdie, then suggested Danny and Sam join him on the deck for a glass of his prized Macallan.

Nell turned on the dishwasher and began washing wineglasses.

"I'm feeling discombobulated," Cass said, picking up a towel. "My mom always used that word when the universe felt off-kilter."

Izzy sat down at the island, her feet slightly swollen. Her face was drawn. "I think there's more to all this, and it frightens me. Things are definitely off-kilter."

"Yes, there's more to this than finding out there was a side to Justin we didn't know about. There's his killer, someone who's still out there somewhere, someone who took a life," Birdie said. "And it's thrown us all off. Izzy, your sixth sense, or seventh, or whatever it is, was on target. Something is not right in the universe."

Izzy's hands moved to the shape that now defined her. "I just ache for Janie. She's a brave gal—but she's a mess right now. She took Justin into her life. And now—now it's all shattered."

"You're right," Nell said. She wiped off the island, moving the empty jewelry envelope and several napkins to the side counter. "She's strong, but she'll need all her friends."

"And a break from being questioned by the police. I don't care if they're doing their job or not," Cass said. "That's enough to break anyone. She's grieving for the guy, and at the same time she's furious with him, and then there's suspicion that she wanted him dead. That's heavy stuff."

There was unspoken agreement, and then Birdie spoke again. "We all agree things are off-kilter—and that poor girl can't begin to put her life together until the person who did this is found. There's no room in any of our lives for the kind of fear that's created this black cloud over Sea Harbor. And it's certainly not the town we want to bring Izzy and Sam's baby into."

For a moment the only sounds in the kitchen were the wind, the dishwasher, and the comforting, familiar voices floating in from the deck.

Off-kilter.

Not the kind of world to bring a baby into.

Birdie was the first to speak. "I'm tired, dear ones. But tomorrow I will be bright and chipper, ready to continue this conversation and to knit an entire arm onto the beautiful romper I am knitting for baby Perry. Last night's knitting session barely counted, and that baby will be wearing jeans and T-shirts before Nell finishes her blanket if we don't get to it. We need time to knit . . . and we need time to think. Time to breathe fresh air."

Nell peeled off her gloves and turned around. "Birdie, as usual, is absolutely right."

"I'm in. Tomorrow?" Cass said.

"Yes, tomorrow," Birdie said. "On my veranda. Bring your knitting."

Of course, they all agreed.

Another agreement was made, too, this one in that silent way of old friendships. An agreement confirmed with a look and a nod of the head; as their needles worked magic and soft yarn turned into tiny baby garments, their minds would be working, too—and not on creating new patterns or figuring out a difficult entrelac pattern.

Their minds would be focused on figuring out a murder.

Chapter 16

Birdie's Ravenswood estate was the perfect place to be, no matter the weather, no matter the occasion. The home was both grandiose and as comfortable as an old friend. And Birdie shared it generously.

Today, a slight afternoon breeze blew in off the ocean while the sun warmed the veranda flagstones. "Like baked Alaska," Birdie said, opening the veranda doors. "Warm and cold."

Nell pulled her cardigan around her shoulders and settled into one of Birdie's steamer chairs, its teak frame polished to a high gloss. The Favazza home, with its gardens and verandas and patios, had the most magnificent view in Sea Harbor. The veranda faced the harbor, and Birdie claimed that on clear days she could see all the way out to the community center and Sunrise Island beyond. At night, one looked out on a sea of lights.

"Ella made her famous chicken salad," she said, motioning for Cass and Izzy to settle in.

"And Gabby?"

"She's off somewhere. Said it was a surprise. Gabby is full of surprises these days."

And her surprises were keeping her nonna young, something her friends loved to see.

"I ran into Tommy on my way over here," Nell said. She pulled her baby blanket out of the bag and stretched it across her knees.

"He's worried about Janie. But even more worried that the police have hit a dead end."

"No suspects?" Cass asked.

"Apparently lots of them. At least people who had a grudge against Justin. Everyone he stole from, like Gus McClucken, people whose businesses suffered because of him—"

"Like Archie Brandley," Izzy said.

Nell nodded. "And each day the police come up with new names. They talked to Martin Seltzer late yesterday."

"Janie said Lily Virgilio was very upset about that," Izzy said. "She told the police that he couldn't possibly have done anything to Justin."

"She probably doesn't want the clinic drawn into such a mess," Birdie said. She finished one sleeve on her romper for the baby and smoothed it out with the tip of her finger.

"I understand that. But I saw Martin yesterday," Nell said, "and he was very vocal about Justin. He thought he deserved what he got."

"Not very smart of him. That won't exactly clear him of suspicion," Izzy said. "Janie said there was terrible friction between those two, and she wasn't sure why. Dr. Seltzer's complaints didn't seem to merit that much hatred."

Nell replayed Martin's dagger-throwing look at Justin's back the day of Izzy's doctor's appointment. "And then he mumbled something about Justin not being around for long, or his days being numbered, or something like that."

"Around the clinic?" Cass said. She put down the small fisherman's sweater, its cables beginning to take shape. "Janie said he wanted Justin fired."

"I suppose that's what he meant. But . . ." But could it have been worse? She remembered the look on his face, and then again at McClucken's. Martin hated Justin Dorsey and he didn't care who knew it.

"This is hard for us because we don't want anyone we know to be guilty of something so awful," Birdie said. "But someone is. Someone killed Justin, and it might very well have been someone we know." She paused and looked out at the harbor, the blue of the sky, the billowing sails in the distance. "In fact, it probably is. If there's been a stranger lurking around here, we'd surely have known it."

Izzy lifted the edge of Nell's blanket and rubbed it against her cheek, as if feeling her baby wrapped up in it. The tiny seed stitches were soft against her skin. "Did Tommy mention if they'd questioned Franklin Danvers?"

Birdie frowned. "Franklin . . . ? That's a little like questioning the mayor or pope, isn't it?"

"He thought Justin was bothering Tamara—and Tamara confirmed it. She said he frightened her."

Birdie frowned. "Justin may have been many things, but frightening wasn't one of them."

"Izzy has a point. She said Justin *touched* her. That would make any husband upset. And Franklin is ferocious these days when it comes to protecting his pregnant wife," Nell said. "Franklin complained to the chief when Tommy didn't arrest Justin that day on the beach."

Izzy's needles clicked away as she talked. She'd finished the booties and was on to a tiny hat, tissue soft and with a wide brim to protect the baby from the sun. "That was silly for Franklin to be so upset. Kind of stupid for Justin to go surfing there, I guess, but still, all the kids do it."

"Including yourself," Nell said with a smile.

Izzy laughed. "Tamara said Justin came on to her, but of all the things we've heard about him, that one just doesn't seem right. I truly can't imagine him coming on to Tamara Danvers."

"So you think she made it up?" Cass asked.

But why she'd do that was a mystery. "Unless," Cass answered herself, "she wanted Franklin to think he had. Who knows? Sometimes people do silly things. Maybe jealous husbands buy more jewelry."

"I think that explanation makes more sense," Nell said. "I don't mean to call her a liar, but sometimes she might exaggerate a bit."

"We're pummeling poor Tommy with questions," Cass said, "and while we're doing that, we're skipping directly over him."

"Who?"

"Tommy," Cass said. "I know—all of us know—that Tommy Porter is the nicest guy around. But he also wanted Justin Dorsey gone from here. Maybe more than any of the others. He hated the way he was screwing with Janie's life. He had a beer with Danny the other night, and Danny said he was almost obsessed with the guy."

The silence that followed was sobering, as truth often was. Tommy Porter loved Janie, a fact that was clear to every one of them. But his relationship with Janie had been strained by Justin Dorsey's entry into it. And there didn't seem to be much he could do about it.

Finally Birdie spoke again. "So our list of people grows," she said. "But so do the questions. Where was he, who did he talk to that week before he was killed? The day before he was killed? Was he bothered about something? Why did Martin dislike him so? Did he steal from him?"

"Yes!" Nell said suddenly. "Martin Seltzer said exactly that yesterday. He said Justin was a thief, that he took things that weren't his."

"So what was it? Janie doesn't seem to know. I wonder who does. Maybe we could pry something out of Henrietta. She seems to be chumming up nicely to the doctor," Cass said. "I suppose the police are asking these same questions, but they might not realize that this has to be resolved so baby Perry can be born."

"Maybe because we know Justin a little better—we certainly saw plenty of him the week before he was killed—our questions will be slightly different," Nell said.

"And we liked him," Izzy said. "That brings a different perspective to it. Somehow I feel the answer to all this is right in front of us. So close that it's frightening."

"Certainly the police care as deeply about finding the killer as we do," Birdie said. "But they don't knit. They don't look at patterns like we do."

Nell looked down at her baby blanket and gently touched the tiny seed stitches with the tip of her finger. "They might not see connections the way we do, the loose threads, the surprising way that sometimes a sweater design comes together before your very eyes, but at first you can't see it."

"Yes," Izzy jumped in, warming to the analogy. "So you keep on frogging where you have to, reworking rows. You just need to keep on knitting, and then, voilà! There it is."

You just need to keep on knitting. Nell picked up her cable needle and began to slip the next group of stitches onto it. She imagined the baby, bundled in the warmth of the soft yarn, tucked in his stroller as Izzy ran behind him over the smooth sand. Carefree. Something that was sorely missing in their lives right now. No one was taking early walks or runs on Paley's Cove. Not alone. Not now. Not until a murderer had a face and was securely behind bars.

The opening of the veranda's doors was followed by a breeze and flurry of black hair as Gabby rushed out. She carried a bowl of chicken salad. Behind her, Ella balanced a tray full of plates, forks, and sweet-smelling corn bread.

"I thought you were out and about," Birdie said, smiling up into Gabby's face.

"I *was* out and about." Gabby gave Birdie a quick kiss and grinned hellos to each of them. She set the bowl down and glanced at Ella, then laughed. "Okay, I'll come clean. Ella knows all my secrets. She told me she'd hold back some of the chicken salad and save it for me, so I came back for it. She's amazing, she puts capers and olives and avocados in it. How cool is that?"

"Great. So you'll stay and eat with us?" Cass scooted over on the chaise. "Come sit, twerp."

"Nope. Not today, Cass. Ella packed up some salad and corn bread for me, and I'm taking it to my friends."

"Which friends?" Birdie began spooning the salad onto plates.

But instead of an answer, she got a breezy hug and a grin. Gabby moved toward the door. "Oh, no, you don't, Nonna. No getting secrets out of me. It's a surprise. But wait, here's a clue." She paused and held up one finger in the air. "I got a new hat today." Then she wrinkled up her nose until the freckles danced, gave another wave, and was gone, her doelike body sailing through the door, singing something about cowboys, her voice full and happy.

"We need a dash of that," Nell said, watching her through the window doors. "Gabby knows how to handle life."

"And death, maybe," Birdie said. "She has an uncanny way of dealing with it."

Nell passed around the basket of warm corn bread. Beyond them, out in the harbor, horns were blowing, vying with the gulls for airtime. And farther out in the open sea, a parade of sailboats moved gracefully in the breeze.

"How did it happen that Justin went on that dive?" Cass asked, picking up the conversation. "What did he do that Saturday before?"

They all thought back one week, one short week. A lifetime ago.

"Janie moved the last of her things into the apartment that day," Izzy said. "And Justin was there, then borrowed her car. But we don't know what he did before or after she banished him."

"He called me," Birdie said. "And after that, he met with someone. A 'business transaction.'"

"And later, he came to the Ocean's Edge," Nell said. "And brought along a roll of bills."

"You said he was talking to Tyler at the bar?" Birdie said.

Nell nodded. "And there seemed to be more to their conversation than just a friendly hello. He was telling him something."

"Tyler was a part of the dive group," Cass said. "Maybe they were coordinating or Justin was asking for a ride, or whatever."

"No, he had Janie's car. But maybe he needed a place to stay?" Izzy suggested.

The thought of Justin spending time under Esther Gibson's roof somehow made them all laugh.

While they were enjoying the scenario, Ella came out to collect the salad plates and announced that Chief Jerry Thompson was in the front hallway, looking fine and handsome in his uniform.

Would Birdie like her to serve coffee and lemon bars while they all chatted?

Chapter 17

Ella's announcement brought with it a scurrying of bodies, as if the chief of the Sea Harbor police was about to catch the women at something nefarious. What they felt, they admitted later, was guilt. They were, after all, trying to do his job.

But by the time Jerry walked through the doors, they were calm and collected, with yarn scattered everywhere and needles clicking.

"Sorry to interrupt, ladies," he said, forking his fingers through his graying hair. "I was on my way home and had to pass right by here. I should have called first, I know, but Ben thought it'd be okay to just drop by."

"Ben?" Nell frowned. Ben and Sam went out early that morning, something to do with the sailing class they were going to teach later in the summer. "Checking locations," Ben had told her.

"He and Sam came down to the station this morning." Jerry nodded at Izzy. "That's how I knew you'd all be over here at Birdie's fine place." He looked around the veranda and back at the house, and shook his head. "Birdie, this is an amazing place you have here. Beautiful. Sonny Favazza must have loved his lady exceedingly to build so grand a place for her."

Everyone in Sea Harbor knew the story of Sonny and Birdie's romance and the home he built for her. When the young Sonny swept Birdie off her feet all those years ago, he used the family land high on the hill as the place to begin their life together.

"Thank you, Jerry. Coffee and a lemon bar?" She handed him the plate.

When Jerry was finally settled with the plate balanced on his knees and a cup of Ella's strong coffee beside him, he launched into the reason he'd come.

"It's the Dorsey murder," he began. And for the next twenty minutes, while the knitters sat uncharacteristically quiet, he gave them a report of all the hours and work that had already gone into finding Justin's killer.

The list of folks interviewed was a long one. And the list of alibis short, but that was understandable. "The equipment had been checked Saturday morning. Gus and Andy dropped it off in the storage shed Saturday night around dinnertime. They locked it up and left. So that leaves the gear unattended in Gus' store that day— and during the night when it was locked in the shed."

Nell frowned. "So you're not sure when it was tampered with?"

"Although we haven't made it public, we think it was at night." He looked around, then went on. "That left lots of time for someone to go down and fiddle with the dive tanks before the early-morning dive. Most people were asleep for some of those hours. But we're looking at it from all angles. And we have our arms around it pretty tight. We *will* find the guy who did this. That's a promise."

"Jerry, why are you telling us this?" Nell asked. The fact that he'd been with Ben was not a good sign. "There's more, isn't there?"

Jerry took the last bite of his lemon bar and declared it the best he'd ever had. Then he said, "It's not confidential, what I've told you. You'll read it in the paper. People want to know what's going on. They have a right to that.

"And yes, you're right. There's more. But before we get into that, I'm here because you've got people caring about you who think you may be wading off into waters that aren't yours to wade in. This is murder. It's serious business—we try to calm people down in the reports that get printed, but it can be dangerous, and

I wanted to tell you that myself because . . . well, because I know each one of you. And I know you want this to all be over as much as I do and . . . well, and sometimes you think you can speed it up a little."

He wiped his brow and looked at each of them. "You can't."

Nell watched the frustration on his face. Poor Jerry. He was doing Ben and Sam a favor, figuring a warning coming from him would bear more weight. She smiled at him and hoped it held a thank-you. Then she said, "You said there was more?"

"Yes. You'll read about this, too." He paused for longer than was comfortable, and Birdie finally cleared her throat, urging the police chief to speak.

"You all know old Horace Stevenson?"

"Of course," Birdie said. "He's older than I am. We oldies stick together."

"Yes, well, you know he lives down there on Paley's Cove. A small house, you've all seen it from the beach."

They nodded. Everyone knew Horace. They all knew Red, too, and were strangely comforted that he and Horace had each other. The dog had even been known to pull a young child out of a strong current one summer. Nell thought of her conversation with him the day before—and his anger over a murder in Paley's Cove. She wondered if that was what the chief was going to talk to them about. Perhaps Horace knew more than he had said yesterday

Izzy spoke up. "Horace and I are friends, and Sam, too." She thought about Sam helping the old man, fixing a broken step. "We share a love of the cove, I guess. He told me that he used to walk that beach with his wife every single day, rain or snow or shine, and after he buried her at sea, he just kept doing it, and the sand became his mandala."

Jerry looked at her. "What's that?"

"A mandala—like the Tibetan monks build out of colored sand—intricate geometric patterns. When they're all finished, they collect the sand and pour it into a river, sending it on its way to the ocean. Horace said it represents the transitory nature of life. He and Red create designs in the sand with their footprints—a mandala in his wife Ruth's memory. And then the tide comes in and takes it away, out to the world—out to his Ruth, he says."

They were silent for a few minutes, thinking about the old man and his dog. And of his wife, honored every day by Horace and Red.

"I knew the old man loved that cove and the beach. It was almost sacred to him. Now I know why," Jerry said.

"You're talking about him as if he's not there anymore," Nell said.

Jerry coughed once, then said, "Horace died last night—or early this morning. We're not sure exactly when. Right outside his house, sitting on the porch in that old rocking chair."

Izzy's face fell.

"Oh, I'm so sorry," Nell said. She looked over at Izzy.

Jerry followed her look. "Actually, Sam and Ben were the ones who found him." He looked up, his bushy eyebrows lifting, as if that explained everything. "They noticed Red running in circles along the beach, howling something awful. They were looking for a good place to teach the Boys' Club lifesaving class or some such thing—but I suppose you know that."

Izzy and Nell nodded. Every summer Ben and Sam taught sailing to underprivileged kids. Lifesaving was the first step, and they needed just the right beach.

"Was it a heart attack?" Birdie asked. "Perhaps he just drifted off. That would be a lovely way to go—sitting on his porch, his faithful dog at his side. We should all be so fortunate."

"We don't know yet how he died. It may have been a heart attack. But a strange thing happened when the emergency medical fellows moved him—a key fell out of his pocket. We thought it was his house key at first, though everyone knew Harold never locked that place up, not ever.

"Then Sam thought he recognized it. It looked like the key Andy

Risso used to lock up that supply shed where they'd stored the dive equipment that night."

"And?" Cass asked.

"Yeah." Jerry shook his head. "And that's exactly what it was. The key fit."

Chapter 18

A call to Ben's cell phone on her way home confirmed for Nell and Izzy the basic facts of what had happened, but Ben said they'd talk more later. He and Sam had to make a few statements to the police and then deal with a pile of things they'd left undone on the boat. But they'd make sure they were finished in time for the concert and would meet them there.

Saturday night. The first Fractured Fish concert of the summer. They had almost forgotten about it as they'd struggled to make sense of what Chief Thompson said—or, as Birdie put it, "didn't say."

"The concert," Nell said to Ben. "Of course."

And Izzy agreed, though the thought of Paley's Cove without its sentinel made her terribly sad. It would be good to be with friends and neighbors.

Cass and Danny arrived at the seaside park shortly before Nell and Izzy, and had already claimed a patch of grass not too far from the water, slightly removed from the open area where Frisbees would be flying and balloons twisted into animal shapes.

"Perfect," Izzy said as she helped Cass spread out several old blankets.

Danny pulled over a cooler of beer and a stack of camp chairs. He opened one for Izzy. "Here, princess," he said. "Take advantage of it. Once that baby comes, all the attention will be redirected."

Izzy laughed and lowered herself into the chair.

Nell pointed over to where Franklin and Tamara Danvers sat on comfortable cushioned chairs. Izzy waved. Tamara looked unusually quiet, but Franklin doffed his straw hat back and smiled a hello.

"Nice that Franklin's becoming more a part of the town," Izzy murmured.

"Does Tamara look all right to you?" Nell asked. The two women shaded their eyes and tried to look over unobtrusively.

"I can't tell. She's probably tired. She's still in that stage where it grabs you by the throat and won't let go," Izzy said.

"I wonder if they know about Horace. He walked in their backyard every day."

"I've seen Tamara talking with him," Izzy said. "And Franklin, too. He'd even walk along the beach with him now and then."

Birdie made her way over a few minutes later. "I came with Ella and Harold," she said. "Gabby absolutely insisted they come. She told them they needed to get out more or they'd atrophy. She has Harold wrapped around her little finger."

"Of course she does," Cass said. "Where are Ben and Sam?"

"Right here." Their shadows fell over the blanket. Their faces were weary.

Danny grabbed cold beers and sodas for everyone. Ben hugged Nell and unfolded a chair next to her.

"Here's what we know. Sam and I were scouting out beaches for lifesaving classes when we spotted Red in Paley's Cove, literally running in circles. When he spotted us, he tore across the sand and sat in front of us until we stopped. Then he looked toward Horace's house, got up and ran a little, sat again, and stared at us. And he kept doing this until we followed him. At which point he tore across the beach toward the house, stopping every now and then to make sure we were behind him."

"He's an amazing dog," Sam said, popping the lid off his bottle.

"Horace was on the porch—like the chief told you. And that's about all we know." He lowered himself into the chair.

"We asked the chief about the key in old Horace's pocket," Cass said. "What did it mean? How was it important? But all we got was police talk that basically told us nothing."

"That's because he doesn't have much to say about it," Sam said. He took a long swig of beer.

"The implication is that Horace Stephenson had something to do with Justin Dorsey's death."

"That's crazy," Izzy said.

"Ridiculous," Birdie added. "What would that old man know about murdering anyone?"

"Not to mention motive. Lots of people were furious with Justin, but I can't imagine Horace would be," Izzy said.

"Of course," Nell said, sitting up straight in the chair. She knew for a fact that he was upset about Justin's death. "He was angry about Justin's death. He told us—" She repeated the conversation they'd had the day before in front of McClucken's hardware store. "One thing he said that I hadn't thought much about but that seems strange now, in retrospect, since no one has said for a fact that the equipment was tampered with while in the shed . . ."

"What's that?" Ben leaned forward.

"He spoke as if it were a fact that someone had definitely gone into the shed during the night. There wasn't any doubt in his words."

"That was yesterday?" Ben asked. "The police need to hear that."

Sam agreed. "Horace didn't talk much, but when he did, it was never trivial, always interesting. He didn't see much with those old eyes, but that didn't keep him from knowing everything that went on around him."

Izzy smiled sadly. "That's for sure. One day I came up behind him and he greeted me by name without turning around. It was my perfume, he said. He used to buy L'Air du Temps for his wife. He said I was the only 'regular' on the beach who wore that kind, and he seemed happy about that. I think sweet Red taught him the fine art of seeing through scent."

Sam's head dropped as if Izzy's words punched him into remembering something important. "Sweet Red," he whispered to himself. He looked over at Izzy and covered her hand with his. His fingers wound around hers, holding them tight.

"Horace doesn't have any family, Iz. None. Sweet Red, you said? Well, he is sweet. And he was upset, a mess. Imagine, being there all night or for however long, with his master still as stone, not responding to his nudging wet nose. . . ."

Nell leaned forward in her chair. Her eyes widened. "Oh, Sam, you didn't. . . ."

Everyone stared at Sam, then turned and looked at Izzy.

Izzy's head spun around. She looked at Sam, her eyes locking into his.

"Hey, Iz," Sam said, "I should have talked to you. . . ."

Izzy lifted one hand to his face, then caressed his cheek. She leaned over and kissed him full on the lips. Long and hard. When she finally pulled away, she said to anyone who was listening, her eyes never leaving Sam's, "Do you know that Red once saved a little girl from drowning? I will buy him the softest dog bed I can find. Made of down feathers, if possible."

Sam released the air trapped in his lungs and wrapped his arms around her tightly.

The vet was checking him out, he told her. They could pick him up early next week.

"So . . . ," Ben said, showing some relief himself, having been complicit in the adoption decision. "Back to Horace. I agree, he's an unlikely murderer. But the old man actually did know a lot about scuba equipment. He used to be a diver himself, years ago. Jerry said that's why they lived in that little house near the water. And why he stayed. Reminded him of the old days. He loved to watch the divers. So as far as knowing how to mess up someone's equipment goes, Horace could probably have done that with his eyes closed."

"And in addition, there was a scuba equipment book on his kitchen table, Jerry said. He had turned down pages on descriptions of the cylinders and valves," Sam added. "They took it in for evidence."

"So, what," Cass said, leaning close, "they think Horace killed Justin, then died of remorse?"

"Or just died," Ben said. "He was old, maybe had a heart condition. They don't know yet."

"Well, we all know it would be a huge relief for the town if Horace Stevenson turns out to be the murderer," Birdie said. "It would tie everything up very nicely, complete with bow." But her voice expressed great certainty that this would not, indeed, be the case.

The whistling screech of the microphone being tested broke into the conversation, and Willow joined their blanket, the black-haired fiber artist folding herself down onto it with the agility of a gymnast. "The show's about to begin," she said, her back as straight as a ballerina's and her eyes bright, focused on the man at the microphone who had become very important in her life over the past months.

The park area was filled with people. Kids and dogs ran freely and small boats dropped their anchors in the harbor to listen. Jane and Ham Brewster came over and sat next to Willow, taking beers from the cooler and chips from the basket Danny passed around.

Nell nudged Ben and pointed toward one of the park benches where Janie and Tommy Porter sat together, their bodies pressed close, their eyes on each other. "That's good to see," she whispered.

"Where's Gabby?" Willow asked, scanning the crowd. "She usually comes into the gallery on Saturdays, but I haven't seen her all day."

Birdie was puzzled. "I assumed she was with you."

Willow shook her head no. "But I know she's met a bunch of kids her age over at the yacht club and at her knitting class. They all think Gabby is famous."

"She is," her grandmother said.

The boom of Pete's voice came over the loudspeakers, quieting the crowd. He introduced Merry Jackson on the keyboard, who flipped her long blond braid in the air as the crowd cheered and whistled. The owner of the Artist's Palate became transformed when she walked onstage, leaving her business persona behind. More shouts and claps greeted ponytailed Andy Risso's drumroll. Songs for young and old, Pete promised, and they'd begin with a medley of old covers. Soon the gazebo and the green were rocking with "Mr. Tambourine Man," "American Pie," "I Love Rock and Roll," and a whole collection of sixties and seventies music that had people swaying and Frisbees soaring across the grass.

The sky was nearly dark when Pete stood up at the microphone again and quieted the crowd. "Folks," he said, "we'll be taking a short break after the next number." He held out his arms dramatically. "But wait—don't move yet. Those Porta Potties can wait. We have something very special for you tonight. The Fractured Fish is proud to introduce to you a sensational new artist with a voice that will wrap around your souls."

Andy began a low rumble on the drum, Merry trilled her fingers up and down the keyboard, and Pete grabbed his guitar and turned toward the steps of the gazebo. "Introducing. . . . our very own . . . Gabrielle Marietti!"

The crowd cheered as a grinning Gabby, a cowboy hat taming her wild black hair, ran up the gazebo steps. She grinned at Pete, then searched the crowd, finally finding Birdie. With a tip of her cowboy hat in her nonna's direction, she began belting out the lyrics to "My Heroes Have Always Been Cowboys," joined by Merry on the chorus, with Andy keeping the rhythm on his drums and Pete's guitar filling in the rest. They were a dynamic quartet, pulling the crowd to their feet.

Gabby's voice was rich and clear. Only the expression on her face and the gleeful young body were signs that the voice belonged to a ten-year-old.

Nell looked over at Birdie as Gabby sang.

Her complete surprise had given way to another, more intense emotion: her love for this child who had dropped into her life with the suddenness of spring rain. She wiped away a tear and sat as straight as her small decades-old body allowed.

A short distance from the gazebo, sitting on a bench, Harold and Ella Sampson reflected Birdie's emotion, their faces beaming as if they had given birth to this child themselves. Ella clutched a tissue in her hand while her body swayed back and forth to the music.

The crowd began clapping along, which only added fuel to Gabby's performance. When the song finally ended, she grabbed her hat and swooped it low, her body bending until her head nearly touched the floor. And then she finished her act in pure ten-year-old fashion by throwing her arms around Pete the guitarist until he nearly toppled over backward.

In the next minute Gabby flew off the gazebo, across the grass, and raced toward Birdie, her cowboy hat back on her head, her face alive with expectation.

"Well, Nonna? Whattaya think? How'd I do?"

Birdie's voice was choked, her eyes moist, as she hugged her close.

"So, where did you learn to sing like that, young lady?" Ben asked.

Gabby pulled away from Birdie and giggled. Then she pointed to the band members, now chugging cold water beside the stage. "And Tyler helped, too." She pointed over to Tyler Gibson and Kevin Sullivan, standing next to the gazebo, talking to the band members. "They both took off work tonight just to hear me sing. Here's what happened. You know how I sing all the time? Well, the other day I was down at the harbor fishing with Tyler and Kevin and they heard me singing. They were egging me on, but it was fun. We didn't catch anything that day, but they said they didn't care because we had a great time and they loved my singing, especially the old Beatles songs, like 'Yellow Submarine.' And so Tyler told Pete about it, and Pete told Merry and Andy, and then they invited me to hang out with them while they practiced one day, and well . . . well, the rest is history!" She jumped up and waved wildly at Kevin and Tyler.

The two men worked their way through the patchwork of blankets and chairs to Gabby's side. "Well, if it isn't the amazing Ms.

Marietti," Tyler said, drawing more giggles from the freshly minted star as he and Kevin congratulated her with high fives.

"I hear you helped start Gabby on her road to stardom," Birdie said to Tyler.

Tyler laughed. "This little gal did it all herself. Kevin and I just listened."

Soon Gabby drifted off to enjoy her new fame, and Tyler crouched down on the blanket beside Birdie and Nell. "I heard about old man Stevenson. He was a friend of Grams and Gramps. She's upset." He nodded over at Ben and Sam, who were talking to some neighbors. "She said Sam and Ben found him."

As dispatcher, Esther Gibson was always the first to get the calls. But she was also discreet in what was passed along. If she'd told her grandson, it meant the news of Horace's death was general knowledge.

"Horace was a sweet man," Birdie said.

"Yeah. I remember him from when I was a kid. He lived down there near Paley's Cove, right?"

Nell nodded.

"Was it a heart attack?" Tyler asked.

Ben turned toward the conversation. "He was in his eighties. So that's always the first consideration."

"They'll do an autopsy," Sam said. "Then they'll know for sure."

"An autopsy?" Tyler's eyebrows lifted in surprise. "Why would they do an autopsy? He was old."

"It's routine when they don't know the cause of death. And he wasn't under a doctor's care. Also . . ." Ben paused, then stopped himself. "Well, it's routine, that's all."

Routine and there had been a murder just yards away from where the old man died.

"First the murder, now this," Kevin said.

"Murder?" Tyler looked up.

"You know. Justin Dorsey."

"Oh, yeah, I wasn't thinking, I guess." He shook his head. "I was there that day. . . ." Tyler fell silent. He looked off toward the water, as if picturing Paley's Cove in his mind.

"Let's hope this gets put to rest and the rest of the summer moves along with only good things happening," Birdie said.

"I'm for that," Tyler said. "Grams said there's not much news about the guy who killed Dorsey."

"At least nothing that's reported," Nell said.

"The police are working hard, as your grandmother knows better than anyone," Ben said. "They keep some things under their hats, though, things that might compromise the case. But they'll solve it; they'll get it done."

"Sure," Tyler said. "Good."

When the microphone began its warm-up whistle, attention turned back to the gazebo and another round of numbers by the Fractured Fish. The cleared area in front of the gazebo was filled now with dancing bodies, from toddlers to teens to Ella and Harold. Gabby stood out as always, minus her cowboy hat, her hair flying in all directions.

Nell sat back in her camp chair, watching the movement of the dancers and the stars lightening up the black sky above. All around her people hummed or sang along, strains of "Don't Stop Believing," and "Sweet Caroline" floating all around them. It was a heady sensation, the sounds of summer.

Kevin had wandered off to find a lobster roll, and Tyler left, too, walking toward a group of young women waving to him from a blanket near the water. A ladies' man, everyone said. And he seemed to be that, though perhaps without intent. Tyler had a touch of Justin in him, a kind of naiveté. He seemed to take life easily, enjoyed whatever came his way. Even his looks were simply there, nothing he really had anything to do with or cared that much about, though they certainly paved his way in crowds.

Tamara Danvers was sitting alone now, with Franklin off talking to some people down at the shore. She, too, was watching the handsome bartender as he made his way across the green.

When Tyler noticed her watching him, the familiar wide smile spread across his face and he detoured in her direction, his long strides bringing him to her side. But Tamara was up and out of her chair in an instant.

Words were exchanged, Tyler looked confused, and in the next instant, Tamara spun around and walked down to the edge of the harbor, where Franklin Danvers introduced her to some friends on a boat.

"Tamara doesn't seem to share our affection for Tyler Gibson," Nell said.

"I noticed that," Birdie answered, watching the banker's wife as she put her hand on her husband's arm, then glanced back in Tyler's direction.

"Probably good for Tyler's ego," Cass said.

When Ben suggested a short while later that they pack up and take off before he fell asleep on the blanket, Izzy nodded happily.

"What's happened to my fun-loving wife?" Sam asked with exaggerated angst.

"I'm never having babies if it's going to diminish my wild nightlife," Cass joked.

"Never?" Danny asked. "Wild nightlife sometimes has been known to—"

"Enough," Cass shushed him with a laugh. She took his arm and announced they were off to Gracie's Lobster Shack. The band was meeting them later, "Long after you old people are sawing z's."

Birdie went off in search of her granddaughter and her ride, and the others said their good-byes, making their way through the crowded park to their cars.

"It's nice to see Jerry Thompson get a break now and then," Nell said, pointing to a car moving through the lot in their direction.

"But it looks like he's coming, not going," Ben said, shielding his eyes from the glare of the lights.

Jerry pulled to a stop alongside Ben and rolled down the window.

"You're a little late, Jerry. You missed a great show."

Jerry nodded, but his face was grave. "Sorry I missed it. No rest for the wicked, I guess."

"What's up?"

"I just phoned my deputy and he's here in this crowd some-where. I needed to talk to him about a new development."

"That doesn't sound good."

"Nope, it's not." He leaned back in the car seat with a sigh, his eyes briefly closing. "Not good at all. I was half hoping I'd run into you. Some nights, it's nice to see an old friend. Softens things somehow."

Ben nodded. He had known Jerry Thompson since they were kids on the yacht club sailing team, and though Ben wasn't born on Cape Ann, he and Jerry had a shared sensibility for the land, the people, and the life.

Jerry leaned forward, one elbow on the window frame.

"So . . . Horace Stevenson is your guy?"

Jerry's face told Ben how wrong he was.

"Old Horace was murdered," he said.

Chapter 19

It was a lethal combination of alcohol and drugs, the alcohol being a single malt whiskey that Horace drank on his porch with a nightly regularity matched only by his walks along the beach with Red.

"My sleeping pill," he told anyone who happened to stop by, and then he would offer them a glass. "Better than those blasted drugs."

He'd sit in the old rocking chair, his fingers wrapped around the stubby glass, until the aches of being old subsided and sleep seemed imminent.

But that night the whiskey had an extra kick, enough morphine to kill a horse, Jerry said, a fact kept discreetly away from reporters. It was a miserable-tasting whiskey, in most people's opinion, thick and dark, so Horace probably never noticed.

Sometimes staying close to home is the best option. Especially after a murder. That's when the news, if it hadn't made the morning paper, would leak out in bits and pieces. No one knew for sure what was true and what was rumor. Questions would be tossed back and forth without any hope of answers. The uneasy, uncomfortable rumblings before the storm arrived.

To avoid all that, Ben and Nell decided on an early Sunday

breakfast at Annabelle's, before the restaurant filled with friends and neighbors, with gossip and concern.

But a call from Izzy stopped them before they got out of the house.

"The baby?" Ben mouthed when he realized who it was.

Nell laughed and shook her head.

"Beach time," Izzy said. "We'll bring blankets, coffee, and a nice surprise."

"Paley's Cove," Nell mused as she and Ben drove around the bend toward the northern part of the shoreline. "The last time I was here, Izzy wasn't herself. Something was bothering her. And then all the things that have happened down here since. I'm surprised she didn't suggest the yacht club or Long Beach or Good Harbor." Perhaps Izzy had turned the corner and those darker days were behind her. Perhaps it meant the baby wouldn't be long in coming. And perhaps the surprise would be names for the baby, something Izzy and Sam had held close and quiet all these months.

The car rounded the final curve, and the cove came into view. It was nearly empty this early on a Sunday, but eerily bright, with shards of sunlight cutting into the ice blue water. They didn't see signs of Sam or Izzy at first, not until they'd parked near the stone wall and walked out onto the flat sand.

They heard them before they saw them. Laughter, a whistle. And then a barefoot pregnant woman, her hair loose and flying about her bare shoulders, running along the sand in a tank top and shorts. A sandy-haired man flinging a gnarled piece of driftwood into the sea.

And the long golden hair of a dog moving with the wind as he leapt into the cold water, then ran back to shore, his coat now slick and smooth against his body and a sea-soaked branch between his white teeth.

Izzy waved, and then they ran—all three of them—across the smooth sand to Ben and Nell.

"I couldn't wait," Izzy said.

Red sat down between the two tall figures, his tail thumping on the wet sand, his tongue hanging out as he panted heavily.

"We called the vet," Sam said, "and she agreed to spring Red early, not make him stay caged until tomorrow. He's in great shape; Horace took good care of his buddy."

"We thought bringing him down here for a while where he lived most of his life would make him more comfortable."

"I think it worked," Ben said, scratching the dog behind his ears. "He seems pretty comfortable to me."

"He knows something is amiss, for sure—he keeps looking up at the house," Sam said, pointing across the street to the small Stevenson house. It sat on a lane off the main road, but faced the sea, its nondescript siding and low picket fence blending into the landscape so most people wouldn't look twice at it—unless you were looking for it, or for the old man who sat on its porch watching the world go by.

"But we've been distracting him, walking Horace's daily route, getting him used to us on a path he knows."

Izzy pointed down toward the far end of the cove where the rocks began in earnest and the land rose to anchor the Cliffside mansions. "Our blanket is down there."

Nell slipped off her sandals and hooked a finger through the straps. They walked leisurely down the beach, the wind blowing salty air across the stretch of sand and Red leading the way. Every now and then he'd run to chase a gull or catch Sam's Frisbee, then happily return to the group.

In the distance, beyond the blanket, was the diving shed, once a boathouse, tucked into the side of the rise in land. Nell glanced over as they got closer, then looked away, finding it made her uncomfortable. Unbidden images came into her head of Sam and the others coming up from the early-morning dive minus Justin Dorsey, who lay dead in the water.

"The storage building was painted a few days ago," Sam said. "The gray blends in perfectly with the rocks. It's not so noticeable."

"Franklin mentioned doing that. Probably a good idea." Ben looked over at the shed. "He thought it'd make it less obvious, less of an 'attraction,' if a crime scene can be called that."

"He wants to erase the memory of that bad dive so the divers will keep coming back. It's such a great spot. In fact, Danvers bought the supplies we used that day, then donated them back to the dive shop to use to train other would-be divers, kids who couldn't afford them otherwise. He wants to start some kind of program," Sam said. "The guy thinks of more than stocks and bonds, believe it or not."

"Maybe it's the prospect of fatherhood," Izzy said. "See what a nice guy it's made out of you?" She eased herself down on the blanket.

Sam threw the Frisbee at her, but Red barked cheerfully and caught it cleanly before it landed on Izzy's disappearing lap.

"Justin's death affected Franklin," Ben said. "He felt some responsibility, I guess, because that land is technically Danvers property."

"And he had given him such a hard time not long before Justin was murdered," Izzy added.

"So that's his shed that the diving club uses?" Nell asked.

Sam nodded. "As far as I know, it's only used now as a place for the divers to keep their equipment."

"Is it always locked?"

"Far's I know. Franklin's a stickler for security. Andy Risso has keys to it, Gus McClucken. And the Danverses, of course."

Ben looked back toward the small house on the lane. "And Horace Stevenson," he said.

They all followed his look, as if somehow the connection between the two places would appear in the sand, like the imaginary lines on a TV screen showing the line of scrimmage. And the key would go sliding along it, back and forth.

"It must have been pretty awful for Red that night," Izzy said. The dog sat close beside her, straight and alert, as if assessing the conversation.

"You two have done a good thing here, giving him a home," Ben said. "It would have made the old man happy, not to mention what it's doing for Red."

Red's tail flapped against the sand.

Izzy picked up a floppy straw hat from the blanket and pulled it onto her head, one hand pressing it down as she looked back toward the sea. "Maybe we needed him as much as he needed us." She wrapped an arm around the dog. Red pressed his wet nose against her skin.

"So, who else lives on that lane?" Sam asked as he and Ben looked back at Horace's house, then started walking toward the beach-access road for a better look. "Anyone who might have seen anything?"

Nell followed. "There aren't any streetlights up there."

"Right. Horace didn't sleep much at night. So he could have been sitting out here any time of night."

Izzy thought back. "Friday night. We were all out on your deck that night, Uncle Ben. The sky was pitch-black. No moon. A perfect night to not be seen."

Ben looked hard at the house, taking it all in. "Jerry thinks the person who killed Horace wanted it to look like a suicide. And to look like Horace had killed Justin. Hence the key and the scuba book they found on the table."

"And why exactly would he do that?" Nell asked.

"Right. Why? The police had had some reports that Justin hung out down here. People saw him on his bike more than a few times."

Nell looked at Izzy. "We saw him here one morning, Izzy and I, remember?"

"He had a surfboard. Is that what people reported?"

"No. One of the neighbors who lived at the other end of the cove, over near the steps, saw him sometimes in the evening, just sitting on the steps. She'd be out on her porch and noticed that it was the same person every night, but not much more. She recognized that old yellow bike Janie gave him."

"Who was he with?" Nell asked.

"Alone, the neighbor said."

"That doesn't give Horace a motive for killing him," Nell said.

"I wonder," Izzy said, pulling herself up from the blanket and a sleeping Red. "This beach was almost sacred ground for Red and Horace. What if Justin was doing something . . . I don't know what, maybe something Horace considered offensive or wrong? We know Justin wasn't an altar boy."

They fell silent for a minute, trying to dig deep to imagine what that might be.

"But what would he see?" Nell asked. "His eyesight was so bad."

"I don't know. But Horace had ways of seeing, somehow, that didn't need eyes."

Nell walked toward the road, looking over at Horace's house. "It doesn't sound like the killer was a professional, if Jerry figured out so quickly that it wasn't a suicide or a natural death."

"Yes," Ben said. "He said as much. It was very amateurish. Not thought out. Desperate, in a way. And Justin's murder was similarly orchestrated. It worked, Justin died, but it didn't appear to be carefully planned, according to Jerry."

"It was just someone who wanted Justin dead." Izzy rubbed her bare arms. "It's worse somehow, knowing it was just a person. A person like us."

She looked back at the blanket. As if sensing her look, Red sat up suddenly, then shot off the blanket and raced toward them, a flying ball of fur.

Izzy leaned toward him and reached out her hand, but Red didn't break his run. In the next second he had shot across the street, heading for Horace's house.

Sam and Ben ran to stop him, calling out his name, and trying to catch up to him before he reached the tape.

But neither of the men was a match for a dog wanting his home, and by the time they'd made their way up the walkway, Red had torn the yellow tape to shreds and was sitting on the front porch of his old house, his tail thumping on the wood.

"Hi, sweet Red," Izzy said, walking slowly up to her dog, holding out her hand for him to sniff.

Sam and Ben looked through the window. The house was small and the police probably had done what needed to be done. A large lock was on the door. Horace had never had one of his own, and now that no one lived there and the inside was nearly empty, the house was locked up tighter than a drum. Murder, like life, had its ironies.

Red jumped off the porch and rummaged in the sandy yard, kicking up dirt and sniffing near a tuft of sea grass. A place where Horace had walked, perhaps, his scent still lingering in the yard. Or someone else's scent, perhaps?

Izzy walked over to scratch his head, then bent low where he'd pushed aside his own water dish, then dug a hole. "It's some kind of vial," she said.

Ben looked down, pulled a tissue from his pocket, and picked it up.

The label had been peeled away, but a small patch of it still remained.

He slipped it into his pocket. "I'll drop it off with Jerry. It could be the missing morphine container."

"Or an old prescription of Horace's," Izzy said.

"Or nothing at all," Nell said.

Ben looked over at Red.

If only the gentle golden dog could talk.

Chapter 20

B y Monday, not only did the *Sea Harbor Gazette* have a front-page story about the awful murder of the quiet man who walked the beach, but Mary Pisano had written a column about those involved. However, since so little was known about the murder, Mary concentrated on the dog.

> *It speaks to the generosity of our fine town that in these sad times, dear Horace Stevenson's best friend and companion, Red, has found a home. Izzy and Sam Perry—who are about to have a child of their own—have generously taken the orphaned golden retriever into their loving home, where he will be treated with the same love and respect that Horace bestowed upon him. These are the kinds of people who live in Sea Harbor. This is our town. Loving. Compassionate. Generous. Openhearted.*
>
> *And just as dear Red once saved a child from drowning off Paley's Cove, we, the citizens of Sea Harbor, must save our town from drowning because of the Paley's Cove murders. And we will. We will come together, we will examine everything we have seen and heard in the last two weeks. No matter how small and meaningless it may seem, this is how we will find the perpetrator of this crime and bring peace back to our amazing town.*

"Dear Mary," Birdie said. "Izzy and Sam will be embarrassed, but perhaps her words will unearth something. Who knows?"

"She has more to say than the poor reporter who tried to write about the murder," Cass said. She sat across from Birdie and Nell on Coffee's patio, steaming mugs of dark roast and the morning paper on the table between them. Nell told them about the vial Izzy found—and the results that it definitely held morphine at one time. Whose . . . and how it got in Horace's front yard . . . and whether it was the drug that ended up in the glass of whiskey were still unknowns.

The article included a short paragraph that covered Horace Stevenson's long life: his marriage to his true love, Ruth Adams Stevenson, her death a few years ago. His occupation as assistant manager of McClucken's Hardware Store. His hobbies—bird-watching and walking along Paley's Cove with his dog, Red, tracking patterns in the sand.

And the rest was a reporter's attempt, without any factual information, to connect the murder of an old man, slowing down in life, to that of a young man, off and running with the world at his fingertips.

"The only connection the reporter could make to the two was that Horace used to scuba dive and Justin died while diving," Cass said.

"And the location," Birdie said.

"Jerry must have been very closemouthed to the press," Nell said. "The article said it was definitely a murder, but not how or where."

"I suppose that's best for now, though it will leak out. Those things do," Birdie said. She took a drink of her coffee, then held her head back to catch the breeze, her eyes half closed. Spikes of white hair fluttered around her small face. "I liked the old man," she said. "And Ruth, too. His death in itself was sad, but that is the cycle of life, and Horace had had a happy life. But now—turning that death into a murder tarnishes all of it. It's such an awful thing. It's poisonous. It's . . ."

"Scary," Willow Adams said. She pulled out a chair and sat down, slipping a huge backpack from her narrow shoulders. "Do you think there's a connection, like that reporter is trying to say?"

Her thick eyebrows lifted into black bangs as she looked at Nell. "What does Ben say?"

"Oh, sweetie, not much. It's all up in the air right now, I think." Nell patted Willow's hand in a motherly way. Ever since the young artist, lost and waiflike, had shown up in Izzy's yarn shop several years ago, the knitters had taken her into their hearts and their lives. And there she stayed, moving into the studio her father had bequeathed to her and becoming a successful artist in her own right. No one could remember now, nor wanted to remember, a time when Willow hadn't been a part of their lives.

"Horace hardly ever left Paley's Cove. He was either sitting on his porch watching birds or walking the beach with Red. He was a contented guy, or so it seemed to me, anyway," Cass said. "It's hard to imagine him doing anything that would get him murdered."

"But something did," Birdie said. She looked beyond Willow to the table beneath the maple tree, where Mary Pisano sat, her computer on her knees.

Mary looked up, smiled, and took that as an invitation. She closed her laptop and walked over, her sneakers silent on the brick patio. "I don't know anything, if that's what you're wondering. Esther Gibson said she took chowder and bread out to Horace now and then and they'd talk while he ate. He didn't always recognize her face, but he knew her voice immediately—that and that Emeraude cologne she always wears were giveaways, he told her. Recently she said he was complaining about things going on in the cove."

"What kinds of things?"

"I don't really know, but Esther said she didn't take him too seriously. She knew that the college kids and friends would gather there at night sometimes, her Tyler included. She assumed it was that. Probably innocent fun but too much noise for his sensitive ears. Horace hated loud noises. But it was probably nothing. The thing is, his murder *is* *something*, something really bad. And coming so close to Justin's, it has the whole town on fear alert. What are we going to do about it?"

"Maybe you've done something already, dear," Birdie said. "That was a lovely column you wrote."

Mary pushed away the compliment. "It was a great thing for Izzy and Sam to do, what with the baby coming and all."

"And speaking of Izzy, the baby, the dog . . . I promised her I'd help her get some things she needs for Red. Like food, a bed." Nell checked her watch.

Mary laughed. "Maybe we should have a shower for him."

"No, no, no," Birdie said, pushing back her chair. "Two showers would definitely send Izzy over the edge."

Mary hugged them off, saying she had to get back to work. Not only did she have a bed-and-breakfast to run, but ever since her column went online, she was deluged with comments that needed replies. And Mary would reply to every single one.

They made their way through the patio crowd, buzzing with today's news, and studiously avoided eye contact with neighbors and friends, knowing they'd draw conversations they would rather avoid. No one knew much, and somehow talk about suppositions and hypotheses didn't appeal to any of them.

Willow grabbed her bike from the stand outside the patio gate and hopped on. "The shower is next weekend. You all ready?" She wriggled her backpack into place and was off, flying down the road toward Canary Cove.

Nell waved at Gus McClucken, leaning against his post outside the hardware store.

He waved back with a shake of his head. He'd heard the news, they could see.

"He looks older," Cass said quietly. "I think it has gotten to him."

But Gus mustered a smile as they came closer and called out, "I just talked to Izzy—great dog. Good decision."

They laughed and crossed the street to Izzy's shop, hoping he was right.

Mae met them at the door. "Can you believe it? Now we have two mascots. Jillian and Rose are beside themselves."

She pointed to the steps leading to the back room. "The menagerie is that way."

"I don't know why I feel we should whisper," Birdie said. "This isn't a baby we're coming to see."

Izzy appeared in the archway and waved them down. "Wait till you see this. Hurry."

In front of the fireplace, on a stack of blankets Izzy had pulled from the closet, was Red, looking like an advertisement for L.L.Bean. And curled up as tightly as a calico cat could curl was Purl, her small body pressed against the dog's chest.

"Shhh," Jillian Anderson said. "They're sleeping."

Her twin sister, Rose, was sitting alongside the curled-up animals, snapping pictures with her iPhone. "Can you like believe it?" she whispered between snaps.

"Barely," Nell laughed. "Picture-perfect, that's for sure."

Izzy hugged Nell. "Isn't Red beautiful? And Purl loves him, so we know he'll fit in. I just called Janie and she's taking a break to come see the two of them."

She looked at Nell. "And then we're off? Mae says she can spare me. With Jill and Rose here, I'm just a piece of furniture."

The teenage twins laughed.

"We're just better at helping Gabby with her class than you are," Rose said. "We know the lingo, Iz."

It was true, Izzy had told them. There were plenty of teens who signed up for Gabby's new hat class, and having the high school twins around made Mae and Izzy both feel better. They sometimes forgot Gabby was only ten.

"Who's available to help me outfit my dog?" Izzy asked.

"It's my day off," Cass said. "What better way to spend it? But only if I get some Red time at the end of it."

They walked to the front of the store, nodding at a steady stream of customers filling wicker baskets with skeins of yarn and new bamboo needles.

"Congratulations, Izzy," Tamara Danvers called out from behind a display of supersoft merino. "Red is a wonderful dog."

"You know him?"

Tamara stepped from behind the display. She wore a strapless sundress, bright blue, that showed off her golden tan. "The Stevenson house is just down the hill from us. Horace and Red walked that beach all the time."

"Sure, I forgot you lived close," Izzy said.

Izzy waved good-bye to Mae and led the way to the alley. "We can take my car. Sam brought it over this morning. We finally got it back from Pickard's Auto. Sam said I should probably drive it some."

"What was wrong?" Cass asked.

Izzy explained about the broken trunk lock. "It seems ages ago, not just days. But anyway, they fixed it. But not before agreeing with Sam that I must have taken some serious tools to it when I was trying to open it."

"Did you? You're not very mechanical, Iz," Cass said, walking over to the car.

"Thanks, Cass. But no, I didn't. Jeez. But it was definitely messed up. I couldn't say anything to Sam because he would have called the national guard in, but I think maybe he was right. It looked like someone tampered with it. But why would anyone want to get in my trunk? It doesn't make sense."

"Hey, guys, what's up?" Janie walked across the street, her plastic name tag pinned to a crisp white blouse. Her hair was pulled back today, and as much of it as possible captured in a silver clasp. "I came to meet Red and see how Purl's doing—and maybe to take a quick twenty-minute nap before I go back to work."

"Not sleeping, Janie?" Nell asked.

"Not so much. Just when it seems it might be getting better, something else happens."

"You mean Horace?" Birdie said.

Of course she did. There'd be more questions, more distress.

Nell touched her arm. "It will get better, I promise."

"Well, one thing that will make you smile is inside the shop," Izzy said, pulling out her keys. "We're off to get Red some supplies."

Cass looked back at the trunk. "Iz, you better try the trunk before we leave, just to be sure. I don't want to be carrying a dog bed on my lap. Those scratches look serious."

"Skeptic," Izzy murmured, and walked to the trunk, opening it on the first try.

Inside, exactly where she had tossed it days ago, was an infant car seat, toppled over on its side.

Izzy gasped.

"What is it?" Nell moved to her side and looked inside the trunk.

"Are you all right, Izzy?" Janie asked.

Izzy took a deep breath. "So much has happened the last few days that I had almost forgotten about this. This infant seat . . . I kept seeing it when I was running over on Paley's Cove beach. It wouldn't go away, it was there day after day and I couldn't get it off my mind. I started having nightmares about it. There was never a baby, a mother. Just this car seat. Finally one night—it was raining, I remember—I couldn't stand looking at it anymore, so I drove over and tossed it in the trunk. And then, a couple of days later, I couldn't open it. And I nearly forgot about the car seat—"

By now they were all standing at the rear of Izzy's car. Cass pulled the carrier out, along with a handful of sand. A yellow knit blanket snagged on the lock and hung there, wrinkled and dirty.

"It's filthy," Cass said.

"It smells," Birdie added.

"It's mine," Janie said, her voice barely a whisper.

Chapter 21

$\mathcal{J}$anie looked unsteady, and Izzy suggested they take her upstairs, rather than into the crowded shop.

Nell got a glass of ice water, Birdie a washcloth, and rather than leave it in the alleyway, Izzy and Cass brought the car seat and blanket into Janie's apartment.

"I'm fine, honest," Janie said. She stared at the infant carrier, now sitting near the coffee table. Finally she reached over and pulled it to her, then tipped it toward her so she could see the top. "See this?"

They looked over at an orange oval-shaped sticker, stuck to the top. Someone had written $5 on it with a Sharpie.

"That's a garage sale sticker. I've bought lots of car seats—but for some reason, I remember this one. It was almost new and I talked the lady down to three dollars. Maybe that's why I remember it. . . ."

She fingered the yellow blanket that had been tucked inside, a soft knit that was now lumpy and matted from rain and sand. "Remember this yarn, Izzy? It was so beautiful."

Izzy nodded. "We got it in last winter, right?"

"Yes. You received a whole shipment and Dr. Lily bought me some because I was so crazy about it and she didn't want me spending all my money on things I gave to the free clinic. The twins had made a huge window display to show the yarn off. It came in every color of the rainbow, and that's how they featured it—a giant rainbow that spanned the shop window—and all of it was created from skeins of this gorgeous angora yarn. They had a yellow brick road beneath it."

Izzy smiled, remembering it. The display had brought in more customers than expected and they had sold out of the yarn almost completely, a bonus month for the small shop.

"It's not so gorgeous now, I'm afraid," Nell said, fingering the edges of the sad-looking blanket. It was torn in several places, with frayed edges disguising the once-lovely angora yarn. "I remember the yarn because it came in just as I was getting used to the idea that Izzy truly was pregnant. I bought it in nearly every color to celebrate."

"I made three baby blankets out it," Janie said. "But only one yellow one. I thought I'd lost it, or that maybe I was just forgetful and had taken it to the Community Center."

The question was sitting there in the middle of the room, unasked. The silence became louder and louder—and finally Birdie looked at Janie. "How did your blanket and your garage sale car seat end up on the beach at Paley's Cove?"

Janie sat still, her back slightly bent and her eyes on the blanket as if it would tell them everything they needed to know. When she looked up, her eyes held sincere bewilderment. "I don't know."

"But . . . ," Nell said.

They all knew the single word was really a question.

Janie answered, "But Justin always carted around my garage sale items for me. And stored them in a room at the clinic. He knew where everything was, so he would be the likely person to have taken it or given it to someone. And yet that makes absolutely no sense."

It didn't make sense, not to any of them.

"Assuming he took it, there's no easy explanation for how it ended up at Paley's Cove," Birdie said. Her voice was gentle and firm at once, in that way Birdie had of laying things out for consideration without being threatening. "Justin was a conundrum to all of us. And why he'd leave an infant seat on a beach is a mystery we may never solve. . . ."

Although the sentence ended, the thought did not, just as Birdie intended.

Janie perked up immediately. Her back straightened and her eyes and mind focused on Birdie's words. "No, I think we have to solve it, Birdie. If only to learn more about Justin—who he was and what he was about and why he did the things he did. And maybe that will help us figure out who killed him."

Nell watched Birdie, her wise friend, who knew the decision to look into the car seat further should be Janie's decision—and not anyone else's. It was Janie who should decide to peel off more layers of the young man she had cared for and protected.

Janie ran her fingers over the padding inside the car seat. "I always wash these as soon as I bring them home. They can be absolutely filthy. I remember washing this one because it was really pretty clean and didn't take long. It looked like it hadn't been used much, maybe a grandparent's extra car seat or something—and it wasn't out of date, so we could still use it for moms at the free clinic. Then Justin helped me stash it in the clinic room where Lily lets me keep things. And then . . . then it left my mind." She lifted the carrier to the coffee table while Izzy shook out the blanket.

"It smells bad," Izzy said.

"It does," Janie said, wrinkling her nose. She unhooked the buckles that held the cushion to the seat and pulled it out. Beneath the cushion, along with twigs and dried leaves and mud, was a wad of bills—curled up and held together by a rubber band.

Janie took off the band and smoothed out a large stash of ten- and twenty-dollar bills.

Cass ran her finger along a row of crumbled leaves that had collected in the curve of the seat. She lifted up her finger and sniffed the orange residue that stuck to her skin.

She looked up. "You know what this is?" But Izzy wasn't really asking a question. She stared again at the residue on her finger and said carefully, "It's pot."

When no one responded, she repeated it. "It's marijuana. Grass.

Cannabis. Whatever you want to call it. It looks to me like Justin Dorsey might have been delivering pot on Paley's Cove—and Janie's innocent car seat was an accomplice."

They all stared at the car seat, then the crumbled debris that lay in the bottom. It was crazy, ludicrous. But the odor was distinctive and definitely coming from the carrier.

Janie shook her head, a deep frown settling into her forehead. "No matter what's in that car seat, I know for a fact that Justin didn't do drugs," she said. "He got sick once when he was in foster care—seriously sick. It turned out to be an allergy to marijuana and some other plants that affected him internally. They made him bleed. He went to Doc Hamilton for a checkup when he came to town, and he confirmed it. Justin never touched it again. I've researched it, and it's all true."

They listened carefully to Janie. Then Cass looked again at the carrier. "We could be way off base about this. But it seems he was collecting either the money or the pot. And if you're right, Janie, about him being allergic, it looks like he was on the selling end."

"But . . ."

There were too many buts to deal with, so they let them lie there, unanswered, but another layer had been peeled off Justin Dorsey, one that only led to many more questions—and a visit to the police.

"This might be exactly what we need to lead us to the killer," Nell said.

Janie looked worried. "I wonder . . . where could he have gotten it? Justin spent so much time around me, I would have known, I think, if he'd been meeting with someone or growing something himself."

She glanced at her watch, then yelped and jumped off the couch. "I need to get back to work. We have a packed schedule today and I can't leave Dr. Lily in the lurch." She looked down at the seat. "But I don't really want to leave this here."

"And you shouldn't," Nell said. "This needs to be in the proper hands."

They were on an errand run anyway, so Izzy suggested they

drop it by the police station, along with the information they'd put together. And hopefully, the police would be able to piece it together in a way that made better sense.

"But it makes *no* sense," Ben said when Izzy had finished telling the story, complete with the car seat being checked in at the police station as if it, too, might be guilty of some crime.

They were sitting at a round table on the yacht club patio—Izzy and Sam, Ben and Nell, waiting for the Monday Night Seafood Buffet to open. Danny and Cass had picked up Birdie and arrived a few minutes late, but just in time for a tray of flavored teas and cocktails to arrive at the table.

"It'll be interesting to hear what Jerry says about this," Ben said.

"What was Justin thinking?" Sam said. "Using a car seat to deliver pot? That's the craziest thing I ever heard."

"I guess he thought it was a family beach—at least during the day—and a car seat wouldn't be noticed. Justin seems to have spent a lot of time at Paley's Cove, so it'd be easy for him to drop the product and collect the cash," Nell said.

"It's a dramatic way to do an exchange," Cass said. "But then, Justin was a little dramatic. He probably saw it on some TV show and liked the idea of an elaborate plan. Besides, if someone found the seat and the stash, a surfer dude would be the last person they'd connect to an infant seat."

"Crazy, maybe, but it worked," Izzy said. "I was the only one who paid any attention to the carrier sitting there day after day. And I only noticed it because my hormones were flying high and anything that reminded me of a baby sent me looking for one."

"You never mentioned the car seat to me," Nell said.

"No, I guess I didn't mention it—though we walked down there together one morning. I couldn't bring myself to go down there alone that day, so you innocently came along—and sure enough, there it was. I don't think you even noticed it, but it was kind of like a nightmare for me. It bothered me so much, but once I tossed it in my trunk, it was as if the worry—and the car seat—was gone. From my mind, at least."

"Do you remember what day you picked it up? Was it recently?" Cass said.

"It was Thursday night, after knitting. The night Janie, Justin, and Tommy moved things upstairs into the apartment."

"I remember that night," Cass said. "It poured later on. Janie was trying to beat the rain."

Suddenly Sam sat forward and looked over at Izzy, the pieces coming together. "Your trunk, Izzy—the damaged lock. It was around that time, right?"

Izzy thought back through the days. It wasn't that long ago, yet time had taken on strange proportions. "Yes, you're right," she said. "It was around that same time. Maybe the next day."

"So you tossed the seat into your trunk—*after* someone took out what they wanted and left cash in payment. And Justin, naturally, wanted that cash."

"But you messed it up. You interrupted an 'operation,' Iz," Cass said. "Call in Rizzoli and Isles."

"That's it. That must be what happened," Sam said.

"Justin would have been worried about the rain that night. If the pot was there, it could have gotten wet. And if the money was left and not secured—it could have been washed away. Justin needed to get over there fast."

Nell remembered the night clearly. She had watched Justin through the window of the yarn shop. He had that fancy motorcycle he was trying out and seemed perfectly content to ride off on it. Not being included in Tommy and Janie's plans for that night hadn't bothered him because he had his own plans.

Izzy was tugging at her own memory of that night. "When I drove away from the beach, I saw someone on a motorcycle—at least I thought it was a bike because it only had one light, but it was raining super hard."

"Someone was watching—probably upset—while a pivotal piece of the transaction was tossed into a trunk," Ben said.

"*Your* trunk, Izzy," Sam said. "And someone—namely, Justin—would have recognized your car."

"So later that night, he came to claim what was rightfully his," Izzy said. "He tried to break into my car that night. . . ." She glared at Sam.

"Okay, Iz. Apologies given. Sorry about the sledgehammer."

Izzy smiled smugly.

"But how does this connect to Justin's murder?" Birdie took a sip of wine and sat back in the chair. "If people were paying him and he was delivering, who would want to kill him?"

"We don't know where he was getting the marijuana," Nell said. "Janie has no idea where it might have come from. Justin was with her so much of the time that she's sure she would have known if he'd been growing it himself. Not to mention there wasn't any place he could have done that. Mrs. Bridge would know immediately. She had a run-in with a boarder about that very thing a year ago and has guarded her backyard diligently ever since."

"So who?" Cass asked. "Who could have been supplying it to Justin?"

"And why?" Ben said. "Why not just get rid of it yourself and keep the profits? Why hire someone like Justin to be the middle man?"

They carried the unanswered questions to the buffet table, and returned with plates piled high with crab legs, fried clams, fresh-boiled lobster, and lemon-baked cod. Caesar salads appeared at their places, along with baskets of warm crusty rolls and tubs of sweet butter.

Liz Santos, the yacht club manager and Birdie's next-door neighbor, appeared at their table. "I heard about Horace Stevenson. It's so sad." She looked over at Ben. "Jerry Thompson is in the bar and looks haggard, as if he hasn't slept in days. Poor guy. It's all weighing heavily on him. People are worried, anxious."

"I'm glad to hear Jerry is at least taking a break," Ben said. "Tell him I'll stop by to say hello."

Liz nodded. She looked around at the dining tables, quickly filling up both inside and on the veranda. "It's strange how murder can be good for business, at least a business like ours. I think people have this intense need to be together. We're booked solid tonight."

Which is exactly what the group of them had done, Nell realized. "Did Horace ever come in here?" she asked.

"Not often, not after his wife died. But he did come by a week or so ago. We had a summer lunch on the patio with man's best friend. The dogs got kibbles and the owners got clam chowder. Red was in heaven. When I asked Horace how things were over at Paley's Cove, he became agitated. He said it wasn't the way it used to be when his Ruth was alive. Daytime was still for the kids, but he claimed there was too much going on at night and early morning. He refused to elaborate, so I dropped it, but later I remembered that the scuba diver died not far from his place. I thought maybe that was what he meant."

A waiter motioned to Liz that she was needed inside, and she hurried off, promising to stop back later if she could.

"I wonder if he knew what Justin was doing," Nell said, trying to think through the implications.

"Could be," Danny said. "But that wouldn't explain Justin's death. Turning him in to the police so they'd put a stop to it would be a lot easier than killing Justin. And it wouldn't explain his own death, either, for that matter—unless anyone thinks Justin could have come back from the dead to do one more deed."

"Only in your stories, Brandley," Cass said. "But what if the person supplying Justin was somehow involved, like maybe Horace knew who he was, too?"

So many ifs. Far too many to put into any kind of order. Tenuous, floaty pieces of yarn that could break with a strong tug.

Liz sent the waitress over with an extra platter of lobster and crab legs, and for a while, the food pushed the uncomfortable unknowns away and allowed lighter conversation and laughter to move about the table. They were replaying Gabby's performance with the Fractured Fish when a shadow fell across the table.

"Evening, folks." Franklin Danvers' deep, resonant voice greeted them. Tamara stood beside him, smiling a hello.

Franklin looked across the table at Sam, apologizing to the others for interrupting and talking business. "But I need a photographer," he said.

Sam looked puzzled.

"You know, family-archives kind of photos."

Sam was discreet in his answer, politely recommending a photographer who'd be much better at that than he was. "I'm no good at family portraits, Franklin," he said. "Now, give me an ocean or a Hinckley sailboat or a crowd of people who don't know or care that I'm there, madly clicking away, that's another story."

"I know what you do, Perry." Franklin's laugh was short and friendly, but clearly intended to suggest he not be second-guessed. "I don't mean that kind of family photo. I mean *family* as in the Danvers family estate. The house, the cottages, the view from the terrace. No one has ever visually recorded our estate, and I'm beginning to be sentimental in my old age. Perhaps it's the prospect of fatherhood, who knows? But no matter, the Danvers family has a long tradition here—my grandfather was here before the town of Sea Harbor existed, and I think his estate needs to be visually recorded."

Sam nodded, taking in Franklin's new information with more attention. "Sure, let's talk about it. I'm interested," he said. "Your place is certainly a part of history. It's a nice idea."

Nell glanced over at Tamara. Her makeup was perfect, her white silk slacks creased, and a black flowered top flowed over her breasts and just to her waist, showing the tiniest bit of skin between the hem and the waist of her slacks. She looked beautiful and fit, but either she was losing her tan or something else was wrong. "Would you like to sit down?" Nell asked.

Tamara managed a smile. "Thanks, but we have a table waiting."

"It's not been an easy time on Paley's Cove—or anywhere, for that matter," Birdie said. "It must be especially distressing for those of you up in the Cliffside neighborhood."

"You mean the murders, of course," Franklin said. His expression was somber. "Horace Stevenson was a decent man. I enjoyed talking to him. I didn't mind when he and Red extended their walk along our beach. It was a pleasant sight and he always cleaned up after the animal."

"He may have been walking the beach that night before the dive," Birdie said. "It must have been awful for him to know he was so close to a crime being committed."

"How so?" Franklin asked.

"No one knows for sure. Someone got in the dive house that night. Birdie's simply replaying what might have happened," Ben said.

Franklin was quiet, seeming to record the information. His face showed little emotion.

Beside him, Tamara's hand reached for the back of Birdie's chair. "He was a lovely man. And very knowledgeable about diving. He used to sit on our veranda and talk about the different places he'd gone to dive when he was young."

"I can't make any sense out of his murder," Franklin said. "Not an old man like that. What reason would anyone possibly have?"

"I'm sure the police will try to find a connection between him and Justin," Birdie said. "Two murders so close to each other geographically and temporally makes one wonder. And both such unlikely candidates—not that anyone would be a good candidate for murder."

Franklin tensed at the mention of Justin's name. Then he spoke frankly. "You're right, Birdie. No one should be a candidate for murder. But there was something about that Dorsey boy that bothered me from the first time I met him. And now it seems it bothered someone else as well. He was a troublemaker."

He looked at Tamara, then back to the others. "Tamara can tell you. He wouldn't leave her alone, came on to her every chance he got. It wasn't decent."

Tamara looked embarrassed, her voice soft. "I didn't want to get the young man in trouble—I knew Janie was trying to help him, getting him a job at the clinic. But he shouldn't have been working there. I saw him following patients with his eyes, giving them looks. I talked to Dr. Seltzer about it and he agreed, telling me Justin had his nose in everything. Franklin is right, Justin was not the kind of person who would go far in this world."

Although her color had come back slightly, Tamara still looked unsteady, and she tightened her grip on the chair.

Franklin took her arm gently. "I think I need to get my wife a cup of tea," he said. With the other hand he slipped Sam a business card, then escorted his wife across the veranda to a table for two.

"That's odd," Izzy said. Her eyes followed the couple across the room.

"What?"

"All of it. For starters, the friendship between those two and old Horace. It seems unlikely. Horace was so unpretentious and simple. The thought of him chatting with the Danverses on their private beach is kind of hard to imagine."

"And what was all that about Justin? Putting the make on Lily's patients?" Cass said.

"I can't imagine that. I certainly never got that impression about Justin," Izzy said. "Dr. Lily would have booted him out immediately, don't you think? I think maybe Tamara exaggerates."

"Or maybe she was simply trying to force the attention away from Justin's attraction to her, if that's what it was," Birdie said.

The lemon tortes arrived, drizzled with a kirsch-infused raspberry sauce. And in an attempt to match the conversation with the decadent dessert, talk turned back to more enjoyable topics—a new exhibit at the Brewsters' gallery and Ben and Sam's great new sailing crew, sure to win this summer's regatta. A shower for Izzy.

Nell pushed her plate away and moved in and out of the conversation, looking over to the table near the railing, lit now with flickering candlelight. Franklin Danvers was holding his wife's hand across the table as Tamara talked, her face looking more animated. Like a woman holding her husband close, Nell thought.

She thought of old Horace sitting on the Danverses' magnificent veranda, looking out to sea. It *was* an incongruous scene to imagine, the kind of photograph Sam would love to come upon and snap undetected—a trio of unlikely subjects, he might call it.

Chapter 22

*J*erry Thompson was getting ready to leave just as Nell and Ben, the last to leave their table, came upon him in the lounge. The chief had waited for them, he said, not wanting to interrupt their dinner. He'd come over to the club to watch the sunset, nurse a Scotch, and clear his head.

"Did it work?" Ben had asked.

The question brought a chuckle from the tired face. "Maybe, maybe a little." Then he thanked Nell for bringing the car seat to the station and explaining to the officers on duty what had happened.

"It's such a goofy thing, in a way," he said. "The guys at the station didn't know what to make of it, a couple of them wanted to laugh—using an infant seat this way? It's definitely a first. But knowing that the person who concocted the harebrained scheme was murdered changes the perspective a bit. It loses its humor fast."

Jerry had agreed with Nell and Ben that Justin Dorsey and his crazy antics were a different kettle of fish—maybe the odd or unexpected was normal for him.

They walked out to the parking lot together and stood beneath the lamplight, enjoying the cool, clean breeze. The sound of waves washing up against the shore mixed with soft instrumental music floating out from the bar. Night sounds and cool air. A good backdrop for cleaning out cobwebs, Jerry said. Talking with friends was good for that, too.

The fact that Justin was involved in this marijuana deal, whether or not he used it himself, would give the police a new direction—hopefully one with some resolution and not more blind alleys. On the surface, it was still difficult to find a motive for murder—what Justin was doing was wrong, but small potatoes when compared to other crimes. It was practically pocket change—ten- and twenty-dollar bills.

Pocket change. Nell thought back to the night at the bar and the money Kevin had described seeing. It didn't sound like pocket change. "Jerry, what was in that fanny pack Justin sometimes wore?"

Jerry looked puzzled.

"He buckled it around his waist, probably used it as a wallet. Maybe cigarettes."

"I know what you mean, Nell, but don't recall ever seeing it. We went through his belongings carefully. No fanny pack far's I know."

Maybe he'd given it to someone, or no longer had a use for it, Nell thought. But she'd double-check, too. Perhaps Janie remembered seeing it. And maybe it didn't matter at all.

"The thing is," the chief was saying to Ben, "we don't know what kind of people Justin was dealing with. Naive kids or another sort altogether? If someone thought Justin had ripped him off or was unbalanced in some way, who knows what might happen?" The whole thing was troubling, knowing Justin had been successful in carrying this off down at a public beach. And whoever was getting him the stuff certainly didn't belong in Sea Harbor.

So the big question, they all agreed, was the identity of this supplier. That took the whole thing to a new level. Justin was unpredictable and not very truthful, and alienating someone who might be dangerous was now a possibility. Finding the man who gave him the goods needed to be a top consideration. But the best route to that end was to talk to the people Justin had rendezvoused with over an innocent baby carrier. Whoever they were.

And maybe Horace Stevenson and his dog, Red, on an innocent walk down the beach, had come upon something not meant for his eyes.

Before they finally parted ways that night, Jerry told them they'd examined the morphine vial carefully and it definitely came from Doc Hamilton's dispensary. They were working on fingerprints, but it had been rubbed by the sand and he wasn't sure what they'd come up with. Then, pulling his car keys out of his pocket, he assured them that no matter how fragmented it all seemed right now, the police *would* find the person who had killed Justin Dorsey and Horace Stevenson. These cases would not be relegated to a cardboard file box in a storeroom somewhere, leaving a lingering fear that would hover over the community until finally enough time passed that it morphed into a blurry memory—two tragic happenings that ruined a summer before they became cold, nearly forgotten cases.

"So the person who sold it to Justin is the person we need to find?" Cass asked. She hoisted a lobster trap off a wooden platform and set it down between her and Izzy.

It had been Gabby's suggestion that they all go down to the dock Tuesday and give Cass an hour or two of help—maybe over a lunch hour? Better than eating in some dark café, Gabby had said, though not one of them could name such a place in Sea Harbor. Some new buoys needed to be marked with the license numbers, and there were a couple of broken traps. And Pete got a new GPS that she was dying to learn how to use.

Although Gabby didn't say it, they all knew it to be true that ever since her performance with the Fractured Fish, she loved being around the band, and endearing herself to them just might get her another gig. Pete was an excellent place to start. Besides, she was crazy about him and claimed him as the big brother she never had.

"Has anyone else noticed how our famous young singer volunteers us to work, then slips off to help Pete with the cushier jobs?" Izzy teased.

Gabby stuck her head out of the boat's cabin where she and Pete were fiddling with the GPS. The wind sent her hair flying as her infectious laugh filled the space between them, and then just as quickly she disappeared inside.

"She's fascinated with all this boat stuff. And Pete, too," Birdie said, unwrapping the sandwiches she and Nell had picked up at Garozzo's deli. "I don't know what her dad will say when she asks for lobster gear for Christmas."

"Or a microphone and a chance to be on *American Idol*." Izzy opened the small hatch on the side of the trap and smoothed the torn vinyl with a piece of light sandpaper. "She's a special kid, for sure. I can't imagine our lives before Gabby." She shifted on the hard floor of the dock, trying to assume her usual pretzellike position. "Geesh, this is getting hard," she said, looking down at herself.

Cass eyed her warily. "Are you sure that baby isn't coming today? This isn't the best spot to have a baby—although we do have a new machine on the boat that boils water."

"Thanks, Cass. But I think I can make it to dry land without borrowing your fancy trap cooker. Besides, the baby's not coming today."

"You know that how?"

"I'm not ready. The universe isn't ready. But it's getting there. Which brings me back to Justin's supplier, or whatever it is you call him."

"Well, that was Jerry's thinking last night," Nell said. "That finding the person Justin went to for his supply was key. If there was a conflict between Justin and this person, it could be a huge lead."

"You mean this person could be the one who murdered Justin?" Birdie said, pulling bundles of white-wrapped sandwiches from her bag.

"Yes." Nell took bottles of iced tea from the cooler and passed them around, while Birdie handed off a bag of sandwiches to Pete and Gabby. "Justin had a knack for making people mad—even people who cared about him. Imagine if it was someone who didn't care about him."

Izzy wiped her hands on a wet rag and unwrapped a giant hoagie. "Oh, my—Harry came through again." She pushed a thin slice of provolone, sandwiched in between pieces of forest ham, sliced mushrooms, and red onion, back into the pocket of bread. "Heaven," she said, her eyes closing as she sank her teeth into the thick sandwich.

"I think you eat as much as I do these days," Cass said.

"And you don't like it because there are never any leftovers for you to take home."

"I suppose you could say that." Cass tossed her a piece of paper towel. "You're a mess. There's sauce on your chin."

A silence fell over the group as they bit into the fat crusty sandwiches and chewed ravenously, as if no one in the group had eaten for days. In the background, instrumental music rolled down the green incline from the Ocean's Edge bar.

Nell wiped sauce from the corner of her mouth and looked over at the luncheon crowd on the restaurant's porch, unable from that distance to distinguish faces, though she was sure if she waved, someone she knew would be receiving the gesture.

Then her face lit up. "Tyler," she said.

Birdie looked up to the porch. "If you can see the bartender from here, you have superhuman eyesight, my dear."

"No, I'm remembering that night Justin showed up at the bar. Janie was worried he was there for a drink, but it wasn't that."

"I remember it, too," Izzy said, "mostly because you and Janie were watching him so closely that I felt sorry for him. But he didn't get a drink, he just talked to Ty, right?"

"That's my memory. They talked, but then Justin pulled something from his fanny pack and set it on the bar. Money, I think. Kevin saw something similar that night. But it makes me wonder how much Tyler knows about Justin's side job. Those two were friends—of a sort, anyway."

"Maybe that's all they were, just friends," Birdie said.

"I asked Tyler about it once and he kind of shied away from it.

He admitted knowing him, but seemed to move on to other topics when I asked him about it."

"So you think he might have been buying from Justin?" Izzy asked.

"It's possible."

"Tyler is kind of a party guy," Cass admitted. "He's a good kid, I think. But I can see him getting caught up in it. Ty finds it hard to say no to anyone—and he's fun to be with. Have you watched the way women flock to him? He loves all that."

"Except for Tamara Danvers," Nell said.

"Tamara?" Cass tested the gates on another trap.

"Well, it's only an observation," Nell said. "He tried to get her attention at the Edge one night, and she brushed him off as if he had the plague. Tyler isn't used to that, I don't think. At least that's what I read on his face."

"Hmm," Cass said. "Interesting."

"She did the same thing at the Fractured Fish concert," Birdie said. "Nell and I are letting our people-watching habits get a bit out of hand, but I did notice him that night, wandering down her way while Franklin was somewhere else."

Nell remembered, too.

Izzy said, "I would think Tamara would like the attention."

They admitted she was conscious of how she looked and, as Birdie said, was quite adept at highlighting her significant assets. So her reaction to Tyler was strange, shunning him as she did.

Izzy folded up her sandwich wrappings and shoved them back into the bag. "But back to Tyler. We should ask Pete if he knows anything. He knows that crowd."

"True. And even if Tyler wasn't involved, he still might know something," Izzy said. "He's down on the beach whenever he isn't at the bar. There's always gossip flying around with the volleyballs."

Pete came over and stepped around the lobster traps. He grabbed the extra sandwich from the bag before his sister could reach it. "Are you guys aware that voices carry clearly on water?"

His eyebrows lifted while he chewed a gigantic mouthful of ham and provolone.

He took another bite and went on. "I don't know if Ty was buying anything from Justin, but there's talk going around that the police will want to talk to a bunch of those guys—maybe even Andy and me."

"You, too?" Cass said. "Ma will kill you if you're wasting money and your mind fooling around with stuff like that."

Pete offered Izzy a hand and helped her to her feet. He looked at his sister calmly. "As would a lovely woman in my life named Willow, who scares me almost as much as Ma. No worries," he said.

He leaned his head to one side and looked at Izzy, then her tummy, concern creasing his brow. "You sure that baby's arrival isn't imminent. Like now?"

"People need to stop telling me when and where I'll have this baby," Izzy grumped.

Gabby ran up to catch the end of the sentence. "Baby? What? What's happening?"

They all laughed and Birdie promised Gabby she'd know the instant anything was happening. But as Izzy reminded them all, "It won't be today. I have a class to teach—and so do you, young lady," she said to Gabby. "Come, your fans await you."

Pete and Cass piled up the lobster traps and announced they were taking off across the harbor to buy more bait.

"We've been abandoned," Birdie said, watching them walk toward Pete's pickup truck.

Nell looked across the water at the Ocean's Edge. The noontime crowd had thinned some, though tourists often ate late. Nell could see waitresses moving around between the tables. "The sandwiches were great," she said, checking her watch. "But I think I need dessert."

Birdie followed her look. "And a glass of iced tea at the outdoor bar. Perfect, in my book." They slipped on their sunglasses and walked back down the dock, the sea breeze ruffling their hair and adding a snap to their steps. "Cagney and Lacy?" Birdie suggested.

"It works for me," Nell said.

Jeffrey Meara greeted them at the door. "Now, where have you been all my life, you two beautiful ladies? Haven't seen you here in nearly a week."

"Jeffrey, you old flirt." Birdie pecked him on the cheek as she looked around the restaurant." It looks like business is good, even in the middle of the day."

"And tonight it'll be packed. Kevin is bringing 'em in in droves. Had a whole tourist bus from Boston come up here just to have lunch. He's making us all famous."

"What's this guy saying about me?" Kevin Sullivan walked up behind them. He had exchanged his apron and toque for a pair of jeans and a plaid shirt and dangled a ring of car keys from one finger.

"Just singing your praises, dear," Birdie said.

"Are you here for a late lunch?" Kevin looked around for a hostess to find them a table. "I'm off but will be sure you're taken care of."

"No, not lunch today," Nell said. "Just dessert. Is Tyler Gibson working?"

Kevin nodded. "I'm keeping his nose to the grindstone for a few days. He's been taking time off, lured away by too many party invitations—then he looks like something the cat dragged in the next day."

"Will we be disturbing things if we go back to say hello?"

"You two? Never. Make yourselves at home. Tell Ty I said the dessert and drinks are on the house." He waved to Jeffrey and headed out the door.

They made their way back around the tables and booths and through the wide-open doors to the outdoor bar. A few men sat at the end of the bar watching the television. Tyler Gibson stood nearby, one eye on the baseball game while he wiped glasses and set them on shelves. A waitress was back and forth, serving drinks and delivering bowls of chips to guests seated at the tall cocktail tables.

Birdie waved at Tyler and he made his way down the length of the bar.

"Ladies," he greeted them warmly. "What's your pleasure?"

"You are, Tyler. Along with iced tea."

Tyler's returning smile was hesitant.

"We'd like to talk if you have a minute," Nell explained.

"Me?"

"It's about Justin Dorsey's murder," Birdie said.

Tyler's smile disappeared and he glanced around the lounge area, then back at the men watching the game. "A couple minutes, max," he said. "We're a little busy and it's almost time for the cocktail crowd." His smile was too bright and never reached his eyes. "Don't want to get fired."

"Of course not, dear," Birdie said. "We don't want that, either. This will take just a minute or two."

Nell started in. "I'm sure everyone knows by now that Justin Dorsey was selling marijuana." She wondered how specific they should be with him, but it didn't seem to matter. Tyler just stared at them with a blank look on his face.

"I'm sure you've heard the rumors flying around the beach," Birdie continued.

"Well, sure," he said.

"We're trying to find out a little more about what he was doing, who was involved, that sort of thing," Nell said. "We think it might help the police find the person who killed him."

"Well, sure," he said again.

He forked his fingers through his hair and shifted from one foot to another. "Hey, you're thirsty. Sorry." He spun around, filled two tall glasses with iced tea, and stuck a lemon slice on each rim. They slid a little forcefully across the bar, tea sloshing over the side, but

Tyler didn't seem to notice. He drummed his fingers, then glanced down at the cocktail waitress standing at the other end. She was talking to the men watching the game.

"Oh, jeez," he said. "Duty calls. Just one sec while I fill Stacey's drink order and I'll be right back."

He fairly flew down the length of the bar. "Poor Tyler. He thinks we're going to arrest him."

"Or worse, tell his grandmother," Nell said.

A waitress walked by with a tray of desserts, and Birdie picked out a single piece of carrot cake. "Two forks, please," she said, then turned back to Nell. "I believe this is Kevin's mother's recipe. Cream cheese frosting. Sinful, as is appropriate."

Nell laughed and took a bite, then wondered aloud how they could make Tyler feel more comfortable while they talked to him. "I think he was starting to perspire," she said.

They looked back down the bar. A few more men had joined the others watching the game.

"So much for making him comfortable," Birdie said.

Stacey, the young cocktail waitress, was now behind the bar, stirring a pitcher of margaritas with one hand and sliding a beer across the bar.

Tyler Gibson was nowhere in sight.

Chapter 23

Hours later, as the sky turned purple and tiny lights flickered on up and down Harbor Road, Izzy, Nell, Cass, and Birdie found a parking spot and walked across Harbor Road toward Jake Risso's Gull Tavern.

Meet us for Tuesday night baseball at the bar, Ben had written in a text.

"So that was the end of that," Birdie said, detailing their afternoon sleuthing adventure to Izzy and Cass. "But the carrot cake was the best I've ever had."

"You don't think he left town, do you?" Izzy said. "What was he thinking? And being intimidated by you and Aunt Nell? That's goofy."

Cass was perplexed. "Tyler's a sweet guy, but he's definitely a sandwich short of a picnic. Maybe he just panicked and did the first thing that popped into his head—disappear. He used to do that with his mom when he was a kid and got into trouble. I actually found him under his bed one time."

"The problem is, it makes him look guilty," Nell said. "He definitely didn't want to talk to us, even though just days ago he was asking all kinds of questions about Horace Stevenson's death. But once it seemed we wanted to ask him questions about himself, he froze."

The door to the Gull was open, letting in breezes while the noise from the crowd rolled out onto the sidewalk.

"Why did we let the men talk us into this?" Izzy asked, peering into the crowded, noisy bar.

"Because Jake's food is passable and it means none of us will have to cook tonight," Cass said.

That was part of it, they agreed. And the other part was that being home alone these nights wasn't something any of them cherished.

Ben waved to them as they came in the door, then pointed above the heads of those around him to the corner booth that Jake always saved for them. Iced water was already poured and a basket of fried calamari and plenty of napkins sat in the middle.

Nell had called Ben on her cell and filled him in on what had happened. In his calm, collected way, he had downplayed it, suggesting that maybe Tyler's shift had ended and he wanted to get home.

But he was wrong this time. Tyler left because he didn't want to talk to them. Even the cocktail waitress stumbled when trying to explain his sudden exit. *"He . . . he had to see someone,"* she had mumbled.

"A man about a horse, no doubt," Birdie had said sweetly back to her, bringing a smile to the uncomfortable young woman's face.

Nell looked around at the crowded room. It was packed with a mixture of townsfolk and visitors, sunburned young women in halter tops and weathered fishermen, friends and neighbors and strangers. Many were at the bar, three deep, cheering on the mighty Sox, most of them drinking beer to drown out the strikes and outs, and some just sitting along the window bar with giant baskets of clams and calamari and crisp, cheesy fries in front of them. When her eyes adjusted to the light, she spotted Pete over in a corner. Willow was with him, along with a group of friends. But not Tyler Gibson.

Perhaps Cass was right—he took a slow boat to China. Or Gloucester, maybe.

Nell noticed a shaft of light coming from the wooden steps

leading up to the roof. "How about we go up on the roof? Stars, moon, no television, a cool breeze." The rooftop seating was a new addition to Jake's bar, a casual area with long tables and benches for those who didn't like the din and swell of bodies below. Izzy, Birdie, and Cass were up the steps before Nell had the words out of her mouth. She mouthed over the crowd to Ben where they'd be, then asked a waiter to bring up their food and drinks.

Andy Risso walked out from behind the bar and waved the waitress away. "I'll do it, Nell," he said, piling the basket and glasses onto a tray and following her up.

"Can't say I blame you—it's nice up here," he said. Andy had always been one of Nell's favorite Sea Harbor kids, ever since he was a young boy running errands for Ben's father. And now he was all grown up and still one of her favorites. When he was studying English literature in college, he'd come home for vacations and sit with Nell on Coffee's patio, discussing Gertrude Stein and other literary expatriates roaming around inside his head. She loved the intelligence and wit that lived beneath his drummer's hands and blond ponytail. He was somewhat of a Renaissance man, not unlike her own husband—and that was the ultimate compliment, the young drummer had told her.

"How're things in the bar, Andy?" Nell asked, a mundane question. *Fine*, he would say.

But instead, Andy said, "Not great. Too many rumors, too much talk about all the bad things coming down on us. And when it gets late, my dad and I worry about folks getting home okay. When you don't know what's going on, you think the worst. It's like some evil shadow lurking around, just waiting to pounce. Can't say I like it."

He set down the tray. "People are just plain wary, even in here where people come to relax and get rid of worries."

"What are the rumors?" Izzy asked.

"I don't hear everything, but when a kid is murdered and there doesn't seem to be a logical reason, people make things up. Some think that Dorsey was murdered because he cheated someone. But no one knows *who* that could be, so people are looking at each other in a different light. *Is it that guy? Or maybe him?* Like who would kill a foolish kid, even if he was selling grass, if that's what was going on. Who would do that? A madman. Someone deranged?" He looked around, waved at some people coming up on the roof, then leaned his palms flat on the table. "None of it computes, if you ask me. Most folks around here would rather have our fantastic beer than what he was selling, anyway."

"What about Tyler?" Izzy asked.

"Gibson?"

"Yes," Nell said.

Andy thought about it. "I'm not sure what you're asking me. He's a nice kid. Guys like him. Ladies love him. I even saw the ice princess flirting with him here one night."

"Ice princess?"

"Sorry. Sometimes my dad's crassness rubs off on me. That's what he calls her because she never smiles at him. Tami Danvers. She was in here drinking with some girlfriends one night—this was weeks ago. She doesn't come in here anymore. I think we're too plebeian. Anyway, she thought Tyler was hot stuff. He charms 'em, young and old."

Cass frowned at him. "And who are you calling *old*, twerp? Tamara Danvers isn't that old. And what's with the 'Tami'?"

"You'll never be old, Ms. Halloran." He swatted Cass with a napkin. "And no, the lady and I aren't on a first-name basis. Her friends were calling her Tami.

"Anyway," Andy went on, "Tyler is a good guy, but kind of a pushover. He's up for anything, easily talked into things."

Several other parties clambered up the steps and Andy looked over, motioned toward an empty table on the other side of the roof. Then he looked back at the women.

"I'm shirking my duty. I'd better send someone up to take orders. Peace." He lifted one hand in the air, then disappeared down the stairs into a sea of bodies below.

Sam came up to be sure they were all okay. He announced it was the top of the sixth, game was tied, and then he looked around, hoping someone would send him back down to the game.

Izzy complied.

They ordered BLTs, knowing a tie game could go on forever, and settled back into the night. Overhead a deep purple sky was slowly melting into an inky black canopy, the moon slipped into place, and Venus shone brightly. It was a magical night.

And maybe a dangerous one.

Cass nibbled on a piece of calamari. "Andy's take on the murder is interesting," she said. "It clearly makes no sense to him."

"We're all trying to be logical, moving from point A to point B. That's what we do—but maybe the path to the killer is a more circuitous one, like that complicated shawl we all knit for Izzy's wedding. It went in a circle, not a straight line." Birdie looked up at the sky. "What a wondrous vantage point those stars have. If only—"

The sound of heavy steps on the staircase made them guess if it would be Sam or Ben bringing them an update that they weren't very interested in.

But it was neither.

Coming through the rooftop door, his hands shoved in his pockets and his blond hair covered with a crooked Sox hat, was Tyler Gibson. He looked over at their table, his face somber.

"Andy said you guys were all up here," he said.

"Andy was right," Birdie said. She smiled warmly at him, and Tyler, looking more confident, walked over to the table.

"Would you like to sit down?" Birdie said. "We have a few pieces of calamari left. That doesn't often happen with Cass around."

Tyler looked over at his old babysitter and tried to smile, but it came out crooked, uncomfortable. "No, thanks," he said.

He was the lone kid called into the principal's office, and standing offered a faster escape once the riot act was read.

"I came up to say I'm sorry," he said, meeting their eyes this time. "I was stupid to leave you both sitting there at the bar."

"It wasn't a very smart thing to do," Birdie said.

"I just didn't know what to say to you, is the thing. I didn't know what you knew or what you didn't know, or what you wanted to know. And my grams is going to shoot me when she finds out about this."

"Esther Gibson is one of the most fair and loving women I know," Birdie said. "Don't sell your grandmother short."

"Maybe we should start at the beginning," Nell said. "What is it you don't want her to know?"

"This whole mess. Grams is the best. She does a lot for me. This won't go over well."

"What mess?" Nell asked.

He took a deep breath, and for a brief moment they could picture him in front of Cass the babysitter, getting caught stealing beer from his parents' bar.

"Okay, you already know that I knew Justin Dorsey. He was all over town, always trying to make an extra buck, trying to sell us watches he'd hocked from somewhere, just weird things. He was all about making money. Had big plans to open a dive shop, he said.

"Then one night he saw us down at the beach and he told some of the girls that he could get some grass, if they wanted it. It's summer, there were parties on the beach, so they teased him a little, then said sure, but Justin had devised this crazy plan of delivering it that they wouldn't go along with. So they asked me if I'd get it for them. They were afraid of getting caught, I guess. They said they'd give me the money. So I said sure. Justin's crazy scheme was to put it in a kid's car seat at the beach. Then I'd put money there in exchange. Cover it up with the blanket, he told me. Goofy, we all thought, but we humored him."

"Where was he getting it?" Birdie asked.

Ty lifted his shoulders in a small shrug. "I don't know. It was small amounts. There wasn't much money involved."

He shuffled his weight from foot to foot. "It was foolish."

Birdie agreed. "And what raises this to a level much higher than being 'foolish' is that the young man was murdered. When you left the restaurant today, it made you look guilty. Didn't you think of that?"

Tyler looked around, nodded to some girls at the next table, then let his smile fade into nothingness. He looked at all of them, but finally focused on Birdie, his eyes locking into hers.

Believe me, his eyes said.

"I heard that Izzy had found the car seat. And I knew you were all asking questions about it. I thought . . . hell, I don't know what I thought. Everyone's talking about Justin being murdered and who might have done it. I may have been the last person to see him the night before he died. Me or the old man."

"Old man?" Nell asked.

"The guy who died. He was down there all the time, like a guard or something, walking the beach."

"Do you think he knew what was going on?"

"Maybe, but what he really didn't like were the bonfires and beer cans and sometimes there'd be some fireworks. I think they hurt his dog's ears. He said that it was his beach and we were desecrating it with our noise. He couldn't see much, but I'm pretty sure he smelled the girls smoking the stuff."

They listened and filed the information away. Then Birdie said, "All right, then. Go on with why you disappeared from the bar today."

"Well, like I said, I didn't know what you were going to ask and I was scared. Justin and I were mixed up in something that we shouldn't have been—him and me. And then . . . then the kid gets murdered, and I'm right there with him then, too. Doing a dive down at the beach. Fiddling with the same equipment. So what kind of alibi could I possibly have? None."

He paused for a breath, and the shade of red on his cheeks deepened to crimson. He swallowed hard. His voice was heavy. "You gotta believe me, Birdie. I didn't murder anybody. I couldn't ever murder anybody. I *liked* the kid. I just did a dumb thing. Nobody got hurt." He looked over at Cass. "You know me, Cass. You have to believe me."

"So that's why you ran off today?" Birdie said. "We're not the police, you know." Her words carried a gentleness that drew Tyler's attention back to her.

He was silent for so long they thought he hadn't heard Birdie. But finally he looked up, his face drawn and sad. "I didn't want you to tell Grams. If I didn't talk to you, you'd have nothing to tell her."

From the floor below, the crowd cheered wildly as the Sox hit one out of Fenway. The building shook all the way to the rafters, sending gulls flapping their wings wildly as they exited the rooftop bar.

Birdie's voice was matter-of-fact. Practical. And warm. "Esther will find out, Tyler. You know that. Justin has been murdered. Anything that touched his life these last weeks will be dissected, inspected, all those things. So she'll find out. Even if she didn't work at the police department, she'd find out. But don't you think perhaps you should be the one to tell her?"

Tyler listened carefully. Finally he nodded.

"Did Justin give you any idea where he got the stuff?" Cass said.

He looked down at the floor as he sorted through his thoughts. "It was . . . it just didn't seem important. He said it was easy, no need to worry about where. He said something weird. He said the stuff was 'organic.' But the thing is, he got it, and we bought it. But he did tell me. . . ."

The noise from the lower level settled down. On the roof the sound of returning gulls mingled with conversations.

"Tell you what?" Cass asked.

"That it was over."

"What was over?" Nell asked.

"The whole thing. Everything. He came by the bar when I was working that night—the night before he died—and he told me that the pickup that night would be the last. He was pretty dramatic about it, like I might be upset, but the only reason we even played his game was that he made it so easy for us—he was like a salesman, giving us a deal. But this was it, he said. The end of the road."

They sat in silence for a minute. Finally Izzy asked, "Did he say why it was the last time?"

Tyler nodded. "Yeah, he did. He said he had bigger fish to fry—and the fire was hot."

Chapter 24

The appearance of a waitress had given Tyler an out, but instead of disappearing, he prudently suggested he leave them alone to enjoy their sandwiches, then excused himself.

They'd all laughed a little, just to ease his discomfort, and Birdie suggested he go home and get some sleep; he looked exhausted.

"Do you believe him?" Izzy asked as he disappeared below.

"Which part?" Cass asked.

"That it was all over anyway, and Justin had bigger plans. What did he say? Bigger fish to fry?"

"Maybe he was desperate to change the subject and move the emphasis from what was happening at the beach to something that didn't involve him," Nell said. "We'd have absolutely no way of knowing if it was true."

"A possibility." Birdie swallowed a bite of sandwich. "Do we believe him? Yes, we need to start with that question. Was Tyler just protecting Tyler? Or was he telling the truth?"

They all liked him, which made answering the question more difficult. And his grandmother was a friend.

Finally Izzy answered her own question. "I do. I believe him. I think he was so scared he wasn't thinking clearly. Someone who would be that afraid of the four of us couldn't possibly kill anyone. Right?"

"Besides, what motive would he have?" Cass asked.

"That's true—it's hard to come up with one. But that's only true if you believe him," Nell said. "If you don't, if he's lying about the friendly way he and Justin parted company, about the last deal being fair and square, then there might be a motive."

"What would it be?" Izzy asked.

"I think any time you're dealing with money in this way, you're at risk. Tyler was taking money from the women, then dealing with Justin—he was right in the middle. Maybe somehow Justin was cheating all of them—giving them something inferior, and he had put Tyler right in the middle of it."

"So he got back at him by murdering him?" Birdie said. "Why wouldn't he simply find Justin and demand the money back?"

That thought silenced everyone for a short while, though as they all knew, motives for murder didn't always lend themselves readily to reason.

Finally Nell said, "Perhaps he was concerned that Justin would threaten to tell everyone what was going on. Ty couldn't bear the thought of Esther knowing." But it was a flimsy motive, they all agreed.

The night had turned chilly and Izzy shivered, pulling her loose-knit hoodie tightly around her. "He must be regretting the day he met Justin. I think Janie reached that point, too."

"We're skirting the most interesting thing Tyler said," Birdie took a sip of water and continued. "He said *Justin had bigger fish to fry.*"

Nell nodded. She pushed the basket of calamari toward Izzy. "I agree. And I agree with Izzy. I don't think Ty made any of it up. It doesn't make sense for him to do that. And I can hear Justin saying those exact words. *He had bigger fish to fry.*"

"If he was beginning to make money somewhere else—*more* money—it would explain some things," Birdie said. She picked up the pitcher Andy had left on the table, and filled everyone's glasses. "He'd been spending a lot of money in the few days right before his death. Money, according to Janie, that he couldn't possibly have earned legitimately. A complete set of original stoneware, for example, that cost him hundreds of dollars. And a hefty donation to a charity. From what Tyler said, that wasn't the kind of money that changed hands via the baby seat. Tens and twenties, he said."

"Jane said he paid for the pottery with one-hundred-dollar bills."

"Don't forget the motorcycle he showed up on the night before he died," Nell said. "You're absolutely right, Birdie. He wasn't getting that kind of money from the kids on the beach—and we know now he didn't get it from your necklace."

"As big and gaudy as the piece of jewelry was, it wasn't worth the kind of money Justin was spending."

"Suppose the person supplying him was moving on to something else? Some activity that was bringing in more money. It seems to go back again to the great unknown, the mysterious person in Justin's life. Someone he knew. Talked to. Met with."

"Conspired with."

Their minds immediately went to work dissecting the town, the neighborhood, the artists' colony, searching for someone they'd seen Justin with, someone who might have facilitated the whole awful mess . . . someone who might have killed him.

But every single person who came to mind was someone they knew. Janie. Tommy Porter. Archie Brandley. Lily Virgilio. Dr. Seltzer. And now, rising like hot air to the top of the pile, there was Tyler Gibson.

But targeting someone they might know—and even like—was a task that soon brought Izzy to her feet. "It's time for me to roll on home," she said, patting her stomach. "Junior and I can't think anymore."

As if on cue, Sam appeared in the doorway. "Came to claim my best girl," he said. "Ready, Iz?"

It was time to call it a night, everyone agreed. They stood and made their way single file down the stairway into the mass of bodies below.

Ben and Danny were waiting at the bottom, heatedly discussing the missed fly ball to left field, which they quickly tabled when the women appeared. Ben cleared a path through the crowded bar and out to the sidewalk. The smell of fried fish and fries diminished with each step.

"A long day?" Ben wrapped an arm around Nell's shoulder.

She nodded and waved good-bye to the others. "They all seem long right now."

"Long and muddled," Ben agreed, turning the key in the ignition. "Murder has a nasty way of doing that."

He made a U-turn, then drove north on Harbor Road, his CRV operating on instinct and heading toward Sandswept Lane. To home, to bed.

As they drove past McClucken's Hardware Store, Ben slowed down. "Look over there," he said.

Nell looked. Sitting on a bench in front of the store was a lone figure. He was leaning forward, his elbows on his knees, and his hands holding his head as if it would topple to the ground without support. Tyler Gibson looked as if he had just lost his best friend.

Ben and Nell slept soundly, and awoke to a day saturated in sunshine.

Perhaps it's an omen, Birdie said, showing up at the Endicotts' door for a cup of coffee. She and Gabby had come over on their bikes, new ones that Birdie had ordered off the Internet, she said proudly. "They call them city bikes."

Gabby was in and out, gulping down the glass of orange juice Ben offered her. "Baby shower planning," she said. Lots to do. Jane and Willow needed her.

She was gone before Ben had filled three mugs with coffee.

"Now you see her, now you don't," Birdie said. "But such energy she leaves in her wake."

"You're loving it, aren't you?" Nell said. "Every minute of it."

"I love her. And her spirit. Somehow that makes me see life a little differently. Gabby doesn't shy away from anything, whether it's horrible or joyful. It's all part of life's great tasty soup."

Nell listened and kept her own thoughts private. Gabby's spirit was energizing, that was true, but Birdie wasn't learning from Gabby. Gabby was absorbing her nonna's spirit—a fine tribute to the wise woman who had welcomed the young girl into her life. And Birdie was simply seeing it reflected in a new, younger light.

Nell slid the cream across the island.

"I think we're looking in all the wrong places," Birdie said, moving on to the reason she had stopped by—that and Ben's scones, she said.

"We?" Ben took the scones out of the oven and slid them onto a plate. Fresh blueberries oozed from a tiny slit in the side of a pastry.

Birdie reached over and scooped it up with her finger. "All right, Ben, have it your way. The police, all of us. A big *we*. But I think this business with Ty and Justin and selling pot to a group of college kids might be a distraction."

"From what?" Ben asked, but Nell knew where Birdie was going. The same thoughts had accompanied her early-morning shower.

"Well, that's what we need to find out. But let's start with the money. Justin had a lot of money that last week or so, and from what Tyler said, it didn't come from him and his girlfriends. So whoever Justin was working with must have provided him with a bigger, more lucrative opportunity. And one that must have allowed more chances for him to mess it up. . . ."

"And get himself murdered." Ben handed them each a fork and a plate with a flaky scone and a dollop of Greek yogurt on top.

"Yes," Birdie said. "Exactly. And from what we're hearing lately, Horace Stevenson didn't always mind his own business. He and Red knew everything that went on down at Paley's Cove."

"Which could be what got him killed."

"Of course there's a big unknown here. Two, actually," Birdie admitted. She cut into the scone and smiled her thanks to Ben. "You do make good scones—definitely not one of the unknowns."

"The two unknowns, then," Ben said, helping himself to the last scone.

"Number one, *what* is this more lucrative project that lured away our friend Justin? We know it wasn't the necklace. And it wasn't the pot, at least not what was being sold to the kids on the beach."

"Which brings us back to the question we always come back to," Nell finished.

"*Who,*" Birdie said, finishing her scone and putting the plate in the sink.

"Who," Nell repeated.

"Yes. Who. Now ponder that, my friends, while I take me and my bike down to Gus McClucken's to find out what this dive shop is that seems to feature quite prominently in all this. It's time we got a little proactive, don't you think?"

And with that, as was Birdie's way, she was gone, out the front door with Nell's "good-bye" hanging in the air behind her.

A habit, Nell realized with a smile, that young Gabby was mastering quite nicely, too.

Chapter 25

*N*ell invited herself to go with Izzy to the Virgilio Clinic later that Wednesday.

She knew Izzy wouldn't mind; she liked the company, especially when Sam wasn't available. And Nell loved the chance to listen to Lily talk about the baby, to watch Izzy's face glow. And of course she'd go to the ends of the earth to hear the baby's heartbeat, a miraculous moment that seemed to put the entire universe back on its proper orbit—at least for those few precious seconds.

But today Nell had another reason, although she couldn't even put it into words. Justin's connection to the clinic had been playing at the edges of her mind, as if it were somehow an important part of this puzzle that would lead them to his killer. It was Birdie who started her on this track, and perhaps Tyler Gibson—their contention that maybe they were looking in all the wrong places to find the person who killed Justin Dorsey. Maybe their concentration on his activity at Paley's Cove was as transitory as the sand that was washed away by the tide.

Working for Dr. Lily was the only job Justin hadn't completely messed up, Janie had said—even though there were other staff members who hadn't been completely happy with him. It seemed an odd job for him to enjoy: not a bustling restaurant where he'd see friends and meet people, or working down at the docks or on one of the many fishing boats looking for summer help—things you'd think a young man would enjoy. But a *women's clinic* of all places. What had engaged him so there?

Jerry Thompson had told Ben they had completely ruled out these murders being random events. There was no vagrant theory or psychopath theory, not an accidental encounter. It was purposeful—the mechanical failure on Justin's regulator and the drug in Horace's whiskey. Intentional. Purposeful.

The words had sounded ugly when Ben repeated them. Someone wanted Justin dead. Someone wanted Horace dead. And it was probably, circumstances told them, the same person. Justin *did* something. Horace *knew* something. It was a theory that made sense, but left big yawning gaps searching for answers.

Maybe looking around a place where Justin worked, Nell thought, trying to follow in his footsteps and mine his thoughts, figuring out what made him tick—maybe those things would give them a hint of what he had done to get himself murdered.

Izzy picked up Nell in midafternoon and, before she got in the car, announced that they had an extra companion. Words were hardly necessary, though. Before Nell reached the car door, a long golden snout in the open back window broke into a canine grin. Izzy quickly assured her that Red would wait in the car when they got to the medical office. He had attached himself to Izzy's Volkswagen—and riding in the backseat with the window partly open and his nose sticking out was a magnificent treat that Izzy simply couldn't deny him.

"You're spoiling him," Nell said as they walked into the clinic.

Izzy glanced back at the car. Red was seated comfortably in the backseat, the window open a crack. "Yes," she said happily. "I'm getting in practice. Dogs and babies should be spoiled. I expect you to do your share, too."

Nell had every intention of doing her share. She followed Izzy through the door.

Janie was on the phone, her back to them, when they walked into the reception area. But her words were distinct and audible in the empty waiting room.

"I know how difficult this is," she said. Each word was professional—but softened with compassion. "Yes, stay on the couch, take it easy—and call us back in an hour if there isn't a change, or sooner if you need to." She listened, nodded as if the caller could feel her assurance, and then told the unseen person that everything would be all right.

Nell listened to the tone in her voice, remembering back to a wintery night when Birdie had slipped and fallen on Harbor Road. Janie had appeared, her voice filled with that same compassion and caring.

She hung up and turned around, slipping a smile back into place.

Izzy glanced at the phone. "I hope everything's okay."

"It will be. Sometimes things don't work out the way we plan," she said. "And when that happens, well, there's a reason. But it's difficult just the same—more for some people than for others. I think this patient will be fine. I'm not so sure about the father, though."

Then she changed the subject and her smile grew warmer. "Seeing you two is always a good thing. It brightens my day."

"If you need another day brightener, Red is out in the car. If you get a second, he'd love to see you and lick your hand."

Janie laughed. "I love Red. He's amazing, Iz. If you ever need a dog sitter, please call on me and Purl. In fact, I found the coolest plaid dog bed at a garage sale. I'm going to wash it and keep it in the apartment for Red's visits."

Janie seemed in better shape than the day before, Nell thought, although she admitted to Izzy earlier that she had had nightmares about baby carriers. But the nurse's smile was back, and her voice more confident. A few light lines appeared about her eyes, ones that spoke to life's trials. Ones Janie had earned.

They walked through the reception area to the inner offices.

Nell paused inside the door and glanced into the library and records room where she'd seen Justin so diligently filing that day, humming, happy. As if he had the world at his fingertips. She half expected to see his head bobbing to the music pumping through his headphones. How long ago was that? Time was difficult to mark these days. Tuesdays, Saturdays, Thursdays—they all merged together in a blur. Instead of the days being neatly marked by the weekend, they were marked by murders, something that turned the calendar into a jumbled maze.

"Is this where Justin worked most of the time?" she asked.

Janie nodded. "Yes and no. There are computers in all the offices and the examining room around the clinic, and he was great at fixing them. So he kind of wandered around everywhere, I guess you'd say, much to Dr. Seltzer's annoyance."

"He didn't like Justin much, did he?"

Janie lowered her voice and turned her back to the long hallway leading to the examining rooms. "No, he hated him. Especially the last month or so. I tried to keep them apart because even the sight of Justin seemed to upset him."

"Did Justin feel the same way about him?"

"No. Justin said the doc was 'a great dude'—his words, not mine." She covered a sad laugh and whispered as they walked into the examining room, "Calling Dr. Seltzer a 'dude' never seemed quite right—but it was so Justin."

"Do you know what Dr. Seltzer's main complaint about Justin was?"

"Where should I start? Mostly he thought Justin nosed into things that were none of his business. He complained to Dr. Lily about it all the time. He said she was too trusting, and the way Justin nosed into things was way out of line. He swore he saw Justin listening outside his office one day when he was talking to a patient, but Dr. Lily told him Justin was just waiting to get in to fix a computer—and that was the truth.

"Then the next day he came up with the idea that Justin wasn't just fixing computers, he might have been reading personal files, too. Dr. Lily made sure everyone used pass codes on patient records after that."

"I know he was upset with Justin that day we were here—and you were, too," Nell said.

Janie thought back to that day. The same day Justin had unwisely washed Izzy's windows—or tried to. The same day he was messing around in the filing room. She nodded at the recollection. "I was furious with him that day. The thing Dr. Seltzer hated the most was when Justin would sneak out to smoke. First he'd done it out in the parking lot, but Dr. Lily said it looked bad for the clinic. Then he discovered the steps to the widow's walk and he'd go up there to smoke. The widow's walk was strictly off-limits to all of us. Dangerous, even, Dr. Lily said. Not just the smoking itself, but the railing up there was weak and could break—and no one ever went up there. Until Justin, of course. And to make it worse, Dr. Seltzer's apartment is on the second floor, so Justin had to sneak past the apartment back door to get up there. But somehow he managed to do it, until Dr. Lily caught him coming down the stairs one day. She was angry and I think came close to firing him.

"So he promised he wouldn't do it again, but I know he went up there anyway. It was that awful smoking habit he had. I hated it. That day you were here was one of those times I caught him doing it. The door to the stairway was ajar and I could smell the cigarette smoke on his shirt, so I knew he'd been up there. It was the straw that broke the camel's back."

"Those things don't seem so awful," Izzy said, slipping up onto the examining table. "I mean, for Dr. Seltzer to dislike him as much as he does."

"No, I guess not. Except it wasn't Justin's place to say what the rules were. He just worked here," Janie said sadly. She slipped Izzy's file into the holder on the door, ushered them into the room, and said she'd be back later.

Dr. Lily's exam was brief and efficient, and then the three of them took turns listening through the stethoscope to the heartbeats, the quick and exhilarating thumps indicating, in Nell's mind, that baby Perry was a happy baby, eager to meet his mom and dad.

Nell rubbed her goose bumps into submission.

"It won't be long now, Izzy," Lily said. "You've started to dilate, so it could be any day. But you just never know about babies. They have minds of their own and can surprise you—it could be a couple weeks. Some like to stay in there a little longer, where it's warm and safe."

Nell and Izzy looked at each other, reading each other's thoughts.

Yes, above all, this baby would be kept warm and safe.

The bark that snaked around the corner of the examining room wasn't loud, but definitely distinct. The flurry of fur that followed nearly knocked Nell onto the chair. But it was Izzy whom Red wanted, and Izzy he found.

"Sorry," Sam said, shamefaced, as he trailed Red into the room. "I had a little extra time and knew Izzy was here, so I stopped in to hear my baby's report. Izzy isn't always detailed enough for me." He leaned over Red and kissed Izzy on the top of her head. "Janie was saying hello to Red through the car window and suggested we bring him in for a drink—"

"It was hot in the car," Janie said, reappearing in the doorway. "He needed some hydration. Dogs are eighty percent water, you know."

Lily was down on one knee, scratching the dog behind his ears. "He's a sweet dog. Horace loved him so. Sweet dog. Sweet man."

"It's interesting that in life Horace appeared to be almost a recluse. But in death we're finding he had a wide array of friends," Nell said. "Everyone seems to have known him."

Lily laughed. "I love Paley's Cove. My—Dr. Seltzer and I walk there often. And Horace was always welcoming, though I do think he considered that sandy stretch his property. We were a little worried about his eyesight and brought him drops sometimes, even suggesting surgery. But he'd have none of it. He said he got along fine. And then he'd prove it by naming a bush or even the kind of sunscreen someone running by was wearing. He didn't miss much."

Nell laughed. "He'll be missed."

"Agreed." The male voice came from the doorway. Martin Seltzer stood there, slightly stooped but with a smile on his face, his eyes on Red. He was rewarded immediately by a short bark as Red moved across the room to his side, waiting for a pat.

Nell watched the interaction with a mixture of pleasure and surprise. Red clearly was fond of both Lily and Martin. She wondered how many other friends he'd made during his years of walking the beach at Paley's Cove. His presence seemed to bring life to Martin Seltzer.

"Goldens are great," the older doctor said. "Best pets in the world. We had one years ago." He looked over at Lily, then back to the dog. "They love you no matter what, right, Red?"

His eyes were on the dog and his voice was slightly muffled, as if speaking to himself and the dog, no one else.

Lily watched him with an unusual expression on her face. Then she cleared her throat and said briskly, "All right, now, back to work, everyone. We've a baby to check."

Martin disappeared and Janie urged Red to follow her down the hall to her office.

Lily closed the door and looked at Sam, somehow knowing that he was the one who would be peppering her with questions.

Nell sat back in a corner, listening to Sam's litany of questions and Lily's patient responses as she attempted to satisfy the new father's insatiable quest for information about all things baby. Sam had embraced the role fully, and was fast becoming an expert on coaching, breathing techniques, and relaxation methods. Her thoughts turned to the phone call they'd overheard, a husband who apparently wouldn't have that experience, at least not now, not as planned. She presumed it was a miscarriage Janie was dealing with. A difficult event—but not the end of dreams. She and Ben were certainly testimony to that.

It wasn't until Janie rapped on the door and pushed it open that they realized they'd been there for nearly half an hour.

"Is Red in here?" she asked.

"No," Izzy said, slipping on her shoes. "He's not with you?"

"He was sleeping in my office. I left to pick up some things from the dispensary, and when I came back, he was gone. But no worries, he's here someplace." Janie forced a calmness into her voice. "No one would let him outside, so we know he's safe."

She headed down the hall, nearly colliding with Martin, who listened to the concern, then joined in the search. Several patients, in the office for quick weigh-ins or to pick up medicine or vitamins, offered reports of hearing Red in one hall or another, and someone saw a waving golden tail disappearing around a corner. But Red seemed to have disappeared.

"Martin, please check down in Dr. Hamilton's section of the building and we'll cover these rooms."

Nell walked into the break room, but the only one inside was a nurse's aide. She hadn't seen a dog, she said, though she thought she had heard one a little earlier.

Nell heard a frantic yelp from Janie, and hurried into the hall, stopping short at the look on Janie's face.

A narrow door at the end of the hall was partially open, a curving flight of stairs visible through the opening.

Justin's escape route for a quick smoke.

"No, he couldn't have," Janie said, but not believing her own words, she headed toward the stairs with Sam and Nell in close pursuit. The stairs wound upward to the second floor and the closed door that opened into Martin Seltzer's apartment. From there the staircase narrowed and grew steep, twisting around like a belfry passage, until finally a door appeared with a sliver of light falling onto the wooden step.

"It's open," Janie whispered, then pushed it wider and stepped out into daylight.

The widow's walk was postcard perfect, a wooden platform surrounded by an ornate white railing. In the distance clouds billowed and puffed over a whitecapped sea, gulls floated overhead, their wings moving in slow motion, and the sounds of traffic were a muted hum in the background. In the center of the walk was a raised garden, tilled and weeded, filled with lush spiky plants.

And on the other side of the garden, lying in the sun, was Red.

Janie ran around the herb garden to the sleepy dog. "Red, you silly old dog, you worried us," she cried, relief rushing her words.

Sam yelled down to Izzy that Red was fine, they'd be down in a second, then walked over to Nell. She was standing at the edge of the roof, looking down over the town of Sea Harbor. It lay at their feet like a tapestry. "Breathtaking," she murmured.

On the other side of the widow's walk, Janie was kneeling next to the dog, peering into his eyes, a deep frown on her forehead. Red pushed himself up, then wobbled toward Nell and Sam, his tail moving back and forth against the raised garden wall. "Something's wrong with him," Janie said. "His eyes are droopy. I think he's sick."

"Red?" Sam walked over to his side and crouched down, holding the dog's nose in his palm. "You okay, boy?"

Red's tail flapped, but his feet didn't seem to move in harmony, and he stumbled once, then continued walking toward the rooftop door. Sam followed close behind, watching him carefully as he made his way across the widow's walk. Just before he reached the door, his head dropped low and he gagged slightly, as if he was going to vomit. But he recovered and made it to the door.

Nell looked over at the garden. "I think he's been eating the herbs."

Sam looked over, frowned, then picked the dog up in his arms and carried him down two stories to the clinic offices.

Lily and Izzy were waiting. "He's sick," Sam said, and followed Lily into an empty examining room.

Martin Seltzer came hurrying down the hallway. "You found him," he said, then stopped short as he looked into the room at the woozy dog. "Where was he?"

"On the roof," Lily said, grabbing a slender flashlight and shining it into Red's eyes.

Martin paled, then moved around Izzy and Sam and gently moved Lily out of the way. He took the flashlight from her and looked into the dog's mouth, checked his eyes, and finally released the breath trapped in his chest. "He'll be okay. I'll watch him for a bit, just to be sure." He looked toward the hallway, where a worried Janie stood. "Janie, would you please get him a bowl of water?"

Janie rushed off.

Lily stared at Martin. "What is it? What's wrong with him?"

For a long, awkward minute, Martin stared back at Lily, as if her questions were an affront to him. At first his look had an edge of anger about it. But that faded almost instantly, and his long face grew longer.

"He'll be fine after a while. It wasn't that much."

"Exactly *what* wasn't that much? What made him sick?"

Martin's answer was firm, but his words short and heavy. "He ate a few cannabis leaves."

Chapter 26

For a long moment the only sound in the office was Red's heavy panting, then the thump of his tail as he basked in the attention all around him.

Then voices were raised, with Izzy's being the loudest.

"Pot? My dog ate pot?" she said in disbelief.

"He couldn't have eaten much," Martin said, his efficient, professional manner returning as he brushed Red's fur with his palm, caressing him gently, his fingers gently prying open his mouth. "In fact, I'm sure of it."

Lily stood near the wall, immobile, her eyes on the older doctor, her hands curled into fists at her sides. Finally she asked, "You were growing cannabis on the roof?"

"A small plot," he answered, his eyes remaining fixed on Red.

Izzy and Sam looked at each other. Awkwardness as thick as Red's coat settled on the room, blocking out the air.

Janie walked into the silence carrying a bowl of water. She looked around, handed it to Martin, and hurried back out.

Nell followed her into the hallway. The rush of fresh air cooled her face and slowed her heartbeat.

Janie watched her in silence, her arms crossed.

"Red will be fine," Nell said finally. "Really fine."

"Did he say pot?" Janie asked. Her eyes filled her entire face. "Is that what he said, Nell?"

Nell nodded. And all around them, puzzle pieces crashed to the floor with a deafening roar, a sound so loud Nell had an irrational urge to press her palms against her ears to block it out.

They left the clinic a short while later, once Martin assured them that Red was fine to ride in the car. He said to give him plenty of water and not to worry if he didn't want to eat today.

The older doctor seemed to know what he was talking about; no one questioned him.

Sam followed Izzy and Nell in his car as they headed to the Endicotts'. Nell had called ahead and suggested Ben start mixing up a batch of martinis. They were on their way home and it had been a long day.

Cass was there when they arrived, asking Ben's advice on a new business plan for the Halloran Lobster Company—but she tossed it aside quickly in favor of hearing about a long day that called for martinis.

The sound of Nell's voice, Ben had said, indicated something was up.

After assuring them that everything was fine with baby Perry, they all gathered in the comfortable chairs surrounding the old wooden coffee table. Ben had done his due diligence and it now held napkins, cheese and pita bread, a plate of olives and pickles.

Nell kissed him soundly. "Perfect," she said.

"Okay, I can't stand the suspense," Cass said. "Spill everything." She slipped off her sandals and pulled her feet up beneath her on the slipcovered chair.

Sam began, filling them in on Red's adventure at the clinic.

Red, for his part, curled up at Izzy's feet, happy and content with the bowl of water Nell had brought him.

Cass was stunned at the story, Ben circumspect. But both found it rather astounding that there was a crop of cannabis growing on the Virgilio Clinic's roof.

"I'm sure both Martin and Lily's first thought was Red. But once they knew he was going to be okay, what did they say? How did they explain it all?" Ben asked.

"Dr. Seltzer said very little," Nell said.

"And Dr. Lily didn't say much, either, " Izzy said. "At least not while we were there. They didn't refer to the garden or how it got there, except to acknowledge that Red must have eaten flowers from the plants. It was clear the garden was a total surprise to Lily."

"Sam, Janie, and I found Red asleep, right next to the plants," Nell said. "The dots practically connected themselves. No one questioned what caused his wobbly demeanor."

"But volumes were being spoken in the looks that passed between Lily and Seltzer. You could almost see sparks flying across the room," Sam said. He began spreading wedges of pita bread with Brie.

"But the thing that rang bells and shouted out at us was what was really going on up there. Justin Dorsey's frequent travels to the roof weren't just to smoke cigarettes—he was going up there to fill his orders for Tyler Gibson and friends," Izzy said. "Martin Seltzer was his supplier."

Nell frowned. "Well, not exactly. I think that's where Justin got it, but I doubt if Martin gave it to him. He disliked Justin intensely and was adamant that he leave the clinic, be fired, disappear. The force of his dislike surprised me at the time. It somehow didn't seem merited by his claims that Justin was lazy and snooped around too much. But this sheds light on it. The reason he was desperate to get rid of Justin was that he was stealing from him."

"That makes sense, Aunt Nell. Dr. Seltzer knew what Justin was doing, but he couldn't tell Lily because he didn't want her to know about the garden. So instead he tried to get Justin fired for other reasons."

"But kindhearted Lily kept giving him more chances, so he kept taking more pot," Cass said.

"So . . . ," Cass said, nibbling on a cornichon. "So what recourse did Dr. Seltzer have left?"

Ben leaned forward, his elbows on his knees, trying to think through the situation objectively. "Moving too quickly can be dangerous. Think about it. Did Martin say the garden was his? If not, how do you know that it is? Maybe he's covering for someone else who works there? It could even be Janie who planted it or someone who works in the family practice with Doc Hamilton in the family clinic? I was in for a checkup recently and he has a new crew of nurses and assistants, even a medical student doing a summer internship." He poured several martinis and passed them around. "Jumping to conclusions can be dangerous."

They fell into silence, replaying the scene in their minds as they considered Ben's comment. Somehow, being there at the clinic, the deduction had been obvious. But when Ben questioned it objectively in the calmness of their home—none of them had an answer.

And then Sam shook his head. "No, it had to have been Martin's. I'm sure of it. Body language, if nothing else. It was obvious Lily didn't know about the plants and didn't recognize the symptoms Red had. Martin did. As soon as he heard where Red had been, he knew immediately what had happened."

Nell and Izzy agreed.

"Here's something else," Nell said, thinking back over recent conversations with Martin. "Gus McClucken told me what a good gardener Martin was, only buying the best materials. At the time I was curious about where his garden was. He isn't over at the community garden, and there isn't enough yard around the clinic for a garden—most of what was the yard is now a parking lot." She thought back over the conversation they'd had, standing there with Henrietta O'Neal. "He used *organic* fertilizer," Gus said.

"And that's what Tyler said." Cass sat forward, excited now. "He said Justin said the stuff was *organic*."

"Okay," Ben said. "If you're right, quiet Martin Seltzer was growing cannabis on the roof of the clinic." He rubbed three fingers against his cheek the way he did when trying to figure something out. He topped off Sam's martini, then poured Izzy some lemonade.

"Martin Seltzer," Nell murmured.

"He hated Justin," Izzy said.

But no one wanted to push it to the next step, although it was on everyone's mind.

"Okay, I'll ask it," Cass said. "Did Martin Seltzer kill Justin? Was that the only way he could keep him from stealing—and maybe revealing—his little hobby?"

Izzy looked down at Red. Then she looked around at the circle of faces. "But he was so good with Red," she said. "He likes him."

No one answered.

Maybe he liked dogs—and not much else.

"I think we need to leave our emotions out of the equation," Nell said. "Except for Henrietta O'Neal—and maybe Gus McClucken—Martin didn't seem to have many friends here. But we can't jump to conclusions. I've often found Martin intimidating, but I think it's simply that he's not talkative. Maybe shyness, I don't know. I saw a hint of humor in him the other day. Also, it's difficult to imagine that anyone in Lily's clinic would be guilty of something so awful."

"It's difficult to think anyone in Sea Harbor is capable of doing anything so awful," Cass said. "That's why we keep walking into walls. We don't want this bad guy to be anyone we know."

Ben took a deep breath. When he started to talk, it was with the same clear, cogent tone he used to help boards formulate new mission statements or business plans. Clear, calm, precise. "We need to call Jerry Thompson in on this," he said. "He needs to know about the garden, the relationships, the animosity between the two men. He may know some of that from interviews he's done with Justin's coworkers. But I doubt if he knows about the garden on the roof. It's tied so closely to Justin, all of it. It may be the break he's been waiting for."

Of course it was, but the idea of casting suspicion on Lily's wonderful clinic was an ugly thought.

"Any hypotheses about how Horace Stevenson fits into this?" Cass asked.

"I always thought Horace was a bit removed from Sea Harbor, but more and more I'm realizing that a lot of people knew him. Lots of people stopped to talk to him—"

"He guarded that beach religiously," Cass said. "It isn't too far a jump to imagine that Horace heard things going on in Paley's Cove, things that might incriminate whoever killed Justin."

The sudden ringing of the doorbell startled them into quiet.

Nell got up quickly, nearly stumbling over Red on her way to the door. Talk of murder seemed to sharpen nerves, even in the calm peace of the Endicott family room.

Lily Virgilio stood on the step, her hair slightly mussed. Her face was pale.

"It's been a rough day, Lily," Nell said, giving her a slight hug and ushering her inside.

Lily attempted a response but settled for a nod and a small smile. She walked into the family room, apologizing for the interruption as she looked around at the sea of faces. "But I'm glad you're all here."

Her eyes sought out Izzy and Sam. "Janie overheard you say you were coming here—"

It was then that she spotted Red at Izzy's feet and quickly knelt down beside him, rubbing his head.

"How is he?"

"Fine." Izzy smiled. "He's really fine. Come sit, Dr. Lily."

"Lily, please call me Lily," she said. She looked around the room and tried to muster a smile. "Although I imagine there are more colorful names you might want to call me today."

"Oh, nonsense," Nell said, and patted the cushion next to her. "Sit with us."

Ben put a drink in her hand. "First, relax. Then we'll call names," he said with a smile.

Lily's responding smile was short-lived. "I'm not sure how to start, but there are a few things I need to say. You all deserve an explanation."

"Well, it was definitely an interesting afternoon," Nell said, trying to lighten the discussion. "And—at least in the case of Red—all's well that end's well."

"Yes," Lily said. "And if this kind of scene was destined to play out at the clinic, I'm fortunate it was with people like you—understanding and generous people—and I hope that what I'm going to say will . . . will make some kind of sense to you."

She glanced down at Red, held his eyes briefly, then went on, as if the golden retriever had given her the push she needed. "I've burst in like this for a few reasons. I think I counted three on the drive over, though you never know—by the time I'm through that number may have grown." A quick smile came and went.

"First, I owe you a profound apology for what happened to Red." She looked at Izzy. "Having your dog get sick in your own doctor's office is not something one expects to happen, nor should it."

She took a sip of her drink, then set the glass back on the table and continued. "Second, I want to promise you that this won't happen again. Ever. To anyone. It will be taken care of." Her voice dropped and she looked again at Red.

There seemed to be more of a message than the words detailed. *It will be taken care of.* The garden will be dug up? Or a lock put on the door. Or no dogs allowed in the clinic? Or . . . Dr. Seltzer will be fired?

But Lily didn't elaborate.

She was quiet for so long that Nell wondered if she had said what she came to say. That was it. It was only two things, but the poor woman looked spent, as if she wanted nothing more than for the day to end.

Just as Nell was about to suggest more crackers and cheese, Lily began again.

"There's one more thing. This last thing . . . it's a favor, really. An enormous favor. And I would never be so presumptuous to ask it if it weren't so important to me—and if I didn't consider you friends."

They looked at her with concern and warmth—and curiosity.

Lily was a fine person, one they respected and liked. Of course they'd help her in any way they could.

Until she asked.

"I'm asking you to keep what happened this afternoon quiet. To not speak of it to anyone, including the police."

The only sound in the room was the ticking of Ben's parents' grandfather clock in the front hallway, its echo suddenly louder than a church bell.

Ben cleared his throat, looked down at his hands thoughtfully, measuring his words. Finally he spoke. "I wasn't there today, Lily, so I'm probably not among those you're really here to speak to, at least not directly. But what was discovered at the clinic today—the garden on your roof, the marijuana plants—is important. You have to know that the police will need to know about the garden. Not because Red indulged himself. And not because it's there, above your clinic. That wouldn't be any of our business under normal circumstances.

"But these aren't normal circumstances. It's more than likely that Justin Dorsey stole from those plants and passed the goods along." He paused, then nailed down the lid of the coffin, causing all of them to wince. "And then Justin Dorsey was murdered."

Lily didn't wince. She was quiet, letting Ben finish. Only her face, as white as the Brie rind on the cheese plate, reflected her agony.

"This may be an important piece of a murder investigation. The police have to know."

Lily took a deep breath, then said, "I understand everything you've said, Ben. But there are other factors. Things that convince me with the utmost certainty that the garden, whatever Justin took from it or didn't take from it, has nothing, absolutely nothing to do with his murder. Things aren't always the way they seem."

"That's certainly true enough," Nell said. "But what if Ben's right, Lily? Think about it. Martin Seltzer knew what was going on in your clinic. He knew Justin was taking those plants and he was angry about it. He tried to get you to fire Justin. He hated him. He wanted him gone. He's told a dozen people that. You . . . you could be in danger."

For a minute they thought Lily was going to fold up into herself right there on the comfortable slipcovered couch. But instead, she straightened up, took a deep breath, and looked around the table, meeting their eyes.

"No," she said. "I'm not in any danger. And yes, he didn't like Justin, that's absolutely true. I didn't fully realize why until today because I didn't know about the garden. But the one thing I do know is that I am not in any danger and he didn't have anything to do with Justin's murder. Nothing. I promise you that. And that's why you can't tell the police about this. They will think exactly what you are thinking right now. That Martin Seltzer was involved in a murder. They will investigate him and make his life miserable. And he's already had enough of that."

"Lily, how can you be sure Martin didn't have anything to do with it?" It was Sam, his voice gentle. Reasonable. Sincere.

Lily looked him in the eye. Her words came from deep in her throat and were tinged with pain, but spoken with solid, unbreakable assurance.

"Because he's my father," she said.

Chapter 27

$\mathcal{S}$omeone's cell phone, hidden in a purse or pocket, rang, but it went unanswered, its sound intrusive in the quiet room. A couple more followed at uneven intervals, then silence.

Ben refilled glasses and sat back in his chair. Lily took the tissue Izzy offered her. Sam's arm looped around Izzy's shoulder, as if to assure her that things would be okay. This, too, would pass.

Finally Lily took a deep breath and thanked them all for not dismissing her completely, at least not yet.

"Of course not, Lily," Nell said. She had busied herself in the kitchen and returned with turkey rolls, a platter of bruschetta, more olives and pickles, warm bread, and cheese. "It's been a long day."

Lily ventured a slight laugh. "And it's about to get longer, I'm afraid. My story isn't a short one. We may well need nourishment."

Izzy laughed, and she and Cass began filling plates for everyone. "We're good listeners," she said. "Especially with Aunt Nell's turkey rolls in our mouths."

Lily took a sip of water and started in. "Martin Seltzer was an anesthesiologist for many years in a small town in western Massachusetts. He also taught at the local college. He was brilliant—in all aspects of medicine, not just anesthesia. My mother used to tease him that he specialized in that because it gave him the most time to study all the other areas. He loved the research, the genetics, the multitude of tests available to patients. He was an excellent doctor—until my mother died. That's when he started drinking.

"As it progressed, my sister and I worried and fretted and did everything we could to get him to stop. I was a doctor; I knew how dangerous it was. But nothing seemed to work, and then he began going to work while drinking. Like some alcoholics, he was very good at hiding it. His associates didn't even know. He seemed steady and in control.

"But my sister and I were afraid something terrible would happen, that he'd kill someone on the operating table. Finally, when he refused to admit he had a problem or to get help, we were left with only one recourse: to report him to the medical board. It was awful, the most difficult thing I've ever done in my life. He wouldn't comply with the program the board put in place for him and he lost his license, along with a part of his soul and lots of friends. Everyone in the town knew about it—it even made some larger newspapers. It was a horrible time for all of us— for several years he didn't speak to my sister or me. But finally we worked through it and he got the help he needed. By the time I got divorced and moved here, he was having some health problems, so I invited him to come with me. I convinced him I needed his help in setting up the clinic, though mostly my sister and I wanted him near family. He agreed to come on one condition—that I didn't reveal our relationship. He was still ashamed of everything that had happened, and somehow he thought if people knew—if someone here, somehow, had heard and remembered the story—it would reflect poorly on me. I didn't agree, but sometimes you give in, you know?" She brushed her hair back from her cheek. Her eyes damp. "With my father I've always had to pick my battles carefully."

"So he doesn't really work in the clinic?" Izzy said. "I thought . . . I remember Janie telling me once that if there was anything I didn't understand, Dr. Seltzer was available to talk to. But I guess I never asked her what she meant. You were always so wonderful about explaining everything yourself."

"And you, Izzy, are one of those patients who practically ends up with an honorary M.D., reading books, learning everything you can about your pregnancy, but not everyone is like that. And some patients need to have more testing than you required, or simply want it for their own peace of mind.

"My father doesn't work in the clinic as a practicing physician. But he would lose his mind doing nothing. So he spends a lot of time talking to patients, answering questions, explaining all the tests and lab work. He loves all of that—it's like he's back in the classroom again. And the patients who talk to him are impressed and appreciative—he's actually a very good listener, kind of like a priest in the confessional sometimes." She smiled with a daughter's pride, and shades of pink made their way to her cheeks. "He's truly brilliant."

"That explains many things," Nell said softly. Lily's story had touched each of them, but in a way, it almost made the situation for Lily's father worse. Martin Seltzer had suffered through such difficulties in his life. How do such experiences affect a man's psyche, his mind? His emotional control?

"Justin truly came in and disrupted that life," Izzy said.

"Yes . . . Justin," Lily said, her tone expressing what she wouldn't say out loud—that she regretted the day she let Janie talk her into hiring him.

"Justin and my father's relationship was everything you said it was. My father didn't like him. He thought he was no good. But he never told me about the garden, so I didn't realize the depth of his bad feelings toward Justin and that they were born of Justin's intrusion into a part of my father's private life. Then pillaging it as he did. If I had known, of course, I would have let Justin go immediately. But my father didn't want me to know about the garden. He thought it would be one more disappointment, one more thing he had done that might reflect poorly on me." She shook her head. A soft auburn wave fell across her cheek and she pushed it back absently, her thoughts moving to other events, other moments. "So many misunderstandings, so many heartaches . . . ," she murmured, more to herself than the group around her.

"Were you . . . were you surprised that your father had planted a garden up there?" Izzy asked.

Lily smiled at her. "You're being kind, Izzy. You mean, why did he plant pot on the roof of our clinic? A fair question—but there's an easy answer, though not a happy one." She took a drink and then leaned back into the cushions for the first time since she had sat down. "My father has cancer. It's under control right now, but painful at times. He has an oncologist in Boston, but Dr. Hamilton is caring for him here—he and I share a clinic dispensary, as you probably know, and he prescribed morphine for the pain. But my father hated the way it made him feel—dizzy and disoriented. He couldn't be completely present to the patients seeking his advice and his knowledge. So he experimented with the cannabis without telling me. It has helped ease the pain, he told me, and it allows him to be more active."

"No wonder he was so upset with Justin," Sam said. "He was depleting the supply, probably having no idea of your father's need."

"I suppose that was a part of it. But I think my father's anger went beyond the fact that Justin was stealing it from him. After you left today, he told me that when he found out Justin was selling it, he was livid. He could hardly contain himself. He had gotten to the point that he was going to tell me all about it, about the garden, everything, so we could confront Justin and do whatever had to be done."

"But someone murdered Justin before you had a chance," Cass said.

"Yes." She looked at them, her eyes filling. "But it wasn't my father. He didn't kill him."

Ben refilled glasses again and Nell got up and switched on the low lights near the fireplace. Outside, the sky was growing dark.

Nell looked at Lily, feeling a rush of compassion for the anguished doctor. "Lily, you know the police won't stop looking for the person from whom Justin got the plants. They think that it's a key to his murder, and maybe Horace Stevenson's, too. A critical missing piece to this awful puzzle."

"Yes, I know that. But my hope is that as they search for that person, they'll find the real murderer and never have to approach my father. They can't possibly know about the garden, unless . . ." Her words dropped off, but those that went unspoken roared in the quiet room.

Unless someone sitting in this room tells them.

They never had to answer Lily's question, to affirm or negate her request, though they would talk about it later.

What would they have done? The police needed to know about this. It would be their duty, their responsibility, to report it. But Lily was their friend, Izzy's doctor, and a kind and lovely woman who spoke from her heart.

But as much as each one of them wanted to believe her, they knew that the strength of a daughter's love could melt cold, steely facts into something else in the blink of an eye.

What would they have said if they'd had to answer her question?

But the Endicotts' phone rang soon after Lily pleaded for their silence, during the time they were each assembling their own thoughts, wondering how to respond.

It was Janie Levin on the phone, asking for Lily. She had tried calling cell phones—Lily's and Izzy's and Nell's, the only numbers she had on her own phone—but when no one answered, Tommy suggested she call the landline number, and he had given it to her. She said she had foolishly forgotten that some people still use landlines—not just offices and shops . . . and police stations.

Nell listened to Janie's rush of words—a nervous flow. Then she put Lily on the phone.

Lily mostly listened, as Nell had done, but the words that Lily heard were ones that once again robbed the doctor of all the color that had slowly made its way back into her cheeks.

Tears stung her eyes. She blinked them away before turning back to the others.

"My rather brazen request is no longer of consequence," she said. "My father called the police himself. They're at the clinic now."

Sam and Ben both drove back to the clinic with Lily, brushing aside her protests.

"I was there, Lily," Sam said. "I might be able to help clarify what happened today." And then he reminded her that Ben was a good friend of Jerry Thompson and it never hurt to have Ben Endicott in your back pocket, which drew a smile from the doctor.

By the time the men returned, Cass had left to join Danny on Harbor Road for dinner, and Izzy was nearly asleep, curled up as best she could on the couch. She awoke with a start when the two men walked in.

"As Lily expected, Martin Seltzer will now be closely investigated," Ben said. "He's definitely a suspect. Jerry assured Lily he would go easy on her dad, as easy as he could. The fact that he called the police, knowing it would put him in the spotlight, will be in his favor."

Sam added, "The garden was the least of their concerns. For now, anyway, they won't bring any charges against him for growing the cannabis. Jerry's wife died of cancer. He's sensitive to that part of the story—"

"But it would certainly be a preferable charge to that of murder," Izzy said.

The thought was sobering. *Far preferable.* Nell had thrown together a goat cheese pizza and brewed a pot of coffee, and the four of them moved out to the deck and the blanketing comfort of a velvet sky.

"It's complicated, for sure," Ben said. "In the meantime the guys took lots of photos, and recorded in detail Justin's days of employment, times he was spotted going back and forth from the rooftop. It was hard on Janie, and after she answered lots of questions, Jerry excused her and Lily sent her home with Tommy."

"What a spot for Tommy to be in, being on the force—and clearly in love with Janie, and right smack in the middle of this mess," Izzy said. She caught a strand of melted cheese on her finger and licked it off.

"Janie's tough, just like you," Sam said, wrapping one arm around her. "Jerry doesn't have Tommy working on this case, although I think for Janie's sake he'd move a granite boulder to find the murderer and put this all behind them. It can't be easy on a relationship."

"How did Martin handle everything?"

"It was difficult," Ben said.

Sam agreed. "The man looked wiped, but he was determined not to have Lily hide his sins, as he put it. There was real affection between the two of them, each trying to protect the other. I got the feeling it had been a long time since that had been expressed."

"I noticed that, too," Ben said. "As for Justin, Martin made it clear he had nothing to do with his murder, though they would find a handful of people in town who had heard him say he'd like to have done the deed."

"That's not good," Nell said.

"No," Ben agreed. "Not at all. Martin had motive, opportunity. And, as Jerry told me when we left, he also had 'know-how.' He was an anesthesiologist—he'd have no trouble manipulating a diving tank regulator."

"So the police will go after him," Izzy said, feeling suddenly sad.

"What an awful thing for Lily," Nell said, reading her thoughts.

"Knowing all this, it's not hard to understand why she came over here. She was desperate that it wouldn't come to this," Izzy said.

Ben agreed, finishing off his piece of pizza. He got up and returned with the coffeepot and a plate of oatmeal cookies. "Yeah. It's hard. I don't know what to think."

"Some residents may hope it's Martin. Everyone loves Lily, but may not be so fond of him," Nell said.

"Except for Henrietta," Izzy said. "I wonder . . ."

"What?" Sam said.

"Henrietta doesn't take things lying down. If she's a friend of Martin's, he couldn't have a better person having his back. I wonder what she will say about this."

It would take them a little less than twenty-four hours to find out.

Chapter 28

Henrietta stood in the shadows at the top step to the knitting room, softly tapping her cane in perfect four/four time. Her white head swiveled side to side as she took stock of the room a few steps below.

Behind her, Mae Anderson bustled about, preparing to close the shop, one eye on the back of the formidable five-foot-tall woman who had bustled into the shop minutes before with fire in her eyes.

Unaware of being watched, Nell stood at the table, uncovering a pan of baked potatoes. Steam curled up in front of her face. Nearby, Izzy turned up the vocals of Marvin Gaye singing about mountains.

Birdie was seated in her favorite chair near the fireplace, talking to Cass. Her small arthritic fingers moved rapidly, stitch after stitch, bringing shape to the remaining arm in baby Perry's romper.

Only sweet Purl, curled up on Cass' lap, was watching Henrietta watch them.

Finally Henrietta increased her taps, now loud and insistent, drawing everyone's attention away from their business and to herself. Before anyone had a chance to say hello, she moved down the steps and over to Nell's side.

"Baked potatoes." She frowned, peering into the pan. "Word on the street is that there is a gourmet spread in this room every Thursday night. But baked potatoes?"

"Twice baked," Nell said. "And stuffed with chunks of fresh

crab in an amazing, if I do say so myself, cheesy wine sauce. We have extra. Try one. It may surprise you."

"Aren't the Irish supposed to like potatoes?" Izzy asked.

"No," Henrietta said, leaning her cane against the bookcase and eyeing the potatoes again, "but I will try anything once, dearie. And I do enjoy fresh crab."

In minutes they were seated around the table, plates of crispy-skin stuffed potatoes and Caesar salad in front of them. Birdie had poured wine and water, and everyone was glancing at Henrietta expectantly as they dug their forks into the creamy potatoes. Why was she here?

"I'm barging in, now, aren't I?"

"Yes," Cass said. "But you've been known to do worse, Henrietta. And you are always fun to have around. But what's up? Why are you here?"

Henrietta laughed, a booming sound that went straight up to the ceiling. "And wouldn't you know the frankness would come from a Halloran? We Irish understand each other." She winked at Cass and wiped a dribble of sour cream from her ample chin. Then she put down her fork and took a sip of wine, and her round face grew serious.

"It's this ridiculous notion that Martin Seltzer could have hurt anyone, much less a young pip-squeak like Justin Dorsey or an old fogey like Horace. Of course he didn't. It's ridiculous, so that's why I'm here, though I suspect you had anticipated as much. What are we going to do about it?" White eyebrows shot up above lively blue eyes.

Nell wiped her hands on a napkin. Somehow knitting seemed more satisfying right now than eating. She took the baby blanket from her bag and settled it across her lap. The sections were coming together now, tiny seed stitches bordering the soft yellow cables.

Henrietta leaned over and looked at the yarn. "Lovely," she said.

"What makes you so sure Martin didn't have anything to do with either of those events?" Birdie asked. "He had every reason in the world to want Justin out of the way."

"Of course he did. The little upstart was stealing from him. Him and some other people, mind you. But I won't go into that. But to kill for that?" She wiped her hands and leaned over to touch the silky angora blend Birdie was knitting into a hat to match the baby's romper. "Angora. Now, isn't that the loveliest thing?" She touched the working ball of yarn, her expression as soft as the yarn.

"He had motive, incentive, capability," Cass said. "And what was his alibi?"

"Alibi, schmalibi," Henrietta said, dismissing the thought with a wave of her hand. "No one has much of an alibi for murders that take place in the dead of night. He was sleeping. Just like all those other people the police have been questioning." She looked over at Birdie's ball of yarn again. "They're fuzzy alibis, all of them, just like that angora yarn of yours, Birdie. Angora alibis, they are, the whole boatload of them. You can see right through them. Give any one of them a strong tug and they'll snap apart. Unless Martin was by chance off for the night with some floozy and can get her to stand up for him. But he's not that kind of man, now, is he?"

She sat back, satisfied with her speech. Short chubby arms crossed over her chest.

Nell leaned forward, her fingers working on another section of seed stitches. "I have a question, Henrietta, which may or not be relevant. But I saw you go up to Martin at the Fractured Fish concert Saturday night, and you all but swatted him. It seemed to me he'd be the last person you wanted to stand by. You seemed very angry, as if Martin had done something awful. And now you're saying that's not possible."

"Well, he had done something . . . and he hadn't. But neither the *had* nor the *hadn't* equaled murder. I had smelled it on him that night—the pot. Once you understand that scent, it stays with you. And I was fiery mad. He was going to get that lovely Lily Virgilio into trouble, smoking pot in her clinic. So I gave him hell and he just stood there and took it. Then he came around to me later and told me privately what was up with it, that he was fighting the pain of his cancer, and I understood. In fact, I told him to move his little garden to my house if it would be safer. He was considering it."

Nell held back a smile. Henrietta's familiarity with the product might well have come from a rather wild youth.

"Esther Gibson called me first thing today and told me that the police had Martin in the station all morning long. *All morning*, can you imagine? The poor man doesn't eat as it is, and there he sat, being pummeled with questions." She took a drink of wine, but it was clear she wasn't finished, so the others busied themselves finishing up and knitting, waiting.

She looked at Nell. "I know our dear Ben has some influence with the chief of police, whom I've always supported, by the way, even though his political leanings are sometimes askew."

"They're friends, Henrietta, but he doesn't have any influence on him. Besides, Jerry isn't that kind of person—nor is Ben. Jerry is investigating this as best he can. If Martin is innocent, he will find that out."

"And in the meantime the poor man will waste away to nothing. But I understand about Ben not interfering, of course I do. I'm not suggesting anything like that. I'd never risk my relationship with that dear husband of yours by asking him to compromise himself. So I'll ask the rest of you instead."

Cass laughed out loud.

Henrietta went on as if she hadn't heard. "You're right that Jerry Thompson will eventually find Martin innocent because he is, but in the meantime we're all in this miserable state and it simply has to end." She pointed at Izzy. "Just look at you, Izzy, about to give birth to a darlin' baby boy—and what with Sea Harbor in this sorry state. It's not right, not healthy."

"We all agree with you," Birdie said, working a row of mint green yarn into the tiny hat. She squinted through her glasses as she counted her stitches. "At least about the fact that this needs to be settled soon. As for the sex of Izzy's baby, unless you have access to some secret source unavailable to us, we don't know that it's a boy.

And as for Martin Seltzer, I want to believe he is innocent. But I think we need more information before that happens."

"Then we shall get it." Henrietta pushed herself from her chair and worked her way across the room toward her cane, talking loudly as she went. "We'll put our heads together and we'll find out who did this." She stood at the bottom of the steps, about to take her leave, puffed up, like Patton leaving his troops. "You know what they say," she said. "It takes a village to do whatever. And we'll do it soon." And then she was gone, tapping her way toward the front door, where Mae patiently waited for her to leave, then locked the door behind her.

Cass held out her glass. "Birdie, after that, I need another splash of your pinot."

Izzy was already wiping off the coffee table to make room for yarn and needles and scissors.

She sat back down and pulled out the hooded sweater she was working on. With five pair of booties wrapped in tissue in the baby's room, she needed diversion—and a slouchy sweater would be the perfect thing to wear while rocking baby Perry on a breezy fall day. "Everything in me wants to agree with Henrietta and Dr. Lily about Martin Seltzer," she said. "But the odds are sure stacked up against him. Whether it's instinct or emotion—or maybe all the little things that don't add up—I don't know, but nothing in me says he's our guy. Janie said he was great with patients, so understanding. Franklin Danvers even spent time with him, she said, and he listened like a schoolkid, even taking notes."

"That's an interesting mental image, isn't it?" Birdie said, smiling. "What about Tamara?"

"Oh, she was another one of his fans. He even stayed late one night, just because Tamara needed to talk."

"We were so sure that finding Justin's supplier would be the beginning of the end. Now we've found his source—and he wasn't that at all, at least not in the official sense of the word," Birdie said. "But I still think we're moving ahead, not totally losing ground."

"It seems we keep making our way back to the clinic. . . ." It was Izzy speaking, her face pulled together in a serious thought. "But one thing Lily said last night has been troubling me. Something I'm sure the police have latched on to. She said her father had a prescription for morphine."

Nell finished her row of seed stitches and ran her hand over the soft sunlit yarn, the small knots defining the blanket's edge. "Yes. And morphine killed Horace," she said, her voice as soft as the blanket. More dots . . . more connections.

Birdie set her knitting needles down, not liking the direction in which Izzy's astute reminder was taking them. "So Martin Seltzer had access to the drug that killed Horace; that doesn't mean he used it."

Izzy looked over at Nell. "Remember that day Janie interrupted my appointment with Lily, telling her something was missing? Janie told me later it was a mistake, that it was a prescription Lily had for Dr. Seltzer and she had forgotten to sign it out. For a minute, Janie said, she and Lily both thought it was something Justin had messed up, but thank heavens, it wasn't. It created tension in the clinic, though."

Nell remembered.

"And then Janie mentioned medicine missing *again*—this time a few days after Justin was killed. The second time it was for real. Justin clearly was off the hook. I don't know if it was resolved the second time. Janie would know."

They looked up at the ceiling. Janie was home. They had heard the footsteps on the staircase earlier. Izzy reached for her cell phone and gave her a call.

Janie joined them in minutes, her sweats and shirt indicating she was in for the night. "I needed company tonight. Tommy's working, so thank you. I was waiting for Purl to come up and join me."

Birdie patted the chair next to her, and Janie curled up in it, accepting the glass of wine Izzy offered and making room for the calico cat that landed on her lap. She laid out her own knitting project, a soft cream-colored blanket with tiny alphabet blocks along the edge. Purl eyed the ball of yarn with great yearning—and minor restraint. Janie tsked him and removed his paw from the soft yarn.

Izzy came over and plopped a box down near the coffee table. "This isn't why we invited you down, Janie, but I almost forgot about this. Mrs. Bridge left it—it's what was left in Justin's room. I keep forgetting to give it to you. She said it was just old clothes, but she thought you should be the one to get rid of it. Do you want me to do it?"

Janie stared at the box. She started to say yes, then changed her mind and pulled open the flap. "Maybe Father Northcutt's clothing drive?" she said, pulling out an old shirt and some socks.

Izzy looked into the box. A glint of silver caught her eye and she pulled out a leather belt with a large silver buckle.

Janie looked at it. "That's nice. I don't think I ever saw Justin wear it—"

Izzy ran her fingers over the buckle. "That's probably because it wasn't his." She held it up and read the initials. TAG.

Cass laughed. "It's Tyler Gibson's. Has to be. His middle name is Arthur and the kids used to tease him and call him Tag."

Nell took the belt and looked at it. "It looks like Tyler," she said.

"Do you suppose Justin stole that, too?" Janie said.

"It's hard to steal a belt off someone, Janie," Nell said. She slipped it into her purse. "But I'll see that Tyler gets it back. Maybe they were at the beach or something and he left it behind. Justin was probably going to return it."

They all nodded, as if they believed Nell's explanation. But however the belt had ended up in Justin's belongings, Tyler would now get it back. And Nell, perhaps, would get another bit of helpful information, whatever that might be.

"And I'll take care of the rest of this stuff," Izzy said, pushing the box aside.

"That reminds me of something," Nell said. "Janie, do you remember that fanny pack Justin sometimes wore?"

"Sure. I got it at a garage sale. One dollar."

"Do you know where it is?"

Janie shook her head. "I know he had it that Saturday when he
left here. Oh, and we both saw him with it that night at the Edge. It
wasn't very attractive but he seemed attached to it."

"Well, if you see it, would you let me know?"

Janie agreed and pulled out her knitting. "This is my therapy,"
she said. "But then, you all understand that."

"We do. It's therapy and sometimes helps us put things into perspective," Nell said. "It's like thinking through a knitting pattern,
looking at it from one side, then the other, imagining what it will
look like in the end."

"So you do that with life."

"And, unfortunately, death," Birdie said. "We're trying to figure
all this out. You have certainly been thrown into the middle of everything once again. These last couple of days must have been difficult."

"It's poor Dr. Seltzer I feel sorry for," Janie said. "I don't know
him very well—and I sure didn't know he was Dr. Lily's dad—but
this is all scary. Tommy says it will work out. But how can it? Everything points to him. He certainly made it known how he felt about
Justin. And now we know he had good reasons for his feelings."

"Do you think he killed him?" Birdie asked gently.

"No." Her response was quick, the kind that comes from the
heart and not always the mind. "I love Dr. Lily, I guess that's why.
But I can't imagine . . . I can't let myself imagine he did it. He has
this other side, you know. He didn't talk much to me, but some of
our patients really liked him. He was a great teacher and loved medicine, so he'd sit and answer questions about all the different tests
and blood work results. Some of them confided in him about worries
and things. He was like a priest or something. He could talk medicine all day long. It sounds crazy, I know, because he wasn't the best

conversationalist outside of work. But give him a patient with a question or problem and he would talk for hours. It pleased Dr. Lily so much, and I didn't know why. But now I do."

"You told us the other night that things had been tense at the clinic," Izzy said. "I used to think of the clinic as my little island of repose. I'd walk through those doors and forget everything about my real life. All of you were comforting and you cared only about me and my baby. But it changed. . . ."

Janie was nodding across from her. "The last couple weeks, things were strained, I know. Part of it for me was Justin. And maybe you felt that. Now we know there was more going on—the garden, Justin helping himself. But there was more, I think. I can't put my finger on it—"

"You mentioned missing medications," Nell said.

"Yeah, there was that—just a week ago. It was Friday, I remember, because we had a lot of patients scheduled, both for Dr. Lily and people who wanted to talk to Dr. Seltzer. I hadn't slept the night before and was so tired. Then that—that drug disappeared."

"Do you think Martin took it?" Nell asked

Janie looked up, surprised at the question. "Oh, no. It was taken from his office. Dr. Lily had me pick it up from the dispensary and put it on his desk that morning. It was *his* medicine, even though we know now he didn't often take it. But it disappeared from his desk. He noticed it that afternoon."

"Did you ever find it?" Birdie asked.

"No. We searched everywhere. It was definitely gone."

"What medicine was it?" Cass asked.

"Morphine."

"So the morphine that *may* have been used to kill Horace *may* have come from Martin Seltzer's office," Nell said after Purl and Janie had gone back upstairs.

"Assuming what Martin said was true and he wasn't just covering his own tracks," Birdie said.

"But why would he even need to do that? Lily thought he was using the morphine for himself—so he could have used it on Horace and no one would have known the difference. He had it legitimately. Reporting it was a responsible thing to do. You don't want morphine disappearing out the clinic door without knowing who has it."

"That's right! Cass, you're so smart," Izzy said.

"And beautiful," Cass said.

Birdie laughed. "All right, then, who would have had access to Martin's office?" Her needles worked along the rim of the baby hat. "Clinic staff, cleaning staff, patients, delivery people?"

"It's really a busy place," Izzy said. "And Janie said it was especially busy that Friday. Sometimes Dr. Lily's patients bring family members or friends, too—like Nell and Sam came with me."

"And Red," Nell said.

Izzy laughed. "Yes. And Red. And this summer Lily has some medical students coming in a couple times a week. There's a parade of folks in and out. I often schedule late appointments so I can avoid the frantic times, but I know from Janie how crazy it gets."

"So we know someone in that parade left the office that day with morphine."

"Janie said it was the Friday after Justin died," Cass said.

Izzy glanced at a calendar on the wall. It was filled with happy events—knitting classes, knitting nights, special yarn studio events. But the Friday after Justin was murdered was blank. Nothing going on at the yarn shop that day.

It was Friday—dinner on the Endicott deck.

And the night that Janie came by with Birdie's stolen necklace.

The night that Horace Stevenson was killed.

Chapter 29

Izzy offered to help Sam with the equipment he needed to take to the Danvers place for the photo shoot. Nell offered to go along, too. Izzy shouldn't be carrying anything too heavy, she said.

"Neither of you fools me for one New York second. You want to see what's behind that stone wall." Sam idled the car as the heavy iron gate to the Danvers estate slowly swung open.

Franklin Danvers was waiting in the drive, dressed in a three-piece suit and an elegant silk tie. His surprise at Sam's crew was evident on his face, but he said little, ushering them into the home. He was polite but unsmiling, serious and businesslike, and lacking the more relaxed personality they'd seen recently. He seemed preoccupied.

Tamara sat on a chair in the entryway and stood when they walked in. She wore tight black slacks and a silk flowered top that billowed out when she walked, outlining the sleek body beneath. She smiled and greeted them warmly. "Sam, you're kind to do this. It will mean a lot to all the Danverses, as well as to the town. This is a magnificent manor."

Beside her, Franklin simply nodded and ushered them all into a walnut-paneled library, where he handed Sam a map of the house and several documents on the art and furniture. He had highlighted the rooms and objects appropriate for photographing. Izzy took the papers and began leafing through them as Sam took out one of his cameras and snapped a few shots for practice.

"Beautiful library," he said to Franklin, his eye coveting the plethora of collections. On one wall they ranged from the classics to finance to management. Another was filled with history books, and there was a section on hunting, scuba diving, sailing, and deep-sea fishing manuals. A third wall held tools of the trade—a magnificent mounted bow and arrow, a glass case of guns and fishing knives, and a magnificent mounted flounder on a polished teak board. "I suspect you're a man who rarely gets bored."

"No. Not usually, although I have little time for most of these things now. Borrow any books you want," Franklin said. He looked over at one shelf, frowned, then walked over to a shelf of scuba diving books and pushed the books closer to fill an empty space.

Franklin Danvers was a perfectionist. Nell smiled, wondering what he'd think of Ben's library—every shelf filled with books of different shape, size, and subject matter. Some piled on top of each other.

Franklin led them to the back of the house first, then through leaded glass doors, out to a terrace that seemed to sweep around the entire back and sides of the house. A manicured lawn separated it from wide flagstone steps leading down to the beach. Several other homes, smaller in size but elegant in appearance, were visible off to the sides, discreetly separated from the main house by manicured gardens and walkways.

But it was the view that took their breath away.

"Amazing," Izzy said, her breath catching as she looked out over the water. In one direction, the skyline of Boston was a hazy land-scape, and closer in, the long, winding shoreline, like a serpent's tail—Paley's Cove, the artists' colony, Anya Angelina Park. Nell walked over to the edge and looked to the right, out over the beach where they'd first met Red, where Horace Stevenson's house was tucked off to the side.

Franklin was standing slightly apart from them, looking out over the water and Paley's Cove as if it were the first time he'd seen the view. Nell thought about going over to talk to him, but it was clear he was caught up in his own world—an interruption would be an intrusion. Perhaps he was thinking about business problems or had regretted his idea of a photo shoot of his home, but whatever the reason, the looser, more relaxed Franklin they'd seen in recent days was definitely not present today.

"Maybe we will host a Gatsby-like party when the pictures are framed," Tamara said. "We'll frame your original photographs and display them." She looked around for Franklin, spotted him near the edge of the veranda, and motioned to him. "Come, darling, let's start with a photograph of the two of us, right here on our magnificent terrace."

Franklin frowned, and Nell looked over at Sam. It wasn't exactly the kind of photo Sam was expecting to take, but it probably made sense to have a shot of the people who actually lived in the house. And then they'd move to the dozens of grand rooms that made the Danvers estate a Sea Harbor landmark.

It took Sam a little over two hours to move through the entire house, his practiced eye immediately zeroing in on the best light, the perfect angle, and the things that would be of interest to an audience who cared about history.

When he was finished inside, they walked outside again and down to the beach, where Sam set his camera on another tripod and focused it back up at the house, a giant silhouette against the blue sky.

"What's that?" Izzy asked, pointing to a heavy wooden door that appeared to be built right into the granite foundation at beach level.

"A servants' entrance," Tamara said. "In earlier times the servants used it to come to a corner of the beach reserved for them. Their beach was around those boulders." When they walked around to the other side of the granite wall, Nell recognized the spot immediately, although from this angle it looked different than it did from Paley's Beach.

"It's the dive spot," Sam said, surprised. It had looked different to him, too. He pointed to a small building, once a boathouse, that blended into the rocks. "And there's the dive shack, as we call it."

"But nothing you want photographs of," Franklin Danvers said, surprising them as he rejoined the group. He'd come out the thick wooden door built into the foundation of the house. "The police did their share of that. I may tear it down and build a new one."

"The new paint job was a good idea," Sam said. "It's generous of you to let the dive club use the place."

"I enjoy diving, that's all. It's a good place to teach it."

"Tamara mentioned you might be going on a dive this summer—someplace a little more exotic," Izzy said.

Franklin frowned, then shrugged, as if he had far more important things on his mind than taking Tamara on a trip. He looked as if he was about to say something, then seemed to change his mind and instead said to Sam, "I understand they have finally found the murderer."

Tamara edged closer to her husband. Her eyes were wide. "What?"

"That's not true, Franklin," Sam said. "They have some new leads."

"Dr. Seltzer," Franklin said, ignoring Sam's assessment, his voice cold, strained. "It's shocking to think there was a murderer roaming around in that clinic. Someone we spoke with, got advice from."

"Dr. Martin . . . ?" Tamara said, her words trailing off as she struggled to process the information. "But . . ."

"He hasn't been accused of anything," Nell said. "They've learned a little more about Justin's activities, but they have not arrested Dr. Seltzer."

The news of Martin Seltzer's secret garden and Justin's connection to it hadn't hit the papers yet. Ben said Jerry Thompson was going to try to hold it back—at least until they had more information. But Franklin Danvers was a different breed. Nell suspected there was little in Sea Harbor he didn't know about. She watched his face, cold and accusatory now.

Tamara moved closer to her husband. "Dr. Seltzer . . . killed Justin? That's awful."

Tamara held tight to Franklin's arm, the news of Martin Seltzer clearly a surprise to her.

"As Nell said," Sam repeated, "he hasn't been accused of killing anyone. It would be wrong and destructive for that rumor to get around before the police have done their work."

"What kinds of activities was Justin involved in?" Tamara asked again. She looked frightened.

No one answered and Tamara looked at Franklin, as if he would surely know.

Franklin was silent.

"The news about the clinic might worry you, Tamara, but don't let it," Izzy said. "It's a very safe place to go. There's no reason any of this should affect Dr. Lily's patients. She's a wonderful obstetrician, the very best. You and I are both in good hands."

Izzy's words were met with silence.

Tamara's eyes were still on Franklin, watching him carefully as if waiting for instructions.

"We have little need for that clinic now," Franklin said. His words were clipped, precise.

Tamara frowned. "But, Franklin—"

"No," he said, stopping her words.

They all looked at him.

"Tamara is no longer pregnant," he said. Then turned and walked away.

Chapter 30

Izzy had finally agreed to slow down her exercise routine. Shorter distances and a much slower pace, she promised.

Nell put her to the test by suggesting a Saturday walk to Canary Cove. Birdie and Cass would meet them there for breakfast. And finally some time to talk. It was probably the only time they would have that day. Saturdays were busy for all of them, especially this one, with Izzy's shower scheduled for that evening.

Izzy was all for it. "If I'm going to move this baby and me anywhere today, there needs to be food at the end of it. Aunt Nell, you are wise and all-knowing."

It was an easy pace that kept them both moving—and ended up on the Artist's Palate deck with hot coffee and freshly squeezed orange juice waiting for them.

Birdie had spread the morning paper out on the picnic table. Next to her, Cass drank her second cup of coffee.

"Well? What does it say?"

"Not much. It's vague. It says the police have determined Justin Dorsey was not dealing with a bigger market. It was a homemade supply—a dead end, essentially."

"Ben is afraid that Martin's name will emerge in all this if something else doesn't happen soon." Nell wiped her forehead with a napkin. "The police are combing his background. He still—on paper, anyway—is the most likely suspect. Apparently Tyler has been asked to stick around. Janie was questioned again. But if they could fill in a few more gaps, something concrete that would put him on the beach or Horace's house, Martin would be arrested."

"And yet there's this lurking unknown out there," Nell said. "Justin's 'bigger fish to fry' comment. Justin was getting a large amount of money from someone, and it wasn't Martin Seltzer. We can't ignore that. There is someone else out there." She sat down next to Izzy and with two fingers plucked her damp T-shirt away from her skin, then released it.

"I think it's just too vague for the police to deal with," Birdie said. "Justin was known to brag a bit. They may be thinking that's all it meant."

"But he was getting money from somewhere," Izzy said. She took a drink of orange juice and looked down at what Sam now called their little basketball. The baby was moving from one side to the other, keeping up with the music Merry had pumping out of the restaurant's loudspeakers.

"Morning music," Merry called over to them, then jiggled her way to their table to the Black Eyed Peas singing "Tonight's gonna be a good night."

"Okay, little Perry," Merry said, patting Izzy's tummy, "you'll like this, I promise." She set a tray of beer steins in front of them, filled with fruit, yogurt, and granola. Sprigs of mint were tucked on top.

"Who would have thought you'd be responsible for turning all these artists into health food devotees?" Birdie said. "I am very proud of you, dear."

Merry's laughter was as huge as her voice was when she soloed with the Fractured Fish. Her restaurant, known for its hamburgers, fries, and twenty-seven brands of beer, was primarily a bar and grill with a large deck and bar outside, but Merry had changed that. She credited Ham Brewster for the transformation—the idea came to her as a result of his bad habits. One morning he stopped by, begging for a cup of coffee before opening his gallery. Then he pulled a bag of chips off the rack on the bar. *"Chips,"* Merry had said. *"For breakfast!"* Merry's healthy breakfasts soon followed and the artists now insisted that their bad cholesterol had been lowered to the bottom of the sea, thanks to Merry Jackson.

"So, here's the thing," Merry said, wedging her body in between Birdie and Cass, her palms pressed flat on the table and her eyes scanning the newspaper article. "If Justin was only making pocket change off the college kids down at Paley's Cove, where was he making his big bucks? He left me a fifty-dollar tip for a hamburger a few days before he died. Can you believe that? I called him back, thinking he'd made a mistake, but he just produced that dimpled grin of his and said I deserved it. I told him that was true, but could *he* afford it?" Her large eyes looked around the table. "He was getting money somewhere," she said. "Where?" Then she glanced over her shoulder at a new wave of customers and frowned. "Okay, later," she said, and was off across the deck, her long blond braid bouncing between her shoulder blades.

"That's exactly the right question to ask," Birdie said. "It's those bigger fish. . . ."

"I agree. But before we get to it, tell us about yesterday's photo shoot," Cass said. "I can't wait any longer to know what lies behind that electric fence."

Friday-night dinner on the deck the night before hadn't happened—a rare event, but a board dinner at the yacht club and a photography exhibit had sent all of them in different directions. Consequently, Birdie had insisted on the morning rendezvous at the Artist's Palate to catch up.

They began with Merry's granola and the Danverses' sad news.

"Apparently the miscarriage happened Wednesday, the day we were in the clinic. We overheard the phone call, but Janie, of course, didn't tell us who she was talking to."

"I talked to Janie last night," Izzy said, "and she said Tamara was handling the miscarriage fine. She'd gone to the hospital Wednesday night, and was home the next day. She was almost *too* fine, Janie said—which was the impression Nell and I got when we saw her yesterday."

"I think the news hit Franklin the hardest," Nell said. "We saw him again at the board dinner last night, and he seemed genuinely distraught. He apologized for being so abrupt at the photo shoot, but I suppose he can't be blamed for that."

"Was Tamara there?" Izzy asked.

"Yes. And she was in great shape. Literally and figuratively. She was very social, talking to everyone. Much healthier than she looked last week. She seemed . . . well, almost relieved. Maybe she wasn't ready to be pregnant."

"And as for the photo shoot, Sam got his photographs and I think Franklin was satisfied with the photos. But as for other things . . . ," Izzy said.

Izzy looked at Nell. "What did you think, Aunt Nell? I thought his comments on Martin being the murderer were way too forceful."

Nell agreed. "He seemed convinced that the police had finally targeted the right man, even though Sam tried to tell him it wasn't a closed case."

"Maybe he's like everyone else in town and wants it over with," Cass said.

"Or maybe he has other reasons," Nell said slowly. "He disliked Justin as much as Martin did."

"He certainly had easy access to the dive shed," Izzy said. She then told the others about the servants' beach, a concept that had Cass groaning. "Haven't we gotten beyond such things?"

"Hopefully," Birdie said. "And it sounds like the Danverses have, too. Letting the dive club teach new divers on their property was a generous thing to do." She waved at Esther Gibson, getting up from a nearby table.

Esther walked over, her large frame shadowing them. "A tableful of my favorite ladies," she said.

"What brings you here so early, Esther?" Nell said.

"Merry's breakfast. I need something to carry me through the morning. Something healthy."

"A difficult morning?"

Esther's smile was weary. "No, not really. Tyler is taking care of my table at the market, and that takes a load off. I'm trying to keep the boy out of trouble."

"He's a good fellow," Birdie said.

"And not really a boy," Cass suggested.

"Of course he's not a boy, Catherine, you're right. But he's gotten himself in a heap of trouble this summer, as you well know." She held up her hands and shook her head. "Yes, he came and talked to me, apparently at your wise nudging. And I know, I know, he has a good heart, but he doesn't think further than that handsome nose of his sometimes. First the business down at the beach. And then the other foolish things."

"What other foolish things?" Izzy asked.

"Oh, just foolishness. When he first came back to town, he was partying too much, he and his old friends, and hanging out at the Gull. Staying out all night sometimes. Dalliances, in my mind. But you're right, Cass—he's a man, not a child, so Richard and I wore earplugs to bed and let him lead his life." She shook her head. "He's a pushover when it comes to women, that's for sure. They can twist him around their fingers faster than you can cast on a row." She shook her head.

"But after he got the job at the Ocean's Edge, Kevin promised he'd keep him busy and the partying slowed down. But always in the background was that Justin Dorsey—a whole other story." She sighed and threw up her hands again.

"It must be difficult for you, working at the police station, with all this going on around you," Birdie said.

"Oh, the chief tries to keep it from me, but I hear Tyler's name being tossed around. Can't help hearing it. He made a mistake. But he's a dear boy. He truly is. I think Jerry is beginning to see that, too."

"The new developments at the clinic have probably taken some attention off him," Nell said, hoping it was true. They all loved Esther, and hated for her to have this worry on her shoulders. "For starters, Justin was getting large sums of money from someone, and you know that couldn't have been Tyler."

"Well, now, isn't that the truth?" Esther managed a laugh, her chins moving up and down. "I think you're right—that whole mess over at sweet Dr. Virgilio's place is getting a lot more attention than my grandson, though the shadow is still there, lurking over him like a black cloud—and it won't go away until we have someone behind bars."

"That cloud is huge—it's hanging over the entire town," Birdie said. "It's time to blow it away."

Esther agreed with a hearty sigh. She looked over at Izzy. "Now, how's that lovely dog, Izzy? Old Horace loved that dog mightily and he's right this very minute grinning down on you for taking him in. It's a shame what happened to Red at the clinic."

Nell watched the concern on her face. Of course Esther would have heard about Red, about the garden. Esther Gibson knew everything that happened in Sea Harbor. She was also a friend of Horace's. She kept all events carefully filed away in her head—and those that needed to be kept under lock and key were handled appropriately.

"He's fine, Esther. It's just a shame Dr. Lily's clinic had to be pulled into this. And an even bigger shame that her father is being investigated."

Esther's white head bobbed in agreement. "I don't know what to think about that man. Can't make up my mind. But Henrietta O'Neal is convinced beyond a doubt that he's innocent."

"And?" Birdie said.

Esther's lips lifted in a half smile. "And have you—has *anyone*—ever crossed our Henrietta?" She looked at each of them, her eyebrows lifted. Then she grinned and waved good-bye, making her way slowly across the deck.

"She has a point," Birdie laughed.

"Okay, then, let's accept that Dr. Seltzer is innocent, at least for now," Cass said, "even though he had motive and opportunity."

"He also had money to meet a blackmailer's demands, something Tyler didn't have," Nell said.

"Even so, let's go with Henrietta for now. He's innocent. Besides, I can't imagine him doing something that would bring complete shame on his family," Izzy said.

"So let's move on," Cass said. "I can't get my mind off Justin's comment that he had bigger fish to fry. That, and the fact that as of the week before he died, he was able to donate a thousand dollars to the church, buy Janie expensive pottery, and consider buying that bike. It sounds to me like the bigger fish were already in the fire."

"So . . . ," Birdie said, pulling a pen and a yellow pad out of her purse. "Justin already had money that week before he died . . . and that Saturday, just hours before he died, he was meeting someone—the mysterious 'business transaction' person. Perhaps to get more money?" She jotted the day down, and then added dollar signs.

"But who would hire Justin and pay him that kind of money?" Cass wondered aloud. "And to do what?"

"Justin wanted to make money fast—and without doing much work," Nell said.

If Izzy hadn't been weighted down by baby Perry, she might have jumped off the bench. Instead, it was her voice that rose above the table like a firecracker. "Blackmail?" she said.

Blackmail.

Easy. Fast. And very dangerous.

"Goodness," Birdie said. "Perhaps . . . perhaps this is the elephant in the room, something so big, so present, that we never considered it."

They accepted the coffee refills Merry sent over, then stared at Birdie's pad. *Blackmail* was written across the page in her distinctive scrawl.

Perhaps the thought had been there, vaguely, unarticulated, when they realized Justin's newfound wealth couldn't have come from Dr. Seltzer's garden. But it was so removed from the path they'd been traveling down that it hadn't reached the light of day.

"From everything we now know about Justin, blackmail—even though it's such a foolish thing to do—would be something he'd try."

"Maybe *because* it's such a foolish thing," Izzy said. "Justin seems to have had a knack for acting foolish."

"That opens up a new kettle of fish," Cass said. *"Who?"*

"And *why?*" Nell poured more half-and-half in her coffee and stirred it absently.

"What could Justin possibly have on someone that would allow that kind of money to exchange hands?" Birdie asked.

"And why give him some money and then kill him?" Izzy asked.

"I think that's easy," Cass said. "But maybe it's because I live with a mystery writer. It was a great and easy way to make money. And if it worked for him once or twice, why not go back and get some more?"

"And whoever was at the other end of it could see that Justin might be coming around forever," Birdie said. "So he killed him."

They all agreed with Birdie's succinct windup.

"But Birdie's question is key," Nell said. "What could he possibly have on someone that would merit big payoffs . . . and then end in murder? He knew something that someone was absolutely determined to keep quiet."

Cass began listing things, a clear reflection of reading Danny's books:

Crooked business dealings. A secret in someone's past?

"An affair?"

She looked up. "Franklin Danvers certainly has a way of getting beautiful women. He was out of town not so long ago. . . ."

"And he's rich," Izzy said. "But he seems to control the world, so I would think even if he had an affair, it wouldn't be motive for murder."

They lapsed into silence, thinking back over the days since they first met Janie's cousin. Thinking of the people he had met, the places where he'd worked, hung out. The information he might have gleaned.

"He was, in Martin Seltzer's words, a snoop. An eavesdropper. He listened to people's conversations at the clinic. Janie said it was a habit and probably had something to do with his life in foster homes, trying to figure out when the foster parents were going to send him back."

"So maybe he heard something that he thought that person would want kept confidential. Would *pay* to keep confidential," Cass said.

"Someone with money, and someone who knew enough about dive tanks to manipulate them."

"Which brings me to a stop I made at McClucken's Hardware this week," Birdie said. "Gus was kind enough to show me around the dive shop. His sweet son, Alan, is running it and he was there, too. He told me all sorts of people come in there—more than you can shake a stick at, was how Gus put it. Ladies, men. He said we have lots of divers around here, not just the tourists, and the Danverses see to it that they have a place to learn how to get licenses and practice, right down there on that little stretch of beach. He sings Franklin Danvers' praises to heaven and back.

"As for the tanks, they were all checked and ready to go. I wondered who knew who was participating in the dive. Alan said the list was posted on the wall."

"So . . . lots of people would know that Justin was diving."

Birdie nodded. "All the divers who didn't have their own gear had come in to be checked. Franklin and his wife had come in that Saturday, too, making sure everything was set and paying for the rentals. He'd also reminded Alan to put names on the equipment so the divers would know whose was whose early the next morning."

Birdie stopped talking. Then looked down at her own list. "Interesting," she mused, then made a note that the equipment had been marked.

At Franklin's suggestion.

They imagined the shed, tucked into the side of the hill.

And Horace Stevenson, walking the beach that night, unable to sleep.

The pieces were falling in place, however clumsily. What was needed, Birdie said, was a spotlight on one shadowy figure, the one slipping into the dive shed.

And visiting Horace and Red on a dark June night.

The night that changed their summer.

Chapter 31

It had been planned for weeks and weeks. But somehow Izzy's shower had snuck up on them, a wonderful ray of light in the middle of too many dreary days. Nell was concerned early on that it was planned too close to Izzy's due date, but Izzy assured her it was perfect timing. Something to look forward to and keep her eyes off the calendar.

Nell removed the bag of gifts from the back of her car. "Canary Cove is anchoring our day," she said, locking the car door.

"And in a lovely way," Birdie said. "Gabby is so excited about this shower you would think she had engineered it all herself."

They walked away from the parking lot and through the community garden, already redolent with spinach and lettuce, new potatoes and herbs.

Beyond the garden, the sea-worn galleries that housed the Canary Cove artists were lit up like New Year's Eve. The shops were open and busy, a favorite haunt for tourists on Saturday nights. Music, drinks, food, and marvelous art.

And tonight, for those eagerly awaiting the birth of baby Perry, there'd be a special event—a shower in Willow Adams' Fishtail Gallery and garden.

"Willow promised it would be a small group, just close friends," Nell said.

Birdie's laughter tinkled like the bells above the gallery doors.

"Shall we lay a bet on that? I can't imagine narrowing Izzy's friends down to a few."

Nell laughed. "Then I'm glad we decided to wait until the baby is here to give Izzy our knitted treasures. The children's book shower is a great idea, but it will be nice to have our own moment with the baby."

All along Canary Cove Road, people moved in and out of the open doors of the galleries. In the far distance, from the Artist's Palate deck, guitars played and drums kept up the beat. People laughed and talked and carried bags with the gallery's name silk-screened on the sides.

They spotted Izzy and Cass standing just below Willow's gallery sign—a carved fish hung from two brass chains. Its tail was painted in brilliant colors and the words THE FISHTAIL GALLERY were carved into the body.

Izzy's cheeks were pink, her eyes bright.

"Good day?" Nell asked, hugging her niece.

Izzy nodded, knowing exactly what her aunt was asking. "Nothing happening. But soon. I feel it. I think the clouds are about to lift."

"I feel that way, too, Izzy. I do," Birdie said. "We're almost ready to welcome this sweet baby into our world. The pieces are finally falling into place."

Although it wasn't the right time to pursue their morning discussion, they knew that they were sharing the same ideas. Knitting had done that to them—allowed them entry into each other's thoughts, even when they didn't say the words out loud. The stitches would come together, the yarn would remain taut, and by the time they were ready to bind off, the whole pattern—complicated as it might have been—would make startling sense.

Even if they needed to do a bit of frogging along the way.

Inside the gallery, the crowd was upbeat and chatty, and the foursome worked their way through to the back, where a small private lounge and garden beyond was reserved for the baby shower.

Gabby spotted them and rushed over. "You're here!" she said, her eyes bright. She hugged Izzy tightly.

Willow came up behind her. "I'm so glad to see you. A tiny fear floated around me all day that maybe you'd decide to have a baby tonight instead."

"And miss this party?" Izzy said, hugging her. "Never."

They followed Willow through to a cozy lounge in the back that Willow used to talk with new artists and plan exhibits. The room was already milling with friends and family, and in the center stood a nearly life-sized wooden giraffe, uniquely designed and carved years before by Willow's deceased father. Today it was surrounded by colorful books in all sizes and shapes. And all along the walls, on the arms of chairs, and in open spaces between the guests were papier-mâché figures, painted in brilliant colors, representing characters from the books: Ferdinand the Bull, the Cat in the Hat, Paddington Bear, and Winnie the Pooh.

It was magnificent, childhood come alive.

"For baby Perry," Willow said. "As you can see—" She looked over at a group of wild things, grinning in all their glory, with Max in the center. "The Canary Cove artists have been busy."

Izzy's hands went to her mouth. Tears stung her eyes. The giraffe was an heirloom, she knew, a cherished one, and the sentiment behind the gift was enormous. Not only would her baby have a giraffe to look over him or her, but a parade of her favorite childhood friends to keep him from ever—ever—being alone during a lonely night.

She hugged Willow tightly, then moved on to greet more friends as they walked in amazement among baby Perry's new nursery friends.

"Now outside with you," Jane Brewster announced. "Gracie's lobster rolls, Kevin's cucumber cups, calamari, and drinks. Come." She took Izzy by the hand and led her out the lounge door and down the flagstone path to the secret haven that Willow's dad had created years before. The secluded garden was located between the gallery and Aidan's home, where Willow now lived. It was tucked away in the middle of wild roses and sea grass, nearly hidden from view except for the low garden lights along the pathway. Tiny sea urchins and mermaids, carved from wood or fired in an oven, were hidden in the grasses or hanging from small magnolia trees along the curved pathways.

The garden was crowded, as Birdie predicted. She looked at Nell knowingly. No one wanted anyone to feel left out, Willow whispered to their backs. "I guess it got a little crazy."

They assured her it would be fine with Izzy. She'd be going home with a whole library of books and treasures, all from people who loved this new baby even before he or she arrived.

"But crowded as it may be," Willow said, "I promised Izzy it would be short—no late nights for this mama."

Izzy turned around, having caught the last words, and mouthed a thank-you over the tops of several heads. She headed for a stone bench and a small table that held a pitcher of iced tea. Laura Danvers squeezed down beside her and poured her a glass.

"Can't believe it, Iz. The baby is almost here."

"I can believe it. These last few weeks have been long ones."

"Sure, I know. It's been a mess. But Elliot's uncle says it's about over."

"He seems to think that. But I don't know how he can be sure."

"Maybe he just wants to close the whole chapter. He's pretty down on the clinic right now, too. Not a happy week for him."

Nell brought over a plate of cucumber cups and set them down on the table. "You're talking about Franklin?"

Laura nodded.

"It's a hard time for him. I know how much he wanted that baby."

"He did." Laura was quiet for a minute. She looked around, assured that others were engaged in their own conversations, and said, "You know, he's a strange man in some ways. I don't think many people really know him, me included. He's done things that have puzzled the family, but he's the patriarch now, so no one questions him. And he has all that money. That helps put people in their place fast."

"What kind of things?" Birdie asked, sitting down next to Nell.

Laura looked around. She spotted Tamara on the edge of the crowd and nodded in her direction.

"Tamara's here?" Izzy said, surprised.

"She heard about it and asked to come. I hope that's okay, Iz—"

"Sure, of course. I just didn't think she'd—"

"Didn't think she'd be up for a baby shower after just having a miscarriage? Wrong." The word held an extra layer of meaning when it slipped from Laura's mouth, not something Laura normally did. "Franklin marrying Tamara was one of the questionable things he's done, at least to some family members. They didn't exactly run in the same circles."

"How did they meet?"

"At a business conference in Boston. She was teaching exercise routines for the spouses, and Uncle Franklin was the keynote speaker. He hadn't been divorced from his last wife very long, and Tamara made sure he wasn't lonely. Or so the family rumor goes.

"Franklin has a condo in Boston that he uses when he's in town, and in no time she had moved in. She's quite convincing. And he's . . . who knows? He's rich, and he likes his power. Not just over his business, but over everything."

"Ben thinks highly of Franklin," Nell said.

"I know. I like him, too. I just don't always understand him. Maybe . . . maybe when he realizes that money isn't the answer to everything, the real Franklin will come out."

"It must be hard for people like that," Izzy said. "He was so tough on Justin one day. And then yesterday, condemning Martin Seltzer so harshly without real proof."

"Franklin doesn't like things that come apart, or fray, or aren't orderly. He wants things to line up perfectly, and having Justin just come onto his property like that and upset Tamara would be unnerving for him. And this whole murder, to have it dangling over our heads—it's disconcerting to all of us, but to Franklin it's somehow worse. It unsettles him. It's just the way he's wired. We rarely visit at his house because I'm always afraid the girls will mess something up. He's used to putting things in their place and making them right."

Nell thought about his frustration with the library book the day before. Such a little thing. A missing book that messed up the scuba diving shelf's order. He seemed agitated by it. A missing book . . . She looked at Birdie and Izzy, wanted to say something, then turned her attention back to Laura and tucked the thought away.

"Well, you can bring those beautiful girls over to my house anytime," Birdie said.

Laura grinned, then grew serious again. "When he married Tamara, Elliot and I worried a little. He'd already been married twice, and they hadn't been easy marriages. Franklin couldn't tolerate his wives looking at other men or having male friends. He was just like his own father, Elliot said. There were rules, and then there were rules."

"Do you know why his marriages didn't work out?" Birdie asked.

They all knew it was a personal question. But somehow in the light of two murders, nothing seemed sacred. And Laura clearly wanted to talk.

"You probably heard the same rumors I did, Birdie. Even though the Danvers family keeps things under wraps, things leak out. His first wife had no idea what she was in for. She was from New York, loved that life, the museums, the city. And she felt isolated up here. She told me once that she never knew having children was a part of the plan. And I'm not sure about Elizabeth, his second wife. She was younger than Tamara, and lonely, I think. There was talk she had a male friend, and well, I don't know the truth of it, but I do know that in Franklin's mind, infidelity is as unforgivable as murder."

She looked over at Tamara again. "Yet I sometimes feel sorry for his spouse, whoever she might be. She occupies a room in his life, a corner, but not the whole mansion. That would make me lonely."

Tamara stood alone now on the edge of the crowd, drinking wine, her face calm and composed. Was she lonely? Nell wondered. Tamara seemed more self-sufficient, the sort of person who would take control and not allow unwanted feelings to mar her life.

Before Nell could turn away, Tamara's eyes met hers. She held Nell's gaze for a minute, then smiled. It was an unreadable smile, Nell thought later. But before she could return it, Tamara moved out of sight.

Willow kept true to her word, and before an hour had passed, she and Jane carried decorated wicker baskets, brimming with books, into the room and set them down in front of Izzy. Everyone's favorite book. A library of children's classics.

"All we need is a baby," Izzy said, her voice thick with emotion.

Gabby followed with a basket of creams, shower gels, lotions, scented candles, bottles of bubble bath, and fresh-smelling soaps. "Everyone brought their favorite scent or soap or whatever," she said, setting it down on the table. "It's to pamper our Izzy. Baby Perry is special . . . but so are you."

After Izzy expressed her thanks and the food was nearly gone, the crowd thinned quickly, some drifting off to enjoy the art festivities on Canary Road, others, like Izzy Perry, to go home.

Ben, Danny, Sam, and Ham Brewster had been hanging out at the Artist's Palate, listening to Pete and the Fractured Fish play a medley of eighties tunes. They moved across the street, bottles of beer in their hands, moving to the beat.

Mild-mannered Danny Brandley was pumped. "Love that fist-thumping rock," he said. His legs were moving, his eyes closed, as he grabbed Cass and twirled her around on the sidewalk, belting out the lyrics to "Eye of the Tiger."

"Stop," Izzy cried, her laughter causing hiccups and tears streaming down her face. "Oh, Sam, take me away from all this."

Ben offered to pack up Izzy's presents and they sent Sam and

Izzy and Cass and Danny on their way to their car, watching from the curb as they moved down the middle of the street, Danny still singing, his arm looped around Cass, Sam and Izzy entwined. Heads back, the air above filled with their laughter.

"What great gifts they are," Nell said, a rush of emotion flooding her chest.

"Yes," Ben said. "And speaking of gifts, I'm off to get your car, Nellie. I will trust the two of you to guard Izzy's presents. Back shortly."

Birdie went into the gallery briefly while Nell stood beneath the fishtail sign, thinking back over the lovely shower. Special people. It had been an enjoyable evening, and in spite of the conversation with Laura, a welcome respite from thoughts of murder.

While gallery lights flickered out all up and down Canary Cove Road, the music was reaching its peak, rolling down the road now like a full spring rain. Nell watched the crowd filling the Palate deck. Several guests from the shower were already there, standing near the rail. Tamara Danvers was crossing the street alongside a young woman who had been helping out in Willow's gallery.

A little farther down, standing alone in the shadow of the Artist's Palate sign, was Tyler Gibson, leaning against the wall as he watched Tamara Danvers—or perhaps the woman with her—move up the steps.

The belt buckle. Nell started to call to him. She'd never returned it. It was still heavy and cumbersome, taking up too much room in her everyday bag. Which was sitting on her bed at home. She lowered her hand. *Tomorrow or Monday.* She'd return it soon. And perhaps Tyler would know how it got mixed up in Justin's belonging. A loose end. A small frayed piece of yarn. Probably unimportant, something that needed to be snipped off.

But maybe not. Nell stared across the street, snippets of conversation racing through her head. Tyler might just be more crucial than they'd given him credit for. Perhaps they'd misread his role completely. The thought sent a chill racing through her.

At that moment, Tyler looked her way—gave a small wave, a nod of his head. Then he disappeared up the stairs and into the press of bodies waiting for tables at the bar and grill.

Chapter 32

*L*aura Danvers brought her oldest daughter, Sara, to Gabby's Sunday-afternoon class. Instead of the lightweight beanie pattern she had taught last summer, Gabby had talked Izzy into an easy headband project. "But it will have my signature flower," Gabby proudly told the class, holding up a large crochet flower that would be attached to the side of the finished band. "And the band will also keep your ears warm," she said.

"Sara is now, at the age of eight, officially grown-up," Laura said, standing in the back of the room with Nell. Birdie was busy passing out patterns, following her granddaughter's directive. "Gabby's class has become a rite of passage."

Laura cradled a cup of hot tea in her hand. It was a gloomy June day, one that forgot it was summer, and instead of the beach, vacationers walked up and down Harbor Road, visited Canary Cove galleries, or hiked over in Ravenswood Park with fleeces and jeans replacing swimsuits. A day for hot tea.

"It's a good day for the kids to be in a knitting shop—safe and warm and cozy," Nell said.

Laura nodded. "Not a lot of that around here lately—safe and cozy. When will this all end? The pointing of fingers, the rumors. Everything. Did you see that poor Tyler Gibson last night? He was hanging outside the Palate like he'd lost his best friend. And Janie and Dr. Lily. What a mess."

Izzy joined them, telling them quietly that Gabby had everything under control, Mae and her nieces were there to help, so why didn't they all go down to Harry's deli? She was starving.

"Occupational hazard," Laura teased, patting her stomach. Then she whispered to her daughter that she'd be just down the street.

"How did your aunt do last night?" Izzy asked as they walked out onto the street. "I barely got a chance to talk to her."

"I think she enjoyed herself. She went out with some friends afterward, which surprised me a little, but people deal with things differently. Maybe that's her way, but . . ."

They waited, knowing there was more to Laura's thought. She seemed to be working through her understanding of her aunt as they talked.

"Tamara was happy about the pregnancy. Franklin, of course, was thrilled. But then a few weeks ago—it was just a few days after the gala at the community center—there was a shift, and she started to act jittery. I thought it was just morning sickness, but now I don't think so. Something was truly bothering her. I took her out to lunch, tried to get her to talk about it, but she insisted things were okay. Janie was puzzled, too, because Tamara's checkups were fine. She didn't even really need checkups, Janie said, but Franklin insisted everything be watched carefully. He was always there with her, right at her side."

"What about Franklin?"

"I don't think he noticed—except during that episode with Justin Dorsey. That upset both of them."

"And then she had a miscarriage," Birdie said.

"Yes. She had just started to act like herself again when that happened. I tried to help her that day, but she said she didn't need any help, that she'd be fine. And she seemed fine. Really fine, in fact."

"Some people like to get through things alone, I guess," Izzy said. "Me? I'd be the opposite."

Laura agreed. "I went through a kind of mourning after I had a miscarriage. I think it was the process of letting go of a dream. But

Tamara doesn't seem to be going through anything. In fact, she's more relaxed than I've seen her in a while. Not so with her husband. Uncle Franklin is having a hard time with it."

"Sam took some photos at their house Friday," Izzy said. "Nell and I tagged along. She seemed fine that day, and happy to be showing us their home. It's a beautiful place."

Laura nodded. "A beautiful museum. But Tamara loves all that."

"Where is she from?" Izzy asked.

"Roxbury," Laura said. "I wouldn't even know that if she hadn't had a friend visit when Franklin was out of town. Tamara had insinuated she was from Brookline. But her friend blew her cover. They both grew up in a neighborhood we wouldn't want to walk through alone, was how her friend described it. Marrying someone like Franklin and leaving that behind was a dream Tamara had had since she was little. Her friend was proud of her because she had finally done it. I don't think Franklin knows where she was raised, even now."

"She doesn't have family?"

"A mother and brother, but she doesn't have anything to do with them."

The rich tomato and garlic odors of Harry's deli interrupted their thoughts and they walked into the tiled entry. The noontime crowd had thinned out, leaving scattered customers at the counter ordering fresh meats and cheeses. Harry waved over the counter and told them to find themselves a booth.

Once they were settled in a back booth, Izzy picked up the conversation. Franklin Danvers' wife intrigued her. And puzzled all of them. "Was it a fairy-tale wedding?"

"No. They got married on the spur of the moment. We hadn't even met Tamara, although Uncle Franklin had us come to the courthouse that day to be witnesses. It was quick and tidy, just like Uncle Franklin likes things."

Harry walked over, wiping his hands on his apron. "Beautiful ladies, what can I get for you today? Chicken cacciatore? Eggplant Parmesan? My magnifico stuffed pork chops?"

They held their stomachs as the list grew longer; then Izzy finally got a word in to stop him. "Harry, stop. How about a plate of those little Italian sandwiches that the summer people have talked you into making?"

He threw up his hands. "Such crazy ideas. *Small* plates, they call them. *Ridicolaggine.*"

They laughed. In Harry's deli, plates were *huge*.

Harry planted his hands on the table. "So, how are you all coping with this mess? Not a way we want to start our summer, is it?"

"No, it isn't, Harry," Birdie said. "Has it affected your business any?"

"We're gonna be okay, but folks don't like roaming around in a town that might have a killer lurking behind a gaslight, you know? I think that Justin kid screwed up his own murder, maybe on purpose, sent the police running in circles. He's probably somewhere up there laughing at all of us."

They looked at him, curious.

"I mean the whole pot-selling thing—that's what everyone's so excited about. Who kills for that? Nobody. Not like that. And not Horace, no matter what the old man saw or thought he saw."

"What did Horace see?" Nell asked. "I'm confused now, Harry."

"Aw, who knows? Horace can't see much, everyone knows that. But, swear on my mother's grave, he can tell when he walks in that door what kind of sauce I'm cooking. Knows it right down to the flakes of basil."

"I've never seen him in here," Birdie said, surprised.

"Only on Fridays. Gus McClucken sometimes brought him in before driving him home with his dog food. Kind of a treat for the old man—none of that small-plate stuff for those two. Great old guy."

"Was he in here last Friday?" Nell asked.

"Sure was. I made a special Bolognese that day. Old Horace knew what it was before he stepped foot through the door."

"And he told you he saw something?" Birdie asked.

"Saw, smell, whatever. He was kind of excited that day, like he had been trying to figure something out for a while, and suddenly it made sense. The lightbulb went on. You know that feeling? Sometimes when I get a sauce just right . . ."

"What made sense, Harry?" Birdie pulled him back to the topic.

"Now, that's the question. I don't know. Something about a channel."

"Channel?"

Harry shrugged. He sliced his hand through the air. "Channel. Like taking your boat through a channel?" He scratched his head. "He said now he knew what he saw. It made sense, he said. The channel. Go figure.

"But whatever. What I'm really saying is this. Horace knew something. And maybe other folks, too. But what is everyone talking about? Selling a little pot on a beach. No one kills for that."

They had no argument with the deli owner. It was almost as if Harry had heard them talking and was echoing their words, forcing them to examine them again. *"We're looking in all the wrong places,"* Birdie had said. Turning over the wrong stones. Nell was convinced of it, and she knew Izzy, Birdie, and Cass were, too.

More now than ever. So what other stones were left to look under? Where were they? And for heaven's sake, what kind of channel did Horace see? One that got him killed?

When no one responded to Harry's assessment, nor changed their orders, he threw his hands in the air again and went to the kitchen to put together the ridiculously sized sandwiches.

Laura checked her watch and said she was going to head back. "I ate lunch. I just came with you for the company. I want to get back and watch Sara learn to knit." Then she added with motherly pride, "It's a big deal. Rite of passage. Her first knitting project."

Izzy liked that. Rite of passage. A good name for her next teen knitting class.

"One more thing before you go," Nell said, "and it's probably none of my business—but I'm curious."

"My favorite kind of question," Laura said.

"Tamara and Franklin got married about a year ago, right?"

"About that."

"They got pregnant quickly."

"I think it was part of the master plan," Laura said. "Uncle Franklin never hid the fact that he wanted an heir, so it was nice that it worked out so quickly. And then, well, a big disappointment. But Tamara is confident the second time will be a charm. Her words, not mine." She grabbed her bag, slipped it over her shoulder, and was off.

Nell watched her walk away, but her thoughts were elsewhere. "Tamara was one of Lily's patients who occasionally talked with Dr. Seltzer. I wonder if Franklin went with her. He seemed awfully sure Seltzer was the murderer. Why do you suppose he was so sure?"

"Or did he *want* Martin Seltzer to be the murderer?" Birdie said. "He made it clear he didn't like Justin. Did he want to get himself out of the spotlight?" She remembered the look Justin had leveled at Franklin that night at the Edge. It wasn't mean, just curious, she thought. A strange look. "I wonder if there was more of a connection between those two than we thought."

The sandwiches came, but they barely tasted them. Their thoughts rolled around the Formica-topped table, bumping into each other, then rolling away until finally Nell called a halt.

"We know where the answer is. It's right there in Lily's clinic. And we've plenty of questions. We just need to find the right one. . . ."

The deli was almost empty now. An old Frank Sinatra song played in the distance, floating on the garlic-scented air. Behind the front counter, Harry hummed along with Old Blue Eyes, his eyes closed, his head back. *Call me . . . irresponsible. . . .*

"That's what Justin was. Irresponsible," Nell said.

"Not a crime, not worth taking a life for," Birdie said.

"Until it was. Until he tried to threaten someone who had too much to lose. And then his irresponsibility was suddenly worth killing for."

Chapter 33

*W*e're looking in all the wrong places. . . .

The words echoed in Izzy's knitting room Monday morning as they sat around the library table, trying to collect the random snatches of conversation and observations made over the long weekend. They had arrived an hour before, brisk showers waking them up, along with Nell's directive that they be clearheaded, alert.

On the table were mugs of hot coffee and half-eaten cinnamon rolls.

None of them doubted that Martin Seltzer had motive and opportunity to kill Justin. And they were just as convinced that he hadn't done it.

And all of them knew that old Harry was right. Justin's murder had nothing to do with stealing pot from a small garden on the clinic roof.

Justin had bigger fish to fry.

"He found out something that no one else knew about. It was important enough that someone would kill to keep him silent," Izzy said. "If we can figure that out . . ."

"I think we will have the murderer," Cass said.

The room fell silent.

A knock on the alley door broke into the silence, and Janie Levin opened it, peeking in. "Hey, can I come in?"

Birdie poured her a cup of coffee and they pulled out a chair.

"I can't stay. I want to get in early today to help Dr. Lily put out fires. It's been crazy." She reached into her large tote and pulled out a beat-up fanny pack. "But look what I found yesterday."

"Where did you find it?" Izzy asked.

"I cleaned my car out, the first time since all this happened, and it was stuck down between the seats. I think Justin probably stuck it there when he went to the dive Sunday. And . . ."

And he never had the chance to retrieve it.

Nell unzipped it and pulled the canvas folds apart. Inside, she fingered dozens of crisp one-hundred-dollar bills.

Cass whistled.

Janie said, "I know. When I saw that money, I nearly fainted. I didn't count it—but there's a lot." She checked her watch. "I need to run, but, Nell, you had asked me to keep an eye out for this—so here it is. I suppose the police or someone will want a look at it—"

"I can take care of that for you, Janie. I'll give it to Ben—or drop it off myself."

Janie waved and was off, prepared for a busy day at the Virgilio Clinic.

"Well," Birdie said, her hands flat on the table.

"This is what we saw at the Edge."

"He was meeting someone that Saturday," Izzy said. "This must have been why it was so important."

"So whoever he was blackmailing gave him money earlier in the week that he used to buy some things—"

"And donate to the church's fund," Izzy added, wanting to soften the crime.

"And then handed this over on Saturday," Nell said. "And probably realized by the second time that there'd be a third, a fourth, and who knows how many requests?"

"So they killed him."

Nell fingered the cables on her baby blanket. The facts were there, but still twisted, just like the blanket. She looked again inside the fanny pack and pulled out the envelope, smoothing it out on the table. She frowned.

"What is it?" Birdie asked.

"I've seen an envelope like this before. In fact, it was sitting on my counter and I shoved it into a drawer just this morning."

"It's a dirty white envelope," Cass said. "So what?"

"No, it's not. It's thicker than most—elegant parchment. Here, feel it. And if you rub your fingers lightly over it, you can feel something."

"Like a water seal?" Izzy asked.

"Maybe." She took the envelope and slipped it back inside the fanny pack. "The one I have is the one that Justin put Birdie's necklace in. I don't know why I didn't throw it out. But I didn't, and I think I'll have a second look at it." She zipped up the fanny pack and slipped it into her bag.

"There's one more thing. After talking to Gus and Harry, I'm convinced Horace saw the person who killed Justin. I think that's what he was trying to say that day in front of the hardware store. He was down there walking the beach that night and saw someone enter the dive shack. But his eyes are so bad he wouldn't have been able to make out features. And he was probably confused. He didn't connect the dots—or maybe couldn't quite process whom he saw—until later in the week. He said something to the effect that it finally made sense."

"So," Cass said, "he was killed, not because he knew whatever it was Justin knew, but because he knew who killed Justin."

"I'm sure of it," Nell said. "It feels right." She looked down at the cable, as if it somehow had the missing stitches, the pieces that would complete the picture, hidden in its twisted shape.

"I have to go out on the *Lady Lobster* today," Cass said. "But let's meet back here later, or maybe I can make it back for your appointment, Iz. I'd love to hear that little bruiser—as well as other things."

Izzy nodded. She glanced down at a half-completed intarsia sweater lying on the table. The loose ends, not yet woven in, stuck out from the sides randomly. "I think we're getting closer. But it's still a little bit like this sweater. We need to weave the ends in."

"There's one more thing," Nell said. "I think it's important."

Cass was headed for the door. She stopped.

"It's Tyler Gibson."

They all looked at Nell.

"I've been piecing conversation snippets together, and Tyler has been a piece of this puzzle from the beginning."

"Because he got mixed up in Justin's crazy scheme," Cass said. "We know that, but it didn't have anything to do with Justin's murder."

"That's right. But maybe something else did."

Cass nodded, as if she had entertained similar thoughts but wasn't sure how to fit them into the puzzle. She walked back to the table and listened while Nell refreshed their memories, lining up pieces of conversations they'd all been privy to over the weeks. They lay there in front of them like pieces of yarn, ready to be stitched into the whole.

For a minute no one said anything. All they could hear were silent chunks of a puzzle falling into place.

Birdie broke their trance. She stood up briskly, wiping crumbs from the table with a napkin. "Murder is awful, plain and simple. No matter who, no matter when or where. But an unsolved murder, a murderer walking casually around our town, is worse. I think we are about to stop the madness."

She looked across the table. "Now, Izzy, we'll pick you up for your appointment this afternoon. Does that work?"

By the time Birdie and Nell left the yarn shop, Mae was unlocking doors and opening windows, and Harbor Road was waking up to a sunny day. The two women turned south and headed to Coffee's. Although they had often tried to teach Izzy, she still made abominable coffee.

"I need a dark roast," Birdie said, and Nell agreed. In addition, Coffee's was the first place they needed to go to tie up a loose end.

Mary Pisano wasn't on the patio with her computer yet, a good thing. The loose ends that might target a murderer were still dangling too freely to be shared, too loose to be believed. They walked into the coffee shop.

Tyler Gibson was two people in front of them in line, just as they hoped he would be. Monday-morning regulars were just that. Tyler hadn't failed them.

They watched him go to a table in the back, then picked up their own cups and followed him.

Kevin was there, his cup half-empty.

The two men looked up, surprised to see they had company.

"May we sit down?" Birdie asked, then pulled out a chair and settled in it, her coffee cup in front of her.

"What's up?" Tyler asked.

"Tyler," Birdie began, "did you kill Justin Dorsey?"

Tyler's face went white. "No, no, I didn't kill anybody. Ever."

"Good, I didn't think so. And see that you don't." She smiled at him.

Nell leaned forward on the table, her hands wrapped around her coffee mug. "Tyler, you told us the other day—and, Kevin, I think you concurred—that you weren't a close friend of Justin's. But you hung around on the beach, parties, that sort of thing. And then there was the—how shall I say it?—'transaction' you had over that car seat. Is that right?"

Tyler didn't answer, but his expression had quickly gone from relieved to suspicious.

"What I'm wondering," Nell said, pulling the monogrammed belt from her purse, "is how this ended up at Mrs. Bridge's boardinghouse in Justin's room." She stretched it out on the table.

Tyler stared at the belt, and then hung his head. Finally he looked up. "Jeez, I'm a screwup, aren't I?"

"But a very sweet one," Birdie said. She patted his hand.

Tyler fingered the monogrammed buckle. "I wondered where it went. It's been missing for a while."

"A couple months is what we figured. Your early days back home."

He nodded. "Sounds right. Like I said, Justin was a friendly guy, very accommodating. But mostly he was interested in making a quick buck."

"So he let people, as Mrs. Bridge put it, 'use' his room?" Nell said.

"I believe she called it a rendezvous," Birdie said.

"Or, as your grandmother would say, a 'dalliance.'"

Kevin got up and told Tyler to be on time for work. He was off to the Ocean's Edge. "No dallying for me," he said, laughing again at his bartender's foibles.

When he was gone, Tyler groaned. "Okay," he said. "It wasn't the greatest move I ever made, but I didn't know that till later. At the time, I thought it might be something real—I hadn't lived here for a few years and I didn't know any of the new people. Especially . . . well. Anyway, I was gullible, I guess. But it's long over. So . . . what do you need to know? I'll come clean."

And he did. Sometimes with more detail than they needed to know.

But as they walked out of the coffee shop, Nell and Birdie looked at each other without saying a word. Tyler Gibson truly was one of the most naive young men they had ever met.

As honest as he had been, it was clear to both of them that Tyler Gibson had no idea at all what his dalliance had wrought.

By the time they had run a few errands and landed back at Nell's, Birdie was starving. She began pulling out Nell's leftovers, wrapping two wedges of a wild mushroom torte in foil and putting them in the toaster oven to heat.

Izzy showed up minutes later. "I couldn't concentrate on work and Mae banished me. She told me to take a nap. Not much chance of that."

"This will take your mind off things," Nell said. She motioned to a basket sitting on the island. "Ben forgot about the basket of lotions when he delivered all the other things to your house."

Izzy fingered the fancy jars and wrapped bars of soap. Each person had brought her own favorite scented lotion or soap and added a short note to the item. "It's like being in the room with all my friends." She rummaged around and found a pot of ginger-scented body lotion. "Here's you, Aunt Nell. I will forever think of you when I smell this wonderful ginger soufflé."

"It was such a nice idea," Birdie said. She took the torte from the oven and began filling plates.

Izzy picked up a green bottle with a bow at the top and laughed. "This is from Esther Gibson, has to be. Horace said he knew when she was half a block away because of her perfume. Emeraude."

"He's right," Birdie said. "Very . . . distinctive."

They laughed and Izzy pulled out a few others, reading the notes. It was a momentary distraction, a welcome bit of ordinariness in an unordinary day.

An elaborately wrapped package caught her eye and she pulled it out and read the card. "May these begin and end your day with the same happiness as they do mine."

Nell busied herself at the sink as Izzy tore off the wrappings.

"She outdid herself," Izzy said. The box was elegant, the Chanel perfume and lotion resting in satin.

Birdie and Nell walked over and looked at it.

And then they stared at the box again.

Horace was right. It all made sense.

Nell headed for the drawer beneath the microwave. Her junk drawer, she called it. The envelope was still there, bumpy from the necklace it had held, and with one corner torn from being shoved in Janie's glove compartment.

Birdie pulled the other one out of the fanny pack, and Izzy cleared a place on the island where they could smooth them out.

"They're the same. And they both have the watermark—"

"Both envelopes probably had money in them. Two payments. He took the money out and grabbed one to put the necklace in when he went to return it to Birdie."

Nell took a pencil and a thin piece of paper from the drawer and carefully placed the paper over the mark. She rubbed the lead back and forth, smoothly and evenly.

They stood back and stared.

"It's probably time to call Ben," Birdie said softly.

Yes, it was time. Nell stepped into the den and called him on his cell. He was going to head down to the police station after a boring lunch with the yacht club's investment officer. He'd pick up the fanny pack on his way and talk to the chief.

"Are we crazy, Ben?" Nell asked.

"There might be some mental deficiencies involved in all this, Nellie," he said, "but they're not yours. Not by a long shot." He paused, his voice dropping the way it did when he was about to say something intimate. "Nell?"

"Yes, my darling. I will be careful."

Chapter 34

They had made one quick stop on the way to Dr. Lily's office—at Izzy's house to feed Red and find out if his nose worked as well as Horace's had.

It did.

It was quiet when Nell and Birdie followed Izzy into the waiting room. Two women sat reading magazines, and a third watched a video on taking care of one's body.

A receptionist looked up and greeted them with a smile and a "please take a seat." Janie, recognizing their voices, immediately appeared in the doorway.

She seemed better each day, Nell thought. Her color had come back and her smile was quick. But the lingering uncertainty of the murder and her loss were still there, a shadow, if not a storm cloud today. Nell wished she felt the same.

On her own shoulders, the shadow felt more like a nor'easter.

Cass walked in behind them. "Do you have room for me, too?"

Janie laughed. "Next visit I think we put Izzy on a big video screen." She checked her watch, then asked Izzy to follow her inside. "If the rest of you don't mind waiting here, I'll take Izzy in and call you when we're ready."

Dr. Lily laughed when they all trailed into the examining room a short while later. It was good to see the weariness lift briefly from her eyes. Babies had a way of doing that.

"I'm happy to report this baby is packing his bags and getting ready for the ride out. It's any day now."

They all clapped, then looked at Izzy. She smiled cautiously. "Not quite ready. We're almost there, though."

"Well, let's check the heartbeat, just to say hello, shall we?" They passed the stethoscope around, each one listening, then acknowledging baby Perry with a loving pat on Izzy's abdomen.

Nell looked over at Lily, patiently watching the ritual. "How are you doing, Lily?" she asked.

Lily leaned up against the wall, hugging her clipboard to her chest. "Honestly? I've had better days."

"And your father?"

"Well—I think he's doing all right. He can't be with patients right now, for obvious reasons. And that's killing him. He spends a lot of time walking back and forth along the beach at Paley's Cove— just like Horace used to do—as if somehow he'll find an answer there. And he's rummaged through all his notes, racking his brain to figure out connections between Justin and him, Justin and this clinic, Justin and the missing morphine, though Justin was already dead when it was taken. It's almost as if he wants to solve the crime himself, as if somehow he should have the key to it. He spent a lifetime doing that in medicine—finding correlations, coming up with hypotheses. I guess he thinks he should be able to do it with something as important as his own future."

"What kinds of connections?" Izzy asked.

"He's obsessed with the idea that someone stole morphine from his office, for starters. He blames himself for that—for leaving it in plain view. He was especially agitated about it these past couple days, even questioning cleaning staff and delivery people, the nurses. Janie is worried about him, and I had to ask him to stop. It was upsetting people so I asked him not to come in for a while. But you can't please everyone. There are still patients wanting to talk to him about their tests—needing his clear, understandable explanations of things. He is so good at that." She looked at the closed door as if she could see it happening. "Just a bit ago one of my scheduled patients came in early, hoping to talk to him. It's a shame."

"It must be terrible for him, knowing he didn't do anything wrong and not being able to do anything about it," Nell said.

"It is. He hears the rumors, though he pretends to ignore them. Yet . . . yet all he seems concerned about is me." Her smile was sad. "It's been a long time since we've had these kinds of emotions between us."

"In the meantime, you're carrying the worry of it all on your shoulders," Birdie said.

Lily nodded. "I know my father. He's dedicated and thoughtful, no matter what kind of appearance he presents. Yes, he went through a bad time in his life, but putting that aside, he cares deeply about life. Being falsely convicted of murdering someone would kill him. I mean that literally. It would, it would kill him."

Her voice quivered slightly, but she continued talking. "I can't imagine who did this to Justin and Horace. It's awful. But my father cannot die in prison for something he didn't do. The police have to find the person who did it. I'll do anything to help make that happen."

"Lily, we agree with you. Your father did not commit these awful crimes. We have a favor to ask of you that might help things," Birdie said. She paused, then said, "Would 'doing anything' include letting us use your computer for a few minutes?"

Lily frowned, thinking, wanting to do anything that might help her father. "Patient records are on the computers. You'd need a password. I . . . I can't let you into those files. They're confidential."

"Of course they are," Nell said quickly. "We wouldn't ask that of you, Lily. Call us crazy, but looking at your appointment calendar might be of great help to us. They'd be on your computer, right?"

"You just want a date check?" She was surprised. "You want to know when patients had appointments . . . ?" She said the words slowly, processing the request, and knowing that Nell and Birdie were not telling her everything—just enough to ask a legitimate favor.

"Yes," Nell said. "Just to see what days people came in to see you, to talk with your father. It won't take any time at all."

"My father has been thinking about calendars himself," she said, more to herself than to the others. She looked up. "Appointments are pretty much public knowledge, I suppose. . . ."

"We thought that might be the case," Nell said, and slipped out the door before Lily could change her mind. Cass followed, offering moral support and technical assistance, should it be needed.

They walked into the reception area where several computers were lined up against a wall, all of them humming and lit up, but without anyone sitting on the chairs in front of them.

Nell and Cass sat next to each other looking at the blue-lit screen.

At the desk, the receptionist who had welcomed them earlier looked over, then busied herself lining up patient files for the nurses to grab.

The calendar program was easy to access. It was arranged by month and had codes that indicated the reason for the visit, the doctor seen, and time in and out. In minutes Nell and Cass had found the pages they needed. Cass clicked PRINT.

The clinic's door opened, but Nell barely heard it as she and Cass watched the printer pushing out their printouts. It wasn't until her name was called that Nell looked up.

Franklin Danvers stood on the other side of the receptionist desk, watching her. Nell's breath caught in her throat.

"Do you work here now, Nell?" His smile was guarded.

Nell straightened up. "Sometimes I feel like I do, I've been in here so often recently."

"Are things all right with Izzy Perry?"

"Yes. She's almost ready to have her baby. Lily is checking her out right now. How is Tamara doing through all this? It's been difficult, I know."

"She has an appointment today, a checkup, just to be sure everything's all right. She insisted on coming back here. But I . . ."

Nell waited for him to go on.

He looked at her, his eyes harder now. "I want to switch doctors. I will insist on it once my wife is pregnant again. Being in a practice that once housed a murderer doesn't seem wise."

The hardness in his voice startled Nell. Behind her, she heard Cass' sharp intake of breath.

Nell folded the printed papers in half and quickly slipped them into her purse. "I'm sorry you feel that way. I think—and I know Izzy and Sam do, too—that this is one of the finest practices on the North Shore. Izzy would never consider leaving here. You . . . you've gotten to know the doctors, you've spoken to Martin—"

His eyebrows pulled together. "How do you know that?" he asked sharply.

"Tamara mentioned once that Martin had been a help to you both, answering questions and explaining things."

Franklin ignored her answer and checked his watch.

Nell stood and looked at him. "Dr. Seltzer isn't in jail, Franklin. He hasn't been accused of anything."

"It's a technicality. He will be. He will be accused of two murders. And then he'll be found guilty and sent away for the rest of his life."

The inner door opened and Tamara appeared in the doorframe, motioning for Franklin to join her. Dr. Lily was ready for them, she said. "She'll answer all your questions, darling."

As Franklin turned away, Tamara noticed Nell and Cass. She smiled at them—a woman-to-woman kind of smile that begged for indulgence. Sometimes men are like that, it said. We humor them.

They gathered at Nell's in the early evening and spread the computer papers out on the table, poring over them, connecting dots as best they could.

And alongside the dates were all the stones they turned over.

A young man who didn't choose his dalliances wisely.

An old man with a gift of smell.

And everything in between, including an innocent shower gift.

Ben had a meeting; then he and Sam would be over with pizza. And then they'd collect everything they had and put it in Jerry Thompson's capable hands for his consideration. And hopefully it would lead to a quick conclusion to the awful beginning of their summer. How much of this Jerry already knew was not known. But one thing was clear. The police concentration right now was on peering into every single aspect and angle of Martin Seltzer's life with a high-powered microscope, looking for a murderer at every turn.

When the truth might be much easier to find. It was all about dates. All about motive.

And if they were right, the motive was clear . . . and the timing tragic.

"Do you think Martin realizes his real role in this?" Cass asked. "I wonder if he . . . if he's figured any of this out himself."

"I don't know," Izzy said. She looked up from scouring Nell's sink. "Lily said he's been obsessed with finding the morphine thief. He's been questioning people who might have had access . . ."

"Questioning people . . . I wonder if that's a good idea," Birdie said. "We have had two murders. We don't want a third. I think that was Horace's mistake. He figured it out, but instead of going to the police, he tried to get an admission of guilt."

Nell dropped the highlighter. She looked at Birdie. "That frightens me, Birdie. I wonder . . . I wonder who he's questioning."

"He could be making his own suppositions," Birdie said. Her words were coming faster now, her tone urgent.

"I don't know." Cass looked down at their list again. "He's too smart to put himself in danger, isn't he? I mean, like you said, two people have already been murdered."

"From what Lily said, danger is the furthest thing from his mind. What he cares about is clearing his name . . . for his daughter's sake."

"Of course he would." Izzy threw down the scouring pad and spun around. Her voice was louder than normal. "He's a dad. He will do anything for his daughter, himself be damned." She wrapped her arms around herself and her baby protectively. "I think he could be putting himself in danger—and he won't care about the danger at all. I already feel that way, and my baby isn't even born yet." She picked up her cell phone and called Lily Virgilio.

Nell tried to call Ben but got his answering machine, his phone off until the meeting ended. She left a brief message.

Birdie was putting on her sweater.

"Dr. Seltzer isn't home," Izzy said, putting her phone in her pocket. "Lily doesn't know where he is, but he was very agitated when she saw him leave a short while ago. It had to end, he said. When she called after him, he said he was going to walk the beach, clear his head, and get some answers. He was through protecting people. Then he disappeared out the door. She was with a patient and couldn't follow him."

Nell looked at her niece, knowing there was more. "What? What else did she say, Izzy?"

"She said that her father owned a gun."

The words were still hanging in the air as Nell pulled out her keys and headed for the door.

"If Martin has connected any of the dots at all, there's only one person he would be going to see."

They dismissed the thought of calling the police and left a message for Sam and Ben instead. It would take too long to make a valid case to some night duty officer who might not be familiar with progress on the case. Ben would call the chief at home.

Nell drove quickly, rounding the bends that led to the beach road. The sky had grown dark while they were poring over their papers, not noticing the time of day. Stars appeared, the moon a sliver of light, hanging low over the water.

At one end of Paley's Cove, a party was gathering force, a small bonfire lighting the sky and suntanned bodies dancing on the packed sand. The smell of hot dogs filled the air. They thought of old Horace. He'd be sitting on his porch, smelling the dogs, listening to the music. "Did he enjoy those nights?" Cass wondered out loud.

If the music wasn't too loud, they guessed he would have. Red, too.

Nell drove on, past the line of parked cars, and pulled in at the farthest end.

Across the road, Horace Stevenson's house sat dark and empty. In front of them, the cliff was silhouetted against the night, the mansions at the top lit with warm lights and television sets, candles on white-clothed dinner tables.

They piled out of the car and walked toward the bend in the path toward the private beach. The servants' beach. The last place Justin Dorsey had taken a breath. A perfect private spot to meet, to not be seen.

To be killed.

The music from the beach silenced their footsteps, but as they neared the granite wall that shielded the Danvers property, they heard faint voices, muted and broken by the sound of the waves crashing against the rocks.

Nell crept closer, her hands pressed against the rock, guiding her way.

"We need to talk. . . ."

It was Martin's voice. Tired—but thick with anger.

They crowded close to the boulder, Nell in the front, crouched down behind a bank of thick wild rosebushes and tangled sea grass. They could see shadows on the beach.

Cass pressed close behind her, and Izzy and Birdie followed, stepping gingerly over the rocky path. They couldn't see much—but they could hear.

They had no plan. No weapons. Just the urgent need to get Martin Seltzer out of the shielded stretch of beach before he killed someone.

The voices continued. "I've nothing to say to you. You're a murderer. You're going to prison for the rest of your life."

For a minute, Nell froze. She thought she heard a click, a gun being cocked?

"No, Martin," she called out, rushing around the side of the boulder, prepared to talk him out of an act he'd regret the rest of his life.

Tamara Danvers and Martin Seltzer turned and stared at her.

"What are you doing here?" Tamara's feckless question was tossed away by a pounding wave.

"Nell, it's okay," Martin said. He put out one hand, as if to shove her back into the night.

But it wasn't okay. It wasn't Martin who held a gun.

It was Tamara Danvers, and she had it aimed directly at Martin Seltzer's heart. She moved as stealthily as a tiger, backing away from the cliff, her back toward the water, as if Martin might try to escape through the sea and she was preparing to stop him.

Nell thought of the women standing behind her. The police were probably on their way. *Talk. Talk,* she told herself.

She looked over at Tamara. A beam of moonlight lit her face. It was calm, controlled. Her hands were steady.

"The baby wasn't Franklin's, it was Tyler Gibson's, wasn't it, Tamara? Poor Tyler, who has no idea he was almost a father."

Tamara allowed a curious smile, as if thinking back to her time with the bartender, somehow enjoying the memory. Her bare feet were planted in the sand, her shadow still. "Yes. The baby that wasn't Franklin's," she murmured. "He wasn't even in the country those nights. I was lonely. An ironic happenstance." Her voice was almost singsong, but with a chilling edge. "I got pregnant. Franklin wanted a baby. It was karma."

"Until it wasn't," Martin said. "Two innocent people killed for no reason."

She nodded. "Yes. It was unfortunate that the miscarriage didn't happen a bit sooner. But that wiped the plate clean, in a way. What if the baby looked like Tyler? It was better this way. I will get pregnant again and give him his heir. Rightfully his, this time."

She fell silent, as if planning in her mind what she would do next. *Talk, Nell*, she told herself again. "Dr. Seltzer was right about Justin's bad habits. He listened at the door, he overheard your conversation."

"And he thought he could make a quick fast buck. And then another. I grew up with kids like that. I know what they are like."

"But Dr. Seltzer didn't know about that, Tamara. He didn't know Justin was blackmailing you. And then, later, he didn't know you'd killed him. And he wouldn't have betrayed your confidence about the pregnancy because he's a good man. He takes that very seriously. How foolish your distrust of people is."

She glanced over at Martin. They were right about Martin's code of ethics. He was like a confessor, Janie had said. A good listener. But once he examined the calendars and knew that Tamara had been in his office the day the morphine was stolen, he had begun to piece it all together.

"People's values change when they're accused of murder," Tamara said. She hadn't taken her eyes off Martin, somehow considering Nell less threatening. "Having him go to prison would be awful for his daughter. I saw him watching her today, hating her worry. Knowing he'd caused it. He'd betray any confidence to protect his Lily."

Her voice was tinged with envy as she talked about a father's love, something she probably had never had herself until Franklin—and his money—came into her life.

"And when he did—when he told the police I was carrying Tyler's baby and desperate for my husband not to find out—they'd look further and find out Justin knew about it . . . that he overheard our private conversation. It wouldn't take long to move along the chain, just like you did, Nell."

"Tamara, this is foolish. Don't make it worse."

Tamara's laugh was unpleasant. "Don't you worry about me,

Nell. Franklin will know exactly what happened here." She glared at Martin. "I told him how you came on to me in the clinic, Dr. Seltzer. How you'd lure me into your office, put your hands on me—"

Martin winced at the awful accusation—one that explained Franklin Danvers' unyielding certainty that Martin Seltzer was a murderer. Tamara had convinced him of that, smoothly, adeptly, probably the same way she'd convinced him to marry her.

"So he bought me this little gun," she said, glancing down. "He'll not be surprised that you came here, looking for me, hoping to satisfy your infatuation. And he won't be surprised if I was so frightened I used the gun he'd carefully taught me how to shoot. And then Nell . . . Nell came to save me and was caught in the cross fire. So unfortunate."

They could hear Martin's harsh laugh. "It was all in vain, you foolish, arrogant woman," he said. "That's the saddest part of all. Both murders. No one would ever have known that the baby you were carrying wasn't your husband's. Tyler Gibson had no idea that a pregnancy had come out of your reckless behavior. No one would ever have connected him to it."

"Just you," Tamara said.

The women standing behind the granite wall could see Tamara's silhouette in the moonlight, but Nell and Martin were hidden from their sight. Cass pushed back into the darkness and texted Ben. *Hurry!*, she wrote.

Nell thought about Tamara's Roxbury childhood, not so different from Justin's, probably. Difficult. But she'd been good at escaping. Good at finding a husband with everything she had never had—

But she wasn't nearly as good at murder.

Nell's breath caught in her lungs, tight and painful. She wondered if the others could hear her heartbeat, loud and raucous to her own ears. And she wondered about Izzy.

"Horace Stevenson's death was a mystery to us for a while," Nell said, filling in the silence. "What could he have known? An old man with bad vision. And then we realized that Horace's vision was bad, but his other senses filled in for him."

"Horace. He was a nice man. I saw him the night I was looking for Justin's gear. And he saw me. He was walking the beach and he waved at me, though he didn't know who it was. He probably thought it was Franklin because they'd often see each other on the beach when they couldn't sleep.

"So after Justin was dead, I'd check on Horace every few days, take him soup, talk to him, just to be sure he didn't know anything. And then last Friday he asked if I'd come by. He needed to talk to me, he said.

"I didn't know for sure why, so I planned ahead."

"You saw Dr. Seltzer that Friday—we checked the calendar. And you took the morphine from his desk. And for good measure, the scuba book you found in Franklin's library."

"Always prepared." She laughed. "I waited until I knew he'd have his whiskey there, then went over to talk. He figured out it wasn't Franklin he saw after all, he told me. It was me he had seen that night going into the dive shed. He was positive of it. So he'd have to tell the authorities, but because we were friends, he wanted to tell me first so I wouldn't be surprised. He truly was a decent fellow. I tried to tell him it couldn't have been me, but he was sure, he said. I could tell from his voice that he was serious—and completely coherent. They might have believed him. It was a chance I couldn't take. He never told me how he was sure, but the certainty was in his voice."

"It was because of your scent," Nell said calmly.

Tamara frowned. "My sense? What does that mean?"

"No, not sense—that's what we thought for a while, too. It was your scent—Chanel Number Five. Just like you gave to Izzy for her shower. We know one another's scents—women especially—but not in an obvious way. Not in the way Harold did. He smelled you there. That's how he was certain it was you. He even knew the name of it, though it sounded more like *channel* when he said it out loud.

And when we let Red smell the perfume on a piece of paper, the dog went wild. That's when we knew that same scent must have visited Horace the night he was murdered. And Red remembered it in horror."

Nell had run out of things to say, and she could see the agitation starting to pinch Tamara's face. Her calm demeanor was disappearing, her grip on the gun tighter.

Nell turned slightly, trying to catch a glimpse of movement, of the women behind the wall.

And then the night lit up as headlights came toward them along the beach. The screech of brakes. And next a rush of blue uniforms, some wading in the water, emerged through the blackness.

Tamara jerked her head, spun around, then raised the gun.

But it wasn't the lights shining in her eyes that stopped her.

Nor the women.

It was Franklin Danvers' voice.

He came through the thick wooden door just behind Martin, the same door Tamara had used to sneak out into the night to make sure Justin's dive was a fatal one.

The voice was fierce and commanding, the figure imposing and stolid. Franklin Danvers walked over to his wife and slapped the gun to the sand.

He kicked it away and waited for a policeman to pick it up and wrap it in plastic. Then, without a word, he walked away from his wife and toward Chief Jerry Thompson, waiting at the side of the granite boulder.

Martin Seltzer slid his back down the side of the stone wall, breathing heavily. Birdie moved quickly to his side, offering comforting words until a young police officer relieved her. He leaned over the older man, handing him a bottle of water and a supporting hand. They'd sent for an ambulance, he said. Just in case. And his daughter was on her way.

Ben and Sam were next, racing across the wet sand. They'd called the police, then driven like madmen toward the beach.

"Izzy?" Sam yelled out into the darkness. "Izzy, where are you?"

Nell spun around.

But Izzy was gone.

"She's up there." A policeman hurrying off to read Tamara Danvers her rights, handcuffs dangling from his belt, pointed back toward the cars lined up at the edge of the beach. "Over there."

They reached her in seconds.

"Anyone coming?" she said calmly, reaching for the car door. "I'm on my way to have a baby."

Then she handed Sam the car keys.

Chapter 35

$\mathcal{N}$othing could deter Laura Danvers from celebrating the new baby—and the fact that the baby herself would attend was a bonus that filled her with great pleasure.

The chosen Saturday was cool and dry, the party set to begin just before sunset—a perfect time to celebrate this new baby, one that the entire town of Sea Harbor, or so it seemed—was welcoming into its arms with love and joy.

Abigail Kathleen Perry had come into the world quickly, once she knew the world was ready for her. In a heartbeat, this tiny baby—with a head of Sam's sandy locks, a sweet round face that seemed to smile as Sam rested her in her mother's arms—changed forever the moment, the day, the summer, and many Sea Harbor lives.

Izzy's parents arrived on the first plane out of Kansas City, and Nell and her sister wept in tandem, sharing this lovely miracle Izzy had brought into the world.

Sam allowed no talk of the past weeks in the birthing room—not when Abigail was present. Only positive, nurturing vibes were to touch his baby girl, he said, and then he held her close and carried her to the window to explain what a wonderful town she was living in, what a wonderful, brave, sometimes foolish mother she had, and how loved she would always be.

· · ·

It was over a glass of wine on Sam and Izzy's deck a week later that they finally revisited the scene, filling in the blanks, though there weren't many of them. It took that long for the men in the knitters' lives to face the danger their wives might have been in. Could have been in. And to allow the night on the beach to be talked about in their presence.

But the joy of sweet Abigail assuaged all things, and the worries were allowed to fade.

The police had uncovered that Tami Ashland was Tamara's given name. She'd been a problem child growing up. No father, just like Justin. And no real sense of right and wrong. *Right* was what Tamara wanted for herself. *Wrong* were people in her life who prevented that. Even her surprise pregnancy—the one-week stand with a handsome, gullible Tyler Gibson while her husband was in Europe—didn't concern her. Her husband wanted a baby, and she would give him one. But when an overly attentive Franklin began asking for every possible precaution and test, she worried some, and talked it over with Martin Seltzer, confiding in him her uncertainty over the baby's father's identity. He assured her everything was fine—the tests Martin had asked for were for other things, not paternity. No one would know.

And somehow, perhaps resulting from a talk between Ben and Jerry Thompson, the police had been able to keep it out of Esther's hearing range and out of Mary Pisano's column that the father *might* have been an unsuspecting Gloucester fellow.

Tyler Gibson might never know. Or he might, if Esther uncovered the truth—and decided that truth was the better part of valor. Perhaps there was an important lesson in it all for her cherished grandson.

But Justin Dorsey, standing outside the door, waiting to fix a computer, did know.

And so Tami's troubles began.

"I don't think any of it bothered her—not even the fact that two people had been needlessly murdered to protect her lie," Nell had said.

"The woman didn't take chances," Birdie concluded, "even if it meant killing an innocent old man."

"Would his testimony have been taken seriously?" Cass wondered.

Ben shrugged. "Who are we to say eyesight is more dependable than scent? Coming from someone like Horace, his words might have been the nail in Tamara's coffin."

But it was over, at last, and on a cool lovely Saturday a few weeks later, exactly at sundown, Laura and Elliot Danvers welcomed Abigail Kathleen Perry, her dog, Red, and her parents, Izzy and Sam, into their home.

The rolling grounds, in a hilly neighborhood overlooking the ocean, were filled with balloons and music—and there would be dancing later, Laura said as she took the tiny Abby into her arms and whirled her out onto the patio. When she handed her back to her father, Laura's face was wet with tears.

"What is it about babies?" she asked, wiping the tears away with the back of her hand.

But they all knew what it was. It was about innocence and joy and a future.

It was about life.

Izzy hugged Laura close. "You're amazing, you know. To do this after the sadness that has been brought to your family."

Laura shook her head. This was exactly what she should be doing. "Uncle Franklin is going to be fine," she said. "We've had some long talks, and even convinced him to stay with us for a couple of nights. Remember what I said about realizing money isn't always the answer? I think he's beginning to get it. Take a look." She nodded toward the stretch of lawn beyond the patio.

Franklin Danvers sat on an old-fashioned swing hanging from two giant maple trees. And on either side of him was one of Laura's young daughters. As Izzy watched, Gabby Marietti approached the swing, her mass of hair haloed by the setting sun. She said something that brought a smile to Franklin's serious face, and then she squeezed in beside them, the girls squealing a welcome.

"Babies and children have healing powers," Laura said simply.

Every room in the Danvers home was filled with vases of bright summer flowers—roses and cape daisies, pink and blue hydrangea blooms, tulips, and pansies from the garden. Children ran freely and a crib was set up in the sunroom, should it be needed.

And on the patio, long tables groaned beneath platters of lobster rolls, calamari, cheesy fries, and bright-colored salads.

Laura's husband, Elliot, was everywhere, fixing drinks, greeting guests, and making sure the platters remained full.

Esther Gibson strolled over to Nell, her eyes misty. "I love babies, you know. And look what they grow up to be. Sweet grandbabies."

They all laughed as she looked over at Tyler Gibson, twisting his legs into a crazy kind of dance with Willow, Pete, and Merry Jackson, his hair flopping to the music.

Ben and Sam ushered them over to a table beneath a tree, where Danny and Cass had filled plates for everyone with lobster rolls and cheesy fries.

Izzy settled down with Abby on her lap, her small, sweet body resting on the yellow cable blanket that Nell had knitted over the months as she'd entertained dreams of this baby, the baby girl who was now the center of their lives. Red sat at her side, dreaming dreams for this child of grace. Simply a miracle, she thought.

Close by, Birdie chatted with Henrietta O'Neal and the man she now introduced as her new gentleman friend. In a rare, uncharacteristic gesture, Martin Seltzer lifted Birdie's hand to his lips and kissed it gently. Then he turned and looked over at the tree—to Cass, to Nell, to Izzy. To Franklin Danvers.

The nod of his head and a slight smile told them what was in his heart and on his mind. And they all nodded back, ridiculously happy that this once-cranky man had been given a new lease on life, for however long that might be. Beside him, watching, Henrietta chuckled, and then she told him it was time to eat. He was as skinny as a rat's tail, she said.

Sam looked around. "My daughter—where is she?"

This time it was Lily who had whisked the baby away. She was standing alone on the edge of the patio, holding the baby in her arms, humming to her. A song perhaps her father or mother had once hummed to her. Their eyes seemed locked together. When Janie and Tommy joined her, they looped their arms around each other, bound together by an infant's smile.

And then Sam was back, taking Abigail into his arms, not able to be away from his daughter for long.

"Attention," Laura said. Behind her Elliot and his girls happily pounded on an old washtub with wooden spoons to hush the crowd.

"The sun is about to set," Laura said, her practiced speaker's voice reaching to the ends of the yard. "It's time to raise our glasses and toast the new baby who has come into our lives. To Abigail Kathleen Perry—peace and love and happiness."

Shouts of "Welcome" echoed throughout the yard as Sam stood proudly with his baby girl in his arms.

"But wait, wait, a surprise," Laura said. She stepped aside and pointed toward the center of the patio, where Pete, Merry, and Andy had set up their equipment and were testing the microphones. They bowed slightly to the applause.

"This is a gift to Abigail Kathleen from the Fractured Fish," Pete said into the microphone. Behind him, Merry trilled chords on her keyboard and Andy rolled the drums.

And then Gabby appeared out of nowhere, her black hair flying. She took the microphone from Pete's hand and lifted her head, her eyes on the baby in Sam Perry's arms. And in a full, rich voice that went clear up to an emerging moon, she belted out "Welcome to the World," filling the air with the lilting song.

Sam pulled Izzy from her chair and wrapped his other arm around her, with tiny Abby cradled between them, her face turned up. Next to them, Red kept the beat, his tail thumping on the grass.

Then they began to dance—the new family, twirling around.

And Gabby sang on: *"Welcome to the world / That will hold you tight."*

Her arms motioned for the others to join in—family and friends, old voices blending with new, welcoming Abby into their lives. "Come dance. Rejoice," her motions said.

"Love is all around you / And here to stay."

Abigail's First Baby Blanket

Yarn: worsted weight. Approximately 1,200 yards
Needles: #10
Cable needle
Gauge: approximately 4 stitches = 1 inch
Seed stitch: K1, P1 across the row. On the next row, knit over the
   purl stitches and purl over the knit stitches.

Section 1:

Cast on 78 stitches. Work in seed stitch for 16 rows.

Row 1: Keep the first 12 stitches in seed stitch, K12, P1, K16, P1, K12,
   P1, K16, P1, K6.
Row 2: P6, K1, P16, K1, P12, K1, P16, K1, P12, keep the last 12 stitches
   in seed stitch.
Rows 3, 5, 7, 11, 13: same as row 1.
Rows 4, 6, 8, 10, 12, 14: same as row 2.
Row 9: seed stitch the first 12 stitches. K12, P1, then slip 8 stitches to
   a cable needle and hold in back. K8, K8 from the cable needle, P1,
   K12, P1, slip 8 stitches to cable needle and hold in back, K8, knit
   8 from cable needle, P1, K6.
Repeat rows 1–14 12 times (or desired length). Work rows 1–4 and
   finish with 16 rows of seed stitch.

Section 2:

Cast on 60 stitches. Work 16 rows of seed stitch.

Row 1: K6, P1, K16, P1, K12, P1, K16, P1, K6.
Row 2: P6, K1, P16, K1, P12, K1, P16, K1, P6.
Rows 3, 5, 7, 11, 13: same as row 1.
Rows 4, 6, 8, 10, 12, 14: same as row 2.
Row 9: K6, P1, slip 8 stitches to the cable needle and hold in back, K8, K8 from the cable needle, P1, K12, P1, slip 8 stitches to the cable needle and hold in back, K8, K8 from the cable needle, P1, K6.
Repeat rows 1–14 12 times or desired length. Work rows 1–4 and finish with 16 rows of seed stitch.

Section 3:

Same as section 1 but do the seed stitch on the opposite edge so you will have a seed stitch border all the way around when finished.

Note:

The sections can be knitted together on a circular needle rather than in separate sections. Cast on the number of stitches for three sections and set up the cables, then continue the instructions for the rest of the blanket. Enjoy!

Designed by Dawn Slugg
Milwaukee, WI 53217

Ben and Nell's Grilled Tuna Steaks
(a Friday-night favorite)

Serves four people. Nell and Ben usually triple the recipe and often make extra aioli sauce.

4 one-inch thick tuna steaks
½ cup mayonnaise
salt and pepper to taste

Marinade
½ cup extra virgin olive oil
2 T red wine vinegar
1 T fresh lemon juice
1 T Dijon mustard
2 T fresh basil
1 T chopped parsley
2 t fresh chopped thyme
3 chopped garlic cloves

Preparation
Mix marinade ingredients in a large bowl.

Put mayonnaise in a medium-size bowl; add 2 T marinade and mix well. Set aioli sauce aside.

Put salt and pepper on tuna steaks and add to the marinade; turn to coat completely. Marinate at room temperature for one hour, turning several times.

Prepare grill. Add steaks and cook about 3 minutes on each side. Top with aioli sauce and serve.

Sally Goldenbaum is a sometime philosophy teacher, a knitter, an editor, and the author of more than two dozen novels. Sally became more serious about knitting with the birth of her first grandchild and the creation of the Seaside Knitters mystery series. Her fictional knitting friends are teaching her the intricacies of women's friendship, the mysteries of small-town living, and the very best way to pick up dropped stitches on a lacy knit shawl.

Chapter 1

Late September
Sea Harbor, Massachusetts

The wind was coming out of the northeast, blustery and heavy with salt. It stung the woman's cheeks, turning them the color of her bright red Windbreaker. Thick strands of hair flew about her face, wild and free—like the sea she was beginning to call home.

After days of warm sun and soft breezes, the weather had suddenly turned. But she loved it in all its disguises—foamy surf crashing against the rocks or water smooth as silk, a chilly wind or sun-warmed sand. Each day was new and amazing and comfortable, as if she'd been born to this place. It had been fortuitous to travel halfway across the country to this strange little town where she knew no one, yet she felt as if she'd finally come home.

She'd awakened that morning to leafy branches banging against the bed-and-breakfast's roof, rattling windows and pulling her attention away from the coffee and blueberry scones the inn's owner had brought to her room. It was a wild sound, unnerving and exciting at once.

Mary Pisano had explained that September was a weatherman's delight. A time of change. A month filled with surprises. An exciting time, she'd said, and then brought Jules another scone.

That was true enough. Already the week had been filled with unexpected happenings—though none a weatherman could predict. The green-shuttered house on Ridge Road was just the beginning. More would come. She felt it deep inside her with a ferocious certainty that would have made her mother uncomfortable. Penelope Ainsley didn't believe in thinking about the past or in secrets or in peeling away layers of anything, other than expensive wallpaper, maybe, during one of her remodeling efforts. Sad things, after all, disappeared if you didn't hold them in your memory.

She told her daughter often that there was only one reality: the one they were living in at that precise moment. Not what was to be . . . or what had been. The past could bring only pain, she'd say, the warning in her voice sharp.

And in those latter days, when Penelope had lain motionless on the white sheets, the bedside table littered with medicine bottles, she'd repeat her mantra with unexpected urgency to her nearly forty-year-old daughter. Live in the day, my darling. Write your own script. The past is gone; let it be. Let it be . . .

During those last days Jules wasn't sure who was talking—the pills or the mother who had loved her so passionately.

But no matter. She would hold her tongue when her mother talked. And then she would follow her own path, a practice honed at an early age and one that served her well.

Thoughts of her mother squeezed her heart. Her lovely, refined, rigid mother, controlled by her parents. She had loved her deeply, but they rarely saw things with the same eye or sensibility. Penelope never wavered in what was correct—the way to act, to talk, to be— never allowing for those shady areas in life where happiness might be found. They were look-alikes, some said, but that was where the similarities ended. One woman sought security at all costs. The other simply wanted to be free and whole. And she couldn't be. Not yet.

Chin tucked to chest, she headed into the wind, climbing the gentle hill to Ridge Road, then turning onto the shady street. *Her* street, as she thought of it. She had intentionally come early, in time to explore before the caller would show up—and before the open house. She quickened her step as she passed the Barroses' place. The small frame house reeked of bad karma. A cranky woman. A weak husband, she suspected. And the grown son. Clarence? Garrett? She'd seen him one day from the road below, standing as still as a rock, looking through binoculars. But the Barroses didn't worry her, not really. She'd turn them into decent neighbors.

Or not.

Some yards ahead, a gray Toyota, the engine quiet, sat at the curb directly in front of the house at 27 Ridge Road. She stopped, startled, and checked her watch again. He was too early.

At first the thought frightened Jules. Maybe the man had ulterior motives for meeting her, maybe ones not as innocent as he'd led her to believe.

No, she scolded herself. Early was fine. The mysterious conversation wouldn't take long, and then she'd spend the extra time exploring the property on her own before the Realtor arrived.

He needed only a few minutes, he'd said when he called. At first, she had tried to put him off, suggesting she stop by the Ocean's Edge the next day—it would be an excuse to have a bowl of the restaurant's mussels, she'd told him, sending her smile across the phone line. Today was bad for her. She had a list of things to do, including this important open house.

Things more important than talking to a man—sweet as he was—whom she barely knew.

But he had been persistent, offering to meet her at the open house so he wouldn't mess up her day. He knew the house well. He'd said the latter words in a way that made her wonder whether he, too, wanted to buy it. Perhaps that was the urgency of meeting her. A worrisome thought. But if that was the case, she'd persuade him otherwise. She was good at convincing men to see things her way.

She walked over to the car window and leaned in, a wide smile in place, a greeting on her lips.

The car was empty.

She stood back and looked around the neighborhood. There were no signs of life along the winding street, and only the relentless wind added movement and sound. She glanced over at the Barroses' house. A curtain in the front window fluttered, then went still.

The watery wind picked up with renewed vigor and slapped a piece of newspaper against her jeans. Jules jumped, a nervous laugh escaping her lips. She pressed a hand against her chest, uncomfortable with the stab of fear that had strained her breathing. Few things frightened her. Certainly not wind . . . a newspaper . . . an empty car.

She looked at the house, trying to dislodge the tightness in her chest. It was beautiful. But so much more than that. It was an unexpected treasure, hidden behind the trees, waiting for her to find it. A key to the life she was looking for.

She was startled the first time she saw it, not believing it was real. The shingles were weathered, the shutters in need of paint. The back swing moving slightly in the breeze. It was a miracle—if you believed in such things. A miracle that she had found it, a miracle that it was to be hers.

Her mother had been wrong in her warnings. There was joy in this house.

Jules glanced at her watch again. Daylight was fading and a flash of lightning lit up the sky in the distance. But she had enough time to explore the back, the view of the sea, the potting shed. She had imagined the porch as wide enough to dance on or to curl up in the old porch swing, a pile of yarn as high as the sky beside her.

She wouldn't allow an irrational fear or a cold wind to color this day. The day was hers, hers to color in rainbows.

And then another thought occurred to her. Perhaps he was here after all, the man she was to meet. Perhaps he, too, was walking about the property, surveying it, imagining it as his own. She looked at the house, listened, then pushed her hands into the pockets of her Windbreaker and walked quickly up the front walk, the ends of a silky knit scarf flapping around her shoulders. If that were the case, she would convince him otherwise. There was no doubt in her mind about that.

The flagstone path led around to the north and Julia followed it past the shuttered windows, the empty flower boxes, the wild rose-bushes. She breathed deeply, pushing against the feeling that still clung to her, prickling and niggling inside her chest.

As she rounded the corner of the house and passed the garage, a gust of wind sliced through the trees and met Jules head-on, sending her scarf flapping to the ground. It snagged on a granite boulder beside the path and she leaned over to pick it up, then stayed there for a minute, one hand on the cold, damp surface of the rock. She steadied herself, breathing in and out, slowly and purposefully, pushing away the sudden fear that threatened to disturb this day.

Her eyes were closed, lashes dark on her wet cheeks. She was aware only of the oxygen filling her lungs, and oblivious to the world beyond it. Deaf to the sounds of the sea crashing against the rocks below, to the roar of the wind. Deaf to what lay ahead.

In her head, all was silent.

Chapter 2

The week before

One week before their September would turn foul and troublesome, a shiver had passed through Nell Endicott. It began in her chest and spiraled out, traveling down her arms to the tips of her fingers and defying the warm, sunny Friday. She pulled her sweater tight, then wrapped her arms around herself.

"Chilly?" Birdie quickened her step, trying to match Nell's longlegged stride.

Before Nell could answer, Birdie shivered, too. "It must be catching," she said.

"A storm, maybe?" Nell looked east, beyond the old pier and parade of pleasure boats heading out to sea. Past Gracie's Lazy Lobster Café and a fleet of lobster boats being repaired in their slips.

The sky was flawless—pristine perfect. No storm was predicted, and the windless day and glassy sea spoke of a lovely Indian summer day.

But sometimes Nell felt things before they actually happened—like unexpected weather or a phone call bringing sudden news—a trait for which her mother took full credit.

"It's genetic, my darlings," Abigail Hunter would tell Nell and her younger sister, Caroline. "A sixth sense. Treat it lovingly and wisely."

Nell's father's reaction was deep laughter and a bear hug for his girls, pulling them close and tousling their hair. Then he'd open his arms and pull their mother into the circle, and tell all of them what a lucky man he was to have such magical ladies in his life.

Nell shifted the bag of knitting hanging from her shoulder, her eyes still looking at the sky.

Birdie looked up, too. "No, it's not a storm," she said. She moved to the edge of the sidewalk to avoid being felled by a redheaded skateboarder racing down Sea Harbor's main street. Large black earphones covered the boy's head, his lips moving to the music pumping into his ears.

"Freddie Wooten, be careful you don't kill yourself," Birdie called out to the skinny young boy's back.

Nell paused at the curb to let the traffic pass. "Are you as curious as I am about why Mary Pisano wants to have coffee with us at this ungodly hour?"

"Not exactly *wants*. She pretty much demanded it. I suspect she's working on some intriguing story for her column and is hoping to pump juicy gossip out of us to flavor it. Perhaps that's what's making us shiver."

Nell laughed and turned her head to wave to Harry Garozzo. The deli owner was standing in front of his store, his white apron already smudged with an orange-colored sauce.

"Pork and porcini mushrooms with Bolognese sauce," Birdie said. "I can smell it. No doubt Harry has been simmering it since dawn."

At that moment a woman in shorts and a T-shirt, a baseball cap barely controlling a mass of flying hair, approached Harry from the opposite direction.

Nell and Birdie watched the deli owner's face open wide as he wrapped Julia Ainsley in a greeting.

Her arms were slender and firm, her legs long and strong like a runner's, her eyes wide and expressive. With a single smile she fastened Harry to the spot as if she'd poured cement beneath his sneakers.

Harry was in heaven.

"A breath of fresh air, that's what he calls her," Birdie said. The octogenarian took Nell's arm and stepped off the curb.

Nell glanced back and laughed. "Harry's always been susceptible to a beautiful woman's charms."

"That woman is odd in that way," Birdie said. "There's a definite magnetism about her. But she doesn't throw it out there to impress anyone. It's simply there."

Before Nell could respond, she heard their names being called and she looked over into the waving arms of Mary Pisano. She was standing just inside Coffee's patio gate, lifting herself on tiptoe in an attempt to increase her less-than-five-foot stature an inch or two.

Patrick O'Malley's café, Coffee's, was nearly always crowded and today was no exception, which was why Mary Pisano was guarding the wrought-iron table ferociously. She pushed open the gate and ushered them in, pointing to the coffee mugs and plate of chocolate éclairs she had used to mark the table as her own.

"I saw you watching Jules come down the street," Mary said, sitting back down and passing napkins to each of them. "She's hard to miss, isn't she? Such a bundle of energy. She's been here just a short time and she already knows that Harry makes the best Bolognese sauce on Cape Ann. She'll probably be the first in history to wrangle his grandmother's recipe out of him."

"She's interesting," Birdie said in her declarative way. "I like her."

"Of course you do. She's talented and smart." Mary passed around the plate of éclairs. "She's the ideal bed-and-breakfast guest—full of life, friendly to the other guests."

Nell looked back across the street. Harry's group had grown. Julia was still there, listening intently to whatever Harry was saying, her hands on her hips, her cap off now and the morning sunlight painting streaks in her dark hair. Karen Hanson, the mayor's wife, and Izzy's friend Laura Danvers had joined in the conversation.

"Attracts people like bees to honey," Mary said around a bite of éclair.

"She's friendly," Nell said.

"Yes. And beautiful. And did I mention how talented she is?"

"You did," Nell said. "Izzy has said as much. She's doing a beautiful job on a cable sweater."

"She's quite a runner. I see her everywhere—the harbor, the backshore. When does the woman have time to knit?" Birdie asked.

Mary wiped the crumbs from the corners of her mouth, her head nodding agreement.

"You're enjoying having her around, I gather." Nell's words were spoken in a tentative way, wondering where Mary was going with the conversation. The text she'd sent the night before had been brief. *Please meet with me on Coffee's patio in the morning. There's something I want to talk to you about.*

Birdie had received the same invitation.

A meeting at Coffee's to talk about Julia Ainsley's fine attributes?

"How long is she vacationing here?" Birdie asked, picking up on Nell's thought, a trick she and Nell had mastered years before.

"Well, now, I don't know exactly. She's a bit mysterious when it comes to planning for the future. And about her past, too, for that matter. I've asked all my usual questions, but I've learned little. I know she'll be here at least a few more weeks." Mary looked at each of them in turn, her eyebrows lifting.

An odd way of wording it, Nell thought.

Mary went on. "But there is something important I've learned about her: Julia Ainsley knows food." Her words were firm, as if her companions might disagree.

"Well, that's good," Birdie said. "So do we. And we've plenty of good restaurants to suggest. I wonder if she's tried Gracie's Lazy Lobster Café yet? It sometimes gets overlooked once the tourists leave."

"No, that's not what I mean." Mary looked at Nell. "She has a knack for presenting things. So I may urge her to stay on long enough, just to get her ideas."

"Long enough for what?" Birdie asked. Perhaps they were finally getting to the reason for the meeting.

"For the anniversary party." She smiled at Nell. "Yours."

Nell put down her coffee cup. "Mary, what are you talking about? Ben and I are planning a casual early-evening event at our house. Appetizers and drinks. No muss, no fuss."

"Nonsense, Nell. No couple plans their own fortieth anniversary celebration. It will be at Ravenswood by the Sea. I've already asked Jules for ideas. And Karen is helping, too."

"Karen?"

"Karen Hanson. Our first lady, that Karen. She's redesigning some rooms in the bed-and-breakfast. She's an excellent designer, you know—her family owned all those high-end stores. And she's good at knowing what people want, which is partly why her husband has been mayor for the last two decades."

Nell looked relieved at the change in conversation, so Birdie picked it up. "But maybe not for long. I hear Beatrice Scaglia is planning to give him a run for his money," she said.

Mary laughed. "Beatrice will keep moving up the political ladder until she's pope, if you ask me, though I'm not sure anyone can beat Stan. He's a good man. But no matter—you're changing the subject on me. We're here to talk about your anniversary party, not politics."

"Mary, I don't think—" Nell began.

"Shush. We've already talked about it."

Mary continued, her voice tamping down Nell's attempt to intervene. She clearly wanted to get her thoughts out on the table without interruption. "Jeffrey Meara from the Ocean's Edge can manage bar duties; maybe Liz Santos from the yacht club will provide staff—"

"Staff?" Nell's summer tan began to disappear.

Mary's small hands waved her into silence. "It will be lovely. A fortieth wedding anniversary should be a time of joy and celebration without any concerns on the honorees' part. That's just the way it is."

The look Birdie passed over Mary's lowered head said it all. *Let it go, my friend. You have absolutely no choice here.*

How true. Once Mary Pisano settled on an idea, she was a dog with a bone, and there wasn't any way they would be able to wrest the anniversary planning away from her, at least not without being bitten.

Nell sighed, then covered her resignation with a smile, wondering how she'd explain to Ben that their laid-back anniversary plans were now in Mary Pisano's hands. "Laid-back" wasn't a word with which Mary easily identified. The talky columnist and owner of Sea Harbor's elegant bed-and-breakfast was not only involved in every inch of Sea Harbor life, she was as resolute and stubborn as a fisherman's wife, which she also was.

"So it's decided, then? Good." Mary took a last drink of coffee, wiped the corners of her satisfied mouth, and pushed out her chair.

"What's decided?" Cass Halloran walked over to the table, balancing a mug of dark roast in one hand and a blueberry scone in the other. She looked tired, even before she pushed her sunglasses to the top of her head, revealing red-rimmed eyes.

Birdie frowned. "Are you all right, Catherine?"

"Fit as a fiddle." Cass set her things on the table, then leaned down and gave Birdie and Nell quick hugs. "I need coffee."

"And I need to write my column," Mary said, standing up and hoisting her backpack between narrow shoulders. She looked over at Cass. "I could use some juicy tidbits. Any gossip heard on the *Lady Lobster*?"

Cass shot Mary a frown. "Why do you ask that?"

"Because my husband is a fisherman just like you and your brother, and I know what goes on out there on the water. Lots of cussing. Some feuding. Nasty tricks now and then. But always plenty of talk."

Cass swallowed a drink of coffee. "Now that we've added more boats and a ton more traps, I'm in the office managing things more often than out on the water. But there's no new gossip that I know of. If I hear anything, you'll be the first to know."

Mary patted her hand. "As it should be, Cass." She wiggled her fingers in a makeshift wave to Birdie and Nell and headed across the patio to the small round table beneath the maple tree, a table for one, reserved for the "About Town" columnist. In minutes, Mary had opened her laptop and settled in, beginning to compose the day's chatty newspaper column. A dearth of gossip was not much of a challenge for Mary—she'd dig something up or applaud someone's good deeds or expound on a favorite cause or pet peeve. The column would be written no matter how little news was circulating around the seaside town—and it would be read by nearly everyone in town.

"So," Birdie said, the soft word drawn out slowly to relax the lines on Cass's face.

Cass managed a smile. "It's been a long day, that's all." She held her cell phone in her hand and glanced down at a message that pinged into view.

"Cass, it's morning. Early morning." Nell looked down to see Danny Brandley's name being dismissed. She was fond of Cass's significant other and had to tamp down the urge to suggest Cass answer it.

"Morning. Night. Just busy. What was Mary in such a heat about?"

Birdie filled her in on Mary's plans for Ben and Nell's anniversary celebration. "And apparently she's recruiting others to help as well."

Cass glanced over at Nell and spoke around a bite of scone. "Oh, jeez, Nell. I'm sorry—"

"It'll be fine. You know Mary."

"She claims it will be simple," Birdie said. "She's already recruiting help, even trying to get a guest to give her ideas."

"Guest?"

"Julia Ainsley."

Cass's head shot up, sending crumbs and blueberries floating through the holes in the wrought-iron table. "What about her?"

"Mary is looking for excuses to keep her around longer. She's asking her for ideas for Nell and Ben's anniversary party."

Cass stopped chewing and stared at Birdie. "Why would she do that?"

Nell answered. "Mary probably thought she was doing us a favor by taking over planning duties." She paused, confused at the look of disapproval on Cass's face. "Cass, it'll be okay."

"No, I mean Jules Ainsley. Izzy says that's what she wants to be called—Jules. She's just here on vacation, passing through, right? Why is she getting involved in our . . . our lives?"

"She and Mary have become friends. And we all know it's hard to say no to Mary."

Cass washed down her scone with coffee, her silence heavy and uncomfortable.

Cass guarded her feelings closely, but she was as unable as a child to hide emotion in her face. Deep lines formed just above her dark eyebrows, creasing her forehead. And her eyes—a color matching the deepest part of the sea—lacked the clarity and curiosity usually found there. Instead they were filled with emotion, her attractive face a study in frustration. "You're upset," Nell said.

Cass turned her head away from the two older friends who were usually like warm blankets to her, always there, always comforting. Always able to lighten her load when the family lobster business became too heavy a weight on her shoulders.

Cass sat still as a granite rock, staring across the street at Harry Garozzo's deli.

Nell and Birdie turned their heads and followed her look. Harry had gone inside, and Laura and Rachel Wooten were nowhere to be seen. Standing just beyond Harry's wide front window were two familiar figures: Danny Brandley and Julia Ainsley, their heads bowed until they almost touched, their conversation shielded in the cave of their nearly joined bodies.